John Needham was born in Rutland in Stamford, Lincolnshire. After study at spent the first twenty-five years of his design and copywriting. Later he purs renovating old houses, to end his career in landscape gardening.

Since retiring he has written three non-fiction books: two on house renovating and an autobiography, *Wishing for the Better*, which is free to read on his website: wordsfromjohn.wordpress.com In fiction he has written *Convergence, Forebears, The One of Us* and *Another Spring*, a short anthology of short stories.

He now lives in west Wales with his spaniel, Sali.

The One of Us

John Needham

Copyright © John Needham 2015
All Rights Reserved

Places and some locations referred to in this work of fiction do exist, but all characters are entirely fictitious and any resemblance to real people, living or dead, is purely coincidental.

For Gwen, who gives support and Jenny, who would have done.

Translations

Welsh words used in the story:

Bach: Small, little. Also used as an endearment, often to children but not necessarily.

Cariad: Love, lover, sweetheart.

Croeso i Gymru: Welcome to Wales.

Diolch: Thank, thanks.

Diolch yn fawr iawn: Thank you very much.

Duw: God, or **Duw Duw!:** The equivalent of saying, 'Good God!' or 'Oh my God!'

Hiraeth: Longing (approximately).

Nos da: Goodnight.

Taid: Grandfather, Granddad.

After

Helen parks her two-year-old Ford Fiesta (dark blue, low mileage, immaculate when she got it although it could do with a good clean now) and looks around for a ticket machine. There doesn't seem to be one. *Fair enough. Haven't the Welsh cottoned on to charging for parking yet? They must be pretty relaxed about it. Not that there's been a great deal of traffic on the roads for the last seventy miles or so, and not that much here in Lampeter for that matter. But this is Saturday afternoon (although admittedly late; going on for a quarter to five) for goodness sake. Northallerton would be heaving. Where is everybody? Not been a nuclear war, has there? Oh well.*

She gathers up her bag, gets out, locks the door and looks around the square, which seems to be given over entirely to car parking, although it's barely a quarter full. It's pretty though; spick and span with small neat terraced houses ranged along three sides, their walls tricked out in various colours like a paint sample card, some of them unapologetically strong. The house is on the north side of the square, Tomos said. Typical man! How the hell is she supposed to know which the north is? She doesn't carry a bloody compass around with her! But he also said, helpfully, that his little house is painted bright blue and that there'll probably be Mair's little red Citroen parked outside. Yes, there it is, to her left, almost directly in front of her. Blue house, red car. That must be it; it must surely be a unique combination of house, car colour and car make. Well, almost. Anyway, glancing around again, there's no other bright blue house to be seen.

She heads towards the house, already feeling a little nervous. *Surely Tomos didn't choose that colour himself, did he,* she thinks, *it's a touch on the excessive side.* She reaches the white plastic door, hesitates a moment, rings the bell.

It's only moments before the door is opened. A small slight blonde girl; black skinny jeans, big bottle-green jumper halfway down her thin thighs stands there, a questioning expression quickly giving way to broad grin.

'Helen?' she says, unnecessarily.

'The same!' Helen grins back. *This must be Mair. Seems nice. Very welcoming anyway.*

'Mair I take it?' She tries to pronounce the name properly, the way Tomos told her.

Mair seems uncertain whether to extend her hand for shaking or open her arms for a hug, so Helen takes the initiative and opens her own, embraces her and pecks a cheek. Well, she's sort of family, after all.

'Lovely to see you,' says Mair, 'I've heard so much about you.'

Then remembers herself. She becomes solemn. 'Er, I'm so sorry . . .' She flounders a little, searching for appropriate words.

'That's okay,' says Helen. 'I know; it's an odd sort of situation. You must have mixed up feelings about it. I'm getting over it, slowly, though.'

Mair says, relieved to be extricated from awkwardness, 'Anyway do come in; it's not very warm out here. Rain coming by the look of that sky.'

She backs into the room (the door opens directly into the snug, low-ceilinged lounge), allowing Helen in, as Tomos rises from the sofa and turns to greet her. It's only the third time she's seen him, actually, and there's the same jolt of surprise, of recognition. *God; you're so incredibly like your brother. I can never get over it. Well, apart from the long hair of course. Apart from that, so like Wayne. Now you're filling out, the sameness is even more pronounced.*

Tomos comes around the end of the sofa, arms open. *He's* not unsure as to the correct welcome, anyway. Helen embraces him. She's not sure how delicate he still is, but he seems remarkably strong, and his kiss on her cheek is generous. The embrace seems to last just slightly too long for propriety; teeters perilously close to the embarrassing, but then he pulls away. His familiar hazel eyes dance.

'Hello Helen. Thanks for coming. Great to see you.'

'And you too Tomos. You look really well.'

'Yes, and I feel it, thanks. A lot better than four months ago, that's for sure.'

'Good! I'm really pleased!'

He indicates the only other seating in the little room, a blue repp covered armchair. 'Sit down, please. Oh; sorry, let's take your coat.' Helen drops her bag down by the armchair and unbuttons, removes her parka. He takes it from her and hands it to Mair ('Hang this up Cariad, you're nearer') who hangs it on the rack by the front door. She sinks down into the armchair as Tomos resumes his seat on the sofa. He's looking at her with that so-familiar, slightly lop-sided grin on his face. He's still not as beefy as Wayne and perhaps never will be. But then poor Tomos is hardly in the Welsh rugby player bracket, far from it.

She relaxes back against the cushions. It's been a long journey. *This is all very comfy.* She smiles back at Tomos. *Look at you, sitting there in your blue sweater, looking almost muscular. Perhaps you will be, given time. You look as if nothing's happened, almost. There's a little colour in your cheeks. And you've got this nice little house. And Mair. Lucky you, Tomos.*

Then catches herself. *Well; lucky now anyway, but you certainly weren't before. It looks as if you're going to be fine, but you must have been through hell.*

Mair pipes up: 'Anyone for tea? Or coffee? What'll it be for you Helen?'

'Oh, tea, please Mair. I'm gasping. Milk, no sugar, thanks.'

Helen stretches her fur-lined (artificial of course) booted feet out in front of her, crossing them at her slightly thick ankles. She'd no idea what sort of weather to expect this far south, but it was still pretty parky back home and had decided to wear them just in case. Needn't have bothered as it's turned out, with the nice fire (well, gas-fired pretend woodstove, by the look of things). She might have to take them off in a bit. Tomos is still looking at her fixedly, still grinning. She almost wishes he'd stop; it's getting a little unnerving. But then the grin deserts his face. He's all solicitousness.

'And you're really okay, are you, Helen?'

Helen sighs; trots out the usual reassurance. 'Yes, I really am fine now Tomos. Can't rewrite the past. You're the one who matters now.'

Part one

Chapter 1
The Two of Me

Julie was determined to have a good Friday night out on this sultry evening in Liverpool in July, 1984. Cheer herself up a bit. It had been a bugger of a day really. The boss on her back all the time because she kept making mistakes with her typing. Three times He'd thrown it back at her for redoing and intimated not-too-subtly that if she didn't brighten up she'd be out.

So tonight it was clubbing. The pulsating lights, the throbbing noise, the booze, a little weed perhaps, the escapism. Every sort of intoxication. Wonderful! Everyday worries relegated to the back seat. They wouldn't entirely go away of course, but they could be ignored for a few happy hours of abandonment. Think about them again next Monday morning. She knew from past experience that it would be sweltering-hot in *Slinky's,* so she'd come suitably if sparingly dressed: her green neon tutu that was little more than a bum warmer, purple mesh top, red D-cup bra. No tights (too hot) and just for once no leg warmers, for the same reason.

With a bit of luck, that hunky bloke might be there again. He had been the previous two times, with his mates, spending much of their time ranged along the wall eying up everything female with varying degrees of approval. She'd tried to catch his eye and give him the come-on but wasn't sure whether he'd taken the hint. He certainly hadn't approached her, yet, anyway. Perhaps he never would. She knew she was no oil painting really (her only significant feature was her chest, but what advantage was a nice pair of knockers if you hadn't got the face to go with them?). She hated her red hair (although admittedly it was easy to change; it was currently blonde except at the roots); hated her freckles (made her look like a ten-year-old); hated her thick eyebrows and her wide pudgy nose But she did her best; spent a good hour in her bedsit putting on her face, trying to enhance nature's sparing legacy.

You could only do what you could do. Perhaps the see-through top might do the trick. She'd deliberately slackened off her bra (it was giving virtually no support at all) so that she would bounce as spectacularly as possible when at maximum gyration. She would almost have been tempted to leave it off entirely, but knew she'd never get past the bouncers on the door, who would have denied her entrance but not before having a good ogle first.

Debbie and Sharon were already there, waiting outside, when she arrived tottering on her platforms. Stupid bloody shoes really, but it was what everyone wore, so you had to. Useless for dancing in really, so all you could do was stand there and bob up and down and sway and wave your arms around. Well, it didn't pretend to be ballroom dancing though, did it? Your feet killed you at the end of the night though. They headed in past the leering bouncers and paid at the kiosk, had a quick check in the Ladies to ensure no repair was needed, left their stuff at the cloakroom and hit the dance floor. It was busy tonight; the floor was crowded already, at the early hour of twenty to ten. What would it be like in a couple of hours' time? And as she'd predicted, it was sweltering. She could feel rivulets of sweat running down her back already. Thank the Holy Mother she wasn't wearing any more.

Madonna was going *Crazy For You* at high decibels as they nudged their way into the bobbing throng. Julie scanned the room. No sign of Mr Good Looking. She felt an irrational stab of disappointment. Still, it was early yet. He was probably still in the pub. Anyway, she needn't get her hopes up. Even if he did appear, he'd likely be as uninterested as before. Why in Heaven's name would he fancy her? She resigned herself to ending the night alone. Again.

But then, an hour and a half later, in the middle of Bruce Springsteen's *Born In The USA,* suddenly there he was, at the end of the room, by the farthest glitter ball, sitting in the raised purple-painted seating area. She hadn't been keeping her eyes peeled. But he didn't seem to be alone. There was a girl with him wearing a tiny pink puffy dress, multi-coloured glass beads and a trowelled-on application of mascara to complement her black perm-curled hair. They seemed to be engaged in earnest conversation. She couldn't hear what they were saying of course because of the distance and Bruce's high-octane paean to America. It did look to be a heated discussion though, judging by the mutual gesticulating.

Julie's supposition seemed to be proved correct when a minute later the girl suddenly slapped Handsome hard in the face, nearly sending him sprawling, came down the staircase and flounced with difficulty through the revellers, heading for the foyer. He watched her departing back for a moment, hand to cheek and mouthing what looked like very creative expletives, and then shrugged theatrically and turned to watch the sweaty carousing throng.

It was then that he spotted her. And to Julie's astonishment began to thread his way towards their little group. Towards her! As he came close she could take in his features properly for the first time. Quite tall; must be knocking on six foot. Broad shouldered; a bit on the swarthy side. Not unlike Brian Ferry, actually, with straight, as-good-as-black hair, sloe-black slightly piggy eyes and a rather long, somewhat aquiline nose. Julie was gratified to realise that he was only looking at her.

He was the first to speak, or rather shout.

'Hiya!'

'Hi!' Julie shouted back.

He wasn't so much looking at her as at her front. He seemed deeply fascinated by it, but then it *was* very mobile. 'You here alone then Luv!?'

Suddenly Julie wished she were. 'No, with my friends!'

She indicated Debbie and Sharon. He glanced at them briefly. They were no great beauties either, and lacked Julie's other attributes. But they knew the unspoken etiquette. If anyone looked as though there was a chance of being picked up, the others would discretely fade away. The girls did so now, moving away on the pretext of going in search of a drink, but not before casting envious glances at Julie and Handsome.

So the two of them were left together. He began to move rhythmically with the music, which had become Tina Turner's *We Don't Need A Hero*. He was good at it; he was a natural, moving easily and smoothly. He made Julie look wooden-footed and as if she had an extra one too.

'What's your name then Luv!?'

'Julie! You?'

'Paul!'

'Good name for Liverpool!'

'Yeah. Not as clever as him though!'

Julie was enchanted. This bloke was cool and droll with it. They danced until the end of the track and then Paul suggested a drink and a sit down. Julie was relieved; she was glad of it. She went up onto the dais to claim a seat as he went for the booze, returning with a pint for himself and lager for her. It was her fourth and she was beginning to feel pleasantly woozy. They sat and chatted, and he offered her a smoke, and she noticed with pleasure that he now spent at least as much time looking at her face as at her front. Julie felt she had to ask about his earlier companion.

'What happened to your friend then?'

'Oh, her? Sandra? Don't think I'll be seeing her again.'

'Why not?'

He took her hand, gripping unnecessarily tightly. 'Don't ask, okay? The slag! It's over.' And with that he changed the subject.

He went for refills and came back with the same again for himself and a gin sling for her. Now Julie felt decidedly unsteady. The room was swimming; the noise oddly muffled, which was odd. Usually the decibels increased as the night wore on. She hoped she wasn't going to puke.

Suddenly he surprised her by saying, 'Jeez, hot in here innit it?' He certainly looked as overheated as Julie felt, judging by the underarm sweat marks on his tee shirt, and he smelled none-too-sweet if she were honest. Not that she minded. It was animal; enticing.

'Yeah; certainly is.'

'Shall we go outside for a bit?'

'That'd be good.' Julie felt she'd pass out if they stayed in here much longer. She doubted whether she could string more than three words together coherently now anyway; she was in no fit state for conversation. Perhaps a little fresh air might help.

Paul finished his half-empty glass in one long gulp and looked at her expectantly. It seemed she had to do the same, and so she did. He got up and she rose, unsteadily, and he led her off the dais and along the side of the dance floor to the foyer. Debbie and Sharon were still dancing and gave her, grinning, the thumbs-up. There was nothing to collect from the cloaks except her bag, which she retrieved as, rather befuddled, she doubted that she would be returning inside.

They left the club, through the former-cinema double glass doors. The bouncers were looking the other way and Paul led her, tottering, into the alley at the side. Julie knew it well from previous experience; it led to the yard at the rear, a dark scruffy wasteland of bins, weeds, vomit and litter. They stopped at the farthest corner, by the last overflowing bin, and Julie sagged back against the grimy brick wall. Paul's hands were straight away on her shoulders, her sides, her flopping chest, cupping her face, all over her, his mouth rough and beery on hers, tongue forcing its way between her lips almost making her gag, but she wanted him, wanted to swallow him whole, take him right down inside. Or was it right *up* inside?

Now his hand was inside her skirt, cupping her bum. He clawed her knickers down, roughly down, bending to pull them tangled, snagging, over one shoe, leaving them hanging like a trophy around the other ankle. He returned his hand as a perch for her bottom and trusting him she sat and wrapped her plump white thighs around the small of his back. He was unzipped and his hot, engorged, urgent member into her before she had time to gasp, let alone say no. His free hand fumbled her top free from her waistband, snaked inside, slithering up hot damp flesh and pushing her loose bra up and aside and squeezing her liberated breast and tweaking her nipple hard, making her cry out in pain, cry out in ecstasy as he thrust hard, deep, in his lust and anger, anger at being thrown over by Sandra, until with an animal grunt he quickly came.

For Julie and Paul it was no more than one minute and forty-eight seconds of unbridled lust, quickly forgotten. They weren't to know that there was an ovum currently in Julie's left fallopian tube, being stroked sedately through to self-destruct in her uterus in due course. (She was never very aware of her menstrual cycle; her period always came as a bit of a surprise.) And Paul, who was even more clueless, wouldn't have known that not so long after taking her so forcefully, there would be hundreds of his spermatozoa milling and wriggling around that cell, each intent on entry, trying for a second microscopic penetration through that tough (for a spermatozoon anyway) membrane of the ovum. Or that one would succeed, to unite its incomplete package of chromosomes with the ovum's, pooling their particular and unique recipes of genes.

Neither would have realised that the resulting zygote was beginning its long miraculous journey to join the ranks of humankind; that it would divide, and divide again, and again. That it would complete the first leg of the journey and reach the temporary sanctuary of the womb. That it would divide yet again, but this time something rare and extraordinary would happen. Eight cells of the now sixteen would, for some inexplicable reason, declare independence and remove themselves fully from the others; take themselves off to begin a quite separate existence. There would be created mutual clones.

And the so vigorously copulating pair in the dingy yard behind Slinky's was quite unaware that the successful spermatozoon had been of the Y-type. The two tiny specks of potential humanity now anchored in the lining of Julie's uterus were monozygotic males.

Growing in her womb were identical twin brothers.

Of course Julie, at any rate, soon became only too aware that something was amiss. Even she knew what a period failing to appear meant. But surely it couldn't be. Could it? Okay; that first time had just happened. It was just one of those things. But after that, as the relationship developed (in Julie's eyes anyway, although Paul's interest didn't seem to extend much beyond three discrete parts of her body) they had always been careful to use rubbers.

At three weeks overdue, having confided her growing anxiety to Becky at work, she was persuaded to buy a home testing kit. She took it home that night, and read the instructions, and sat trying to summon up the courage to go to the bathroom (she couldn't wait until the best time, the following morning), putting it off and putting it off until she was nearly wetting herself, until finally with a thumping heart she screwed up her courage and tested her wee. And of course it changed to the colour she didn't want.

She didn't sleep that night. She wept, long and bitterly. She cursed herself over and over again. Why in the name of Jesus couldn't she have said no? It must have been that first time. Not very likely, true, but it could happen, so she'd heard. And it only needed one time, after all. But Paul had been so insistent; she couldn't have denied him, even if she'd wanted to, which she hadn't. Besides, there'd been a simmering anger in him that night; she could tell. To have refused him might only have resulted in rape. But anyway; what now? The thought of motherhood was appalling.

She knew only too well what a burden it had been for Mammy, bringing up nine children in that miserable little slum of a house in Sligo; Da coming in drunk most evenings and slapping her around (but then still screwing her of course), before he eventually walked out to shack up with a younger model, leaving her to cope alone. She remembered the nights after that; her mother's dead-eyed exhausted look; her siblings' frequent tetchy bickering; the constant red-faced bawling from six-month old brother Seamus, who could never be comforted. She'd been glad to get out of it after she'd left school and come to Liverpool to live with older sister Maeve, who paid for her to do a secretarial course, which was kind of her, but who then took up with a fella who wanted to move in and suddenly three became a crowd, and she had to leave and find her own crummy bedsit.

If those were the joys of motherhood, you could keep them. Besides, seventeen was much too young. She'd seen what being a young mum was like: Sharon's Kylie was one. She was only sixteen, poor kid, and had no life at all since dropping little Brett. Kids were great as long as they were someone else's. But then again; Kylie was a single mum. She had little support. On the other hand she herself had Paul. And he had quite a decent job, at Halewood making Land Rovers so he'd told her. He'd be a good provider. Perhaps it wouldn't be so bad after all. Yeah. He looked as though he might like kids, particularly one of his own. She'd phone him if she could, but for some unknown reason he wouldn't give her his phone number. Bit of a mystery man he was really! So she'd just have to wait until she saw him on Wednesday night for a drink or three; could tell him then after they'd had a few jars and then some energetic How's Your Father later at his flat, after which he'd be in a mellow mood. Hopefully.

Well that was the theory, anyway.

Paul, as always, enjoyed parts one and two of the planned programme. After she'd climbed sated and still trembling off him, disappointed as usual to feel his rapid flaccidity, and flopped down on her back as he reached for cigarettes for them both, she braced herself to bring up the subject. She turned and snuggled close to him, stroking the dark hair that began so soon below his collar bones.

'That was brilliant, you wicked man.'
'Well, gotta keep the ladies happy,' he preened, smugly.
'It really is a great way of making babies, don't you think?'
He stopped, cigarette halfway to mouth, and looked at her

sharply. 'Waddya mean?'

'Well, you know; it's a lovely way to start things off.'

He was staring at her in alarm. 'But we aren't having one. That's what the Johnnies are for! What the fuck are you talking about?'

Julie felt her mouth go dry. 'But don't you think it would be nice?'

He removed his free arm from around her shoulder, crossly. 'No; of course I bloody don't!'

Julie felt a chill of alarm, as if the temperature had just dropped ten degrees. 'But what if we found we were having one?' Her voice had shrivelled; all confidence gone.

He was getting annoyed. 'But we aren't, you silly cow. Why are you going on about it?'

He paused. Half-realisation dawned. 'Hang on a minute. Are you trying to say . . . ?'

'Yes.' Her voice was a whisper.

Paul sat up abruptly, pushing her roughly away; glared down at her.

'Oh Christ no! But how can you be? Fuck's sake!'

'It must have been that first time. I should never have let you!'

He snorted derisively. 'Oh come on; you were gagging for it. You led me on, dressed like that. You slut!'

'No Paul, no; I didn't! Really!' Her tears were flowing in a hot salty torrent now.

He watched her sob, dispassionately. There was no comforting hand on her shoulder or in her hair. There were no soft consoling words.

Eventually he spoke. 'Anyway; what are you going to do about it?'

'Do about it? What do you mean?' she asked; the questions tremulous between gasps.

'Well, get rid of it of course, what do you think?'

'But we'll get married, won't we?'

'Married?' He was incredulous. 'No of course we won't! I don't want to do that and I don't want your sprog either!'

'But it's ours! Yours too!'

'Well I don't bloody want it. Just get rid of it, okay?'

That set her off again. Hands palmed to eyes, face beetroot red, she wept as if her world were ending, completely abandoned to sorrow, all hope evaporated clean away.

Clumsily, belatedly, Paul tried mollification. He ruffled her hair. 'Ah, come on now Jules! What's so wrong with having it got rid of? It happens all the time.'

'No Paul,' she pleaded. 'No! I can't do that. I'm Catholic. It's a sin. No!'

He took his hand away, sneering again. 'Sin? You didn't find it such a mortal sin when you were fucking me did you? Don't make me laugh!' Although he did laugh, but it was bitter, not amused.

Julie had stopped crying again. She had no tears left; just a dull leaden resignation. 'No, I can't have an abortion. My mother would never forgive me. I'm sorry.'

'And it's my body anyway; I'll do what I want with it,' she added bravely.

There was a long silence, as he stared ahead and she buried her face in the pillow. Then he said, calmly, utterly cold, 'Okay then, yes, it's up to you. You can please yourself. Come on, get dressed. I'll take you home.'

And that was the last Julie saw of Paul.

He didn't ask to see her again when he dropped her back at her bedsit. At first she assumed – well, hoped – that he was just angry, or hadn't yet got over the shock of her surprise revelation, or both. He'd surely get over it in a week or two though? He couldn't desert her now. If he didn't want to get married, that was fine. She was okay with that. She didn't want him to feel any more trapped than he perhaps already did. Lots of people lived in sin, as Mammy would put it, nowadays.

But as the days went by, and then the weeks, he made no attempt to get in touch. She looked again in the phone book but he wasn't listed. Must be ex-directory. She started going to *Slinky's* again but he was never there, apart from one night when she saw him enter, have a long and careful look around, walk up onto the dais to get a better sweep, apparently spot her (although she couldn't be sure) and then make a hasty exit. She never saw him there again. She even, pathetically, took the bus to his flat one Saturday afternoon but his car wasn't parked outside, so she sat on his doorstep and waited for nearly three hours until it appeared making its way down the street, but as it got close, instead of slowing down it suddenly accelerated instead and drove straight on past, his head facing resolutely forward. He must have seen her. She walked to the nearest bus top and made her disconsolate way home.

She began to accept that she'd lost him. She couldn't keep kidding herself that he'd suddenly appear, full of remorse for his rejection, and promise to stick by her come what may. She'd been such a stupid little fool. And now here she was, far from home with a kid on the way. How would she ever cope? She didn't even know whether, as a non-Brit, she'd be able to get Social and all the rest of it. But she could hardly turn up back home like the Prodigal Son (no, Daughter) with a baby in tow. Mammy would probably throw her straight out again. She wasn't the most forgiving of mothers.

And she'd never registered with a doctor. Well, she'd never needed to. Again, she wasn't sure if she could anyway, being Irish. Holy Mother of Jesus, what was she going to do? In desperation, she put scruples aside and found the name of a private clinic that did abortions and vasectomies and made an appointment. The doctor there, apparently from the Indian subcontinent, was very kind and examined her carefully and asked when she thought she might have conceived (she'd worked it out from the calendar so could tell him that to the day, anyway) and calculated from *his* calendar on his desk how many weeks gone she was, and seemed a bit surprised in view of the size of her belly, which was already looking quite conspicuously pregnant. He asked her if she was sure, and she said yes, but he still looked dubious.

He said that, judging by the size of her, she must be pretty much at the legal limit for terminations and he couldn't possibly exceed it on pain of losing his license or even being struck off, whatever that meant, but he could fit her in in three days time. Then he told her the fee, which was payable in advance, but she simply hadn't got that much money and told him so, and he said sorry; they weren't a charity and it seemed that her best course of action in that case would be to come to terms with the prospect of being an unmarried mother and possibly go back home to Ireland.

Yes, she thought, after she'd paid the fee for the consultation and walked back home because she was now skint (she'd thrown a sickie to explain her absence from work), perhaps he was right. That did seem the best, or at any rate least worst, option. Perhaps Mammy would be okay about it. And then she wouldn't be going against the Church's teaching. Not in that respect, anyway.

But when, after the following payday (she wasn't too sure how many more there'd be; the boss was beginning to look at her waistline rather suspiciously) when she was back in funds and she summoned up the courage to phone home to Sligo, her hopes were dashed again. Mammy just hit the roof, calling her a tart, a little hussy, a disgrace to the family name, so she was. How could she possibly come back home? Whatever would the neighbours say? She'd had quite enough of being stigmatised herself already, so she had. She'd made her own bed and now she'd have to lie in it.

And so that was that. There'd be no support from that quarter then. All the avenues of escape from her predicament were one by one closing off, as far as Julie could see. Doors were slamming shut. There were few options left, it seemed. The weeks passed and she steadily ballooned. She hated the sight of her distended belly with its curiously engorged navel (why was that?), her swollen uncomfortable breasts with their dark organ-stop nipples, the increasing backache, the morning sickness that made her feel so wretched; and she dreaded the delivery. Please God; perhaps she might miscarry? That would be a solution. If she got through this she'd swear on the Holy Book never to allow another cock near her again, so help her. But then one morning, sitting on the edge of the bed getting dressed, she felt the first faint kick and somehow knew that wouldn't happen either; she would just have to face the trauma of it all.

Of course, before long she was called into the boss's office and handed her cards. Well; given the push anyway. She couldn't actually be formally fired because she hadn't been formally working. And Veronique, her landlady (again informal), who must have been knocking on for fifty but was still on The Game, became aware of her situation pretty smartish. Veronique (real name Mandy) was a kind-hearted soul though. She empathised. She'd been there more than once herself. When the tearful Julie poured out her heart, telling her confidante that she really didn't want the pregnancy, that her boyfriend had deserted her and her mother rejected her too, that she was terrified of motherhood, Veronique/Mandy was all sympathy. 'Yes Luv, I know, believe me,' she comforted, rubbing her knee as they sat in her kitchen drinking tea, 'Life can be an absolute bastard at times.'

She promised the despondent Julie that she'd see her through this. She knew what to do. And she had a friend who delivered babies. She'd be fine.

Christmas came and quickly went again. There was no trekking back to Ireland that year or even spending it with Maeve and boyfriend Tony. Maeve was as disapproving as Mammy and felt put out that she'd squandered good money on a secretarial course for her sister only for the silly little cow to get herself up the duff and have nothing to look forward to now except single parenthood. So it was spent in the ribald company of Veronique/Mandy and her workmates (they having been given three days off from work by Aimee (Andrea), who ran the massage parlour).

And then it was the end of January 1985, followed before she knew where she was by the last knockings of February. Veronique/Mandy became secretly concerned about the size of Julie. For someone about six and a half months gone now, if Julie was to be believed about the conception date it looked like it was going to be one enormous baby. Would her friend Madge be able to cope with the delivery when it came? Okay; Madge was a qualified midwife (albeit a struck-off-for-misconduct one) but even so . . . But then, if the worse came to the worse, there was always an emergency ambulance and A and E to fall back on. If it came to that, they'd just have to concoct some sort of story.

Things were taken out of Veronique's hands a fortnight later though. Late in from the parlour one evening (there having been a particularly demanding last minute customer who wanted Veronique's' 'special,' but he was a regular so they couldn't say no), she was alerted to screams from Julie's room. She ran up the stairs, heart pounding, and rapped on her door before barging straight in. Julie was curled on her bed in a pool of amniotic fluid, red faced and gasping, looking terrified out of her wits.

'Oh Christ,' said Veronique, and ran back downstairs to the phone.

They were waiting, forewarned, incubators at the ready, for the ambulance to arrive. Wayne and Tom quickly carried the tiny bundles inside. Wayne's face was like thunder. He was normally composed and totally unflappable in an emergency, but this had really got to him. He was livid, unsurprisingly really. Jan had had their first only last Tuesday and he was still euphoric about it.

He addressed the team: Marjory Baxter, consultant paediatrician; Bev Rees, paediatric staff nurse; and other members of the night shift.

'How the hell could anyone do this; how *could* they?'

Marjory was cool efficiency personified though. 'Okay; calm down,' she soothed, 'tell us what you've got,' as the babies were swiftly placed in the incubators and relieved of the blankets the ambulance men had swaddled them in. Wayne pulled himself together. 'Found in a ladies' loo, can you believe? Together in a bloody cardboard box, like unwanted kittens or something! Thankfully they were spotted almost straight away, we think. But not before whoever left them had scarpered. Looks as though they're newborns. Not even cleaned up yet. Both got pulses and breathing, but the smaller one's is a bit ragged. Poor little mites!'

The incubators were whisked into paediatric intensive care and Marjory got to work. She examined the smaller one first (although they were both tiny – certainly prems, by a good five weeks, probably). Heart reasonably okay although the beat quite rapid and a touch too shallow. Airways clear but breathing, as the angry ambulance man had said, a bit on the erratic side. Best on oxygen for a while. The larger one was better: heart and lungs really quite good, considering. Both seemed to have all their components, externally anyway. She'd check them more thoroughly later, when they were fully stabilised. She popped bigger baby on the scales. Four pounds two ounces (she still couldn't think in terms of metric, to save her life). Not bad. Then she quickly weighed the smaller one. Three pounds ten. Um; could be better, although she'd seen a lot worse.

She looked at them both carefully as they lay, tidied up now with oversize woollen caps and wearing tiny nappies, safe now in their warm environments. They'd need some colostrum ideally, if there were any available. Apart from their size they looked remarkably similar. Monozygotics, possibly? That might explain the size disparity. Could have been a common placenta, but there was no way of knowing now. One might have been taking more than his share. Interesting. But anyway, it was academic. Unless tests showed up anything really untoward, they should both be okay.

And that was the inauspicious start the brothers had to life. They could so easily have expired even before they'd begun it, had they not been found quickly (when Veronique had peeped cautiously into the Ladies she'd found a cubicle occupied and so dropped the box with its blanket-nest of babies by the wash basins and beaten a hasty retreat back to Madge's waiting car). And had they not been conveyed very quickly indeed by the surprised and appalled ambulance men to hospital. Of course the police were involved, but there were no clues at all as to the identity of the depositor of the tiny human package. The find made both the local and national news and the police went on television appealing for the mother to come forward, because apart from anything else she might need medical help, but they drew a complete blank. With no clue as to their identities, the babies needed names, if only temporary ones. Perhaps the birth mother might eventually come to light (but of course, even if she were discovered, she probably wouldn't have named them anyway as seemingly she didn't want them), but in the meantime they had to be called something.

The paediatric staff discussed it and Marjory suggested naming them for their ambulance men rescuers. Everyone agreed; they were the heroes of the piece. And so Wayne and Tom they became.

In good and caring hands now, they thrived, soon beginning to put on weight. Tom, the smaller sibling, came off oxygen support as his lungs and heart strengthened. And so they spent their first few days in a world into which they'd been thrust rather too soon. And one, sadly, without the welcoming, loving arms of parents. Although, as helpless tiny foundlings, they certainly did not go short of love from everyone in the paediatric unit. Soft-hearted Wayne senior and his colleague Tom became regular visitors on their time off, taking great interest in their namesakes' progress.

The little boys were quite unaware of their inauspicious start in life as they lay in their incubators with no other concerns than sleeping and suckling (although, sadly, not at a breast) and excreting. Never remember the surprise on occasional-midwife Madge's face when tiny Tom arrived first and it was suddenly apparent that there was another to come. (She'd assumed it was just one large, very active baby). Recall that they'd been shown to their exhausted young mother with the question, 'Do you want to keep them?,' and the tearful sideways shake of her perspiring head with its mop of greasy half blonde, half red hair as she turned her anguished face into the pillow and wept bitter, relieved, confused tears.

But they were well out of it, these two little mites with the first wisps of startlingly red hair. Their birth mother didn't keep her vow of celibacy for long, and she would not have coped well with them.

    Instead they would be loved by other, surrogate parents who most certainly did want and love them. Oh yes: they would be loved.

Chapter 2
Divergence

It was time for a family conference. A crucially important one that would have, in all fairness, to involve Lowri. She was only nine years old, but even so. This was nineteen eighty-six for heaven's sake, not the bad old days when children were never consulted. Glyn and Sioned Rees were modern in their outlook, they liked to think. What they were now seriously considering would impact as much on her as themselves. She'd had nine years of being the centre of attention, of being an only child. That might be about to change. So she had every right to an opinion as to whether she wanted to share her parents with a sibling.

But the thing was, it – he or she – wouldn't, couldn't now, be a biological one. Glyn and Sioned had always thought they could be content with Lowri. And of course in one sense they were. Absolutely. She was everything you could wish for in a child: happy, bright, funny, enthusiastic, a joy to be around (most of the time anyway). But nevertheless, wouldn't it be so much nicer, the family be so much more complete, if there were a second child? A brother or sister for Lowri? So long as she wanted to have one, naturally. In the normal way she wouldn't have been consulted of course, but this was different. This was a conscious choice whether or not to expand the family. It didn't involve a physical act and the following miraculous evolution, if you were lucky. It involved instead a solemn assurance to the powers-that-be that you would take a child that someone else hadn't wanted and love and cherish him or her just as much as if she or he were your biological own. It was an enormous commitment and responsibility.

Glyn remembered how it had been after Lowri's far-from-easy birth (which had had to be a caesarean in the end and for a terrifying twenty minutes had threatened Sioned's life too); his mixed up emotions; relief at the eventual safe delivery and saving of his wife's life all swirled up with the joy of the new tiny arrival in his and Sioned's life. After that experience with its emotional overload, their lives had felt complete. It really didn't matter that

Sioned must never risk pregnancy again. He'd willingly submitted to a (rather painful, to be honest) vasectomy. The past eight years had certainly been happy. They'd moved to Liverpool in search of brighter lights than were to be found in west Wales and he'd done quite well in his job as a surveyor at the estate agents.

And yet...

And yet. In recent months Lowri sometimes talked wistfully (or so it seemed) about her little friends having brothers and sisters. And they couldn't help feeling sometimes that she was just a little deprived. Well, disadvantaged anyway. She was probably just a tiny bit spoiled; had never had to learn about sharing. Inevitably.

And then, a few nights ago, they'd looked at a programme on the telly about adoption; about how there was a dearth of potential adoptive parents and how some poor kids had to spend years in institutional care, which was fine as far as it went (the staff did their best) but could never be as good as life in a normal family. Sioned had gone very quiet, and continued pensive later in bed. Glyn knew her so well, could easily divine what she was thinking. She wasn't settling to sleep; something was on her mind.

He knew he'd have to make the first move.

'Penny for them?'

Sioned turned towards him and snuggled close, hand across his chest. 'Oh; you know. Just thinking about those poor little kids.'

'Well they looked well taken care of.'

She sighed. 'Yes I'm sure they were. They looked happy enough. But it's not the same as being in a proper family is it?'

Glyn gave the shoulder his arm was around a squeeze. 'No you're right, Cariad. It isn't . Every child deserves love.'

Sioned lapsed into silence. Then: 'Glyn...'

'Yes?' He could almost have predicted what was coming.

Another silence, and then, cautiously, the words forming reluctantly: 'What if we did that?'

'Did what?'

'Glyn! You know exactly what!'

'What; you mean adopt?'

'Well why not?'

'Duw Duw Sioned! Hang on!'

'No but why not, really? Wouldn't it be nice for Lowri to have a brother or sister?'

'Well, yes, but . . .'

'You know she'd like it!'

'Well no, we don't actually. She's never mentioned it.' Glyn paused. 'Has she?'

'Well not actually in so many words.'

'Then we'd have to ask her opinion. Obviously.'

Glyn could sense her head lifting in the dark to look at him.

'You mean . . . you'd like the idea? Perhaps?'

Glyn grinned. 'Well you've probably got your way as usual, woman!'

Sioned punched him on the chest, quite hard.

'Glyn; be serious! You know we'd have to be in total agreement about this. All three of us!'

He rubbed her shoulder reassuringly. 'Yes, of course we would. Let me think it over. But yes; the idea does appeal, come to think about it.'

'Okay', Sioned said (he could feel her relaxing), you have a long think, and so will I, and we'll talk about it some more, and if we both want to go for it we'll ask Lowri what she thinks. How's that?'

'Yes; sounds good to me. Let's do that.'

Sioned suddenly felt unaccountably amorous.

So now it was crunch time. They were sitting in the lounge, Glyn in an armchair and Sioned and Lowri together on the sofa. There was nothing particularly interesting on telly so it had gone off. Lowri made to get up, announcing that she was going up to her room. Sioned put a restraining hand on her arm. 'Just a minute Cariad; Daddy and I have something we want to talk about with you.' So they told her what they'd been discussing lately, frequently, in the intimacy of their bed. Talking about it over and over again, turning their germinating mutual (yes, it was genuinely mutual now) wish this way and that, upside down, inside out, examining it from every angle, trying to be rational (but finding that difficult, to be honest) as the desire took root. Told her of their settled and agreed idea which over a week's gestation (although perhaps it had lain there dormant, unrecognised for a long time) had become a want, then a need, then a craving. A *hiraeth* indeed. Lowri knew that Mummy couldn't have any more babies of her own (Sioned had had a serious, girl-to-girl conversation with her on the subject some time ago). And so what did she think?

Of course it came as a complete bolt out of the blue to Lowri. The thought had never entered her mind. Sioned's nervous presentation of the notion had ground to an anxious halt. Lowri looked from one parent to the other, lost for once for something to say.

Finally she spoke. 'Oh, right, have you chosen a baby yet then?'

Glyn smiled. *Typical; the child's three steps ahead of herself already.* 'No, not yet Cariad! We're still at the idea stage. Mummy and I just wanted to run it past you first; see what you thought.'

Lowri pondered it some more. *Um. Quite a good idea. Yes, it could be nice.*

'So would it be a boy or girl?'

Sioned spoke now. 'Well, that would be for us to decide. Are you saying you like the idea?'

Lowri felt suddenly that she had immense power. Whether or not another member was added to the family could depend on her. So what did she think, really, deep down? As her parents watched anxiously, she gave the matter yet more thought. *Would I really like a baby sister? Well, perhaps it wouldn't even be a baby. Can you choose how old it is? A baby would be nice though. Then it would be almost as if Mummy had had it herself. Or it could be a baby brother! That would be better still. Yes, that's it. Definitely a baby brother.*

With all the authority and arrogance of a nine-year-old only child she spoke up, boldly, fixing each parent in turn with a condescending expression. 'Yes, I have decided. I would like a baby brother.'

Sioned expelled a huge sigh of relief. Glyn put hand to mouth, concealing a grin, but he was relieved too, to be honest.

Back from hospital and the D and C (the fourth one now!), worn out and utterly dejected, with bitter tears still barely constrained, Maureen went up to bed early. Every time it got worse. Every time, in spite of extra-special care (and the doctors and midwives did really try, give them their due) and although each time they coaxed her unwilling uterus along a bit further (she'd got as far as twenty-one weeks this time; the foetus must have been a recognisable albeit miniscule baby), the result, with the same devastating inevitability, was the same: miscarriage. The discomfort, the morning sickness, but worst of all the anxiety, the holding of breath, the ultra-carefulness, had once again been all for nothing. It was all so unfair. For the umpteenth time since she'd bled and known only too well what that betokened, she surrendered to self-pity and wept.

Jim must have heard, because two minutes later he was poking his head around the bedroom door.

'Alright, Luv?'

An inane question of course. Of course she wasn't alright. He quickly undressed and climbed in beside her, taking her in his arms and letting her sob uncontrollably. After a while she calmed, tears spent.

He spoke, his voice heavy with sorrow and concern. 'We really can't let you go through all this again.'

She answered tiredly, 'No, I couldn't face it. I really couldn't. We'll just have to accept that it's meant to be.'

'No; so it seems.'

Silence fell, oppressive, like a heavy damp fog.

Then Jim said, 'We could always try IVF, with a surrogate mother, perhaps.'

'How do you mean?' Maureen's voice betrayed dubiousness and caution.

'Well, you know. They fertilise one of your eggs with one of my sperm and then implant it in another woman, who actually has it, then she gives the baby to us. Or something like that. You hear of it happening, don't you?' Jim's knowledge of the subject was hazy, to say the least.

'No, I don't think they do that. Why would they need to combine my egg and your sperm artificially? Surely they could just take my fertilised egg and put it in someone else's womb.'

'Don't ask me,' said Jim. 'I just thought I'd heard about it somewhere.'

Maureen wasn't convinced though. 'But anyway, just imagine; why would a woman want to carry someone else's child, and then have it and give it away. What if she found she couldn't part with it?'

'Well I think what usually happens is, the woman's sister does it. So there'd be no risk of that. But I really don't know.'

Maureen laughed humourlessly. 'Oh yeah, right; I can just see our Jane offering to do that, can't you?'

Jim had to admit that it was unlikely. His wife and sister-in-law were not the greatest soul-mates.

'No,' Maureen continued glumly. It just wouldn't happen, and I don't have a wonderfully concerned friend who'd be prepared to go through all that for me either. Certainly no one I could possibly ask. Well you couldn't, could you?'

'No, I suppose not,' Jim had to concede.

'So there you are then. It's not going to happen. No; no way.'

'Oh well,' said Jim. 'It was just a thought.'

They lapsed into silence again. Jim got up, went into the bathroom to wash his face and brush his teeth.

When he came back Maureen was still wide awake, gazing unfocused at the ceiling. Jim wasn't going to let the matter drop. He took her hand, pressed it to his lips then held it against his chest.

'There is one other possibility of course . . .' He left the sentence dangling.

'What's that?'

'Well; what about adoption?'

Maureen looked at him sharply. 'No!'

'Why not?'

'*Why not?* We've just lost another baby and you're suggesting that? Taking on someone else's? How could you Jim!' Her voice was rising, threatening hysteria and more tears.

Jim was quick to contrition. 'I'm sorry Luv. Don't get upset again. Putting my great big foot in it as usual. Sorry.'

Maureen was mollified, but only a little. 'Well it just wouldn't be the same, would it? It wouldn't be our flesh and blood. I want to have *your* baby, not some other man's!'

'Yes, I know Sweetheart. I would have really wanted you to, to have ours. I'd have given anything. And maybe if we tried again, the next time it might happen. But what if it still didn't and this happened yet again? I couldn't put you through it again. Bloody hell; I couldn't put *myself* through it again.'

Maureen sighed. 'No, we couldn't risk it. Not again. It looks like we're fated to be childless.'

'Yes,' Jim agreed sadly. 'It does.'

But Jim had sowed a seed. Three weeks later the subject came up again. There'd been a programme on the box about some famous celebrity who was researching her roots. It wasn't easy for her because she'd been an adopted child and a foundling to boot, she'd learned, and with no knowledge of her birth parents, or possibly just birth mother, researching her ancestry was difficult. She'd confessed disappointment, but looking straight to close-up camera with glistening eyes she'd confessed that she loved her adoptive parents dearly; she couldn't have wished for better ones. She had no regrets, felt no sense of deprivation at all. Smiling bravely, she'd remarked that she might also have been disappointed had she been able to track down her birth parents anyway. She'd formed a deep unbreakable bond of love with Maisie and Sid, whom she regarded totally as her parents. Her interest in her biological parents was only academic, but the Mum and Dad she'd come to regard as her own were real and irreplaceable. After that she'd broken down embarrassingly and after a few moments they'd cut the filming.

Jim had looked slyly at Maureen. Her eyes were shining. She'd turned and looked at him, sensing that his eyes were on her, and given a quivery smile. In that moment, they knew, both individually and collectively, what they wanted to do.

And so, after more earnest discussion, and not really knowing what the procedure was, Maureen had phoned the Social Services Department of the City Council and spoken to a very sympathetic and helpful woman who had put literature in the post. They'd read it together, avidly, and then contacted Social Services again saying they wanted to apply to be adoptive parents. And so they'd embarked on the lengthy process of assessment, home visits with many probing questions by an assigned social worker called Joy (it seemed an appropriate name in the circumstances) and visits to 'workshops' in child care and the particular needs of adopted children.

It had seemed to go on forever, and they'd begun to get a little impatient with Joy, but she'd explained that these things took time: it was a big responsibility the council had to place children with suitable, dependable and loving adoptive parents. Don't worry, she'd said, it looked as if they'd meet all the criteria, whatever that meant. The final decision didn't rest with her but it looked as if they'd be alright. But all the hoops had to be jumped through; it was just the way it was. They confessed to her that, if accepted, they would prefer a small child, a baby even, rather than an older one that might have emotional problems. Joy had looked momentarily disappointed (most would-be adopters said that; the older children, particularly the 'difficult' ones, were always more difficult to place) but had smiled reassuringly then and said yes, that was understandable; they hadn't had the joy of experiencing a baby and small child of their own so they'd obviously want that now. Besides, the younger you started with a child, the better the bonding, usually.

And then, finally, after four months they'd been invited to the assessment panel, before which they'd sat nervously, secretly holding hands under the table as if their very lives depended on it, and then there'd been a nerve-wracking few days before a letter had come telling them officially that, yes, they were considered to be suitable candidates as parents. It was simply a matter now of matching them to the right child.

That had been three weeks ago. Now, today, there was another letter from Joy. There was a little boy, a baby, who looked as if he'd fit their bill. They'd said they would prefer a boy, hadn't they? If they were interested, there would now have to be a series of getting-to-know-you visits to the children's home. *If they were interested indeed!* Maureen's heart hadn't slowed since she'd read the letter. She couldn't wait for Jim to come home!

Glyn and Sioned stood before the ornate iron gates of Strawberry Field Children's Home, both feeling extremely nervous.

'Well this is it, Cariad', said Glyn. 'Moment of truth.'

Sioned reached for and squeezed his hand. 'Yes, certainly is. We're about to commit ourselves, I think.'

'I feel terrified, to be honest with you,' Glyn admitted.

'Me too,' said Sioned.

'Well, come on,' he said, 'let's get it over with. We can always change our minds I suppose if it doesn't feel right.'

They'd been advised not to bring Lowri for this first meeting. Best to keep things simple. They could see the wisdom of that, knowing their daughter. She'd agreed in principle to adopting anyway. So it was just the two of them ringing the doorbell now and trying to calm their heart rates. Knowing that the home was run by the Salvation Army, they were a little surprised when the door was opened by a gentle-faced woman in her forties dressed in normal attire: a straight brown skirt and beige jumper.

'Hello, Mr and Mrs Rees is it? Do come in. I'm Captain Price. But call me Susan.'

'Hello, er . . .'

Their host grinned broadly. 'Yes, you're wondering about the uniform, or the lack of it, aren't you? It's alright; we only wear civvies at the home. Makes it feel more normal for the children. Not too institutional!'

It certainly did feel indistinguishable from any home in a typical upper middle class Victorian house as she led them into a bright cheerful lounge that would doubtless have been a drawing room in grander times. And as they entered the room, still the impression was one of a normal family tableau, with a small group of children playing happily and a young woman who could quite easily have been their mother watching over them with a benevolent expression on her kind face.

Susan Price indicated armchairs. 'Please sit down.'

They sat and took in the gathering. There were five children: a girl and boy of three or so, a solemn little boy who looked to be about two, a girl of perhaps five who was deeply engrossed in dressing a doll and completely ignoring them, and another girl who was possibly around seven. She was sitting on a sofa nursing a baby who had astonishingly red curly hair. Beside her, the young woman was holding what looked like a duplicate, although a little larger by the look of him. And they were dressed differently: one in a tiny pale blue jumpsuit, the other in a lime green one.

Sioned looked at them, fascinated. They must be the ones. They'd been shown photos. Six month-old identical twin boys; both at present available. Glyn had remarked jokingly that it was a bit like choosing from a litter of pups, before she'd thumped him for his pains. They'd said, when declaring a tentative interest, that they didn't feel they could take on two, but their contact at Social Services had said, trying to stifle a look of slight disappointment, that that was fine; she understood, particularly as they already had a biological child of their own. Most would-be adopters said they could only take on one child, and whilst it was a pity that the brothers couldn't be placed together, with there being fewer adopters than adoptees they had to grateful that they could find enough suitable ones at all.

Susan walked over and took the larger twin from Tracey, the

young woman, and brought him to Sioned. Glyn left his chair and came to kneel beside her.

'This is Wayne. Say hello to the nice lady Wayne!'

But the baby was having none of it. As he was handed over his bottom lip began to tremble, he screwed up his eyes, paused and bawled, astonishingly loudly. Shocked, Sioned tried pacification. 'Ah, come on Bach; it's alright. Shush! There there!' She tried cuddling but the baby wouldn't be comforted.

'Let me try,' Glyn offered, and leaned to take the howling baby. He came to him, but was no more impressed than he'd been with Sioned. He could make an extraordinarily loud noise for such a little person. Glyn's baby-mollifying skills were no more effective than Sioned's. After a minute or two of this, with no cessation in sight, Susan took him back and returned him to Tracey. The cure was almost instant. He buried his face in her ample bosom, put a thumb into his mouth and quietened, peering now and then with great suspicion at the alarming strangers.

A pall of embarrassment fell. Susan had a plan though. She left the room, returning with several tiny tubs of pink yogurt and plastic spoons, which were distributed amongst the children but not the babies. 'This usually works,' she said, 'hasn't failed yet anyway'.

No, I'll bet, Sioned mused. *It worked pretty well with our Lowri too.*

Susan had given two of the yogurts to Glyn, and he peeled the foil top from one. She said, 'Do you want to try with Tommy this time?' as without waiting for an answer she took the other baby from his minder and brought him over to Glyn.

'Give him a mouthful to try,' she commanded, holding the baby down to him, chubby legs dangling, as Glyn spooned some of the bright pink goo into the tiny rosebud mouth. It worked wonders. This baby's reaction to a stranger was quite different from his sibling's. His facial expression shifted in rapid succession from surprise, to delight as the sweetness hit, to determination as he stretched for the tub. Susan plonked him on Sioned's lap as Glyn quickly fed him another spoonful, and thus the connection was made, between culinary gratification and these strange people.

As Sioned held him, remembering the cuddliness and sweet baby scent of a six-month-old, Glyn fed him the rest of the yogurt and then gave him the tub to messily play with. Of course it went into his mouth too, and spilled the remnants onto her blouse, but she couldn't have cared less. On the basis of this intimacy, she would have chosen Tommy above Wayne there and then. But she and Glyn had to be fair minded and give the other baby equal consideration, and so Tommy was reluctantly handed back and the process repeated with his more timid sibling. But it worked with Wayne too. Even in *his* tiny unformed mind he was aware, vaguely, of missing out on something, and when he too was tempted with yogurt he quickly overcame his fear. Now he too sat confidently in Sioned's lap and received the ambrosia with alacrity.

Susan handed Tommy back again, this time to Glyn, and for the next half hour they nursed and played with a baby each. Sioned looked at the other children. They were eyeing her and Glyn with, what, envy? Did they have a sense that they were simply spectators in this curious game of choose-your-baby? Had would-be mothers and fathers visited and appraised any of them, but found them not to their liking? Certainly, none of them were as beautiful as the twins – not that that mattered of course. Well why should it? They were all children who needed every child's birthright: love. She wondered what sort of backgrounds they had to their short lives that had led them to be spending an interlude in the care of authority. Neglect possibly? Or inadequate parents? (or parent, singular?) Or even cruelty and abuse? Duw; she'd rather not even think about that. Poor little mites.

Their hour's visit quickly passed (there'd been tea and biscuits half way through, during the consumption of which they'd had to content themselves with just watching the babies), and Susan gently signalled its end by taking the twins from them. She showed them out. They hovered on the doorstep, reluctant to leave.

'Well there they are then. Fine little chaps aren't they?'

Sioned and Glyn nodded in fervent agreement.

'I expect you'll be in touch with Social Services now, when you've chosen one, although I don't envy you. It'll be a hard choice I would imagine.'

'Yes, it certainly will be,' Glyn agreed. 'It would be tempting to say we'll take them both, but we don't feel we can commit to that. It would be even more of a responsibility. And there's our daughter to think about.'

'Yes; you're quite right. I do understand. Anyway, if or when you've come to a decision, we'll arrange another, longer visit. There have to be a few, a process of getting-to-know-you, as I'm sure you've been told, before they'll release a child.'

Glyn promised Susan they'd be back in the near future, hopefully bringing Lowri if that was alright, (to which Susan affirmed yes; absolutely), and they took their leave. Driving home they talked it over. They must consider their choice carefully; not be too starry-eyed about it. It was an important decision, with a lot at stake.

'Duw, it's difficult to choose,' Glyn said.

'Yes,' said Sioned, 'of course it is. But going on first impressions, which one would you go for?'

Glyn glanced at her and smiled. 'Really tough, isn't it? They're both great. But I suppose Tommy just has the edge, perhaps. He wasn't at all shy about coming to us'

Sioned laughed. 'Yes, but that was partly the lure of the yogurt you know.'

She briefly covered his hand resting on the gear knob.

'But yes; I agree.'

Jim had hardly got in through the door and had a chance to call hello before Maureen was at him, waving the letter from Social Services, her eyes round with excitement.

'We've got a child!'

Jim laughed. 'Steady on Luv! Let me get inside the house then!'

He went and hung up his coat and then wandered through into the kitchen to sit at the table. That was their custom. He'd sit watching his wife as she finished cooking the dinner, lending a hand now and then, chatting about the day's events, the goings-on at work; asking about hers. He often thought her part-time (mornings only) job at the solicitors sounded more interesting than his: keeping the production lines running smoothly at the factory. She followed him through, still clutching the official missive as if it were notification that they'd won millions.

Thoughts of preparing dinner forgotten, she sat down opposite, on the only other chair at the small table, and spread the papers in front of him.

'Look, there's a photo. Isn't he sweet?'

Jim picked it up to study. It showed a baby nearing the walking stage, taken in what looked like quite an elegant living room. He was being held up to pose, standing in red dungarees between the knees of a seated young, plump, smiling woman. You might have thought him fairly unremarkable with his regular features beginning to foretell the looks of an average-looking child. Had it not been for his shock of vivid curly ginger-red hair. He'd presumably been prompted to, because his mouth was set in a grin that nevertheless hinted at shyness behind the beginnings of freckles.

Maureen began a rapid-fire commentary. 'His name is Wayne. He's one of identical twins. He's ten months old. He's living at Strawberry Field Children's Home . . .'

Jim interrupted. 'Oh, is that the place run by the Sally Army?'

'Yes, that's it. That place in Woolton. As immortalised by the Beatles. It's supposed to be a really nice home, apparently.'

'You say he's one of twins?'

'So it says here. But the other one's gone; already taken.'

'Really? I wonder why they weren't taken together.'

'Dunno. Perhaps the people just didn't want two.'

'Um; seems a shame,' said Jim. 'I thought they liked to keep siblings together.'

'Well maybe it was Hobson's Choice.' Maureen was getting a little irritated. 'Anyway, never mind that. Whatever the reason, they're offering him to us. Aren't you pleased?'

'Oh yes; don't get me wrong. Yes, he looks a grand little chap, doesn't he?'

'Yes. He's gorgeous. Look at that hair!'

'He'll probably get teased about that when he's bigger,' Jim remarked. 'Kids can be little sods sometimes.'

'Yes, well. He'll get lots of love to make up for it.'

Realising what she just said she caught herself, laughing. 'What?'

'Well, listen to me. I'm talking as if he's already ours!'

Jim laughed too. 'Better believe it Luv; I think he probably is, all bar the shouting.'

And with that, as Maureen reluctantly rose to absent-mindedly continue getting dinner ready, he reached for the literature.

They were as surprised by Susan's appearance when she answered the door as Glyn and Sioned had been four months earlier. Susan was well used to explaining it though, and led them into the lounge. There was a slightly different contingent of children now. The seven-year-old girl had gone and so had the self-contained little five-year-old female. And of course one tiny red-haired twin had gone. Replacing them there was a ten-year boy with a haunted, nervous expression on his face and a new baby in the care of Tracey, who was engaged in giving him or her a bottle.

Maureen would not have known about the turn-round of course and was only interested in one person present. He was currently up on wobbly legs, holding on determinedly to the edge of the sofa, concentrating hard on staying vertical. He'd had many lapses already resulting in a sudden sit down (although his bottom was of course well padded), and he meant to get the hang of this strange new bipedal thing.

The couple took the armchairs and Susan walked over to the sofa and took a chubby little hand in hers. 'Come along little man,' she coaxed, 'let's see if you can walk over to see these nice people.'

The baby took four tottering steps towards his would-be parents but then collapsed on the fifth. Maureen clapped her hands in delight. 'There's a clever boy; you nearly made it!'

Little Wayne was a trier though if nothing else. Hauled back onto his feet he continued his staggering progress, heading for Maureen, until at the last one Susan removed her hand and he fell forward into her arms. He was less timid now since the reward therapy, which had been repeated a month ago when prospective parents came to view (although they hadn't shown sufficient interest, Susan had reported back), and there were no tears. Maureen hauled his surprisingly heavy little body onto her lap. Oh; but it felt so *good!* It had been a while since she'd nursed a baby. *When was the last time? When Jane had Millie? Yes, that was it. But that was ages ago.*

'Hello Wayne,' she cooed. 'How are you then?' *What on earth did you say to babies?* She realised with a shock, a twinge of sadness, that she hadn't had a great deal of practice, not having seen a great deal of her sister.

Jim moved across and knelt by the chair. He moved a tentative finger to tickle the baby's belly. Any excuse to touch. He was struggling a little for words too. It was so difficult talking to a baby who couldn't talk back. Although you would have this problem anyway, right from day one, if you'd had a baby in the normal way.

But then you would just gradually get into the way of it; a verbalising relationship would grow as the baby slowly acquired language. So coming to it like this, being suddenly thrown in at the deep end, was bound to be difficult, he guessed. A thought suddenly struck: what if they were adopting a child from overseas; from a non-English-speaking country? That wouldn't exactly be easy either, but people did it, and presumably successfully. This ought to be simple compared with that. He felt a slight surge of panic. They couldn't just sit here staring at the child. They were supposed to be in getting-to-know-you mode. He was aware of Susan's eyes on him, registering his reactions. If they muffed this it would surely be reported back, and that would be the end of adopting for the pair of them.

He forced himself to relax. *Come on now you silly bugger. This adopting thing was your idea in the first place after all. Just talk. Say anything! It doesn't matter what; he can't understand you anyway!*

He began to speak, hesitantly at first but then more fluently, until the flow of words became a torrent of all the things he so wanted to say; had wanted to say for so long.

'Well now, little man. Would you like to come and live with us, do you think? We'd really like to have you. Think of all the fun things we could do together. There could be footy. I bet you'll like that when you're a bit bigger. We'd support City of course, not Everton! And you'll love it in the winter, when there's snow and we can do snowmen and tobogganing, and in the summer when we go to the seaside, to Southport or even to Prestatyn, and do sandcastles and all that and I'll teach you to swim and ride a bike and you can come mountain walking with us and your mummy will love you absolutely to bits and so will I because you'll be so precious to us so we'll keep you safe and sound and . . .'

He ground to a halt, embarrassed and emotional. Everyone was staring at him: Maureen with soft glistening eyes, the baby on her lap open-mouthed and solemn as if taking it all in, and Susan, who was smiling encouragingly.

'Oh, sorry, got a bit carried away there.'

It was Susan who spoke next. 'Don't worry Mr Harrison. I think you've just sold yourself and Mrs Harrison splendidly!'

Chapter 3
Tomos

Sioned sat on the sofa watching TV with her two-year-old, red-haired son lying in the curve of her shoulder. Lowri sat inches away, sharing the intimacy. She loved the moments like this, when he was clean and warm and sweet-smelling and sleepy and wonderfully cuddly from his bath, when they had a precious half hour before Glyn carried him up Wooden Hill to his bed and a bedtime story. Told in Welsh, of course. It was their first language (although they were also perfectly fluent in English, naturally; a fact their neighbours could never fully get their heads around). Well, they saw absolutely no point in not bringing him up to speak Welsh, even if they did live in England now. It was the language they'd been brought up to instinctively speak, by default; to think in. Why should it be any different for their little boy, just because he'd been born in England? Although, technically speaking, as he'd been born in England and had had his birth registered by the Social Services in Liverpool, he was English.

He was learning both languages, although at the moment, having more exposure to Welsh, he had a better vocabulary in that than English. But he would become fully bi-lingual – after all, Lowri had. And it had been a perfectly natural process for 'Tommy' to segue into 'Tomos.' Speaking of learning, Lowri was all set to start the big school, the Comprehensive, this September. How time had flown. In a couple of years she'd be a teenager, and then probably the gap would widen between her and her little brother as she put aside childish things. Sioned hoped it wouldn't be too much (and later as they both accumulated years, the proportional difference would shrink anyway), as Tomos certainly adored his big sister.

And the feeling did seem to be mutual. She and Glyn had been a tiny bit apprehensive that the novelty of having a ready-made baby brother would fade after a while with Lowri, as the reality of competition for her parents' attention sank home, but not a bit of it. Sioned thought back, smiling nostalgically; to that second visit to

Strawberry Field taking Lowri with them this time. Of course they'd described Tomos in great detail on her insistence after the first visit (although she'd seen the photos of course) and she'd looked forward to the event like looking forward to Christmas. That second time they'd seen Tomos in another room, just the four of them plus Susan, who seemed to be quietly assessing their interaction) and Tomos had been perfectly happy to be with them. He hadn't minded the presence of Lowri, another stranger, either, and she'd engaged in an excited squealing game involving bashing various brightly coloured plastic shapes into corresponding female ones (although Tomos hadn't always appreciated that they were supposed to match). As Sioned and Glyn had looked on, delighted and relieved, it quickly became apparent that the siblings-to-be would hit it off.

After three more visits when each time Tomos had seemed more pleased to see them than the last, a favourable report had been submitted to the powers-that-be regarding their suitability to adopt that particular child. After a final nerve-wracking interview with the adoption committee, followed by an agonising wait outside in the corridor sitting on hard uncomfortable chairs, the body with the power to create happiness or bestow crushing disappointment had deliberated, agreed that they ticked all boxes and the adoption had been approved. It still couldn't quite be for real though, because there was the excitement of decorating the baby's room and buying him a cot, pushchair and all the other essential paraphernalia for toddlers. Superstitiously, Sioned hadn't dared risk preparing his room or buying his essentials until they knew for certain that he would really be theirs. She just didn't want to take the emotional risk.

What a joyous homecoming it had been though! They (and he) were used by now to doing things like feeding and changing him, having had practice at Strawberry Field as their visits were gradually extended, and that evening all three of them (Glyn and Lowri weren't going to lose out; no way!) had collectively bathed and put him to bed in his teddy-bear-wallpapered room, clutching a proper one as a welcoming gift, and he'd settled to sleep as good as gold. Sioned smiled again, remembering that first night. If she'd crept quietly up the stairs to peep in at him once, just to make sure he really was with them now, she must have done it ten times. Not that Glyn was much better. He'd suddenly needed to visit the bathroom an inordinate number of times too.

Sioned was shaken from her reverie by Glyn lifting Tomos from her lap.

'Come along Bach, time for your bed. Give Mammy a kiss.' Sioned closed pursed lips with her son's, exchanging a dry soft kiss for a sloppy wet one.

'Good boy. And now Lowri,' he said, as he held him down to his big sister. Tomos bestowed a similar one upon her and Lowri wiped her mouth, smiling fondly, and said 'Nos da little man,' turning back to the television programme.

Glyn carried the sleepy child upstairs, leaving them to their television. Ten minutes later the phone rang. Sioned reached across to the side table to lift the receiver.

'Hello?' she began in English, but then switched to Welsh when she recognised the voice on the line.

'Oh, hello Mam. How are things?'

Sioned exchanged the usual beginning-of-conversation pleasantries with her mother then fell into listening mode (it was always easier, otherwise it was a constant battle to get a word in).

'Oh...'

'Right...'

'Really?...'

'Oh dear...'

'Duw duw...'

And so it went on. Gradually the smile slipped from Sioned's lips and her expression became grave. The mostly one-sided chat went on for three quarters of an hour. Her responses became murmurs of disbelief, then shock, then sympathy, then attempts at familial support. At last it ended, with a few words from Lowri to her gran and a final goodbye, and she replaced the receiver. She sank back into the cushions of the sofa, puffing her cheeks out as if glad to have ended a difficult conversation.

Glyn had not failed to notice. He'd turned the volume on the television low (Lowri hadn't thought to quieten it in considerateness and he'd had to do so on returning downstairs after the bedtime story) when it seemed to be a serious conversation.

'Something wrong Cariad?'

She gave him a thin smile, glancing at Lowri who was waving

her arm theatrically, making signals to turn the volume back up.

'It's my dad. He's . . . a little poorly.'

'Oh, what is it?'

Sioned looked uncomfortable. 'I'll tell you later.'

And she did, when Lowri went up to bed at nine-thirty and they were alone. She told how her father had been having worrying symptoms of late, and had finally been dragged reluctantly (lot of fuss about nothing!) to the doctor, who had examined him thoroughly and then looked very serious and referred him to Swansea for 'tests' and to see an oncologist. She'd had the feeling something was a little amiss when speaking to her mam the last time; felt she was holding something back, that there was something sinister lurking just out of sight.

Her brother Guto had driven them there and the consultant, after doing an even more thorough examination and studying the scan and other test results, had told them gently that it was pancreatic cancer, metastasised elsewhere in the abdomen too and too extensively spread for surgery to be an option. There was the possibility, apparently, of very aggressive radio- and chemotherapy, but the oncologist was of the opinion that the discomfort of it probably wasn't justified by the few extra months that would be gained. Palliative care might be the best thing. But of course it was up to her father. It was his decision.

Sioned paused in the telling, overwhelmed with sadness and pity for her dad. Glyn joined her on the sofa and took her hand, caressing it gently.

'Poor Idris. Poor man. So what's happening now?'

Sioned sighed. 'Well, he's going to give the treatment a try it seems. See if he can cope with it. Now he's cursing himself for not going to the doctor earlier, Mam says.'

'Yes. But we all do it don't we? Us men do anyway. Hate going to the doctor in case it's something trivial and we look a fool.'

Sioned had sunk into a pit of gloom. Tears were probably not far away, only being held in check by anger.

'Oh Dad! You're a fool for just leaving it, never mind making a fool of yourself with the doctor! Stupid, stupid man!'

Glyn was lost for words of comfort. Whatever he might say would just sound inadequate. So he said nothing; simply stroked her hand.

'And the thing is,' Sioned continued morosely, 'we're stuck up here in Liverpool, miles away, and there's my dad perhaps with just months left, but we don't know how long, and what will my mam do when . . . when . . .'

The tears finally came and she sobbed quietly as Glyn's arms went around her. Glyn's heart went out to his wife. He remembered how he'd felt when his mother had died unexpectedly, soon after moving to Liverpool; the guilt at being so far away and unable to give very much practical support on top of the pain of loss. Although his father was strong enough to manage alone, as it happened; had seemed to adapt to widower-hood alright. It might be a different matter for Annie, his mother-in-law, though. She was a timid little woman and not exactly an exemplar of stout, just-getting-on-with-it self-reliance. Yes, there was Guto, but he didn't really live on the doorstep either, being forty-odd miles away in Swansea too (where he had some high-powered job at DVLA . There seemed to be only one sensible solution.

'Well what if we move back to Wales Cariad?'

'But how could we do that Glyn?' Sioned sniffed, 'what about your job and everything?'

'Oh, I'm sure I could find something in Lampeter. Or the surrounding area, anyway. The job at Bentley's isn't all that wonderful; I could leave it tomorrow and never look back, to be honest with you.'

'But it's a good job. You'd never get that sort of money back home.'

'Well no, perhaps not. But money's not everything is it? Family matters more.'

'Oh Glyn; it would be nice. Well, not nice exactly, in the circumstances. But you know what I mean.' She paused, taking in the possibility offered; beginning to weigh pros and cons. 'There's Lowri's schooling to think of, of course.'

'Well as far as that goes, this might be a good time to make the move, with her going to the big school in September. She'll have to be changing schools anyway.'

'Is this what you'd want though Cariad? We've begun to make a life in Liverpool. There are better career opportunities here. Are you happy here?'

Glyn smiled ruefully; gave her a squeeze. 'I can take it or leave it really, quite frankly. Yeah, it seemed a good idea eight years ago, and it was great landing that job at the time, but it would be nice to go back home. Don't you think?'

'Yes, said Sioned quietly. 'I do. I really do.'

The following weekend they drove down to Talsarn, taking the familiar route not visited enough in recent years, Sioned now thought guiltily (apart from the last two Christmases and Easter last year, after Tomos had come into their lives): down to Chester, sweeping around the ancient city with its touristy half-timbered centre on the outer dual carriageway, diving off onto the A483, soon crossing into Wales past the welcoming *Croeso y Gymru* sign, then down, down through Wrexham and Chirk, dipping back into England for ten miles to skirt Shropshire's Oswestry. Then back into their homeland at Llanymynech; on through the soft green hills of mid Wales, by Welshpool and Newtown to Langurig, there to turn right through the mountains on the way to Aberystwyth.

They could have gone all the way there and then taken the coast road south – there was little difference in the distance – but today they turned south before then, through the visitor honey pot of Devil's Bridge and on through the wild hinterland seaward of the Cambrian spine of Wales to Tregaron, and soon after that along a minor road to sleepy Talsarn.

They were shocked when they reached Sioned's parents' house to find how poorly Idris looked. The weight had fallen from him, leaving behind a gaunt shadow. His bushy eyebrowed, craggy face with its Roman nose that had once held a certain dignity of bearing now simply looked wan and worn out. But he was determinedly cheerful when he insisted on rising from his chintzy chair in the familiar living room of the substantial family cottage (a farmhouse in days gone by) to greet them. Sioned felt afraid to hug him too tightly in case she shattered his fragile-looking ribcage, as she held tears precariously under control. He made a great fuss of Lowri and even more so of Tomos (he'd craved a grandson for years but eventually had had to stop wishing, only to be pleasantly surprised on learning that they'd adopted).

They sat and told Iris and Annie of their decision to move back home. At first Idris would have none of it. 'No, Glyn, you've got your good job in Liverpool. You don't want to throw that away for me! That's really why you're coming back, isn't it?'

'But Dad,' Sioned said gently, 'it's something we've been thinking of doing for some time now.'

'And we want Tomos to grow up Welsh,' she added, knowing her father's proud nationalist streak. He'd only ever voted Plaid Cymru, not even Labour.

'Well, I can't fault you on that Bach,' Idris conceded, immediately forgetting that he'd extolled the virtues of leaving Wales to 'get on' just a few moments previously.

Sioned thought she detected a faint look of relief, of secret gratitude now that he'd made his token objection, in his tired, rheumy eyes. She glanced sideways at her mother. Annie's eyes were filmed with wetness and she was fumbling for the hankie up her sleeve.

'But what will you do about a house and a job?' Idris continued, looking back to Glyn, playing Devil's Advocate against their plan a little longer because he felt he should.

'Oh, I'm sure there'll be something work-wise. It doesn't necessarily have to be in surveying. And we can rent a place for a while, because we'd obviously have to wait for the Liverpool house to sell; we couldn't buy down here until that had happened. Have you got this week's *County Times*? It'd be interesting to see what's on the market and what jobs are going.'

So that was it. Idris could see that his daughter and son-in-law were adamant. He wasn't so stupid in his old age that he couldn't see what they were up to. Bless them. It would be so much better for Annie afterwards. She wouldn't be able to rely on Guto all that much, with the best will in the world, as he was making a life for himself in Swansea. Not that he wasn't a good boy. But you had to be practical.

Annie got up to finish getting the late lunch ready and Sioned went into the kitchen too, from which wonderful odours of Welsh lamb and mint sauce were emanating, to lend a hand. And discuss the coming crisis, of course. Idris slumped back in his armchair and gazed tiredly, fondly at his grandchildren ranged along the sofa. Lowri was regarding him with a composite expression of curiosity, affection and concern. She'd been briefed that Granddad was very poorly, and might look different, and she and Tomos weren't to get too noisy just this once. It might bother poor Granddad. And she wasn't to ask about his illness, okay? Tomos was gazing at him too with an expression simply of curiosity. He was such a solemn little child.

Idris returned his gaze with a smile. Tomos, slightly uncertainly, grinned back.

'I still can't get over that hair. Such a strong colour. It's really growing now,' Idris remarked. 'I wonder where he got it from; his mam or dad? Looks as if they might have been Irish, doesn't it?'

'We've no idea, obviously,' Glyn replied. 'As you know, he was a foundling.'

He could speak frankly in front of Lowri. They'd told her all they knew themselves about her little brother. Well she was getting a big girl and she'd always been mature beyond her years.

'Sioned wants to let it grow long,' Glyn continued, passing the responsibility for their son's appearance to his wife. But it *was* the prevailing style of course.

Idris's thoughts were still on Tomos's provenance though. 'Yes, that was terrible though wasn't it? Just being left like that. Duw Duw.' He glanced, disconcerted, at Lowri. The child didn't seem in any way perturbed though. But then Sioned and her husband had always had a modern attitude to his granddaughter. This was 1987 after all. And it was fine, as long as it wasn't carried too far.

He spoke to Lowri now. 'And you'll be going to the big school in September then Bach? Are you looking forward to it?'

'Lowri smiled shyly. 'Yes, think so' Taid.'

Idris laughed. 'What do you mean, you think so? You'll love it, a bright girl like you. You're too big for the infants' school now!'

Glyn interjected. 'That's another reason for making the move soon. It would be good if Lowri just had one change of school, which she's got to have anyway, rather than two if we leave things for much longer.'

'Yes, and also of course she'd switch to a Welsh speaking school. That would be good.'

'Yes, that's right.'

Iris looked at his son-in-law, voice quieter now. 'Look, Glyn. I know just why you and our Sioned are doing this. And I do appreciate it. Not so much for my own sake. That doesn't really matter now. But for Anwen's. Thank you. Thank you.'

Glyn was lost for a sensible response that wasn't a weak transparent denial of their true motive. All he could mumble was, 'Well, it'll be nice to come back home.'

At least it was a nice crisp bright spring day, not raining, with a pale sun and daffodils splashing the graveyard here and there with their cheerful summer-anticipating yellow. It seemed appropriate somehow; Wales's national flower saluting a passionate Welsh nationalist at his leaving. Sioned was amazed and touched at how many people had turned out; it must have been almost the entire village and many others besides. All the older men were attired in their dark only-for-funerals suits and the surprisingly large number of younger ones, if they didn't possess a suit, had done the best they could, dressing as soberly as their wardrobes allowed. The women were turned out in a monochromatic palette of greys-through-to-black, some even wearing hats with veils.

The women were congregating in a murmuring commiserating group by the chapel door now, while the men, as custom dictated, were at the graveside witnessing the final rites. Sioned had wanted to be there too (she could have left Tomos in the care of Lowri for a little while); she felt she wasn't properly saying goodbye, somehow. But she knew she couldn't. It would have offended the sensibilities of many there, and probably even her mam. She breathed a sigh of relief. Well at least it was over now. She'd been dreading today; had thought she'd never fall asleep last night. Mam seemed to have coped quite well though, really. Certainly no hysterics. But she looked absolutely drained, poor love.

It had been a lovely service. *Cwm Rhondda* had been sung of course (well what else?) and *The day thou gavest Lord is ended.* It had to be that too. She'd forgotten how wonderful a chapel-full of voices sounded, not having been in one in years; all those Welsh tenors and sopranos and baritones and contraltos with one or two gruff sonorous basses blending in soaring emotional harmony. She been reminded oddly, of that CD that Glyn had played for her when they were courting (and many times since) of Thomas's *Under Milk Wood;* of the Reverend Eli Jenkins' comment, 'praise the Lord! We are a musical nation'.

And the eulogy had been lovely, and so had Guto's few words, which he'd struggled to get out before the tears caught up and clamped his throat shut. She'd held herself together, just about, but it had all been too much for Lowri, who'd buried her face in her hands to stifle the noise but you could tell she was sobbing because of the shaking. Well she was twelve years old now and a surprisingly sensitive girl. But Tomos had been fine; as good as gold really. He'd sat quietly on Glyn's lap, regarding these strange goings-on with his usual solemn expression. There'd been no questions piping up at inopportune moments. They could have left him with neighbours of course, but she'd wanted him to be there, although she couldn't quite explain why. Obviously, at only three he couldn't really understand what this was all about or that he'd never see his granddad again. But somehow it just seemed right (although he'd have only a hazy memory of it in years to come) that being just as important a member of the family as everyone else, he should be at the leave-taking too.

Sioned moved to her mother's side. She was surrounded by a clutch of supportive female relatives: Auntie Marged her sister, Cousin Elin and Cousin Patricia. She hadn't seen any of them for ages, particularly Pat, who was the daughter of her father's brother Huw, who had lived in England for years.

'Well that's over with then Mam,' she said, unable to think of anything more appropriate to say but immediately feeling the words were absurdly inadequate.

'Yes, it is Bach. Indeed it is.'

Sioned imagined that if she felt anything like herself, she'd be feeling very relieved indeed, although her mother looked as though she could easily succumb to tears.

'Beautiful words from our Guto, weren't they?'

Annie's eyes sparkled with moisture.

'Ay, lovely. He showed me what he'd written last night. So they wouldn't come as a surprise and upset me too much, he said. He's such a thoughtful boy.'

'Yes he is,' Sioned agreed.

The men were making their way back from the graveside. Guto, looking very smart in a clearly expensive well-cut suit, was in earnest conversation with the minister. They rejoined the ladies. Glyn moved to relieve Sioned of the burden of Tomos. He was a small child but still quite a weight, although Sioned had wanted to hold him. The feel of his little body against her hip was a comfort, in a way.

'Come along big boy,' he said as he took the child, 'you're getting a bit big for your mam to be holding. Tomos was well able to understand their normal Welsh and a basic vocabulary of English too, although he tended to mix the two with casual abandon (Lowri had been just the same).

The family and the many respects-paying guests made their way to the chapel vestry and the alcohol-free refreshments: the sandwiches and rolls, the dainty pretentious sausages on sticks, the Welsh cakes, the bara brith, the strawberry jam sponge cake made by hand as Thomas might have said, the tea, the coffee, the pop for children. Idris Evans, late of this parish, would get a good send off.

Later, back at the cottage (known since anyone could remember as Plas Newydd, New Palace, to distinguish it from Henblas, Old Palace, next door), after a wake that had gone on all afternoon, they could relax a little. The anticipation and then the tension of the sad occasion was dissipated. After putting Tomos to bed (they were staying the night) Sioned assisted by Lowri set about cooking dinner. Annie wanted to do it of course, but she was told in no uncertain terms to sit down and take it easy. It had been a trying, draining, emotional day for her and she looked just about spent.

The meal was eaten with spirits gradually reviving and they lingered at table, reminiscing about Annie's husband and Guto and Sioned's father. Memories were evoked with sadness but were fond. Then, after washing up (Glyn and Guto in charge now) they repaired to the sitting room. Annie quickly fell asleep on the sofa. Sioned gently roused her. 'Come on Mam, have an early night. You look done in.'

Annie opened bleary eyes. 'Yes Cariad. I think I will.' She looked fondly from one to another. 'Thank you my dears; it was a lovely send off.'

Sioned hugged her. 'You're welcome, Mam. Yes it was.'

After hugging everyone else too, Annie made her way up to bed. Everyone relaxed visibly.

'Poor old Mam,' said Sioned.

'Yes,' Guto agreed. 'Forty nine years together was a long time. It's a pity they didn't make the fifty.

'Yes,' Sioned concurred. 'Just four weeks short.' She paused, thinking about that. 'But it wouldn't have been a very happy anniversary, the state Dad was in.'

'No,' Glyn put in. 'Well; at least he's at peace now.'

'Anyway,' said Guto, 'I'm glad you two have moved back, for Mam's sake.'

He looked as though he had something on his mind. 'You know, I've been thinking. This house is a bit big for Mam to rattle around in now. I think she really ought to downsize. Perhaps move into Lampeter. It would be easier for her to get to the shops and everything.'

'That's rather up to Mam, isn't it?' said Sioned, sounding slightly irritated. 'She doesn't need you organising her life Guto.'

Guto raised his hands, palms forwards, placating. *Steady on little sister. I'm only trying to help.* 'Yes, of course it is. I'm just saying; if she wanted to do that, we could help her.'

'How do you mean?'

'Well; you know this house is willed to us two. Which means when Mam goes, either we sell it and split the proceeds or one of us has it and buys the other out of their share. Well I wouldn't want it; there's nothing for me up here. I might move to Cardiff or perhaps even England, the way things are going career-wise. But if Mam did want to move out, she could perhaps sign it over legally to you and Glyn, if you wanted it, at this stage, and you could buy me out of my share.'

'Yes,' Sioned interrupted, impatient, 'but how does that help Mam? Even supposing she wanted to do it?'

'Ah; well here's the thing. I could use the money you bought me out with plus some of my own to buy a little place in Lampeter, then she could stay in it for the rest of her days. It'd be an investment for me, and you'd get this cottage cheaply for whatever you bought me out for. Everyone would be a winner, and Mam would get a more manageable place in town.'

Sioned laughed mirthlessly. 'Well, you've certainly got it all worked out big brother. But apart from Mam, there's the small matter of whether Glyn and me want to go along with this!'

She turned to Glyn. 'What do you think Bach? Would you want to live here?'

Glyn was a little taken aback. This was a suggestion right out of the blue. He was lost for words. But the idea did have some appeal.

He thought about it for a while as Sioned waited expectantly, eyes boring into his.

'Well, yes, it would be quite good; I rather like the idea.' He boomeranged the question back. 'But would *you* really want to?'

Sioned thought about it too. *Yes; why not? It's better than selling our house completely to total strangers, probably English incomers as a second home or something. It'd be good to keep it in the family. And we aren't having much success finding anywhere else to buy that we both fancy, and I'd like to get out of that rented place in Aberaeron. And it'd be nice if Tomos went to the same school I went to.*

'Yes, I'd certainly like it, provided Mam agrees to your madcap idea Guto. But it's entirely down to her of course.'

But then a thought struck Glyn. 'Hang on though, Guto. I doubt whether we've got half the market value of Plas Newydd to give you at the moment. I should imagine a good-sized detached house in a village like this would be worth getting on for a hundred thousand. We only ended up with thirty-seven on the Liverpool house after repaying the mortgage.'

Guto was magnanimous. 'That's okay,' he laughed, 'I'd be happy with thirty-five, so you'd still be left with a little. We don't have to split it exactly down the middle. And you two need a family home after all, whereas I don't, particularly. Sam and I are fine in our flat, and as I say, we could be on the move in the future. Think about it anyway.'

Glyn and Sioned definitely did think about it, and talk about it at great length in bed that night. It was certainly a tempting proposition of Guto's. Provided of course Mam did want to move into town with its greater convenience in all sorts of ways, it was like a gift from heaven. A detached three-bedroomed country place for effectively thirty-five thousand: that was a gift horse not to be looked in the mouth at all. Sioned was overwhelmed by her brother's generosity. She'd always assumed that, as male heir, the house would automatically pass to him. She hadn't even considered that the legacy would be divided between them. But then this was nineteen eighty-seven after all, not the Dark Ages. And it would be wonderful to come back here. The place held such memories. To bring her own children up here too – well; it simply hadn't occurred to her as a possibility. It was the stuff of dreams.

As for Glyn, his thoughts were more pragmatic of course. It had certainly proved difficult so far to find a place that they both really liked in equal measure and he'd always thought this a nice place with plenty of potential to improve it. It could do with a good renovating job doing on it really (Idris and Annie had done nothing to it for donkeys' years). A new kitchen and bathroom perhaps? Sioned would love those. And it was well placed for getting to work in Aberaeron, which looked like his place of employment for some time to come since landing the job in the estate agents there. Equally, if anything better should come up in Lampeter, that was just as easily commuterable-to as Aberaeron. And as for the fact that they were in effect swapping their dull modern house in Liverpool for a place in the country without the burden of a mortgage; well, they'd be fools to turn it down, wouldn't they?

It did just depend on Annie though . . .

In the event, Anwen May Evans (née Morgan) thought it a wonderful idea. They had thought she would baulk at the idea of leaving the home she'd shared with Idris for all but six of their forty-nine years together (he having inherited it from his farmer parents, although he hadn't followed them into that), but not a bit of it. The idea of a little house in Lampeter just big enough and easy to manage was appealing, most decidedly. Yes indeed. She seemed to have found a new sense of independence after two-thirds of a lifetime spent as a timid, wouldn't-say-boo-to-a-goose little spouse. And she was surprisingly unsentimental about Plas Newydd. But then, it would be staying in the family anyway and she liked that idea too. And Sioned and Glyn and the grandchildren would be only six miles away if she needed them.

And so Annie, Guto and Glyn (as professional advisor) toured the estate agents in Lampeter (she preferred it to coastal Aberaeron; wasn't a great sea person) and found a nice little terraced house, which was very tidy, Glyn said in the Welsh vernacular, in the colour-variegated square. Guto added five thousand pounds of his own money to Glyn's thirty-five, and there Annie stayed for most of the remaining sixteen years of her life, strolling the streets in her twilight years and making friends at the old folks' day centre, only admitting defeat in the final one and returning to Plas Newydd (Lowri having left home by now, thus freeing up a bedroom) to be cared for by her daughter until heart failure finally took her to the maker she'd believed in all her chapel-going life.

And as for Sioned, she got her new kitchen and bathroom and a facelifted (but sympathetically done) house in general, but the memories were not expunged. And little Tomos got a happy childhood, one very different from what might have been, had his natural father accepted him and his twin. He had almost certainly had a lucky escape, really.

Chapter 4
Wayne

Maureen sat in the armchair watching telly with her two-year-old, red-haired son lying in the curve of her shoulder. Jim sat opposite, gazing at them both fondly. She loved these moments, when he was clean and warm and sweet-smelling and sleepy and cuddly from his bath (which it had been Jim's turn to do tonight but her turn for the bedtime story). After ten minutes *Coronation Street's* closing, laid-back serenade and credits rolled and she bestirred herself to rise. She could happily sit here all night nursing him, no problem. But they mustn't get into bad slovenly habits with the child. Instil a sense of proper reasonable bedtime from the start. That was what the books said. And they'd been waiting so long; they weren't about to mess up and spoil their precious child now.

She rose and took him across to Jim, holding him down with an arm under his belly to keep him tilted. 'Say night-night to Daddy then.'

Jim pressed pursed lips to open ones and exchanged a dry kiss for a wet, sloppy one. He pretended distaste. 'Augh! It's about time you learned to do that properly Sunshine!'

Maureen chided, 'He's only two, Jim; give him a chance!'

Jim laughed. 'Yeah; I know. Only kidding. Night-night Big Boy.' He tousled the damp, absurdly red hair.

She took him up the narrow staircase of their small terraced house in its unremarkable back street, one of very many in Liverpool and many thousands in the North. A street just like *Coronation Street,* in fact.

Ten minutes later, story read and Wayne tucked up clutching his Teddy, she rejoined Jim downstairs. He was engrossed in the next television programme.

'Any more news today at work then?'

He didn't take his eyes off the box, but his expression clouded over instantly. They didn't like discussing serious subjects in front of the child, notwithstanding that he wouldn't have known what they were talking about of course. But he had become such a presence in their lives that it was almost as though he did.

'Well; the rumours are still flying. The union was in with management again today. And when our convenor came out he didn't look at all happy. So I just don't know; I really don't.'

'But how can they even think about closing your site down? Didn't you say the firm was making a good profit?'

'Yeah; that's the union's case. So they tell us.'

'Then why?'

'Don't ask me Luv; I only work there.' Jim tried to keep the bitterness out of his voice, but it was difficult. 'They're just not making *enough* profit it seems; not enough to keep the shareholders happy. Apparently the shares are starting to slide on the Stock Market, or something. Not that I understand all that stuff. I'm only a lowly engineer.'

'Well it all seems very unfair to me,' said Maureen loyally. 'To think of the years you've given that firm.'

Jim snorted. 'Fair? *Fair?* What's that got to do with anything? Its Thatcher's wonderful free market ent it! If you can make even more money by downsizing the English workforce and sending manufacturing overseas to Asia, where you can get away with paying peanuts, you will, I suppose. And to hell with the poor sods you throw out of work in the process.'

'But it's only the Liverpool plant that might be going, isn't it? Couldn't they spread the staff here around the other plants?'

Jim was trying to keep a grip on his patience. 'No Luv, not really. If they did that it wouldn't be downsizing, would it? They wouldn't be saving all these fabulously high wages they pay us, would they?'

They lapsed into an uncomfortable silence, save for the game show on the television.

Jim started again. It wasn't fair to start getting ratty with Maureen. 'Well, there might be some relocation it seems, but there's only so many line engineers they can employ. I don't suppose any of the other plants are actually short staffed as far as that's concerned. They look at us sideways sometimes when we seem not to be doing very much, when we've maintained the lines and everything's running smoothly, as it is.'

Maureen knew there was no point in keeping on. Bickering among themselves wouldn't solve anything. They settled to watch the telly. Perhaps it wouldn't happen anyway. Not to them.

But it did. The following Friday afternoon Jim came home with a face like thunder. Without bothering to say the usual enthusiastic hello to Wayne, he vehemently flung his wage packet down on the table. Maureen didn't have to ask. 'Oh, Jim!'

Jim slumped onto his chair. 'The bastards! *Bastards!*

Wearily he opened the larger-than-normal packet and withdrew the letter, passing it across to her. She picked it up, unfolded it, read. Oddly, it was still a surprise seeing the ill-tidings spelt out. The management very much regretted that, due to the prevailing economic climate and the need to maintain competitiveness, the company had no choice but to rationalise its UK operation. Unfortunately this would mean closure of the Liverpool premises. (No mention was made of relocating some production overseas. Perhaps even the management felt that would be insensitive). This would take effect from the following Friday. There would of course be a generous redundancy package commensurate with number of years employed by the company.

And the company would like to take this opportunity to thank all members of staff . . .

Maureen couldn't read any more. 'Oh Jim! What will we do?'

'Dunno Luv. You tell me. It's a bugger, ent it.'

'But they'll give decent redundancy money, won't they?'

'Oh yeah. But us workers aren't top management leaving with enormous golden goodbyes. We only keep the bloody factories running! There's another paper, look.'

He fished out another sheet and slid it to her. It was a calculation, neatly typed.

'A week's pay for every year worked. So work it out. Nine times two hundred and forty, plus a half-week for each of the two years I did when I started as a teenager. So that's two thousand four hundred.'

'Well it's better than nothing I suppose . . .'

'Bollocks Maureen; it really ent very much!' Jim was seething. He'd never felt so vulnerable; so frightened, and he was lashing out. Basically we've got ten weeks' money – perhaps another four or so if we really tighten us belts – for me to try and find something else.'

'You can sign on though, can't you? Are you allowed to do that if you've got Redundancy?'

Jim sighed tiredly. 'I've no idea Luv. I've never done this before.

I don't know what the rules are.'

They'd forgotten all about their policy of not having heavy conversations in front of the child. Maureen picked him up and plonked him in Jim's lap. That caused his brow to unfurrow a little, anyway.

'You haven't said hello to your son you know!'

Jim smiled and hugged the warm little body to him. 'Sorry Big Boy. And how has your day been? Better than your Dad's, I hope.'

And so they temporarily forgot their worries. After tea it was Jim's turn to read the bedtime story. It was a new one; one involving a startlingly blue elephant and his friend, a pink mouse (a certain amount of license being taken with their relative sizes in the pictures, of course). Jim read the simple story very slowly, pointing at objects as he read their names, encouraging Wayne to absorb their meanings. Some of the tension was leaving; some of the resentment and anger receding. He tried to get Wayne to say elephant, and the child had a valiant stab at it, producing an approximation sounding not unlike 'ellfut.' Well, it wasn't a bad first try. But then, out of the blue, he had a sudden impulse to burst into tears. To take his little boy in his arms and sob, howl at the unfairness of it all. What if he couldn't support this precious little being, for whom they'd waited so long? Bloody company, with its fat-gutted directors sitting round their boardroom table smoking their cigars and guzzling their port, or whatever it was they drank, playing God with peoples' lives. None of them would suffer because of their sodding 'rationalisation' and downsizing. They were on another planet.

But of course the subject didn't go very far away. Later, as they sat only half-watching telly and not taking any of it in, Maureen brought the money question up again.

'Will you look into the thing about whether you can draw benefit and have your Redundancy too?'

Jim smiled tiredly. 'Yes Luv; of course I will. The Union will probably know all the ins and outs of that, I expect.'

'Surely you'd be able to have it and benefit too though. It's not as if you'll be getting a fortune, is it?'

'No,' said Jim grimly. I certainly won't. I'll see what the rules are. If you can only have so much cash in the bank before losing benefit I'll hide anything that's over and above the limit, sod it. Give it to our Malcolm for safe keeping then he can slip it back to us a bit at a time. Or stash it under the mattress.'

'But wouldn't that be illegal?'

'Yes of course it would be bloody illegal! But to hell with the Government. It's their policies that have caused all this! Three million unemployed and now I'm going to be one of them!'

'Well if you have to do that Luv, for God's sake be careful.'

In the event, when the following Friday came and the disgruntled workforce collected its final pay packets, Jim found rather to his surprise that the company had made a small show of considerateness. Along with his week's wages and P45 there was a cheque for £1,400, but the rest of the redundancy money was in the form of twenty fifty-pound notes. Presumably whoever was in charge of the payroll had had a twinge of conscience and known only full well that many people would try to hide some of their redundancy payoff, and had made it easy for them.

That Sunday they had a drive over to see Jim's older brother Malcolm and his wife Sheila, taking the cash. Both Malcolm and Sheila worked at Rowntrees in York and lived in red pantile-roofed Haxby, five miles outside the historic city. They'd been before, the previous Christmas, and Malc and Sheila's offspring, Katie and Bren, as is the way of all little girls, were thrilled at this unexpected chance to see their little cousin again.

Leaving the little ones to their play and the women to prepare a late lunch, Jim and Malcolm discussed the situation. Malcolm was full of sympathy.

'Ay, it's all very well for the bosses to play their nasty games with people's lives ent it? I bet none of those buggers will be getting their marching orders. Oh no. Jobs will be found for them at headquarters, you can bet your life.'

'Yes,' Jim agreed ruefully. 'One law for them and another for the rest of us.'

They lapsed into a moody silence.

'How are things at your place, anyway?' Jim asked, breaking it, more out of politeness than real interest.

'Okay, as far as I know. But then people never stop eating chocolate and the kids never stop eating sweets, do they? Thank God.'

'No, I suppose not,' Jim agreed. He couldn't really imagine indulging in a big box of Black Magic, not now. It sounded an impossible-to-attain luxury.

'It's just plastic buckets they stop buying when times are hard, it seems,' he added, feeling faintly jealous of his big brother's good fortune to work for a firm that made something as apparently important as confectionery.

'Yeah, I know. People have funny priorities don't they?'

'I don't suppose there are any jobs going at your place then are there?'

'What; you mean in line maintenance?'

'Quite frankly Malc, anything would do. I'd work *on* the line if needs be.'

Malcolm laughed, although the subject was far from funny.

'Well you'd be with the ladies then Sunshine. It's hardly men's work is it?'

'Well I wouldn't fucking care about that,' Jim retorted crossly, forgetting he was in the presence of children. 'I can't afford dignity at the moment. Sorry. Excuse the French. It's really getting to me though. I feel so bloody helpless. Like I'm not in charge of my life anymore.'

He stopped. There were tears bubbling not so very far beneath the gossamer surface of self-control again, like lurking demons.

'Yes, you poor bugger,' Malcolm sympathised. 'It's the one thing we all dread ent it? I'm so sorry Bruv; I really am.'

He glanced at little Wayne who was absorbed, oblivious to all grown-up concerns, in play with the girls.

'You and Mo's lives had just taken a turn for the better after all those other bloody awful things, and now this comes along. It's not fair.'

Jim couldn't trust himself to reply. It would probably start him off. Things could get very unmanly. Malcolm tried changing the subject. 'Ee; yon's a grand little chap, right enough. I can't get over that hair!'

'Yeah; amazing ent it?' Jim always felt ridiculously smug when people remarked on it, as if he'd been personally responsible.

'He'll probably get teased about it a time or two when he starts school,' Malcolm remarked, unaware of his insensitivity. Kind-hearted but unperceptive sometimes, he didn't see that the last thing his depression-teetering brother needed just then was negativity.

Jim didn't bother to answer. But he knew what his brother meant. The casual cruelty of children yet to learn tolerance, who challenged any sort of difference. He didn't understand it though. What the hell did it matter what people looked like? And it was only hair colour for God's sake anyway. And a few freckles. Well, quite a lot actually. Anyway, if he ever caught any nasty ignorant snotty-nosed little brats baiting his little boy, they'd get the edge of his tongue and probably a clip round the ear too, whatever the parents thought.

Finally sensing Jim's mood, Malcolm steered the conversation back to the immediate problem.

'Shall I keep an eye open for any jobs coming up at our place?'

'Well yeah; if you could Malc.'

'You wouldn't mind coming back across the Pennines then?'

'No, why should I? Liverpool hasn't done me any favours, it seems. It's what we're being told to do by the bloody Tories ent it; don't riot, get on us bikes and look for work. Even if there ent any. It's a sick joke.'

'Right-oh then,' said Malcolm, 'I'll let you know if anything comes up.'

The young man at the employment exchange perused Jim's bank statements for the last three months and pursed his lips.

'And this is your redundancy money is it?' he asked, prodding the entry of the abnormally large deposit into Jim's current account.

'Yes, that's it,' Jim said, desperately trying not to blush. *Hell, I'm no bloody good at this fraud thing, that's for sure. And it's bloody humiliating, trying to put on an act for this pimply little sod who's got the power of life or death over me. Bet his job's not on 't line. Oh no; he'll have a meal ticket for life.*

The young man regarded him steadily. Jim tried to return his gaze with an expression of childlike innocence. *God; he knows. I'm sure he does.*

'And you don't have a savings account at all?'

Jim tried to affect a nonchalant air. 'No point. I can never afford to save anything, what with paying the mortgage and all.'

The young man became a touch patronising. 'Well I'd seriously recommend that you open one for this lump sum Mr Harrison. Then it can be released slowly to supplement your dole. Leave it swilling around in your current account and it'll be gone in no time.'

Jim tried to contain his irritation. *Cheeky little bugger! Trying to suggest I can't handle my own finances!* 'Yes, I'm sure you're right,' he said weakly. 'I will.'

He waited for the accusation to come: You're hiding money from us aren't you? Where's the rest of it then?

But it didn't. Instead the young man was suddenly empathetic.

'I know, it's tough for you, this, Mr Harrison. I know how you feel. My dad's just been laid off from Halewood. Been there nineteen years and this is how they treat him.'

He leaned forward, conspiratorially, dropping his voice. 'I shouldn't be telling you this, and of course I'm not going to shop him, but I've suggested ways that he can, shall we say, invest some of it so it looks less on his bank statement. Of course I can't advise you on that. More than my job's worth. But I think you take my drift, don't you?'

Jim released a sigh of relief that the young man couldn't have failed to notice. 'Er, yes, right,' he mumbled. He could have wept with gratitude.

The young man drew back again; raised his voice. 'Okay then Mr Harrison. This all looks to be in order. It'll just be a few days and then you'll be able to draw the benefit.'

And so, for the first time in either of their working lives, Jim and Maureen sampled the austerity of life on the dole. Yes, they could supplement it, as much as they dare whilst trying to eke it out as long as possible, with the official redundancy money. But in spite of their efforts to economise, the supplement gradually began to rise as a proportion of the dole. How the hell people managed to survive on that alone, Jim couldn't imagine. They must exist on bread and water. He could well see why people got into debt; borrowing just a little, from a loan shark, probably, to make it through to the next paying out day, then after repaying that finding it was even more difficult the next week, and so taking out a slightly larger loan to get through again, and so on, with things steadily, inexorably, spinning out of control, down into a pit of desperation and despair.

But they were determined not to go there. Surely some sort of work, anything, would crop up before first the official money and then the last contingency, the cash that Malcolm had paid into his building society, ran out? But it was so, so difficult, for all that Jim visited the labour exchange every day, going into town first thing, on the bus to begin with but then walking to save the fare, in the hope that if he were quick off the mark he'd land something, almost anything, before anyone else got it. Of course, everyone else had the same idea too and there would often be a queue outside the building when he got there, like shoppers at the January sales, ready to burst in like an unstoppable human tidal wave when the doors were thrown open.

At first he'd tried to be selective and seek jobs suited to his skills. He didn't really expect to find anything specifically in assembly-line work; any sort of engineering would have done. He got as far as going for a couple of interviews but in both cases there wasn't even a formal letter of rejection to follow the We'll-Let-You-Know end of audience. With far more applicants than jobs available, employers could be very picky. Only the most suitable got taken on. It was survival of the fittest, alright.

He tried setting his sights lower. He applied for a job as a motor mechanic. After all, he could tinker quite competently with his car; do the brakes and all that. But there was no joy there either. They could take on kids and train them up, and pay them peanuts in the meantime. With each week he broadened his scope. Warehouseman. Kitchen assistant (basically a washer-up). Gardener with the Parks Department. Even, still with the council, on the dustcarts.

But every day there was the same disconsolate trudge home to tell Maureen he'd failed. Failed to become the breadwinner again. Become a man again. He became ever more despondent. When he wasn't teetering on the edge of irrational irritability he was trying to fight down tears. Their love life petered out. He just couldn't be bothered, as if weighted by a remorseless lethargy. And he stopped taking an interest in the child, and yet knew he was doing it and hated himself for it.

They sold the car when the insurance and road tax became due together. It was just too big a lump sum to find. It was adverted locally and normally Jim would have been a tough negotiator, not prepared to let anything go for less than what he felt was its true value. But now he couldn't be bothered to haggle. A spotty youth with a very knowing expression lurking beneath his spiky green-dyed hair came and looked and kicked the tyres and looked under the bonnet and peered underneath, and offered £300 less than Jim was asking, expecting that to be the start point for haggling, but Jim meekly said okay, that was fine. The youth couldn't believe his luck.

Christmas arrived, and that made a big dent in the already greatly reduced redundancy money, try as they might to economise. Well there were some things that you just couldn't do without, like a modest turkey, the smallest in the shop. And whilst Jim and Maureen tacitly agreed to give each only token presents, she insisted that Wayne shouldn't go without. At two years and ten months now, he was beginning to understand what Christmas was all about. The way Jim felt, he could just as easily given it a complete miss. Maureen did her best to stimulate a modicum of festive cheer, but it was only a veneer.

It should have been the turn of Malcolm, Sheila and the kids to come to them for the day and stay the night so the men could get some serious drinking done, but for some reason the subject, the assumption, simply never came up in Maureen and Sheila's phone conversations, due probably to embarrassment on both their parts. Sheila was sensitive enough to appreciate that her in-laws wouldn't be able to afford the sort of lavish entertaining they normally laid on, and if she'd suggested instead that she and Malcolm did the honours, it would have undermined Maureen's dignity. Besides which, Jim was so morose nowadays, he would hardly have been the life and soul of the party.

So instead there was a low-key pre-Christmas get together when the York contingent visited. Maureen put on the best meal she could muster (roast beef and Yorkshire pudding; a rarity for them nowadays). Presents (modest in their case) and slightly embarrassed Christmas wishes were exchanged, and they drove home again. Left to shoulder the burden alone, she bought a small tree and looked out last year's decorations and adorned it, helped by a wide-eyed little boy. She was determined to give him as good a time as she could. Coming from proud Liverpool working class stock, she wasn't going to let a little thing like a depressive husband spoil things. Like her mother before her, she just grinned, bore it and got on with it. But thank goodness there was the telly and *Morcambe and Wise* to fall back on that year.

In the New Year Maureen, increasingly worried about Jim's mental wellbeing, almost frogmarched him to the doctor. He would never have gone otherwise. Dr Patel didn't seem at all surprised. He'd been seeing it more and more: dead-eyed men sitting before him, emasculated by the lack of a reason to get out of bed and leave the house in the morning, usually brought to him by anxious wives. He leaned towards Jim and Maureen as they sat side by side facing his desk.

'Tell me how you feel Mr Harrison.'

Jim stared listlessly at the floor. Even speech seemed too much trouble. Maureen prompted gently. 'Jim? Come on Luv. Tell the doctor how you feel.'

The doctor tried to help. 'Do you feel lethargic, er, as if everything's too much of an effort?'

Jim nodded. 'Yeah. That's it.'

'And – I know this is difficult to admit to – inclined to be weepy sometimes?'

Jim nodded again, unwilling to admit it in so many words. The doctor looked at Maureen. 'Any mood swings?'

'Well, er . . .'

'A tendency to unaccountable irritability sometimes?'

'Well, yes, but he's got a lot on his mind at the moment. He doesn't mean it.'

Dr Patel hardly needed to ask more. 'No, no; of course not.'

He looked at Jim. 'If you don't mind my asking, are you in work?'

Maureen did the answering. It was easier. 'No. He lost his job seven months ago.'

The doctor nodded. He almost knew without being told. He continued to look at Jim, a sympathetic smile provoking laugh wrinkles at the corners of his brown eyes.

'You've got a touch of depression. We'll soon get you sorted out. I'll prescribe you something, but you must keep taking it. Even if you start to feel a little better. It's important that you come back to see me so that we can keep an eye on you.'

He looked again at Maureen, as if she were Jim's surrogate

mother. 'Alright Mrs Harrison?' He scribbled an indecipherable prescription. 'Take this to the chemist, and make sure he takes it. And I'll see you both again in a fortnight.'

And that was the turning point. Well, the bottoming out anyway. Jim didn't get any worse. Gradually the insidious, tempting, suicidal feelings (so irrational he would think, looking back later) became less frequent until one day he realised that he hadn't had one for over a week. The root cause of the illness hadn't gone away, but the chemical assistance began gradually to rebalance his brain. He began to come to terms with his status, to look outside himself a little. To recognise that he wasn't the only one on the scrap heap. That it wasn't even that, actually. Not really. Just a bloody awful consequence of the recession that wasn't of his making. He hadn't failed. There were many others (some blokes had large families to support after all) in as bad if not worse a situation as he.

And then a gradual, at first barely perceptible rise started. He began to take notice of Wayne again, to Maureen's great relief. Although the child had retreated from him in recent months, had become self-sufficient; didn't look for recognition or a smile, knowing that there wouldn't be one. There was a mutual re-education in communication needed, encouraged by Maureen. It was a major red-letter day when, for the first time in six months, Jim actually laughed at Wayne's antics and swept him into a hug, to the child's astonishment and his mother's tearful delight. It was a big event too for her a few nights after that when she felt for the first time in ages the hot urgency of his member against her thigh. At the firm insistence of Maureen, he went back regularly with her to the doctor who beamed toothily with genuine pleasure (he was a compassionate man) at his steady improvement as he gradually reduced the dosage of the anti-depressant.

By the end of February most of the Redundancy had gone, but by now Jim felt well enough to trust himself to stay at home as househusband and carer-dad and allow Maureen to go out and do a few hours work on the tills in the local supermarket. She had given up the part-time secretarial work of course when Wayne first arrived and there was none of that sort of thing going just then. Not part-time, anyway. But the small amount of money she brought in was slightly more than they'd allowed themselves out of the

Redundancy, so it was a small net improvement in disposable income. Things seemed just a little better. A little bit.

And then, one evening in April, things became very much better when Malcolm rang to say they were taking on staff at Rowntrees. People with some engineering experience, preferably. He'd been tipped off by his friend Max in Personnel, who usually got to hear about these things before they were advertised (Malcolm had asked him to keep his eyes and ears open). They would be interviewing the following Monday. He could nip over and collect Jim on the Sunday afternoon so he could stay the night and be there bright and early the next day, near the head of the queue in case there was one. Jim did not need twice telling. For the first time in many weeks he visited the barber and Maureen took his best suit out of the mothball-smelling wardrobe and pressed it, and washed and did the same for his reasonably sober cream shirt (the collar points weren't excessively long), and his brown and orange not-too-wide tie.

Lying alone in bed that Sunday night (in Katie's bed in fact; she'd been turfed out to sleep with Bren) Jim rehearsed over and over his answers to the probable questions he might get asked. Well he'd had a steady employment record up until last year's bloody disaster after all; had hardly missed a day's work in his life. And being made redundant certainly hadn't been his fault. And he was a well qualified bloke really. Okay, the jobs on offer were more in the way of general assembly line work rather than maintenance as such, but never mind. He'd always got that extra string to his bow, which made him more useful than most applicants, surely.

But it was nerve-wracking, all the same. So much was riding on this. What if he didn't get a job? He'd have to crawl home to Maureen and say he'd failed. Then there might be another plunge into the pit of despair. No, please God no! He couldn't bear that. He'd been feeling so much better lately; was nearly off the pills altogether. Just a little more fine-tuning, Dr Patel had said the last time he went (and he could go by himself now). But he was sensible enough to know that drugs were only part of the cure. He needed to regain his self-respect too. Get back to living life properly with his wife and little boy.

Ah yes; Wayne! He'd been so wrapped up in his own worries, so steeped in self-pity; he'd neglected and rejected the poor little kid. Hadn't seen the need in the child's eyes, or the grief in Maureen's when she felt her world falling apart. But he really mustn't dwell in the past. There was the future to grasp. He *would* be a provider again, and a proper husband and father. He was bloody determined to be.

And he got one of the jobs. The interviewers (one of them Malcolm's friend Max) seemed impressed by his smart turnout and politeness compared with some of the other applicants, his CV and his obvious competence. They'd asked if he'd be able to cover for the maintenance staff now and then if necessary. Jim had assured them that he could, no problem. So there was an excited phone call home afterwards when Maureen finished her shift (a child minder had been found for Wayne) to tell her news. He could hear her crying with relief on the other end of the line. After Maureen had composed herself and they'd discussed all the implications of this change of luck, they agreed that he would stay with Malcolm for the rest of the week to look around sizing up the housing situation. Suddenly their financial situation seemed rosy. Well comparatively, anyway. By eking out the redundancy money to supplement the unemployment benefit, they'd just about managed to keep paying the mortgage on the Liverpool house and avoid the humiliation of repossession. So they'd be able to put it on the market now and have a little money in hand when the mortgage was repaid.

And they'd been able to leave the other money that Malcolm was looking after untouched, so adding those two together they could nearly find the deposit on a small place in York. Something just to keep them in the property-owning game. Perhaps later they'd be able to upgrade. Before the redundancy had hit they'd been tossing the idea around of adopting another child, possibly a sister for Wayne. Of course after Jim lost his job that idea had gone out of the window, but now it might be revived.

So Jim toured the estate agents in York. He was a little disconcerted to find that prices were quite a lot higher than in Liverpool, but that was hardly surprising really. York was a tourist honey pot and a highly desirable place to live after all. On the other hand, until they really got back on their feet financially they wouldn't be able to run a car, so living in the town where Jim's work was made perfect sense.

That Friday evening, as Jim sat with Malcolm, Sheila and the girls for their last meal before Malcolm took him back home, Jim ruminated over their housing problem.

'It looks like we'll have to rent for a bit until I've done some saving,' he said, slightly disconsolately, 'prices are certainly higher here than in Liverpool. I doubt whether we'd get a deposit together with what we'd get selling our present place and the rest of the Redundancy.'

'Well,' Malcolm pointed out, 'you'll have to do that anyway, until your place is sold.'

'Yeah; true.'

'And as for a deposit, how much do you reckon you'd be short on it?'

Jim pondered. 'Dunno really. All depends on what we'd get for the Liverpool house for one thing, and I don't know how much we'd have to call our own after the mortgage was paid off either.'

'Well, said Malcolm, if it was a matter of finding only a couple of grand or so, I could help you there. With a long term loan. I've got the money. No interest, obviously. Just pay it back as and when you can, at your own pace.'

Jim looked at his brother sharply. 'Hang about Malc, we couldn't ask you to do that. You need the money yourself, I'll be bound.'

Malcolm smiled indulgently. 'It's alright old son. You've just been through a lousy bloody time. What are brothers for if not to help each other out?'

In the event not too much of Malcolm's generously offered financial help was needed. The following Friday evening all three of them travelled to York on the train (a magical experience for Wayne) for a Saturday spent searching for a small flat for Jim, so that Maureen could stay behind in Liverpool overseeing the selling of the house. It sold quite quickly (Jim had always maintained it in immaculate order) for a better price than they'd anticipated and they found a small terraced house that was a little tatty and needed a few jobs doing on it, none of which would be a problem for Jim but which depressed the asking price, and the shortfall on the deposit was only £785. They borrowed that from Malcolm and had repaid it within two years.

So that was how Jim came to return to his county of birth and Maureen left hers. And how little Wayne embarked upon a generally happy childhood, one very different from what might have been, had his natural father accepted him and his twin. He had landed on his feet, as they say.

Chapter 5
Tomos

Tomos wondered what the matter was with Lowri nowadays. She just didn't seem so much fun anymore. They used to be such friends, in spite of her being so much older and being a girl. She seemed so moody most of the time, playing with her food at mealtimes and then disappearing up to her room straight afterwards with the meal often only half-eaten. And then going out so often too. It had been twice this week already and it was only Thursday now. Sunday and Tuesday she'd been out. She never used to do that. Where was there to go in Talsarn after all? And it looked as if she were going out yet again tonight. He was beginning to know the signs. A hurried half-meal. Then up to her room, to emerge an hour later all dolled up and plastered with makeup (looks like a tart, he'd heard Dad mutter, although *he'd* never seen a tart that looked remotely like Lowri) to leave a mumbled promise not to be late hanging in her wake as she disappeared through the door. He'd noticed the looks that passed between his parents; strange indecipherable looks that seemed an odd mixture of amusement and concern.

It was all a puzzle for a nine-year-old. She hadn't played chess with him for ages now (well, last Thursday to be precise) and when after much cajoling she'd agreed to, she'd seemed only half there and he'd won easily. It hadn't been much of a contest; hadn't been very *mind-stretching* for him (he'd read that phrase in a book recently and was looking for an opportunity to use it in an essay at school, although it didn't translate into Welsh very well). And she seemed so short with him much of the time. He couldn't imagine what he'd done wrong. But then girls were funny creatures, even grown-up ones like your sister.

And sure enough, here she was now, looking like one of those presenters off the telly and, *Duw!* She'd dyed her hair! No wonder she'd been so long up in her room, not that Tomos had any idea really how long it took a girl to dye her hair. And it was *orange!*

Glyn glanced at her from his television programme (something on S4C) then did a double-take. He couldn't hide his shock. 'Good grief Lowri, what have you done to your hair?'

She rolled her heavily accentuated eyes theatrically. 'What does it look like? Dyed it. Okay?'

Glyn grinned. 'I can see that. Why didn't you just ask Tomos for some of his though? Would have been cheaper.' He sniggered at his own pun.

Tomos squirmed. He hated being teased, even good-naturedly, about his hair.

'Ha ha; hilarious! Well I wasn't born with his wonderful pre-Raphaelite locks was I?' (Lowri had recently discovered the Victorian artistic Brotherhood.) 'Just plain ordinary mousey brown.'

'Oh, sorry about that Bach, but your mam and I did our best you know.'

Tomos hadn't the faintest idea what they were talking about. What did pre-raff . . . raff, something-or-other mean? And what had Mam and Dad got to do with the colour of Lowri's hair?

'Yes, well, anyway. I'm off out. Won't be late.'

Glyn looked his daughter up and down. *Yes, you're certainly quite a stunner when you're all dressed up now. I suppose we should be getting a little anxious about you now you're a grown woman. But are you grown up inside yet? I doubt it. Just be careful Cariad, that's all.*

But he knew he couldn't keep his little girl in cotton wool; his daughter who was now an attractive shapely big girl, with her olive green turtleneck sweater (that did rather clash with her hair, if he were to be honest) and her skin tight blue jeans. It was time for her to spread her wings, to mix the metaphor.

'Where is it tonight then?'

'Oh, just the usual. Lampeter. Seeing a . . . friend.'

Glyn had noticed the pause. 'Do you want me to run you there?'

'No; it's okay. I'm being picked up.'

Sioned spoke. She was nosier than Glyn. 'Is this a new young man you've got then Bach?'

Lowri grinned. 'Well; maybe. We'll see how it goes.'

Now Sioned was all ears. 'Oh; what's his name? Is he local then?'

Lowri hopped from one foot to the other. 'Look; I must go. He'll be here in a minute. Tell you later.'

And with that she swept grandly out the sitting room. Moments later they heard the front door slam. Glyn sighed and resumed his television programme, trying to pick up the thread again.

'Well I hope this one's better than the last,' Sioned remarked, I never really did like him. What was his name now? Gareth, was it?'

'Mm.'

'A nice enough boy I suppose, but a bit weak really. She needs someone with a bit more about him. Someone who'll stand up to her. Don't you think?'

'Mm.'

'I don't know where she gets her bossiness from really. It's not from either of us is it?'

'Mm.'

Sioned gave up.

Tomos went up to his room. He'd wanted to watch a good documentary about the Romans on BBC 2, but his dad usually had control of the remote control and the default setting was mainly the Welsh language channel. It wasn't fair being the baby of the family sometimes. You never got to do the choosing, unless Dad declared there was nothing worth looking at, tossed the controller to Mam and reached for the newspaper. Mam was good; she sometimes discussed what to watch with you.

He stretched out on his bed and gazed at the ceiling, tracing the fine crack that ran from near the door, passed nearly over his head and petered out near the window. It wasn't fair really. If Lowri could have a television in her room, why couldn't he? Alright, she'd bought it herself, bought it on the never-never (whatever that was) soon after starting work at the out-of-town supermarket (in the office, not on the checkouts) in Lampeter. Well, he could hardly buy one himself, could he? It would take years saving up out of his pocket money, probably. He briefly considered borrowing her TV, sneaking it into his room, but chickened out of the idea. It seemed a little bit like stealing, even though it wasn't, and he knew it took a lot of fiddling around with the areal to get a good picture. If he couldn't restore the setting of it and she found out he'd borrowed it, she'd be livid.

He did want to watch that programme though. It looked much more interesting in the write-up in *Radio Times* than some boring thing about house prices in Wales. Didn't Dad get enough of that all day at work? Perhaps she wouldn't mind if he watched it in her room. He tiptoed across the landing, feeling a little like a thief, and gently opened her bedroom door, nervous even though he'd only just seen her leave the house. He closed it gently behind him. Her room was a shock. It was riotously disordered, not what he'd expected from a girl at all. The clothes she'd returned from work in were scattered over her bed and the floor. Other apparel was heaped in corners, doubtless awaiting washday. Her wardrobe doors were flung open displaying her hippy dresses and slinky blouses bought new this year to keep up with the trends. Her dressing table was a clutter of cosmetics that he could only guess the applications of, apart from lipsticks, which were obvious.

There was an old armchair, now relegated to bedroom use (presumably Mam and Dad had the matching one in their bedroom) which was also adorned, embarrassingly, with several pairs of knickers and a pair of tights, and faced the chest of drawers which was crowned with her small white television. Still hardly daring to breathe, he went over to the set and peered at its controls. He'd have to keep the volume really low or Mam and Dad would hear and think there was an intruder or something and come up and find him here, and then there'd be trouble. He found what looked like the sound knob and turned it fully anticlockwise. Then, still holding his breath, he turned the television on.

To his enormous relief the picture sprang into life after a snowflakey start but the set was silent. He turned the volume knob ever-so-gently clockwise as the sound began to grow, then stopped turning when it was just audible. It was on the wrong channel though. He changed it and went to the chair and began, distastefully, to move the underwear, but then thought better of it. *No; leave it! She'll probably notice if anything's been moved!* He forced himself to sit down on top of a pair of bright red lacy knickers and one leg of a pair of dark brown tights. The sound was barely audible so he couldn't sit back properly and relax, but remained perched forward, straining to listen. This was no good; there would have to be just a little more volume. He got up and turned the sound control just a tiny bit more. Sitting down again further back in the chair, he encountered something small and hard that suddenly became smelly too.

'Oh no!' He leapt up and looked behind. There was a pungent smell and spreading stain beneath the knickers. Working up courage and overcoming his aversion, he pulled them away. There was a small glass bottle of something-or-other on the chair seat. The top was adrift and it was gently leaking into the faded upholstery. He snatched up the bottle and top and quickly stoppered it, but too late. Now what to do? He looked around wildly. There was a box of tissues on the floor by the dressing table. He grabbed a handful and swabbed at both the knickers and chair, but to little effect. The stain might dry before Lowri got back, but the scent would be a dead giveaway.

In a panic, he threw the tissues into the waste paper basket, the perfume bottle on the dressing table, the knickers back on the chair and switching off the television, fled the room. Back in his own room he undressed and climbed miserably into bed. She'd know; know it was him. Perhaps if he offered to buy her a new bottle (how much would it cost though?), she'd let the matter drop; wouldn't tell Mam and Dad. Worrying thus, he fell into a troubled sleep.

But of course he didn't get away with it. The next morning over his corn flakes he tried to be as unobtrusive as possible, but when Lowri came to the table (she was always last) she fixed him with a steely accusatory stare.

'Were you in my room last night young man?'

Tomos managed a mumbled 'No.'

'Well that's strange. The television wasn't as I left it when I got in, and my bottle of Calvin Klein is half empty and the room reeks of it. You have been in there haven't you? What have you been up to, you little bugger?'

'Lowri!' Sioned interjected, pausing halfway to the table with the toast, 'language please!'

Lowri ignored her. 'Come on Tomos, what were you doing in my room?'

'Um, I was just watching your television.'

'Oh really? And did I give you permission to?'

'No.' Tomos's reply was a squeak.

'Okay; well just stay out!'

'Yes, alright.'

Sioned chimed in. 'That wasn't a nice thing to do at all Tomos. Imagine if she'd come into your room. You wouldn't like that would you! Now say sorry to Lowri.'

'Sorry.'

'And what were you doing in her room watching television anyway? Why wouldn't you watch downstairs with us?'

'Because there was something I wanted to watch and you were watching something else. I didn't think she'd mind.'

Lowri resumed her tirade. 'Well I do bloody mind, alright?' Keep out of my room!'

'Yes. Sorry.'

She hadn't finished. 'And another thing. How did my perfume get spilled? It was all over the armchair and my, er . . . Half the bottle's gone.'

'Sorry. It was an accident.'

'*Accident?* What were you doing with it? Nasty little boy!'

'Now steady on Lowri, I'm sure he didn't mean to spill it!' Glyn put in, trying to make peace. Let it drop, will you? It's not the end of the world.'

Lowri rose, feeling a little put out. For Christ's sake, she was the victim in this, not Tomos. Sometimes they seemed to think more of him than her, and she was their real daughter after all.

'Well anyway,' she retorted, still giving Tomos the eye, determined to have the last word, 'I've got to get to work. Just stay out of my room in future!'

She got up leaving her toast half eaten (Tomos eyed it covetously; it had strawberry jam on), walked into the hall, grabbed her coat and bag and left, slamming the front door behind her. The bus would be along shortly. Sioned sighed. She knew what the problem was, recognised the signs; boy trouble. Lowri was either in the first flush of new love or things weren't going very smoothly. The symptoms were similar, really.

She chivvied Tomos. 'Come along Bach; time you were off too. Have you packed your bag? We'll talk about this again tonight. Perhaps Lowri will have calmed down a bit by then.'

Tomos really hoped so.

When he got home from school Sioned (who worked mornings only in a cafe in Aberaeron) sat him down and asked him his side of things.

'So what was so important to watch that you had to sneak into Lowri's room to look at it then?'

Tomos had been dreading this post-mortem all day. 'It was something about the Romans. We've been doing them at school. It looked interesting. And you were watching that other thing.'

Sioned sighed. *Oh, this child with his enquiring mind. Still, mustn't discourage that. Can't fault his taste in television really.*

'But even so Bach, you shouldn't have gone into her room like that. If you'd asked properly she might have let you watch on her television this once.'

Tomos stared at the floor glumly. 'No, don't think she would. She's so moody all the time nowadays. She never wants to play chess with me or anything.'

Sioned could only silently agree. 'Yes, I know. But you have to understand that she's grown up now. Well, nearly. She wants to be out having a life of her own. Her mind's probably full of this new boyfriend, whoever he is.'

'Well, suppose so,' Tomos conceded, but grudgingly.

'And how did you come to spill her perfume?' Sioned continued.

'It was an accident, honestly. The bottle was on the seat of her armchair under her, er, underwear, and the top must have been loose and I sat on it and it spilled. I didn't do it deliberately, really!'

He looked up at Sioned, his green eyes round with pleading. Sioned put hand to mouth to stifle a grin. She had to be serious though.

'Yes, well, Lowri isn't the tidiest of people really, I'll grant you that.'

Tomos nodded sagely.

'Anyway, about the television. I'm sorry about last night Bach. You know how it is with your dad though. He tends to be ruler of the remote control. What if you had a little television for Christmas, perhaps? Would you like that, unless you've other ideas about what you'd like?'

Tomos's eyes lit up. 'Oh, yes, that would be great! Thanks Mam!'

Sioned had to show she wasn't a pushover though. 'But you'd have to be sensible with it. No watching it late at night when you're supposed to be going to sleep.'

'Oh no, I promise I wouldn't. Really!'

'Alright, we'll see what your dad thinks about it then.'

They sat around the flame-dancing woodstove in the sitting

room (it was an October weekend and unseasonably chilly during the day now), a little awkwardly, taking tea and smiling politely at Lowri's boyfriend, Giles. At last Lowri had deigned to bring him to meet them. She'd taken her time about it, Sioned thought. The couple were occupying one end of the sofa and Tomos, looking decidedly uncomfortable, the other.

To be honest, at first impressions she wasn't terribly impressed. Oh yes, he was certainly good looking, in a smouldering-eyed, designer-stubbled sort of way, sitting there with his arm ostentatiously around Lowri's shoulder, manicured hand dangling languidly on her collar bone and his long legs stretched out in front and crossed at the ankles as if he meant to make himself at home. He certainly cut a different sort of figure from the last one, Gareth, who was timid, stuttered a bit and wouldn't have said boo to a goose. Lowri used to dominate him completely, she'd always thought. She was quite glad when Lowri finished with him, for his sake.

Sioned stole a quick glance at Glyn. His smile looked more rictus than genuine. She could imagine what was probably going through his mind. He'd be wondering where on earth Lowri had found this one (well actually they knew; he worked in one of the banks in Carmarthen, on the investment side he'd rather self-importantly told them, and they'd met in a wine bar there). Oh yes, the second-hand (presumably, anyway; it was difficult to tell with the customised number plate) Porsche that currently graced their drive confirmed his important status and looked all very impressive, but she knew Glyn wouldn't be.

This Giles (what a ridiculous name!) had got off to a bad start with Tomos too, grinning at him and calling him a carrot top like his sister, which had made the poor child squirm and Lowri look as though she didn't know where to put herself. He was engaged in a loud condescending conversation now with Glyn about the housing market, doing most of the talking so it was virtually a monologue, as Lowri looked bored and examined her fingernails and poor Tomos fixed her with a blatant can-I-go-now-please? expression on his freckled face. For Tomos to let freedom trump food, he must have been bored.

Seeking escape herself, Sioned rose from her armchair and went into the kitchen to brew more tea. She could feel the poor trapped child's pleading eyes boring into her back and, improvising rapidly, turned and said, 'Come and get some more tea from the top shelf for me will you please Tomos?'

Tomos looked briefly blank then realised it was a ploy, and leaped to help her with alacrity. Sioned closed the kitchen door so that their voices wouldn't carry along the hall. 'Look; I know this is very boring for you Bach. You've been introduced so now you can go out and play or go up to your room if you want.'

Tomos looked very relieved. 'I don't like him at all,' he said, with the disarming honesty of a nine-year-old.

Sioned secretly agreed, but couldn't be seen to do so openly. 'Well, he's probably alright when you get to know him.'

'I don't want to get to know him. He teased me!'

Sioned pulled him into a hug, pressing his troubled little face to her breast. 'Yes I know, Bach. Some people do that. They haven't got much imagination; can't put themselves in other's shoes. I'm sure he was only having a bit of fun though.'

'Well I still don't like it,' Tomos insisted petulantly.

'Yes, well; go and play outside now. And you can choose what television we watch tonight. How's that?'

Tomos's face brightened. He pulled away. 'Yeah, great. I'll go and read my new book now. I don't want to go outside.'

Sioned busied herself making a fresh pot of tea. She smiled to herself, a little grimly. The child had their visitor worked out really. Children were usually more straightforward in their appraisal of people. It was pretty black and white with them. Although quite what Lowri saw in this one, she couldn't imagine. Unless of course it was his glamour; his flashy car and everything. You didn't see a lot of that in this corner of west Wales. No doubt he was on a good salary, which would be appealing to an impressionable eighteen-year-old too.

She sighed, braced herself and took the tray through to the sitting room. Giles was still holding forth loudly in his braying voice.

'. . . My father works in derivatives in the City. We've got a little place down here in Llanybri, near Laugharne, where Dylan Thomas wrote. I keep it warm for them and commute to Carmarthen, which doesn't take long in that baby outside.'

Sioned glanced at Glyn. His irritation was barely concealed. He wouldn't be taking lightly to being educated by this tiresome upstart young Englishman who made no effort at all to pronounce the place names properly and flaunted his affluence so brazenly. And the mention of a second home would really put his back up too. It was a good job her passionate nationalist dad wasn't alive and here now, seeing his granddaughter consorting with the old oppressor. He'd certainly be turning in his grave just up the road if he knew.

Sioned and Glyn had nothing at all against the ordinary English who chose to come and live (and preferably work and contribute to the economy, which to be honest needed all the help it could get), even though most of them didn't learn the language. As Glyn said, when all was said and done we were all British; many Welsh people moved to England seeking better employment opportunities after all. But he really disliked well-heeled outsiders who muscled their way in with their much greater buying power and snapped up country cottages, driving up prices out of the reach of locals and then leaving the places standing empty much of the time. He saw it so often in his line of business.

The tiresome afternoon dragged on as Glyn and Sioned sat and listened to their unwelcome guest, finding it easier to succumb to his incessant prattle and stay silent than hold any sort of two-way conversation. Eventually, at twenty past five, when Sioned was beginning to fear that she might have to offer them dinner, Lowri looked up from her fingernails and announced that they really ought to be going; they were meeting up with some of Giles's friends from London who were down for the weekend. Getting up perhaps just a little too quickly, Sioned and Glyn trotted out the usual parting pleasantries (lovely to meet you; you must come again) and escorted the couple to the door to wave them off as they drove thunderously away, Lowri's arm semaphoring from the open passenger window as they went.

Breathing hugh sighs of relief, Sioned and Glyn returned to the sitting room and sank into their chairs. Glyn spoke first. 'Thank goodness that's over!'

'Duw Duw; yes,' Sioned agreed.

'I wish we could choose our offspring's boyfriends for them, don't you?'

Sioned laughed. 'Yes,' she said wryly, 'perhaps they do have a point in India after all.'

'What a bumptious little prick,' said Glyn (he rarely swore).

'Well, perhaps it won't last,' Sioned said, sounding more hopeful than confident.

'Let's hope so,' said Glyn, fervently.

Sioned went out into the hall and called up the polished oak staircase. 'You can come down Tomos; they've gone!'

She returned to the sitting room and fell back into her chair. 'And poor Tomos didn't like him either!'

'Yes, well, the young fool's not what you'd call sensitive, teasing our Tomos like that.'

Tomos had joined them. He slumped down on the sofa. 'I didn't like him at all,' he repeated to Glyn, determined to make his point.

'Yes, I know,' said Glyn. 'But Lowri has to choose her own friends, whatever we might think.'

'But anyway,' he added 'perhaps it's just first impressions. Perhaps we'll get to like him.'

Although he didn't say it with a great deal of conviction.

Their dilemma was solved a month later though. To everyone's relief there were no more visits, and Lowri's nights out began gradually to tail off. Her mood became ever more sullen, snapping irritably at her parents and ignoring Tomos altogether. Sioned knew the signs; something was going wrong. Hating herself for thinking it, she secretly hoped that the thing was withering on the vine. The nights out dwindled to one a week, the Friday, and then fizzled out completely. The next Friday came around and there was no disappearance to her bedroom with dinner left half-eaten for beautifying.

She did go up to her room, after eating her meal in total silence, but the television went on and there was no appearance a hour later dressed up to the nines. And there she stayed until eleven o' clock, when she emerged to make herself coffee (no asking if anyone else would like one). Sioned followed her into the kitchen, ready to have it out. Well she could only get her head bitten off.

She sat down at the kitchen table, waiting for her moment, as Lowri stood miserably waiting for the kettle to boil.

'You can tell me about it if you want, Cariad.'

Lowri poured the boiling water over the instant granules.

'There's nothing to tell.'

'Really? Are you sure? How are things with Giles?'

Lowri was making her way to the door clutching her mug and a handful of biscuits, but then changed her mind and sat heavily down at the table.

'It's over.' Her voice was quiet, expressionless.

'Oh Lowri; I'm sorry to hear that.'

'No, I don't think you are Mam. I think you're quite relieved really. I'm sure Tomos will be, anyway.'

Sioned let that go. 'But why? What's gone wrong?'

Lowri sighed. 'Well, I suppose it was doomed from the start really. We weren't exactly very similar, were we?'

'No, I suppose not.'

'Come on Mam; you know we weren't. Hardly the same backgrounds. His family from Surrey and his dad something important in the City; little old me from west Wales and my dad an estate agent.'

'Well I hope you aren't ashamed of that Lowri!'

Lowri's blue-green eyes suddenly blazed. 'No, of course I'm not!'

For the first time in many days she allowed herself a smile, if only a wry one.

'No; I suppose it took someone like him, with his smugness and superiority, to make me realise we're every bit as good as the English. I think we sometimes have a little bit of an inferiority complex, don't you?'

'I don't know Bach; I've never thought about it.'

Sioned smiled; looked at her beautiful daughter whose face was animated now. *This is more like it! There's some fire back in your belly. Yes; you be proud of yourself. Make your Taid proud of you!*

Lowri was speaking again, her words tinged with disappointment. 'He seemed so wonderful at first. I couldn't believe my luck that someone like that would be interested in boring country-bumpkin me. But he did really seem to be. And it was good to begin with. He was fun to be with, and I seemed to amuse him too. Or perhaps he was just laughing *at* me, and that's all I was; just an amusing little plaything from the peasantry, or whatever.'

Sioned looked at Lowri fondly. 'Well I can quite understand someone being attracted to you, Cariad. Don't do yourself down. You could have your pick.'

Lowri continued, ignoring that. 'You know it all started to go wrong when he came to tea. First he was rude to Tomos. I could see the poor kid was upset. And then the way he was talking down to you and Dad, not that he let either of you get much of a word in. Did you notice; he never asked Dad about his job or g, or you about anything at all. I was so embarrassed. And then when we left he was making sarcastic comments about you, and then about us to his ghastly friends from London, especially about our language. Including the old thing about us speaking Welsh just to exclude the English.'

'Yes,' Sioned sighed, 'I've never understood why so many of them think that.'

'So anyway, from then on it got steadily worse and he seemed to almost start to despise me, but I couldn't see why, and then I said I wouldn't, um . . .'

Lowri stopped, suddenly on difficult ground. But she had to carry on now. 'He got cross and called me horrible names and I said right, that was it, I didn't want to see him again, and he brought me home then. That was last Friday. I haven't seen him since then and don't want to!'

Sioned felt a rush of sympathy. *Yes child. Boys! Who'd have them? They can be such a bother at your age. I had one or two heartbreaks before I met your dad.*

Lowri was staring, glum, at the mug clasped in her long-fingered hands.

'I don't know Mam; I never get it right do I? Never find the right one.'

Sioned reached across and unpeeled one of her hands; squeezed it.

'Now now; come on Cariad. Don't be sad. I know it's hard just now but there'll be others. There's plenty more fish in the sea, and better ones. A pretty girl like you, you'll be fine. Just wait and see.'

Lowri looked at her mother, her eyes glistening. 'Yes, I expect you're right Mam. I'm sorry I've been a bit of a bitch lately. And to Tomos. I'll be okay.'

'Yes, you will. And it'll be your birthday in a couple of weeks. Nineteen already! It doesn't seem five minutes since you were Tomos's age. You've got to be alright for that.'

'Yes Mam,' said Lowri, smiling wryly, 'I will.'

The next afternoon when Tomos came home from school, Sioned told him the news. The child didn't try to hide his relief.

'Oh, great!'

Sioned chided. 'Well don't sound quite so pleased about it Bach. Lowri's quite upset and disappointed. It's not very nice when you break up. You'll perhaps find that out one day.'

'Sorry Mam. But he really wasn't very nice, was he?'

'Well, no, but it's not for us to say. Lowri must make her own choices.'

'Well anyway, I'm glad she isn't being so horrible to me anymore. She smiled at me this morning!'

'Yes, she'll soon be back to her old self again.'

Tomos had been thinking about Lowri's upcoming birthday. He had a problem about his present for her though. He confided it to his mother.

Sioned looked at him, astonished. 'Oh Bach. That is thoughtful. I'll talk to your dad about it; we'll see what we can do to help.'

Tomos breathed a big sigh of relief.

By the time her birthday came around Lowri felt much better. Her latest disappointment was almost forgotten, consigned to the dustbin of history; the file of life-lessons learned. She entered her last teenage year on a Saturday, which made it all the better. No getting up early to catch the bus to work. She could laze around as much as she wanted. So when she woke at half past eight, having disabled the alarm the night before, she just lay there, gazing around her untidy room.

Yes, you are in a bit of a state, aren't you? Perhaps I'll give you a birthday too; give you a good tidy up. You'll wonder what's hit you! And Mam will wonder why I'm getting the Hoover out too! It doesn't happen all that often, does it? Then a nice idle day. I wonder what my presents are? I hope Mam took the hint when I was pointing out those gorgeous shoes in the catalogue. This isn't quite the way I thought I'd be spending my birthday a few weeks ago though. I thought it would be with Lover Boy. Oh well; never mind. Best out of that anyway. I'm glad I'm not the black sheep of the family anymore. Well, I know I wasn't quite that, but it was as if he was driving a wedge between me and Mam and Dad and Tomos. Poor little kid. I really shouldn't have been so nasty to him. He seems to have forgiven me though. Wonder if Mam's made a Birthday cake? Hope so. I know I'm getting a bit old for them really, but who cares? Well this won't do. Can't stay in bed all day.

Sioned, Glyn and Tomos were sitting waiting patiently at the table when Lowri finally shuffled into the kitchen in her white towelling bathrobe and slippers, hair awry and showing a good half-inch of mousiness at the roots of the ginger (that was another of today's lazy tasks actually; to re-dye it, black).

'Happy Birthday, Lowri!' they chorused, as she plonked herself down in her chair, eyes fixed on the silver paper-wrapped parcel and cards, five, in a tidy pile by her cereal dish. Making herself wait, she tore open the envelopes first. She recognised Mam's writing of course and Tomos's (which was surprisingly neat for a small boy) and also that of her grandmother Anwen and Grandfather Geraint and Uncle Guto. Mam and Dad's card was a reproduction of a Holman Hunt picture (*The Lady of Shallot;* they'd remembered she was into the Pre-Raphaelites) and Tomos's was clearly home-made, probably done at school, depicting sheep in a meadow with a mountainous backdrop. He was no artist really, but it was a sweet thought.

Then she ripped away, excited, the wrapping paper from the parcel. It was an oblong box. Yes! She lifted the lid and pulled away the white tissue paper and there they were: those gorgeous red shoes! She pulled one out; turned it this way and that admiringly, slipped off a mule and tried it on. Perfect! She was thrilled.

'Diolch, Mam!' she cried, knowing she would have done the getting of them, and then 'Diolch, Dad!' remembering who would have done the paying.

She looked around her place at the table. There was nothing from Tomos. *Oh, Duw; he was still offended!*

But he didn't look cross. In fact he was trying to stifle a snigger. He slid off his chair, muttering about having something to do upstairs, and left them. A few minutes later he was back, still wearing his slightly lop-sided grin. He looked at Lowri, eyes dancing with merriment. 'You can go and look in your room now Lowri!'

Irritation instantly flared. 'What did I tell you about . . .'

But then she caught herself. *Steady on, it's your birthday. Leave the kid alone.* She left the table and ran up the stairs as fast as her slippered feet would allow. She burst into her room and looked urgently around, expecting a Happy Birthday banner or something. No; there was nothing. *What's the child talking about?*

Then she spotted it: a curiously-shaped wrapped parcel on the seat of her armchair. There was a note underneath it. It read, *Don't sit on it Lowri! Happy Birthday from Tomos.*

She tore the wrapping paper away. She laughed, eyes pricking a little bit. She might have known. It was a new, full bottle of Calvin Klein perfume, and body talc too.

And two months later Tomos got his wish: a small white television set for Christmas, just like Lowri's.

Chapter 6
Wayne

Wayne wished he had a brother. A brother would have been so much more fun. He imagined so anyway. Poppy was okay, and it wasn't her fault, but she was a *girl*. And there was a bit of a mystery about her. She was six (well, nearly seven) and he was nine. So she must have been born when he was three. He could work that out, quite easily really. But although he could remember a few things, most of them a bit fuzzy, from ages ago when he was five (like his first day at school), he couldn't remember Poppy being with them very much before then. But she must have been, according to his sums. Although wasn't there a faint memory of Mum going out some time before he started school and coming home with a baby? That wasn't how it happened with babies though, was it? He'd heard vague stories at school about babies coming out of their mum's stomachs after they'd been married for a while, and the way they came out, but it just sounded revolting. It couldn't be like that, surely? (He'd seen what Poppy looked like down there a few times (very peculiar!) when she was really little, and it just seemed impossible.)

Someone else had said at school that doctors had to cut women's stomachs open and take the baby out. It had happened like that when his little brother was born. Yes, that seemed much more likely. But anyway, how come that he could never remember Mum getting really fat, the way women did when there was going to be a baby? It didn't make sense. He'd asked Mum about that once, and she'd got a bit strange and said that it would all be explained one day, which just made it all the more mysterious. Memories were funny things though. He tried to really concentrate and think as far back as he possibly could, but the recollections were really difficult to find. There was one really *really* dim half-memory, not really a memory at all, of being in a big room somewhere and being put onto a strange woman's lap and for some reason it had been very frightening and he had cried, but it seemed to be all mixed up with a memory of Mum. It was so confusing.

He was idly thinking those thoughts now, on this sunny day in late July as he sat on the sofa, bored with his comic and the school holiday already, watching Poppy who was on the floor playing some sort of game with her Barbie doll, talking to it as if it were an actual person. Girls did play such stupid games!

He tried his luck with Mum, who was nursing a mug of tea on the arm of her chair and reading what looked like a very boring magazine.

'Can we put t' telly on?'

Poppy piped up too. 'Yes, can we?' She always aped her big brother.

Maureen looked at Wayne as if he'd made an indecent proposal. 'No! Not in the middle of the day. You know you can't!'

'But I'm bored!'

'And I am too!' Poppy echoed.

Maureen regarded her daughter of nearly five years now with some irritation. 'No you're not; you were playing quite happily a moment ago before your brother spoke up!'

'Am,' the child repeated defiantly, nodding her beribboned blonde-haired head for emphasis.

Maureen took a deep breath and exhaled slowly. 'Well why don't you both go out and play? It's a lovely day out there and you're stuck in here under my feet. I want to vacuum this room in a minute anyway.'

'But there's nothing to do out there . . .'

'Oh for God's sake Wayne, of course there is,' Maureen snapped. 'You're a bright boy; use your imagination. Go and have an adventure, or something. But don't get dirty.'

'I'd like to have a venchure,' Poppy put in, not really understanding the concept but determined not to be left out. It sounded fun, whatever it was.

'Oh alright then,' Wayne muttered, throwing his comic aside and getting up. 'I'll go out.'

'And take Poppy with you.'

'Aw; do I have to?'

'Yes, you do have to; don't be selfish. She's your sister!' Wayne went out into the garden and kicked his football around for a while, although it wasn't really much fun with no one to kick it to. Poppy was simply useless; she was too small, couldn't kick and was a girl anyway. He decided to go and look at Willow Beck. The last time he'd seen it was after that really heavy rain two weeks ago when it was in full spate; a brown boiling torrent. He loved seeing it like that; the beck was the only good bit about this new town really. He set off with Poppy trailing in his wake, wishing she hadn't latched onto the adventure idea. Hopefully he wouldn't meet any of the kids from school. He'd only get teased about having her in tow. It was bad enough getting the stupid comments and name calling about his hair. But apart from that, it was alright for them; most of them had brothers, not a stupid sister.

He still hadn't got used to Northallerton really and the excruciating difficulty of making new friends. He knew why they'd had to move here, but it didn't make it any easier having to leave his best friends Darren and Craig behind in York and find new ones. Dad had lost his job at Rowntrees. The firm hadn't been the same since it was taken over by that Swiss firm. He'd been really miserable about that and often snappy with him and Poppy, even though they'd done nothing wrong. Mum had said he was to try and understand; it was horrible losing your job and he'd done so before, which was why they'd moved over here from Liverpool when he was three. It really wasn't that Dad didn't love them, but losing his job had made him very sad.

But then he'd got the portering job, in the town's hospital, that didn't pay so much money, but it was better than nothing and they'd come here. Uprooted him and wrenched him away from his friends. Oh well, he'd just have to make the most of it.

They reached the beck. The water level was quite low again now, murmuring quietly and dappled in a sparkly sort of way by the overhanging trees, and the stones of its rocky bed were bone dry. He found a twig and snapped it in half to make boats for racing; ran upstream for a hundred yards and threw them into the middle of the beck where the water flowed quickest, then ran back to where Poppy was squatting by the beck's side dabbling a stick into the water.

'Yours is t' thin stick,' he said, gifting her that one because it had landed behind the thicker section of twig when it was launched. 'Let's see whose wins.'

He watched as the two pieces of wood made their rapid zigzaggedly way towards them. He was in the lead, by a good stick-length! But then his boat hit a stone and was captured, wriggling in an eddy and the other sailed triumphantly past. Oh no; Poppy would win! He looked around urgently for something to throw at his stick to free it from its miniature whirlpool. There was nothing except the small stones lying submerged on the bed of the beck. He got down on his knees and leaned over the shallow water, lost his balance and toppled in, splashing, grazing hands and forearms painfully as he flung them protectively forward. He lay on the hard knobbly bed of the beck, shocked by the sudden coldness of water on stomach, thighs and knees, almost taking a mouthful, too surprised by the suddenness of it all to cry out.

Downstream, Poppy had witnessed the event. She looked at Wayne, unsure whether to laugh or be frightened. He'd get up after a moment or two though and then she'd know which to do. Sure enough, after what seemed a very long time he got slowly to his feet and climbed out onto the bank. Poppy rose and ran to him, hovering uncertainly as he sat shivering and clutching his skinned arm, still not knowing how she should react though. He was biting his lower lip hard, making it red and trying not to cry. There was a long red streak on his bare left arm and it was bleeding, quite a lot it seemed to Poppy. That decided things for her. She began to wail. Wayne got painfully, soggily to his feet. His teeth were chattering, Poppy noticed.

'Come on,' he winced, we'd better go home,' and set off with Poppy trailing tearfully behind.

Maureen, of course, was not best pleased and not terribly sympathetic. After an assessment of his injuries – mainly just the scrape on his arm which didn't look as though it warranted a trip to A and E, she marched him into the bathroom, turned on the hot and cold bath taps, sat him on the toilet while she removed his sodden, smelly trainers and socks, then when the bath was a quarter full stood him up to remove all his clothes in spite of his protestations (his modesty wasn't deemed a priority), and commanded him to climb in. She found his face flannel and as the bath continued to fill bathed his chest and back and arms, avoiding the wounds.

'How the hell did you come to fall in the beck anyway, you young fool?' she demanded angrily. 'You know you have to be careful there. We've told you about it often enough.'

'I was just leaning over to get a stone out and I lost balance,' Wayne said through still chattering teeth. He was still slightly in shock.

'And why did you want to go grubbing around in water after stones?'

'Dunno. I was just playing.'

Poppy had wandered into the doorway, afraid she might be missing something. 'It was a venchure,' she explained helpfully.

'I'll give you adventure.' Maureen scolded, letting the observation hang, forgetting that it had been her idea in the first place. The child just wasn't safe to be let out sometimes. Look at that bother they'd had last year when he'd fallen out of that tree and broken his arm, before they left York, just before Jim got made redundant again after thinking he'd be with Rowntrees for the rest of his working life. Extra worry about his accident-prone son hadn't exactly helped his mental state.

'Lie down in the bath,' she said, exasperation evaporating a little, 'perhaps it'll stop you shaking.' Wayne shifted his bottom forward and lay back, hands over his privates.

She tousled his ridiculously red hair. 'Then I'll see to your arm and make you some cocoa with plenty of sugar. Then you can stay indoors for the rest of the day young man. You can watch the telly.'

'Thanks Mum.'

Maureen permitted herself a smile. She could never stay cross with him for long. 'I don't know; what are we going to do with you?'

'Can I have cocoa with plenty sugar and watch telly too?' Poppy enquired anxiously.

Maureen sighed. 'Yes, alright then Poppet.'

Kids; who'd have them?

Of course when Jim came home after his shift he was none too pleased about Wayne's latest scrape either. He glared down at his son who was lying on the sofa in his dressing gown with a blanket over his legs, milking his wounded-soldier situation for all it was worth.

'Honestly Wayne, can't you stay out of bother for five minutes? Thank God t' beck were low. You can drown in six inches of water; did you know that?' His accent and dialect had returned now he'd been back on home soil and amongst Yorkshire people a few years.

Wayne shifted uncomfortably. He hated it when Dad was cross. He thought things were alright in that department now that he was back in work and normal life had resumed.

'Sorry Dad. It were an accident, really!'

'Yes, so your mother says. But it were bloody stupid all the same. The water might have been higher; in spate even. And you'd taken our Poppy there too. What if she'd fallen in?'

'I didn't take her. She followed me!'

'Yes, well. I don't see why you two can't play together nicely.'

'And anyway, Wayne pleaded, 'I would have rescued her if she'd fallen in! I wouldn't have let her drown!

Jim's anger softened a little. 'Maybe you would son, or think you would. But rivers can be dangerous, even little ones like Willow Beck.'

Wayne said nothing.

Jim sat down on the end of the sofa and looked exasperatedly, fondly at his son; his always-on-the-go Action Man boy who needed so much excitement, so much stimulation to keep him satisfied. Who when they went walking now he was feeling better again, up on the fells, was straight up the nearest rocky outcrop as quick as you could say Jack Robinson. He really did need something to burn off his energy.

He suddenly had a thought. 'Why don't you join t' Scouts?'

'What?'

'Join t' Scouts. It's quite a good troop they've got in Northallerton, so they say.'

Wayne sounded dubious. 'I don't know . . .'

'Well why not? They do lots of stuff you'd like, I reckon. Camping. Rock climbing. Proper trekking; better than we do because we have to take Poppy into account. I think they do hang gliding, the bigger boys.'

Maureen, only half concentrating on *Coronation Street,* glanced at Jim sharply. 'Jim! Don't put ideas like that in his head! Sounds much too dangerous to me, that does.'

Jim scoffed, but good-naturedly. 'Course it ent Mo. It'd all be well supervised. They have good leaders in that outfit. Any road, that's for the older kids, as I say.'

Maureen wasn't really convinced, but she returned to her soap.

'Anyway,' Jim said, 'why don't you think about it? It'd give you something to do.'
'Yeah; suppose so.'
'Go on, you'd love it. Are any of the kids at school in it?'
'A couple of boys are in cubs, not scouts.'
'Yes, well, same thing. Shall I enquire about it for you?'
'Okay then,' Wayne said, giving in.

As it turned out, Wayne was glad he did. Once over his shyness about meeting new people (although he knew Gary and Simon from school) he took to being a cub scout like a duck to water. He'd found his natural habitat. He loved most of the activities and learned to swim. He liked the outdoor things especially, like exploring on days out with the pack, and best of all he loved the camping: the fun of putting up of tents, the learning how to safely make a fire, the trying not very successfully to cook (but the burned sausages still tasted great) and the top-of-their-voices singing afterwards. He felt proud and important walking to the scout hut wearing his uniform with its steadily growing tally of badges, like junior medal ribbons, on Thursday evenings. And he loved the camaraderie of an all-male community. He felt himself an important part of a greater whole. For the first time no one teased him about his hair or his freckles; he felt fully accepted just for himself, as a proper person.

He made his first real friend. Billy, a tall skinny boy with blond close-cropped hair and spectacles, was six months older than him, nearly ten, and in a few months would be moving up to the proper scouts. Wayne felt very jealous about that. Billy had an older brother, Mick, who was going into the army as soon as he was old enough. At the moment he was a senior scout. He also had a sister, Janet, who was three years older than him but she wasn't interested in scouting. Wayne wished he had an older brother too; someone to look up to, rather than the limpet-like Poppy, who was now even more of an embarrassment really, although he supposed it couldn't be helped. But then he did have his wider family of cubs, he was a member of a pack, so they were sort of brothers really.

That September they went away to a weekend camp in Swaledale. Wayne had walked the Yorkshire fells with his parents (although they'd been fairly gentle ambles because of Poppy) but this was different. This was proper adventure! They arrived at the riverside site, an emerald-green field outside Feetham just before lunch time, and set about erecting their tents. Some of the older boys, the ten-year-olds, were old hands at doing it now and had theirs up in no time although Wayne, who was sharing with Billy, was anxious to keep up and earn kudos from Mr Braithwaite the leader (pot bellied and hairy legged in his voluminous shorts and ably assisted by Mick, Billy's brother), and they weren't far behind.

Then it was time to eat. For their first meal of the weekend they'd been instructed to bring packed lunches from home, which Wayne thought a little disappointing, but never mind, there'd be the fun of cooking on the methylated spirit stoves later. It was okay though; quite good in fact. Mum had done him tuna sandwiches and jam ones, a banana and a Mars bar. The weather didn't look too promising with rather ominous grey clouds gathering over the distant rearing mass of Great Shunner Fell in the west, but they sat outside and ate anyway. Mr Braithwaite had planned a trek up to Crackpot Hall for the afternoon, but first they had to collect firewood whilst the weather was still dry and stash it inside the big communal tent, hoping that the rain would hold off and they'd be able to light a fire outside. (That was the only trouble with arranging events well in advance; you could never really rely on the weather.)

Mick, a taller, darker, thicker-set version of his baby brother, rather bossily led them on a wood gathering sortie. He enjoyed his rank, the superiority of being nearly seventeen to their eight-to-ten and much greater experience in scouts. That one-upmanship over the small kids would be ending soon though when he joined the Yorkshires. Then he'd be a simple squaddie like the other lads. But he couldn't wait to start.

The weather looked as though it had been dry for a few days since and there were plenty of dry-looking branches, windfall casualties from the spring storms, lying under the oaks in the corner of the field. The smaller boys picked up one small branch each.

Mick was scandalised. 'Come on you lot, I want an armful from each of you!' To illustrate his point he picked up a larger branch and thrust it at eight-year-old Denis, the small child fumbling gamely to add it to his paltry load. 'We want us to have a good blaze later!'

Wayne and Billy knew the score though, and chose the largest windfalls, struggling to hold a growing bundle in one arm as they added with the other hand. Mick collected a large armful too (well, you had to be seen to be leading by example) and they made their way back to the tents.

'Well done lads!' chortled the ebullient Pete Braithwaite, his large uneven teeth gashing his rather wild beard, as the band of scavengers gratefully dropped their loads in a pile. 'Let's get this lot under cover and hope t' weather holds off. We'll have a good singsong under t' stars after dinner.'

He glanced heavenwards. 'Well, perhaps no stars, but you know what I mean!' he qualified.

The boys did as instructed, stowing the wood in the large tent that served both as Braithwaite and Mick's sleeping quarters and a meeting place if the weather turned foul.

The minibus disgorged them, tingling with anticipation, at picturesque Keld, tiny and goose-grey at the head of Swaledale on the watershed of the Pennines. Already wearing their walking boots, they donned rucksacks containing extra clothing, emergency rations (Kendal Mint Cake of course; well, you couldn't take any chances) and waterproofs, and with Braithwaite and his lieutenant Mick in the lead set off up the track to the gaunt ruin of Crackpot Hall.

Wayne and Billy plodded side by side, happy in the camaraderie of the pack. This was the life! What could be better, thought Wayne, out with your pals like this. He wondered now why he hadn't thought of joining the scouts before. And there were no girls hanging around either. It was brill! The only downside was; Billy would be joining the proper scouts soon. But then, after another year, he'd be rejoining him. And they could still be friends outside of scouts anyway.

'Good this ent it?' Wayne enthused.

Billy nodded his blonde head vigorously. 'Yeah, cool,' he agreed, a little breathless from the steepening track.

'I hope t' rain holds off so we can have a fire after.'

'Yeah, hope so,' Billy agreed. 'And the singsong. Pete's brought his guitar.'

Wayne was slightly shocked to hear their leader referred to by his Christian name. It seemed a little disrespectful. He was a grown-up after all. But then he'd heard Mick calling him that, although there probably weren't that many years' difference between those two. It looked almost as if Mr Braithwaite had become a leader straight after leaving senior scouts. And perhaps Billy thought he could call him that just because his brother did. He wouldn't dare to himself though.

'I wonder why this place we're going to see is called Crackpot Hall?' Wayne mused.

'Dunno; perhaps they were all crackpots what lived there,' Billy said, giggling at his own levity.

It was only a mile's walk and soon they reached, panting, the tumbledown stone building. The boys immediately began exploring it, darting in and out of the broken walls and doorways, calling to each other in their excitement. Pete and Mick stood to admire the view down into the deep green furrow of Swaledale with the river threading through it like a silver snake, although both had seen it from this vantage point before. Wayne joined them. It seemed the appropriate thing to do. Well, Mum and dad had always taught him to appreciate the rolling heathery landscape of the Dales and Moors and he genuinely did love it. Dad had been talking seductively about a trip to the Lakes next year, just the two of them doing some proper serious mountain walking, leaving the females to do other things down in the valley (well, Poppy wasn't really old enough yet and she'd slow them down too much). Wayne wasn't quite sure how that would fit in with his scouting activities, but he'd damn well make sure it could.

'Ay, this is grand ent it Wayne?' Pete said, doing a long appreciative exhalation, his eyes sweeping the panorama below.

'Ay grand,' Wayne agreed. That summed it up, really.

The other boys were reappearing and Pete gathered them together. 'Right you lot, let's have a little bit of education now, shall we? Anybody know anything about this place?'

'It's where crackpots lived,' Billy chirruped, determined to get full mileage from his pun.

Pete grinned tolerantly as the boys fell about laughing, easily amused.

'Yeah, very funny, clever clogs. Now does anyone really know?'

He was met with blank looks, so he proceeded to tell them (his dad was a teacher after all and knew about such things) that it had been a seventeenth century farmhouse with shippons either end for the beasts, and then later probably a mine office, and mining subsidence had caused it to fall down. He told them that its name didn't mean 'crazy in the head' at all, but the village of the same name along the valley had originally been called Crakepot, from Viking words *kraka,* which meant crow, and *pot,* which meant a pit, so it just meant 'Hole where crows gather.' Billy looked disappointed, although he liked the Viking reference, but then Pete spiced up his lecture with a tale of a wild four-year-old girl called Alice who had lived there in the nineteen-thirties. The boys loved that.

After Pete and Mick had sat awhile drinking thermos flask coffee and the boys had swilled pop, wanting to eat their Mint Cake but being told a firm no (the expedition was not yet over so it still constituted emergency rations, and besides there was still tomorrow to come), the pack made its way back down the track to Keld, the minibus and then to the campsite. The weather was still holding up and looked as though it would continue to for some while yet, so Pete directed that the wood be brought out and stacked ready for fire lighting (which was fine by Mr Truman the farmer who's field it was; he knew the scouts would act responsibly).

They set about cooking their meal, squabbling good-naturedly over who would peel potatoes until Pete decreed that they each do their own, taking it in turns with the peeler. They would be boiled (it was easier) along with tinned peas, and burgers from the cool box could be fried in the big blackened frying pan. Pudding would be tinned fruit and Carnation milk. The potatoes were under-cooked and the burgers burnt (although they got the peas right), but they tasted wonderful all the same. Then came the highlight of the day, the rediscovering of their inner pyromaniac selves: lighting the fire. With it well ablaze they sat cross-legged, cheeks scorching, as Pete inexpertly strummed his guitar and led them (his voice wasn't much better either) in all the favourite scouting songs.

They sat and sang and listened to stories from Pete until long after dark and all the wood was burned, reduced to hot white ash that lifted and blew away like incense. When a chill Yorkshire wind started nibbling at their backs and cold fat blobs of rain began to fall they crawled into their tents and sleeping bags, happy and tired; murmuring and giggling until sleep took them one by one.

Wayne was woken early by rain hammering on the roof of the tent. He peered up at it anxiously in the dim dawn light. The noise was tremendous and the thin fabric was sagging disconcertingly, distended like a large orange balloon. Would it withstand the onslaught? They'd pitched the tent on a slight slope and water was beginning to ooze in at one corner at the higher end. Billy was awake too.

'Good this, ent it?' he enthused.

'What's good about it?'

'Well; exciting ent it. I love rain.'

'Well I don't; you can keep it,' said Wayne, not sharing the enthusiasm.

'Ah, come on. Don't be a misery guts.' Billy wriggled out of his sleeping bag. He was still wearing his uniform. 'Bloody hell, I'm dying for a piss.'

He reached for his rucksack and took his waterproof cagoule out, slipping it over his head.

'You aren't going out in this are you?'

'Well you don't want me to do it in here, do you?' Billy sniggered.

'No, 'course not.'

'Well there you are then.' Billy was reading Mick's book about Captain Scott's final desperate days in Antarctica. He intoned, pretentiously, Captain Oates's heroic last words. 'I'm just going outside. I may be some time.'

He opened the flap and dived out into the teeming rain, making for where they'd established the latrine. Wayne looked at his Mickey Mouse watch (which was beginning to become an embarrassment really, it was for little kids after all). Six twenty. What time would Mr Braithwaite want them up? They wouldn't be able to do much in this rain, surely. He lay and thought about the events of the day before. It'd been great, trekking up to Crackpot Hall with the lads. He did envy Billy though, going up to proper Scouts soon. They did more of this adventurous stuff and other things too like rock climbing. He'd love to do that. Actually he'd like to go all the way up; be a Senior Scout too and perhaps even be a leader one day. It would be great to be in Scouts as a job, do it for a living, but he doubted whether that was possible. Mr Braithwaite – Pete – had an ordinary job he knew, in Ackroyds bookshop. He wasn't a leader all the time.

Wayne mused about this and that for some time, then looked at his watch again. Ten past seven. It'd be getting-up time soon, surely. Then it hit him. Hang about, where was Billy? He did a calculation, using his fingers. Billy had been gone forty minutes. It didn't take that long to have a pee!

Then he heard something, faintly, muffled beneath the rain pounding on the tent. A bird, was it? It came again. He opened the flap and it was repeated a third time. It sounded more like a faint cry now. Billy? Surely not. But it kept coming. Wayne unzipped his rucksack, got out his waterproof and pulled it over his head, put the hood up and ducked out of the tent. Like Billy, there was no need to dress; he'd gone to bed wearing his uniform. He stood in the driving rain, listening. It seemed to be coming from upstream. He went to look at the latrine. There was no one there. He began walking towards the end of the field, following the riverbank towards the source of the sound. It was getting louder now, and now it really did sound like a cry.

There was a gate in the stone wall, by a barn that was also stone built, seeming to grow organically out of the wall. It was ajar and he passed through. And then he saw, up ahead, a figure lying on the ground, wearing a familiar red cagoule.

'Billy?' he shouted.

Immediately there was an answer, stronger now, 'Help!'

Wayne broke into run, slipping and sliding on the sodden grass as the plaintive calls continued. He reached Billy who was lying with his left foot twisted at an improbable angle. He was soaked, shivering violently and sobbing, his face a rictus mask of pain. Wayne knelt down beside his friend. 'What's happened?'

'I fell over and something's happened to my ankle. It really really hurts!' Billy gasped and grimaced, his words punctuated by sobs.

'But what were you doing right out here anyway?'

'I just came for a walk. I was being Captain Oates. I was on my way back when it happened.'

Wayne decided that it wasn't the best time to ask who Captain Oates was. 'Can you stand? I'll help you get back.'

He put his hands under Billy's armpits from behind and tried hauling him to his feet, but it was almost impossible. Billy was a bigger boy. He got him halfway upright and Billy tried putting his foot to the ground, but he screamed in pain and sat quickly down again. It wasn't going to work.

'Don't worry,' Wayne reassured, 'I'll go for help.'

He began running, running, stumbling, afraid of falling over too, as fast as he could, back through the gate, along by the river, back to the bright cluster of tents that seemed a long way away through the rain. It seemed to take forever to close the distance. As he got close, his heart bursting, he began shouting between gasps of breath, 'Pete! Pete!' Inhibitions had gone now. Braithwaite's tousle-haired head popped out of his tent flap.

'Wayne! What the bloody hell?'

'It's Billy! He's back there. He's fallen over and hurt his ankle. I tried to bring him back but I couldn't!'

'Oh Christ! And what were you two doing out in this rain so early in the morning? Oh, never mind. We'll talk about it later. Where is he then?'

Wayne described the location. Mick had now appeared, also fully dressed. He'd heard the commotion.

Pete barked at him, 'Get us waterproofs!'

He ducked back inside the tent and reappeared with the garments. They donned them, and with an order to Wayne to get in his tent and take his wet clothes off and bloody stay put, they set off at a run across the field. When they reached Billy he looked worse. His face was deathly white and he was trembling violently and sobbing, lying in a foetal curl apart from his injured ankle. Pete sank to his knees beside him. This wasn't the time for bollockings about indiscipline. He felt a sudden surge of excitement. Here was the opportunity to demonstrate some leadership skills, show his mettle!

'It's okay Billy. What happened then?'

'I slipped over in t' wet and my ankle went under me and now it really really hurts!' His voice was a pained whisper.

'You stupid idiot! What the fuck where you doing out here anyway?' Mick put in, anger mixed with concern.

Pete silenced him with a save-it for-later look. He looked at Billy's ankle. It certainly looked bad. And the kid was shaking like a leaf. Must be in shock.

'Do you hurt anywhere else? Didn't bang your head did you?'

Billy shook his head mutely. Pete considered the situation. Okay; they always said don't move the patient. As a first-aider, he knew that. But it did appear to be just his ankle. He couldn't leave the poor kid lying out here in the rain much longer waiting for an ambulance to arrive. That could be bloody ages. He decided to risk it. He peeled off his waterproof and his sweater, then got Billy's sodden cagoule off and his sweater onto him followed by his dryer waterproof. He bent and scooped Billy into his arms, lurching slightly at the sudden weight. He looked at Mick.

'Run back to t' farm and tell 'em to phone t' ambulance,' he commanded, enjoying being master of the situation.

Mick didn't need twice telling; he took off like a greyhound as Pete followed, staggering with his load. Back at camp, the wide-eyed cubs were gathered beside Mrs Truman who was waiting, anxious, arms folded over her oil-coated, ample bosom. 'Bring t' lad into t' house to wait, she commanded, pulling age superiority on the now drenched Pete. 'It's warm in t' kitchen. I've turned t' Rayburn up.'

It certainly *was* warmer in there than in a tent. Mrs Truman fussed about getting a thick blanket to swaddle Billy in after removing Pete's waterproof, and offering to make sweet tea. Pete wasn't sure about that; best wait until the ambulance arrive, he said, reasserting authority. It took twenty minutes for the ambulance to come and whisk Billy back to hospital in Richmond, followed by Pete as responsible adult in charge, in the minibus. (Mick had to stay behind, worried, and supervise the cubs). It turned out that the ankle was quite badly broken, both tibia and fibula, and needed an operation, and Billy had a moderate case of hypothermia too. To the rather envious boys who visited him later, he was a wounded hero.

But to the adults, when all the facts were known the real hero of the piece, with his sharp hearing and initiative, was Wayne.

Chapter 7
Tomos

Back from school and up in his room, Tomos flicked on his television. There had been a rumour flying around the school for the last hour and a half about something dreadful going on in America. The teachers had suddenly adopted grave, rather distracted-looking faces. It was something about an aeroplane crashing into a skyscraper. It sounded dreadful. An image flickered into life on the screen and there it was in all its horrific detail; an airliner suddenly appearing from out of shot and ploughing straight into a tall pale grey building to be engulfed in an enormous cloud of smoke. A running caption came up at the bottom of the screen. *Breaking news: airliners collide with World Trade Center New York.*

Tomos sat down on his bed and stared open mouthed. *Duw Duw!*

Then the reporter's voice came in above the constantly repeated pictures (because, presumably, there was no other footage available yet), telling the ghastly story. How there was not one airliner involved but also a second, with pictures of it colliding too, which of course ruled out the possibility of it being a dreadful accident; it was a deliberately intended atrocity of gargantuan proportions. Tomos watched the horror piled unremittingly upon further horror as first one tower and then the other collapsed, surprisingly neatly as if deliberately demolished; then the dust, the mayhem, the panic, the screams, the confusion, the people rushing terrified through the streets trying to get away.

It was almost like some Hollywood disaster movie but it was all too sickeningly clear that this was real. As Tomos watched and listened, all thoughts of homework (he was beginning his A-levels) banished, the rest of the news unfolded. A third plane had hit the Pentagon and a fourth had come down in a field. The President had been hurried aboard Air Force One, to be carried out of harm's way. When Sioned got in from doing her big shop in Lampeter the sitting room television went on too (she'd also heard rumours in the shops) and she too sat transfixed, as it began to emerge that this was the work of Islamic terrorists. And when Glyn arrived home and they sat down to dinner, for the first time ever the kitchen set stayed on with the volume turned up so that they could hear it from the dining room.

Glyn was outraged. He liked to think of himself as a tolerant and broad minded man, but this outrage brought out his most visceral instincts. And he seldom swore; at least not in front of Sioned.

'Bloody terrorists!' he fumed. 'Just what do they think they're achieving by all this barbarity?' he asked Sioned, as if she might know the answer.

'Goodness only knows Cariad,' she said, 'Think of all those poor people. What are they saying now; it might be thousands killed?'

'Yes,' Glyn remarked grimly. 'I can't imagine many people getting out of those ruins alive.'

Tomos felt lost for words. He didn't feel mature enough to voice an opinion, although he felt he ought to have one. He was sixteen after all; nearly a man. He had no problems with Middle-Eastern people, whether the women were veiled or not. Admittedly he didn't know very many, but Hadiqa at school was fine, and certainly friendly. In fact, because she didn't wear the veil and he could see her face, he thought she was actually rather beautiful. Yes, as Dad said, what was their problem really with the West? Alright; he knew all about repressive British colonialism in the past and American commercial colonialism in the present, but even so. That didn't warrant killing and maiming any more than it was justified for the IRA. Why couldn't people just get on together?

Glyn was still holding forth. 'Well I dread to think what America will do after this. They won't take this lying down, that's for certain.'

'Yes, well,' Sioned put in. 'Let's hope there isn't another war because of it. We've had quite enough of those.'

'Duw, yes Cariad,' Glyn agreed. 'We certainly have.'

When Tomos looked back on that time it really seemed to him a sort of coming of age, for all that he was only sixteen. It was as if a major world event, and a pretty seminal one at that, had in some way kick-started his transition from boy to a youth with a nascent world view; it had influenced his developing ethical code considerably. He'd always been a reflective and thoughtful boy though; always been inclined to ponder things, think things through and balance options for himself, like playing chess, rather than accept easy populist views ready-made. And Nine-Eleven, as it had rapidly become known, made him do some rapid opinion-forming.

On the sixth of October, following the Trade Center atrocity, Lowri came home for the weekend with her partner Will. Now that she, like Will, was a lecturer (having ascended straight to that dizzy academic height from post-grad) in sociology at the University of Wales Cardiff, Sioned saw less of her daughter than she would really have liked. But as Glyn pointed out, and he was right of course, their children had to make their own way in the world and Lowri had done very well for herself at university. Her future had to lie in Cardiff at least, possibly even further afield. There was nothing for her really in Lampeter or even Aberystwyth, although they were university towns too. Well, not in her speciality, anyway.

That Sunday over midday dinner (which was praised extravagantly by Will who had been used to rather more basic bachelor fare, mostly out of take- away cartons, in recent years), and in English because Will had no *Cymraeg*, no Welsh, they discussed the burning issue of the day.

Lowri was greatly exercised about it. Sioned watched her fondly *(yes, that's my girl, you're just like your Taid when you get started)* as she waved her Welsh lamb-laden fork about, nearly taking Will's eye out, to emphasise her passionately expressed point.

'It's just crazy. Did Bush really think the Taliban would just hand bin Laden over? No; probably not. He knew he'd be bombing anyway. So now countless innocents, women and children, have to die so that he can give America vengeance!'

'But it was a terrible thing to happen; so cruel,' Sioned put in reasonably. 'All those poor, poor people.'

'Yes of course it was Mam,' Lowri said, just a little patronisingly (she felt she could always best her mother in debate nowadays), 'but what's bombing innocents going to achieve? The perpetrators of the deed are dead anyway, and bin Laden denies being the mastermind. Perhaps he was, perhaps he wasn't. But doing what they're doing won't bring justice.'

'But al-Qaeda needs to been cleared out of Afghanistan surely?' Glyn put in tentatively. (He felt a little intimidated by his daughter's intellect nowadays too, although he admired it greatly.)

'I fear it won't be as easy as that,' said Will, frowning and rippling his high, hair-receding forehead, eyes serious behind their steel rimmed spectacles. 'History shows you can't win simply by destroying your enemy. Not this sort of fanatical guerrilla enemy anyway. It's a many-headed Hydra. It's all very well talking about a war on terror, but all you do is create martyrs and radicalise replacements who keep coming back at you. It's not a solution.'

Tomos listened, rapt. He had to agree with what his clever big sister and her scholarly partner were saying. They spoke good sense and with fairness and compassion, it seemed to him, unlike many of the half-wit boys at school who simply wanted the Coalition to charge in, all guns blazing, never mind that they'd be invading another country, destroying everyone and everything in sight, like some sort of holy crusade. But sitting here with the grownups, he, Tomos Rees was (rather mutely, true) putting the world to rights.

Lowri was speaking again, clusters of words escaping between mouthfuls. 'And what really gets me is: we are getting involved as well. A Labour government for Heaven's sake! Well it's the last time I'll vote for them, I can tell you. It'll be back to Plaid next time!'

Glyn laughed. 'Well it would warm your Taid's heart to hear you say that Bach! I think he'd be right alongside you in criticising Labour there.'

'Yes, he certainly would, bless him,' Sioned agreed.

'CND are organising a demo in protest next Saturday,' Lowri said. 'In London. Will and I are going.'

She looked across at Tomos. 'Why don't you come, Little Brother? Learn some principles?'

'Oh, he couldn't possibly go all that way by himself; not all the way to London,' Sioned put in anxiously.

Lowri scowled at her mother, exasperated. 'Mam! I'm not suggesting that! It's easy. He gets the train from Carmarthen to Cardiff on Friday afternoon after school, stays overnight with Will and me and then we get a train up to Paddington on Saturday morning. No problem!'

She regarded Tomos again. 'What do you reckon?'

Tomos considered it. Briefly. *Oh yes! This could be great fun. Apart from being in a just cause of course. And a trip to London too! Great!*

He looked across at his sister, eyes bright with excitement but trying to appear nonchalant. 'Yeah, I'll come.'

Lowri beamed back. 'Wonderful! Provided you can get to Cardiff, I'll pay your fare to London. We have to get from Paddington to Marble Arch, which is the congregating point, then march from there to Trafalgar Square, where there'll be speakers, and the media recording it all, hopefully.'

Glyn spoke up, keen to lend support. He almost wished he could go too; wished he *dare* go; wished he had as much idealistic zeal as his father-in-law had had and his daughter had now. 'Well I'll help you with the fare to Cardiff Tomos; you just find the bus fare to Carmarthen.'

'Oh, diolch, Dad,' Tomos said, and then, remembering himself, 'and you too, Lowri. Diolch!'

So wrapped up in thoughts was he, Tomos didn't hear a great deal more of the conversation as it gradually drifted onto other topics. His mind was on Lowri's thrilling invitation. *Yes, this will be great. My first demo! Like a proper student. I know I'm not one yet, but it's what students do after all. What an adventure!*

He could barely contain his excitement all that week. Suddenly it felt as though he were entering, looking cautiously about him, the adult world. Friday afternoon seemed to take forever to come around. Back from school, there was no time for dinner as the late afternoon bus (from Aberystwyth and via Talsarn and Lampeter to Carmarthen) had to be caught. In spite of his protests, Sioned made him sandwiches though, in case Lowri didn't feed him when he got to hers. Knowing her, she'd probably forget all about it.

She proved her mother wrong though. Will was waiting with his tiny red Fiat to meet Tomos at Cardiff station and Lowri had ready some sort of exotic pasta dish that he'd never tasted before (Mam never did such things, other than simple spaghetti Bolognaise once in a blue moon when she was feeling really adventurous.) This was how they ate in the sophisticated metropolis of Cardiff, it seemed. Afterwards Lowri proudly showed Tomos the placards she and Will had made, one for each of them, with various legends: WALES SAYS NOT IN MY NAME and NOT THE ANSWER TO 9/11 and STOP THIS WAR NOW. Now, quite suddenly, he felt very grown-up indeed, although a little less so later when, after a nightcap of proper, percolated coffee, Lowri disappeared into the bedroom and re-emerged with a pillow, sheet and quilt, dumping them meaningfully on the grey leather minimalist-styled sofa and decreeing that they should all hit the sack as the train would be leaving early in the morning, before disappearing into the bedroom again with Will in tow.

Tomos removed the bright red cushions from the sofa, made up his bed, stripped down to his underwear, put out the table lamps, groped his way in the total darkness to the sofa and crawled beneath the covers. He didn't think he'd sleep a wink, so wound up with anticipation was he. He lay on his back staring into the blackness, trying to imagine what the demo might be like. Would it turn violent, with protesters attacking the police and getting beaten up for their pains? Surely not; not in this day and age in Britain? But he'd seen footage of protest marches from the past, like the miners' and the poll tax demonstrations, and they'd got very nasty. He really couldn't see himself hurling missiles at the police (after all, they would only be doing their job and keeping order) and certainly not going on the rampage and breaking shop windows or anything like that. Duw, no, please, don't let it be like that. He suddenly felt a slight lurch of panic at the thought that made his chest hurt a tiny bit.

But no, it wouldn't be. Anyway, he'd be with Lowri and Will; they were responsible adults, university lecturers for goodness sake. They wouldn't get into a dangerous situation. Speaking of those two; Lowri might have suggested a fairly early night, but she and Will didn't seem to be going to sleep, judging by the murmuring, then giggling, then mattress-creaking, then moaning, then stifled squeal and more giggling that was coming through the door. Tomos turned on his side and pulled the pillow over his uppermost ear, trying not to imagine what they were doing. Suddenly he felt a like a naive child again.

He must have dropped off eventually though, because the next thing he knew he was opening his eyes to stare uncomfortably down the rather-too-open front of Lowri's bathrobe, beneath which she clearly wore nothing, as she bent and shook him awake.

'Come along young man,' she was saying, in Welsh as Will wasn't present, 'time to get up. We've got a demo to attend!'

'Er, alright . . .'

Lowri grinned at his discomfiture. 'Oh, are you naked under

there?'

'No! I've, um . . .'

His big sister laughed. 'Don't worry; I don't particularly want to see you in your boxers or y-fronts or whatever you wear. Not now you're a big boy, although I saw you often enough in the raw when you were little. I'll leave you to it. You can have the bathroom first.'

Tomos gathered up the discarded clothing from the previous day and his rucksack used at school that contained a change (shirt and pants anyway) and scurried into the bathroom, then realised that he hadn't brought any hygiene or grooming equipment, not even his toothbrush. He'd begun to shave a few months previously but it was more token than necessary really. His ginger beard was little more than a downy red-tinged wisp. He wished he'd been born with the genes for dark hair and then he'd have proper manly stubble, like some of the lads at school. But at least he could go without shaving for a weekend and not look scruffy. He splashed soapy water on his face and left it at that.

An hour later, clutching their placards (Tomos felt just a little self-conscious; he was no exhibitionist), they were waiting on Cardiff station. They were by no means alone. There was already quite a sizeable contingent waiting, most of them young people with woolly hats, a smattering of beards amongst the men and earnest save-the-world faces. They joined them, snowballing the group, as other waiting passengers turned their faces away, embarrassed and in some cases offended by such blatantly unpatriotic behaviour as anti-war demonstrating.

Lowri spotted faces she knew, belonging to two girls and a young man, and shrieked delightedly. 'Patti! Steve! Mair! Great to see you! Didn't know you were into this sort of thing!'

There was a chorus of Hi's from the trio. 'These are some of my students,' Lowri explained to Tomos. Clutching his upper arm proprietorially, she introduced him. 'Guys, this is Tomos, my little brother.' The Hi's were repeated as they smiled at him. Patti was a red-faced girl, slightly plump and large breasted, Steve looked as though he'd only just got up (but then he probably had) with long dark hair sticking out in all directions and several days' growth of stubble, and Mair was short, thin-featured, skinny-legged in tight blue jeans and wore her blonde hair centrally parted and plaited, looking more like a refugee from the *Sound of Music* than an anti-war protester. She wasn't particularly large-chested, Tomos couldn't fail to notice.

Steve was glancing around, eyes darting everywhere. He dropped his voice and spoke urgently to Lowri. 'Don't look now, but I think we're being photographed.'

Unfazed, Lowri promptly did so. A suited man was standing three metres away to their left, trying to blend in with the non-protestor travelling public, pointing a camera directly at them.

'It's okay folks,' she grinned, 'it's probably only Special Branch snapping us, just in case we're dangerous unpatriotic subversives!'

She held the photographer in her stare. 'Let's pose for the nice man, shall we?' She struck a pose, pouting, placard thrust towards the man. Scowling, the policeman, if such he was, lowered his camera and pointed it at another section of the assembled throng.

The train pulled in alongside the platform and the protestors climbed aboard. There were already others there, clustering in chattering groups around tables piled with placards. They must have come from Swansea, possibly Carmarthen; perhaps even remote Haverfordwest in the far west. The thought struck Tomos that he could have travelled this morning really, but then that would have meant doing so alone and he doubted whether he could have handled that. Being under his big sister's wing was the much preferred option. Lowri knew how to handle herself.

Lowri, Will and Tomos found themselves an empty table-and-seats and Patti and Steve joined a couple, clearly protestors, to make a foursome across the aisle. Obviously they were a couple then. That left Mair looking around uncertainly for a seat in the rapidly-filling carriage. Lowri grabbed her arm and pointed at the empty place beside Tomos. 'Here Mair; sit beside our Tomos.'

Tomos squeezed up against the window, making as much space vacant as possible. He wasn't really very good with the opposite sex; had yet to acquire a girlfriend at school although many of the other boys seemed to have managed it alright. He knew what his problem was; lack of confidence and a poor self-image. He couldn't imagine why any girl would be interested in him, with his shyness and quiet, studious ways anyway. And he'd certainly never sat next to an older woman. Duw, if she was a student she must be at least three years older than him, if not more. It was one thing to be paired up with girls at school sometimes; sitting beside one, aware (although he always tried not to dwell on it) of a different sort of body in certain intriguing ways to his next to him, but this was different. This was a social occasion, not school. He wished he'd remembered his washing things now.

As the train jolted into motion he suddenly realised that Mair was talking to him in an accent that was Welsh and not unfamiliar, although not quite a Lampeter one.

'Are you at uni in Cardiff then? I haven't seen you around.'

Ridiculously, he felt himself blushing. 'Er, no; I'm still at school.' (How he hated having to make the admission; it would be so much better credibility-wise to say that he too was a student somewhere.) 'Just starting A-levels.'

Mair laughed. 'Oh, don't tell me about those! I'm glad I'm past that stage. What a struggle they were!'

Tomos suddenly felt dejected. *Yes, go on then. Tell me you'll be graduating next and stepping into some high powered job in Cardiff, or even going to England.* All he could manage was a shy smile in reply. He wished she'd shut up. But she clearly wasn't going to. He could feel her studying his profile.

'Well you do surprise me a bit, to be honest. I had you down for older than you obviously are. I'd have taken you for eighteen or so.'

Tomos took that to be a compliment. He turned to her and grinned. 'Oh, thank you!'

She did too. 'You're welcome! I'm in my first year with your brilliantly clever sister.' She flashed an anxious look at Lowri, suddenly afraid she'd overstepped the mark; been over-familiar. But Lowri just laughed indulgently. 'And a good student you are too, Bach. It's a pleasure and privilege to teach you!'

Tomos relaxed a little; felt a little emboldened. She couldn't be so much older than him then. Two years, perhaps?

'Where are you from?'

She returned her gaze to him. 'Bancyfelin, near Carmarthen. Do you know it?'

'No. I know where Carmarthen is though.'

She laughed again. He liked the sound of it. It sounded slightly gruff and earthy for such a petite person; not what you'd expect at all.

'Well good for you! And you?'

'Sorry?'

'Where are you from?'

'Oh. Talsarn, near Lampeter.'

She was still grinning mischievously. 'Right; and do you know, I know where Lampeter is too! Even visited, although you can see everything there in about two minutes flat.' And isn't Talsarn out on the Aberaeron road?

Her gentle mocking sarcasm went over Tomos's head. Very seriously, he replied, 'Well, just off it actually.' He was impressed. Here was a woman of the world who knew her way around.

'And what are you working towards with your A-levels? Have you decided yet?'

'Well I'd like to do medicine, if I'm good enough.'

Lowri snorted. 'Good enough? Of course you're good enough young man! Anyone who can beat me at chess nine times out of ten is bloody brilliant, I'd say! You'd sail through uni, believe me. You're streets ahead of some of my students, to be honest.' She glanced at Mair. 'Present company excepted, of course.'

Tomos smiled modestly; stole a quick look at Mair. She was looking at him intently with what looked like a hint of admiration in her eyes. She spoke. 'Well if Lowri thinks that Tomos, I'm sure you would.'

Tomos could have kissed her, but he would never have dared.

They arrived at Paddington and most of the demonstrators, those in the know, made their chattering excited way down the Edgware Road. Will knew London too. Much better, he said, to walk the half a mile to Marble Arch than struggle onto buses with their placards. By the time they'd waited for one they could be halfway there on foot. When they arrived, Tomos was astounded to see so many people congregated, waiting for the order to move off. But perhaps it wasn't so surprising. No doubt people had come from all over England and Wales (there was to be a separate demo for Scotland in Glasgow, according to Lowri). And South Wales alone had contributed the best part of a trainful. There must be thousands, he imagined, although he didn't really have a clear idea of what a thousand people looked like. They stood around now in groups, some people chatting happily, others wearing more earnest expressions, psyching themselves up to make their opposition to the military adventure abundantly clear.

Half an hour later (any latecomers would just have make their way to Trafalgar Square as best they could), at a signal from the organisers, the crowd began funnelling itself into a column and set off along a temporarily traffic-free Park Lane. Yellow-vested policemen, who had been waiting patiently, talking and smoking cheerfully in a large group to one side, fell in at intervals beside the column, like escorting tugboats. Tomos could barely contain his excitement. He had got the WALES SAYS NOT IN MY NAME placard, and copying Lowri and Will beside him, now he angled it high against his shoulder and joined in their chants of 'No war' and 'We want peace.' Patti and Steve were on the other side of them. Mair was next to him, he found to his delight, although he wasn't quite sure why. Steve was shouting 'Stop the War!' at the top of his voice, already caught up in the thrill of protest.

Thoughts about the deadly seriousness of the demonstration were banished for the moment from Tomos's mind. This was wonderful, doing something really grown-up! People around him were chanting and shouting too. Some were blowing whistles and a few banging on drums. The noise was almost overwhelming. It was heady; it was passionate; it was intoxicating. The police in their escort stayed poker-faced. If they were sharing the sentiments of the protesters, they certainly weren't showing it. They were probably resenting having their day off cancelled.

Down Park Lane they marched, past the vast green acres of Hyde Park across the opposite carriageway on their right, into Duke of Wellington Place, then down Constitution Hill to the high rococo gates and grandeur of Buckingham Palace. They turned into the wide, die-straight Mall. Crowds were gathering on the pavements, attracted by the commotion. Some cheered their support; others jeered, offended by such a show of lily-livered pacifism. Others simply stared.

Up ahead, a group of shaven-headed, leather-jacked men were hurling abuse at the marchers, who simply ignored them, which simply enraged them further. As they drew level with them, a young man, tattooed about the neck, pot-bellied and scruffy, suddenly lurched into the road, looking very much the worst for drunken wear. Tomos was at the end of the rank and the drunkard made straight for him.

'You fucking wog lover!' he spat into Tomos's face, eyes

unfocused, grabbing for his placard. Tomos started back, surprised and terrified, pain squeezing his chest.

The last words he heard before blackness fell like the snuffing out of a light were Lowri shouting, 'Get off him you bastard!' And then there was nothing.

It seemed (but of course it wasn't) but an instant before his eyelids were struggling, heavy with enormous weight, to open. He was on his back, in a bed, staring up at a bright white light reflecting off a white-tiled ceiling. The din of the demonstration had gone, replaced by a silence punctuated occasionally by distant, calm voices. His forehead, indeed his head generally, hurt like hell. A tube was up his nose and something that felt nice was seeping into his lungs. Looking along his body he discovered more attachments. There were thin cables taped in various places to his bare chest and leading to some sort of machine with lights and displays of graphics and numbers. Another tube led into something taped to the back of his hand. It felt a bit sore, too. A vision hove into his field of view; a face, a dark-skinned female face wearing glasses with frames of almost the same colour. Below the face and the high demure vee of naked neck there was a blue uniform.

She smiled at him from what seemed a great height but was probably not at all. 'Hello sweetheart,' she said gently, 'you're back with us again then.'

'Where . . .?'

'You're okay, just fine. You're in St Mary's Hospital.' She pronounced 'hospital' very oddly.

'Oh . . .'

She took his unencumbered hand, gave it a little squeeze and then kept hold, which felt oddly comforting.

'You fell and banged your head on the pavement. At that demo. Do you remember?'

Tomos just looked at the nurse, vacantly. He didn't remember anything.

She smiled again. 'Okay, never mind. Your sister's here look.'

Tomos felt a hand settle on his shoulder. He looked to his left-hand side. Lowri was sitting by his bed, looking anxious. She must have been there all along.

She spoke, her voice unusually soft, betraying concern. 'Hello

Bach. How are you feeling?'

Tomos felt tears threatening. 'Awful. My head hurts!'

'Yes, I know Cariad.' She massaged his shoulder. 'You did give it a hell of a bang when you went down. If I hadn't been so busy clouting that brute who accosted you with my placard, I might have realised what was happening and caught you in time. I'm sorry.'

Tomos smiled painfully. 'That's alright. What happened anyway?'

'You really can't remember? That moron came at you from the pavement, shouting his mouth off, and you seemed to faint. You just folded up and went down, and smacked your head. Then you just lay still. I thought you were going to get trampled underfoot, but people behind us stopped and formed a barrier to protect you. Duw, Tomos, you really gave us a fright. I thought for a horrible moment you were. . .' Lowri shuddered, remembering the trauma.

She gathered herself and continued. 'Then a policeman came up from behind and took charge. He was brilliant. He called for an ambulance on his phone, and then a policewoman got involved as well, steering all the marchers clear of you. You couldn't be moved, obviously. The ambulance came quite quickly. It suddenly appeared in a side street. They let me come in it with you when I told them who I was.'

'How long have I been here?'

Lowri pouted her lips and exhaled noisily. 'Dunno. Feels like forever. You're in A and E. About an hour, I suppose. They x-rayed you as soon as they brought you in but you're basically okay; nothing broken and no serious damage. Just concussion, they say.'

'What are these things on my chest for?'

'Just to monitor you, I think.'

'And where are the others?'

'Will followed on here, and so did Mair. That was nice of her. They're in the waiting room. I presume Patti and Steve carried on to the rally.'

They were interrupted by a doctor, whom the nurse had summoned when Tomos regained consciousness. Lowri vacated her chair by the bed to allow him near. He was young; looked to be barely into his twenties and judging by his olive skin, brown eyes and shock of thick black hair, clearly originated from the Indian sub-continent. He glanced at the notes at the foot of the bed to remind himself of Tomos's name before speaking.

'Hello Thomas; how are you feeling now?'

'Not too bad, thank you. Head hurts,' Tomos repeated, hoping someone would give him some pain relief.

The doctor smiled indulgently. 'Yes, I am sure it does. We will give you something to make it feel better in a few moments. But you will have a large bruise for a while, I have to say. But first I must do a few tests.'

He held his upturned left hand in front of Tomos's face with the index finger bent down. 'How many fingers am I holding up?'

'Three,' Tomos said.

'Good. Now tell me; what is the name of the Prime Minister, please?'

'Blair. Tony Blair.'

'Yes; excellent!'

The doctor ran a few more cognitive tests and declared himself satisfied. 'Yes, very good.' You have not fractured your skull and you do not seem to have suffered any brain damage. We were slightly concerned about your heart when you came in; you had a very elevated pulse and it was a little erratic but (he glanced at the monitor) it seems to have settled down now. There is nothing to worry about there either.'

Behind him, Lowri breathed an audible sigh of relief.

'We will keep you in overnight just to make sure everything is fine then you will be able to leave tomorrow. Go home and get some rest.'

'Yes, I'll make sure he does that,' Lowri assured.

The doctor removed the oxygen tube, drip and disconnected the monitor and instructed the nurse on pain relief, then with a few parting words turned to go. But then he hesitated. He looked from Lowri to Tomos.

'I believe you were on the demonstration today.'

'Yes we were, before we were rudely interrupted,' said Lowri jocularly.

The doctor did not smile though. 'Well thank you for doing what you did. Perhaps you can get the madness to stop. We are not all terrorists hell-bent on attacking the West, you know.'

A sudden realisation struck Lowri. 'Oh! Forgive my asking, but are you Afghanistani?'

The doctor smiled, although it was confined to his lips. His eyes remained sad, infinitely sad.

'Yes, although I was brought up in Britain. My parents came over in 1980 after the Soviets invaded.'

'This must be a very worrying time for you then,' Lowri said gently. 'Do you have family there?'

'Yes; uncles and aunts and grandparents,'

'I'm so sorry.'

'Yes, only my parents left. For me, England has always been my home, but for my parents, home is still really Afghanistan. Obviously.'

'Of course.'

The doctor smiled ruefully. It's such a tragic country, really. Always being invaded or occupied by evil forces. First Russia, then the Taliban and now perhaps America and Britain. All most people there want is to live in peace.'

'Well take it from me,' said Lowri, 'we don't all want to invade. There have to be better ways to deal with terrorists.'

The doctor smiled sadly again. 'Well thank you for that. And thank you for what you did today.'

Lowri came over to him and touched his arm gently. 'Not at all. Sometimes we have to stand up and be counted.'

She dropped her hand, afraid of offending some cultural sensibility. 'Thank you too for what you did for my brother today.'

Chapter 8
Wayne

Wayne sat in class, mind anywhere but on the lesson (as usual), idly contemplating the back of Helen Micklethwaite's head. She sat directly in front of him, partnering Samantha Parkinson. Well if truth were known, his interest was slightly above the level of casual. He was fascinated by her hair, which was (also as usual) a thick black unruly mop, sticking out in all directions. Did it ever get shown a comb? He wondered what it would be like to run his fingers through it, investigating, stroking the head that lay secretly beneath. You could tell the shape of most girls' heads because they had thin lank hair that simply fell plumb to their shoulders and in some of them halfway down their back too. But with Helen Micklethwaite her skull was a mystery.

It was a warm late May afternoon and for some reason best known to whoever decided those things, the heating was on. Wayne couldn't imagine why (he usually wore just his white shirt and tie at half-mast above his black school uniform trousers, only half tucked in, whatever the time of year, indoors and out, unless it was really cold, like actually snowing). But this unnecessary heat did mean that many of the girls in the room had their blazers off too, including Helen. His eyes dropped thirty centimetres from where her hair ended abruptly and rather untidily in the nape of her neck to the region of her shoulder blades. He liked that part of her too. He liked the way, when she leaned forwards and tautened the fabric of her shirt the silhouette of her rather plump back was squeezed, bulging at the sides, by the constriction of her bra, and the teasing, slight suggestion of the clasp of it.

Of course her body was even more interesting around the front, as she was the sort of slightly plump girl whose chest was well upholstered in proportion. He would never have let himself be caught blatantly staring at her of course, but he couldn't help but notice. Not that his interest in her was purely carnal (he'd read that word somewhere and thought it sounded good, although he wasn't entirely sure of its meaning). If it meant fancying her, no, his interest went further than that. He really did like her; liked the way she would mischievously tease, but never in a cruel way, like some of the kids, who still poked fun at his hair and freckles (and which he still hated). And also the way, when he spoke in class, which wasn't all that often admittedly because he could rarely think of interesting questions to ask and seldom knew the answers to the testing questions the teachers, especially Mr Wallace, would suddenly, randomly, fling at the class, she would gaze at him with those hazel eyes and wrinkle her funny snub nose and seem to hang on his every word.

But he was beginning to get a little desperate. He'd be leaving school in a few weeks' time and then there'd be no more opportunities to make a play for her. Time was running out, so he would have to get his skates on. Work up the courage. Always supposing that she was interested in him, at least. After all, why on earth should she be? Most of the girls made it pretty plain that they weren't; certainly all those *he* was interested in. Apart from anything else though, it was just embarrassing and a bit shaming that, amongst his mates at school, he was almost the only one who hadn't had a girlfriend yet, much less actually had sex with one. Although that seemed a daunting mountain to climb; an impossible dream. No, he'd settle for just going out, and just as importantly being seen to be going out. He wouldn't have used the word himself because it wasn't really in his vocabulary, but it was a matter of prestige.

It was fine when he was with his other set of friends at Scouts. He could really hold his own amongst them; compete on equal terms and often come out on top with anything involving adventure. He was fearless doing rock climbing or canoeing or any of that stuff and he was pretty good at leadership as far as relating to the younger scouts was concerned, but girls were an entirely different matter.

So he was trying to summon up the courage to ask Helen Micklethwaite out, but to do what, quite, was the problem. He knew (he wasn't that stupid) that as a girl who (as far as he knew) had fairly normal girls' interests, she would hardly be interested in anything outdoor. Probably not even walking. There was a youth club in Northallerton where they did dancing and all that, but he couldn't dance. Hadn't a clue about it. So what did that leave? Not a lot. There was no picture house anymore; it was closed down to become a chapel some years back. Well, he'd just have to think of something . . .

Leaning against the wall of the science block, Helen watched Wayne. He was standing, hands in pockets (as usual), his shirt half out of his trousers (also as usual), chatting animatedly to his mates Kevin and Gary. She didn't know what to make of him. She wished she were good at reading signs. Wished she could differentiate between simple straightforward friendliness and something Significant. Every time they happened to pass he'd flash his funny, slightly crooked – but quite sexy, actually – smile and then quickly look down before she had a chance to smile back. Did that imply more than friendly interest?

It was alright for Sue and Becky and Jojo. They were old hands at this sort of thing. Becky and Sue were both on their second boyfriend (in fact, come to think of it, wasn't Becky on her third now she'd started going out with Steve?) and Jojo was deeply in love, or so she insisted, with Ben. And she didn't quite know whether to believe it or not, but Sue was making a big thing of the fact and boring them all rigid (and in her case provoking a little envy of the graphic and intriguing details) with her opinion that her sex life was absolutely wonderful.

Of course Helen joined in the rude banter with her friends, as they dared each other to be more and more outrageous, without quite knowing what she was talking about. Sadly and wistfully, she knew that her interest was purely vicarious; she could not speak from experience at all. She knew she wasn't as conventionally pretty as her mates, with her ridiculously uncontrollable hair and absurd snub nose, and as she had a little bit of a weight problem. She was also only too well aware of her inner, hidden imperfection: her chronic shyness. Although she was able to rationalise that knowledge and know that it sprang from a poor self-image, simply knowing it didn't make it any easier to deal with.

But she did so want to do what other girls did. It was like a basic human right really, wasn't it? Everyone was entitled to a little dignity; a little love. After all, it had happened with big sister Gilly; she was no raving beauty either but she'd got herself a fella. Lucky cow. So why not her? She didn't expect the handsomest, sexiest bloke in Northallerton; she really didn't. She knew her limitations. As long as he was presentable, and kind, and not a moron, that would do for starters, anyway.

She surveyed Wayne, talking to him in thought. *Look at you now, clowning around. You're not such a bad looking lad really, even if you do have an awful lot of freckles. In some places they practically run into each other. Not that it bothers me in the slightest. Neither does your hair. It's like my mop in a way; it certainly can't be ignored, at any rate.*

Helen knew that some of the girls sniggered behind his back about his appearance and one or two of the cruellest amongst them had teased him openly, until they saw the anger in his eyes, the clenching of his jaw and decided they'd best shut up. But then they were just stupid moronic bitches.

As she watched he suddenly looked in her direction, and there it was again; that lopsided grin. She grinned back. He returned to talking with his mates. Did that smile mean anything? Did it? Perhaps she had to take a little initiative. She knew that Wayne was one of the students not staying on to do A-levels, so he'd be leaving in a couple of months. Then there'd be no opportunities to meet. She'd no idea what he did for a social life; where he hung out in the evenings. Not that she'd have been brazen enough to go along to wherever it was and pick him up, or even just make it abundantly clear that she was willing to be. Anyway; perhaps he was like her and didn't do anything very exciting with his spare time. Perhaps they were a couple of timid mice together.

She decided. The next time (if there was one) he looked in her direction she'd give a little wave. Nothing flamboyant or obvious. Just a little, discrete one. Surely that would send a signal. And if he ignored that, well, she was probably wasting her time. But he'd have to get a move on and look at her soon; break would be over in a few minutes. He was larking about with his friends, thumping shoulders, laughing about something, something boy-oriented no doubt .

And then it happened. There was a lull in the frolicking and he looked her way again. Steeling herself she raised one hand and wagged the fingers, twice, and smiled again. He broke into another grin too, and raised a thumb, fingers balled. What the hell did that mean? Boys; honestly! They had all these secret codes. They were a mystery. This time though (or was she imagining it?) he seemed to keep his face turned towards her a little bit longer. But then he was back larking around with his mates, and then the bell rang, calling them to the last afternoon lessons.

Wayne found it even more difficult to concentrate for the final two periods. In English grammar (which he was hopeless at) Helen was sitting behind him so he couldn't catch her eye except by very obviously turning round, and male dignity dictated that he couldn't do that. And the last one, English composition (which he was even worse than hopeless at) was held in the same classroom anyway, so there was still the problem. Well there was nothing for it, he'd just have to hope that little wave had meant something, screw up courage and catch her before she left after school.

Although he still hadn't thought of anything to suggest to do. Well what was there? Youth clubs weren't his thing and he could hardly take her along to Scouts now, could he? Well, only if she seriously wanted to become a Guide, but even then they were separate anyway. And besides it was the wrong night. So it only really left hanging around the town, really.

The lesson came to an end and everyone packed their books away in their rucksacks and bags, making for the door. Wayne rushed to take up a place in the playground. He placed himself strategically between the main doors and the gates and waited, heart thumping as though he'd just run five hundred metres, for Helen to appear. To his great relief, when she did she was alone. She was plodding along eyes downcast, deep in thought it seemed. But then, a metre away, just when he feared she was going to walk straight past, she looked up and registered him at the edge of vision.

She turned her unruly-haired head to look straight at him, green eyes alight, already grinning. Wayne felt his chest lurch, just a little. It was now or never.

'Hi, Helen!'

And she stopped. She actually stopped.

'Hello Wayne!'

Now; what should the next sentence be? 'Erm; are you okay?'

'Yes; great. And you?'

'Yes great,' He parroted, floundering already. She was looking at him intently. Expectantly, was it? The smile was still on her face, her suddenly extremely pretty face. Never mind the snub nose and the plump apple-red cheeks and the ridiculous hair.

He had to keep talking at all costs. 'Erm; I was just wondering. D'you fancy coming out tonight?'

The grin left her face and she regarded him solemnly, as Wayne held his breath. 'Er, okay, what to do?'

He exhaled. 'Erm; dunno really. Like just hang out, you know? Or something.' He could feel himself blushing; knew it would make his freckles look even worse.

Helen spoke, helpfully. 'Perhaps we could go for a walk; something like that?'

Wayne seized on the suggestion enthusiastically. 'Yeah! Great! That'd be good!'

But then Helen spoiled it a bit; put him back on the spot. 'Okay, I'd really like that. Where?'

Wayne had to do some rapid thinking. Nothing too adventurous perhaps? He'd no idea what Helen would regard as a reasonable walk. 'Er; along by Willow Beck? Something like that mebbe?'

'Yeah, fine. Where shall we meet?'

'Top of t' High Street perhaps? Outside Jameson's?'

'Right. What time?'

'Half seven?' Wayne was finding all this decision making tiring.

The smile was back on Helen's face. She looked lovely when she smiled, Wayne thought.

'Okay then. I'll see you then, then.' She giggled at her own repetitiveness. Wayne though that was even more becoming.

'Fine.' He had no idea how to end the conversation.

She came to his rescue. 'Right; I'd better go. Get my homework done. See you later then.'

And with that she left him standing there, wearing a stupid grin and feeling hugely relieved.

Helen tried to apply herself to her homework, but it was a hard-fought battle. Her mind just wasn't on it. It was full of Wayne and she couldn't believe her luck. He'd asked her out! Her first date! Did this count as a date, just going for a walk? She supposed it did. Most of her mates probably wouldn't have thought it very thrilling, but it suited her. She sat in her bedroom going over that encounter at school. Poor Wayne! He'd really been floundering; she could tell. He obviously had no idea what to suggest to do, but actually she liked the idea of a walk, just the two of them, alone. It was much better than simply hanging around the town.

She struggled and finished the homework. After all it was important. She knew she probably wasn't uni material, but she still wanted to get one or two good-grade A-levels at least, as a passport to a half-way decent job. But anyway, enough of the future for the minute; now she had to decide what to wear. Such agonising decisions! Well it would have to be jeans, obviously, if they were going for a walk. Her best ones, and her new trainers. And perhaps her white tee shirt and denim jacket. It was still only May after all; the evenings were still a bit parky. Yes, that should do it. Not too dolled up, practical, but appealing (she hoped) all the same.

She looked out clean underwear, not too saucy (not that she had anything like that, and besides it wouldn't be a consideration anyway, would it? It surely wouldn't come to any sort of petting the first time). She'd be quite grateful just for a kiss, to be honest. She took it and the jeans and tee shirt to the bathroom, stripped off and got under the shower. She studied her water-beaded body with distaste. How she wished she were slimmer. Not anorexic like a model, just not podgy. She hated her large breasts, with their areolas nearly as big as bloody hobnobs (and almost the same texture and colour too). And her soft belly with its almost disappearing navel. She had to lean well forward to see her pubic hair, not that she enjoyed looking at it either. There was too much of it too, a veritable bush, matching her too-thick head hair.

Although, she supposed, it wasn't a matter of what she thought but what Wayne did. But what if, when he got to look (whenever that might be) he didn't like what he saw? That would just be awful. And yet, the thought of him looking, of *touching* even, was quite thrilling and gave her a funny, slightly achey feeling between her legs and made her nipples harden.

She pulled herself up. *No, this is ridiculous! Nothing like that's going to happen tonight anyway! And I'm not such a slut! I'm not like Sue!*

Angry with herself now, she picked up the shampoo bottle and washed her hair vigorously for the second time that day. But the thoughts still kept churning as to whether or not he would really fancy her. When (or if) it came to it, it would, she supposed a little glumly, just remain to be seen. She rinsed and stepped out of the shower, reaching for the bath towel still damp from the morning and rubbing vigorously to dry off. She'd just think of it as a pleasant evening out and expect no more than that. But on the other hand, she could still wish . . .

Wayne was there ready and waiting outside Jameson's (having gobbled down his dinner and rushed straight upstairs to shower, beautify and change, to the astonishment of Jim and Maureen, and then raced into town) at twenty past seven. He was wearing his best jeans, a white tee shirt and the denim jacket he'd had for his birthday. Trying to affect an air of bored nonchalance, he shifted from foot to foot and glanced up and down the High Street, unsure from which direction Helen would come.

When she arrived, at twenty-five past, striding towards him with a wide grin on her face, he was relieved and amused in just about equal measure.

'Snap!'

Her smile evaporated. 'What?'

Now he was grinning like a cat from Cheshire. 'Well, look at us! Dressed just the same! Us just like twins!'

'Oh, yeah!' Helen wasn't always quick on the uptake, but she could give as good as she got. 'Apart from hair. And one or two other things of course!'

Then she caught herself. *God; what am I saying? He'll think I'm common.*

But he just grinned, a bit shyly. 'Okay; right. Shall we go then?'

They sauntered in the direction of Willow Beck. *What now?* Thought Helen. *Do we hold hands? Like, straight away?*

Wayne was thinking just the same thing. He'd no idea how to behave really. So he played safe and kept his hands in his pockets, to Helen's slight disappointment. The next problem was what to talk about. He had no clue about that either. After a minute or so of strained silence, Helen blurted out, 'What do you usually do with yourself of an evening then?'

Grateful for the ice breaking, Wayne said, 'Oh not much normally. I go to Scouts Tuesdays and Thursdays though.'

'Oh, you're in Scouts are you?' Helen said, somewhat unenthusiastically.

'Yeah; it's great! I've been in since I was nine. Well, I was a Cub then. You become a proper Scout when you're eleven.'

'Oh,' Helen repeated, her voice still flat.

It dawned on Wayne that he'd made a bad start. He tried to rescue the situation and backtracked. 'Well, it's okay. It's a bit boring sometimes. Anyway, there's other things in life besides scouting.'

He glanced at her anxiously to gauge her reaction. She grinned back, now slightly reserved. 'Yes, there are. Lots of things. It's nice to have an interest in something though, I suppose.'

'Yeah.' The wind had rather forsaken Wayne's sails now.

They walked on, the silence back. Wayne desperately searched his brain for a topic. All he could come up with was: 'What do *you* do in your spare time then? Do you do hobbies or stuff like that?'

Helen sounded a little dejected. 'No, not really. Just watch telly. Play records and tapes sometimes. I'm pretty boring really, I suppose.'

Wayne would have none of that though. A little too quickly, he reassured her, 'No you're not! Not at all! I don't think so anyway!'

She looked at him hopefully. 'Oh; do you really think so?'

'Yeah; really! I don't suppose my stuff at Scouts would be very interesting to you either.'

Helen said nothing to that. She wanted him to talk about something else. Then she said, 'What are you going to do when you leave school then?'

That was another tricky subject for Wayne. He really had no idea, apart from a half-baked one.

'Dunno really. There's not a lot of work around here. Not unless you've got qualifications anyway. The careers master says there'll probably be some jobs at Tesco's in a couple of months' time, so I might see if there's anything going there. Or I might think about t' army. My mate Billy's just joined.'

He looked at her again, still worried. She was silent once more. 'But I dunno. Haven't made up my mind, really. What do you want to do then?'

Helen brightened. 'Well I'm going to do A-levels. If I do well enough I'd like to do some sort of office work, although my maths isn't brilliant. Or maybe work in the library. That'd be good. I love books. Do you read?'

Wayne squirmed again. She was asking all the wrong questions.

'Yeah, some,' he mumbled.
'Oh? What sort of thing?'
'Well, adventure. Stuff like that.'
'Oh . . .'

Wayne thought he perhaps ought to try another approach; be a little tactile. He took his hand out of his jacket on the side next to her and let it dangle, hopefully. She seemed to have noticed and released hers from her pocket too. He moved half a sideways step closer and their swinging hands began to brush. Emboldened as she didn't flinch away, he took a deep breath and captured her hand in his. She didn't remove it. He breathed out; he squeezed, just ever so gently, and he felt the pressure reciprocated. He looked at her with a mute enquiry. *Is it okay to do this?* Her answering smile seemed to confirm that it was.

They were at the beck now. The fading May sun was falling slowly into the west, obliquely dappling the water through the trees. The ice broken, they were chatting more easily now, about the minutiae of their sixteen-year-old lives, bantering, laughing at each other's weak puns. Wayne let go of Helen's hand and cautiously put it around her shoulder instead and she closed the gap between them, brushing her rather plump hip against his skinny one as they walked, wrapping her freed hand around his back.

Wayne felt for the first time in his life the softness of a female body as a sexual entity; a counterpoint to his hard thin adolescent frame, so different from the remembered comfort of his mother. But that sort of hugging had stopped years ago; he hadn't been touched with any intimacy by his mum since – when? Since that embarrassing incident when he'd fallen in the beck and she'd put him in the bath, like a baby. After he'd joined the Cubs he'd scorned her touch; had neither wanted nor needed it after he'd discovered the new family of male company.

But this was quite different from that. There was a faint but unmistakable perfume coming off her now, which he thought he'd detected before but wasn't quite sure. What was it? Soap, or shampoo, or something really female, like scent? This was exciting, intriguing, tantalising! He could stay here all night with this lovely creature. His groan was aching a little, and he knew from past but solitary experience what that feeling usually lead to. But he mustn't think things like that. Mum had dinned into him about respecting girls; about what could happen if you weren't very careful. But hell, he'd never want to get a girl into trouble, as Mum called it, especially not someone really nice and sweet like Helen. And he didn't want to be a teenage dad either.

They'd gone as far as they could along the river bank now, to where a path led back into the town. He had a surreptitious look at his watch. It was still only five past eight. If they returned now they'd get back before half past. And then what? Just hang around the streets? This was much nicer.

'Do you want to go back yet?' he asked, a little anxiously.

'No; not particularly,' Helen replied.

So they walked, slowly, back the way they'd come, and at the other end, having screwed up his courage for the last ten metres, Wayne got very brave indeed. They paused and made to take the return path, but he stopped her and turned her towards him, holding her gently by the shoulders. She looked up at him with an unfathomable expression on her face. What was it? Expectation? He had no idea.

'Erm . . . Could I . . .'

'What?'

Wayne couldn't bring himself to say the words; just come right out with them. He bent his face towards her. She didn't flinch away. They stayed like that for what felt an eternity to him, just centimetres apart, and then he closed the distance as she shut her eyes and puckered her lips a little in anticipation and finally did it: experienced his first ever, clumsy, kiss. They stayed locked together like that for some time. Her lipsticked mouth smelled oddly minty, until it dawned on him that it was the after-scent of toothpaste. He cursed inwardly. *Bugger! I should have thought of cleaning my teeth!*

But she didn't pull away, until he judged that perhaps it was time to do so and did it himself. They remained looking at each other; both relieved, hearts hammering in two chests. He was still half-expecting her to look away, embarrassed, though.

'That was nice,' he offered tentatively.

'Yes it was,' she agreed. And she sounded as though she meant it.

So he kissed her again, taking her properly in his arms this time, intoxicated by the feel of her, the intimacy of her willing body against his, the perfume, the ache back in his groin again, everything.

And that was how it all began. It wasn't earth-shattering of course; just two young people free of childhood but not yet adult feeling their cautious, nervous, excited, heart-fluttering way to love, or at any rate acceptance, which when you're a mid-teenager is almost the same thing. There was just one more hurdle for Wayne to leap though; asking Helen for a second date, after they'd kissed goodnight back outside Jameson's, as he was from one end of town and she the other and he couldn't pluck up the courage to ask if he could walk her home. But she answered yes readily enough to his blurted question, and they made it the evening after next because it was Scouts for him the next night.

The next day at school he couldn't wait to meet her; exchange a knowing look that said, plainly if only to them, that yes, we're now an item! After that they consorted openly, disappearing together into the town at lunch time, hand-in-hand with a rite of passage safely negotiated, each wearing their new-found status as a badge of self-esteem. Gradually, as on non-scouting evenings together they gained confidence, so their boldness grew. Wayne no longer had to wistfully imagine what lay beneath her shirt or sweater or tee shirt, now he thrillingly felt the heavy softness of her breasts fall into his hands when he found the clasp between her shoulder blades.

 And it was a rapid progression from there to discovering the forbidden, intriguing soft cave between her thighs, as she in turn discovered his hardness as he came, safely if a little frustratingly, well out of harm's way. But that was as far as it went. For Wayne there was still a shackle of restraint holding him back, an inhibition about taking things all the way. His parents' words (they'd both had serious talks with him) on the subject of respecting girls rang cautionary chimes in his ears; held him in a tight cage of self-control.

His loyalties began to divide. Before, he'd found complete fulfilment in the company of his scout friends, But now there was a competing interest. The twice-weekly evening meetings were fine – that still left five in which to be with Helen, but the weekend ones lost some of their adventurous attraction and he began to miss some. Weekends now were often much more satisfyingly spent with his girlfriend. Not that he was altogether giving up outdoor interests anyway. She wasn't like a typical girl. She genuinely enjoyed going for long walks with him, like out to Crow Wood, where they could usually be sure of being safely alone together or sometimes even getting the bus out to Ainderby Steeple and walking all the four miles, through the wood again, back to Northallerton.

The final few weeks of school flew by and the next thing he knew, he was out in the world of work. His GCSE results had not been spectacularly good, as he didn't suppose they would be, and there were few opportunities for unqualified school leavers. As predicted by the careers teacher there were some vacancies at Tesco's though, and that was where, on the seventh of August after a couple of weeks holiday, Wayne went to apply, and because the branch manager felt he was a bright lad who could go places (that was what he said anyway), he landed a job.

Rather to Wayne's relief, he was put to shelf stacking, not working the checkouts. That could follow later, his supervisor said, once he'd settled in and proved his trustworthiness and reliability. Wayne wasn't too sure whether he wanted the responsibility of dealing with customers though, even if it did largely amount to swiping the items through the scanner and not a great deal else, unless customers paid with cash. He found that actually he quite liked the stacking though; there was even less initiative involved in following orders as to which products to bring from the storeroom onto the floor of the store, and if it had limited shelf life bringing the stock already on the shelves to the front and filling up behind. He liked that; it appealed to his sense of orderliness. And of course there was the money too. It wasn't a great deal, but even after giving his mum something for his keep (which he did proudly, feeling suddenly quite grown up), it was quite a lot more than he'd had in pocket money before.

So now, life really was pretty good. He had a steady but not too demanding job, whereas many of the other school leavers, those even less academic than he, hadn't. And he had Helen. He knew she wasn't the brightest star around Northallerton looks-wise, but that didn't matter. She was his girlfriend and she accepted him, red hair, freckles and all; that was the main thing. And with more money in his pocket now he could afford to take her out more. Not that there was a lot to do in Northallerton, but there were always bigger places like Harrogate and York, which had delights like the Pictures. Really, what with the job, money, Helen and the male companionship of Scouts (if a bit reduced nowadays), Wayne felt he had pretty much all his heart could desire.

And then nine-eleven happened. It was a scout evening on that terrible day, and one that Wayne attended, and of course it was the only possible topic of conversation amongst the boys. Since Billy had joined up, his main friend now was David, who came from a large family on the council estate, a couple of streets away from Wayne's home. Whereas Wayne came to scouts almost out of a reluctant sense duty now, for David it was an escape from the noisy overcrowded chaos of family life. His views about the attack and terrorism generally that dreadful day and the war on it declared by the American president eleven days later were straightforward and uncompromising. If Muslims wanted a fight they could have one, as far as David was concerned. He was up for it. He disliked the way there were so many of them in Bradford and places like that (not that he'd ever been there but he'd seen plenty of pictures on the telly). And if they were going to turn round and start attacking the West for no good reason, England had to be defended against them. Like Billy's brother, two of David's older siblings, Steve and Rachel, were regulars in the Yorkshires. He'd been tempted to emulate them for a while now, as he had little idea of what else to do for a job. And now nine-eleven had pretty much made up his mind for him.

Wayne walked home from Scouts two weeks after nine-eleven with David. His friend was still full of George Bush's declaration of war.

'Well he's right ent he?' he said as they sauntered along together. I think we should bomb the buggers. Soften them up and then send in ground troops. Root them all out and shoot the bloody lot of them.'

Wayne would have expressed it in less bloodthirsty terms but he thought, deep down, that David had a point. Sometimes you just had to fight fire with fire. There was no other language that fanatics understood. You couldn't reason with them.

'Yeah,' he agreed, 'I suppose you're right.'

'Too right I am,' David affirmed, with all the self-assurance of a sixteen-year-old who had never been inconveniently troubled with self-doubt.

'Have you thought any more about going in t' army?' Wayne asked

'Yeah; that Trade Center thing made my mind up. What if something like that happened here? We can't let it! I've sent off for all the info about the Yorkshires. You have to send to York for it.'

'Really?'

'Yeah. Well our Steve reckons it's a good life in t' army, any road. So does Rachel. And there's bugger-all else to do for work round here really, is there?'

'Well I got a job okay, at Tesco's.'

David snorted dismissively. 'Well, that's okay if all you want to do with your life is work in a sodding supermarket, but it's not exactly exciting is it?'

Wayne felt a little affronted. At least he'd been able to get a job, which was more than his friend could say.

'I don't mind it,' he said defensively, although not with total conviction now.

'And I bet pay in t' army's better than what you draw an' all. I bet you don't even get t' minimum wage, do you?'

'Well, no; but starters don't anyway.'

'Well I reckon I'll be starting on more than you, that's for sure!' David boasted.

He was getting on Wayne's nerves, talking as though he'd already joined up. Wayne wished he'd just put a sock in it.

Chapter 9
Tomos

Recuperating at home a few evenings later with Mam anxiously waiting on him hand and foot, watching warily for any signs of abnormal brain behaviour (she knew he should never have gone on that demonstration; with feelings running so high there was bound to be trouble), Tomos was surprised when the phone rang, his mother picked up, said 'Hello?' and then, in English, 'Yes, hold on please; I'll get him.'

She leaned across and handed him the phone. It was one of those new-fangled cordless ones, so he didn't have to get up from the sofa and move close to the instrument. 'It's for you Bach.'

Tomos repeated the 'Hello?'

A both unfamiliar and vaguely familiar female voice said, 'Hello, Tomos?'

'Yes, speaking.'

The voice reprised the greeting a second time. 'Hello Tomos, it's Mair. We met on the demo if you remember. Lowri's student?'

Tomos remembered alright. 'Oh, Mair! Hello, how are you?'

'I'm fine,' the voice said. 'I was just ringing to see how you were?' She was one of those people who made every statement a question. He remembered that.

Tomos smiled into the phone. 'I'm okay, thanks. Getting over it. Head doesn't hurt any more, anyway.'

There seemed to be a sigh of relief represented by a pause at the other end. 'Oh good; brilliant! You really had us worried there for a while you know?'

Tomos laughed. 'I think I had *me* worried for a while too! Not to mention Lowri.'

An answering laugh came from the phone. 'Yeah, she certainly was a little freaked out. Poor Lowri. I think she felt very responsible for it all. Not that it was her fault in any way. It was that lout in the crowd suddenly deciding to pick a fight'

A solicitous tone crept into Mair's voice. 'And you really are okay, are you Tomos?'

Tomos was touched by her concern. 'Yes, I really am Mair, thank you. It's nice of you to ring.'

There was silence at the other end of the line. Tomos suddenly felt a little inhibited. He would really rather be talking to this unexpectedly reappeared Mair in private. He got up from the sofa and walked through into the kitchen; sat down at the table.

Then Mair spoke. 'Er, well apart from you coming to grief, it was a good demo, wasn't it?'

'Oh yes,' Tomos enthused, 'It was great!'

'Of course I missed the rally in Trafalgar Square because Will and I followed you to hospital. But Steve and Patti say it was good. Good speakers. Very inspiring.'

'Yes, I bet it was. I'm sorry you missed it just for me.'

Mair sounded just slightly impatient. 'Oh, don't be so silly! We were anxious about you! Of course you had to come first.' Her voice faltered a little. 'You were completely unconscious. I was imagining all sorts of horrible things?'

That made Tomos's throat catch, oddly. 'Really? Were you?'

'Yeah; of course!'

There was another silence. It seemed to be up to Tomos to carry the conversation on.

'Um; well I wonder if our demo will make any difference.'

Mair's voice came back, reanimated. 'Well it hasn't yet. They're still bombing.'

'Yeah; right.'

'There's another demo planned for next month. On the tenth. I won't be going though. Can't afford another rail fare I'm afraid!'

Tomos laughed. 'No, nor me. Anyway, my mum wouldn't let me go again, I don't think!' And then he immediately regretted saying it. It made him sound juvenile.

There was a pause again, as Tomos struggled to keep the conversation moving. But then Mair spoke.

'Anyway, I'm really glad you're okay. No lasting damage.'

'No, not as far as I know, anyway!'

'Great. Right then. Must go. Things to do. See you around then?'

'Er, yes, right . . .'

'Okay then. Bye-ee!'

And with that the line went dead.

Tomos stared at the telephone for a long moment, as if it might spontaneously come back to life, then heaved himself up from the table and returned to the sitting room, replacing the instrument in its dock. Sioned of course was all aroused curiosity. 'Sounded like a nice young girl on the phone . . .' She left the question unasked but Tomos knew perfectly well what it was.

'Yes; that was Mair. She came on the demo with us. She's a student of Lowri's. She rang to see how I was.'

'Ah, there's nice,' Sioned said approvingly. 'A student of our Lowri! I still can't get used to the idea of her having students of her own. It's not so long since she was one herself! Isn't that right Glyn?'

'Mmm,' said Glyn.

Sioned returned to her television programme. Tomos sank back against the cushions of the sofa, his brain buzzing. But the television was a distraction. He got up again. 'I'll go upstairs and do some reading.' He'd never got out of the habit of telling his mother where he was going, even in the house.

Sioned looked at him fondly. 'Alright then Bach. You're alright are you; no more headaches or anything?'

'No, honestly Mam. I'm fine.'

He left his parents looking at their programme, went up to his room and stretched on his bed, hands clasped behind his head, his mind working overtime. *Well; that was unexpected! Didn't think I'd hear from her again. Nice of her to ring. Nice of her to think of me.* He turned that thought over a few times, trying to analyse it. *Is that all it was? Was there anything else there? Did she have a deeper reason for ringing? She was a bit hesitant though. Was she holding things back? Or was it just shyness? Mind you, I can't talk. I'm not the world's best at coming forward, to be perfectly honest. And what did 'see you around' mean? Was it au revoir as opposed to goodbye? Does she want to see me again? Does she? Well now!*

It was a mind-blowing thought. Why else would she say it like that? And yes, her hesitancy must have been shyness. He knew just how she felt as far as that was concerned, after all. What to do now though? He lay staring at the ceiling and the crack that was still there (his dad wasn't the world's best decorator), pondering. Was she expecting some sort of response from him? And if so, what? He couldn't phone her back because she hadn't given out her number (and it didn't occur to him to check the last call received on the phone). A letter then? But then he didn't know her address either. Oh, hell! But hold on; what about a letter via Lowri? Write a letter and send it inside a larger envelope to Lowri, with a covering note asking her to forward it? Yes; he didn't particularly want to involve her, but that was the answer!

He lay and mentally composed a missive, trying phrases for size. He mustn't appear too eager, too presumptuous. But not too vague, too opaque either. Just the right balance; that was the way to go. He got up and went downstairs and rummaged through the bureau, looking for a writing pad and envelope, hoping his mother wouldn't notice and ask awkward questions (but it was alright, she was engrossed in her television programme), then returned to his room. He found a book to rest the pad on and sat in the armchair that had been Lowri's. (It was rather on the large side for his bedroom, but he liked it. It gave his room something of the air of a study.) He began to write,

Dear Mair,
It was really nice to hear from you this evening. Thank you for thinking of me. Yes, I do feel quite well now although that incident is a complete blank. As I said on the phone, there are no more raging headaches now anyway!

Yes, it was a really good demo wasn't it! Let's hope that people like us can make governments see sense. I enjoyed talking to you on the train and marching with you (until I got assaulted, at least!).

I would really like to see you again – hopefully you would like it too? Perhaps we could meet up sometime. I could come to Cardiff – maybe inflict myself on Lowri for a weekend, if she'll put up with me! Then we could get together and do whatever you like doing recreationally. Meanwhile, I'd really like to keep in touch, by letter or Alexander Graham Bell's brilliant invention (or even both!) I may be getting a mobile phone for Christmas; that would make it easier still.

I don't know about you, but I feel we have quite a lot in common and might share quite a lot of interests. We do seem to feel the same about governments taking us to war, anyway!

Well that's all for now. Thanks again for the phone call. I hope to hear from you.
Bye,
Tomos

Tomos read through his words, several times. Did they strike the right tone? It wasn't too forward, too presumptuous, was it? It was so difficult to tell. And just about the right length, was it? Not too long-winded; direct and to the point. Cutting straight to the chase, as the English said? Although he could have written reams, actually. They did so seem to be on the same wavelength. Perhaps now was not the time though. Not yet. Work up to it gradually. Well, the letter seemed to be alright as far as he could tell. He folded the two sheets of Basildon Bond he'd used (well, it looked more elegant to write on just one side of the paper, somehow), put them in the envelope, licked the gum and sealed it. There seemed a certain symbolic finality in doing that, of sealing his fate, even though he could always undo the envelope again. He picked up his ballpoint again and wrote on the envelope, smiling at his own tepid wit,

Mair (?)
Address Unknown!

    Then he wrote a covering note to Lowri. *Lowri, could you do me a huge favour and give enclosed letter to Mair for me please, the next time you see her? I don't know her address, I'm afraid. Thanks!* Now he just had to look in the bureau again tomorrow for a larger envelope then take the morning bus into Lampeter and the post office.

Coming out of the post office and walking to the library to kill time until the midday bus, Tomos calculated how long it might take for Mair to telephone or write back. His letter would reach Lowri tomorrow and she might get it to Mair that same day. It all depended on whether her post came before she left for work, presumably. Supposing it did end up in Lowri's hands in the morning (and after all, she lived in a city where the post probably came early, not at nearly midday like in Talsarn), Mair might just get it sometime tomorrow, depending on when she had a lecture or tutorial with Lowri. So she might even phone tomorrow evening! Tomos smiled to himself imagining the look of surprise on Mair's face when Lowri handed her a mysterious letter saying it was from him. He wished he could be a fly on the wall when it happened.
    Or she might decide that a letter would be better, so if she wrote

tomorrow night, Wednesday, and posted it the next day, it could reach him by Friday. Could he wait that long though?

The following day, time appeared to have slowed to a quarter of its normal pace. The evening seemed to take forever to come around. Tomos hovered never very far from the telephone as if magnetically attracted. Seven o'clock came and went, then seven thirty. At seven forty-two it rang and Tomos's heart skipped a beat. Sioned picked up the receiver as the dock was nearest to her chair, as Tomos waited like a coiled spring to snatch the instrument from her and dash upstairs. But there was only a silence after her 'Hello?' followed by a cold, 'Sorry; not interested thank you,' and an abrupt replacing of the receiver. It was just a nuisance call.

There were no other calls that evening and eventually Tomos went disconsolately to bed. Perhaps she would ring the following evening though. But the next evening there was still nothing; no calls at all in fact, not even of the bothersome variety. There was still the possibility of a letter on Friday though. But all that came through the letter flap after another night of anxiety were two circulars and the electricity bill. And there was still no phone call in the evening, and nor were there a letter or phone call on Saturday. Tomos had sunk into a morass of gloom. There'd be no post on Sunday of course and he'd pretty much given up hope of a phone call by now.

On Monday, having been signed off by the doctor, he returned to school. Concentration on study was a struggle though. Had he made a fool of himself in writing that ridiculous letter, he thought glumly? It all seemed excruciatingly embarrassing now. His first day back was long and difficult. He'd acquired a little of the status of a hero amongst a few students, particularly girls, as his friend James had been to see him during his convalescence and word had got back to school. The war on terror had polarised opinion amongst the idealistic senior students and for those who opposed the bombing, the incident when demonstrating, the getting wounded in a noble cause, imbued Tomos with a little of the glamour of a freedom fighter – or at any rate an activist. But he felt in no mood to wallow in glory, however modest. All that mattered now was Mair and her silence.

But when he walked into the house that afternoon after being delivered back to Talsarn by the school bus, and muttered a subdued hello to Sioned, and went into the kitchen to make himself a mug of coffee, there on the table lay an unopened white envelope addressed in a large loopy script to Tomos Rees! His heart did a minor lurch as he grabbed the letter with trembling fingers and took the stairs two at a time to his room. He flopped into the armchair, panting, and fumbled the envelope open to pull out a single sheet of exercise paper. In an almost childlike hand it read,

Dear Tomos,
Thanks for your letter, which Lowri passed on to me. I really don't know how to write this without hurting your feelings. It looks as though you misunderstood the intention of my phone call last week a little. I'm very sorry Tomos, but I phoned just because I was concerned about you, nothing else. Although I do think you are a really nice guy, honestly (and I think your hair is gorgeous!).

I do actually have a boyfriend at the moment. He didn't come on the demo because he's not really into that sort of thing. So I'm sorry if I gave the impression I was 'available' or something. But I really don't want to complicate things right now. I hope you understand.

I'm certain that you'll have no problems at all finding a girlfriend, Tomos, a good looking and clever and really nice guy like you. Find yourself someone just as nice as you are, promise me. I feel really bad about this.

Take care,

Mair

Sioned was worried about Tomos. He seemed so listless, so lifeless nowadays. She thought she might know what the problem was though. He hadn't been the same since that mysterious letter arrived. It had to be girl trouble; she was convinced of it. She knew the signs; remembered them from Lowri's teenage years. And her own, for that matter.

She hated to see him looking so down. And his trouble, whatever it was, would have to come just now, wouldn't it, just when Glyn and she had resolved to tell him the truth about his parentage? They'd decided years ago that age sixteen might be the best time to tell him, when he was old enough and mature enough to be able to handle the knowledge (they hoped, anyway) but not so old that he could have justifiably resented that they hadn't told him earlier. But ever since he turned sixteen they'd been dithering; afraid to take the plunge and tell him. They couldn't keep putting it off though; it wasn't fair.

When Tomos came home that afternoon looking sad and withdrawn as usual and made to go straight up to his room, Sioned sat him down in the sitting room for a heart-to-heart.

'Are you going to tell me what's troubling you, Bach?'

Tomos studied the carpet. 'It's nothing really,' he muttered dully.

'Oh but it is, isn't it? I can read you like a book. Tell me. Is it anything to do with this, what's her name? Mair?'

'Well, yes.'

Sioned nodded. *I thought so!*

'And? Come on Cariad. Tell your old mam.'

'Well, we met on the demo – well, on Cardiff station actually. And we got on really well. And I thought . . .'

'You thought she was interested in you in . . . that way?' Sioned finished his sentence.

'Yes, well, she came to hospital with me after that thing on the demo. And then rang the other night to see how I was!'

Sioned sighed. 'So she's obviously a very caring person Tomos. But you must have read too much into it.'

'Yes, obviously,' Tomos said bitterly.

'How old is she, do you know?'

'About eighteen I suppose. She's in her first year at uni.'

'Ah.'

'What does "ah" mean? Why should a couple of years make any difference?' Tomos retorted.

Sioned smiled. 'It shouldn't, but it does when you're a teenager, Bach. Would you want to go out with a fourteen-year-old? I don't think so! Your trouble is you're older than your years.'

Tomos smiled wryly and a little bitterly. 'Well, yes, perhaps so. But I can't help that, can I?'

'No, you certainly can't.' Sioned reached across to briefly lay her hand over his. 'And your dad and I wouldn't want you any other way.'

Her face clouded for a moment. Then she took a deep breath, holding it in until her lungs screamed to exhale.

'Er, Tomos. Since we're having this chat. There's something your dad and I have been meaning to talk to you about for a while now. Speaking of you acting like a grown-up: we've left it until now because we wanted you to understand properly, and take it alright and not get upset...'

She faltered. This wasn't going to be easy. She wished she'd waited now for Glyn to share the burden of the disclosure. But it was too late. She'd started now. Tomos had lifted his head to stare at her. 'What are you talking about Mam?'

Sioned met his stare and ploughed on. 'Well, I'll just say this first. I want you to know – and your dad would say just the same – that we do love you Tomos. We do. So very much. From the first day we saw you.'

There was alarm in Tomos's eyes now. 'Mam! What are you saying?'

Sioned felt tears pricking; panic. Duw, she was getting this all wrong. She took another deep breath. 'Tomos! Darling boy! This is so difficult to say!'

'Mam! Will you just say what you have to!'

She tried again. 'Well, have you ever wondered why you're so much younger than Lowri? And why you don't take after either your dad or me?'

'No, not really.' Tomos paused; looked at the carpet. Then realisation began to creep across his face, as the colour left it. He looked back at her, eyes wide with alarm. 'You don't mean...?'

But Sioned could not simply, blandly say the 'yes'. She continued to prevaricate. 'When I had Lowri it was a very difficult birth. It was touch and go that she would make it alive. And it was a close thing for me too. Afterwards we were warned not to risk another pregnancy, and to make sure of it your dad had a vasectomy. We resigned ourselves to having just the one child. For nine years we were quite happy with Lowri. And then one night – I still remember it – we saw a documentary on television, about adoption. All those poor little children wanting homes. And how there was a shortage of people wanting to adopt them.'

She paused to let Tomos take that in, the first installment of a major revelation. She held his look anxiously.

His face still drained, he stared at her open-mouthed.

'So I'm... adopted?' There was a tremor in his voice, tearing the words, making them shrill.

Sioned took his hand again, clasping as if to keep him there, terrified that alienation might steal him away.

'Yes you are, lovely boy,' she whispered.

She could see emotions racing across his face. What were they? Astonishment? Outrage? Anger? Hurt? *No, please, not those!*

But he remained calm, although there was pain dulling his voice when he said, 'So what happened to my proper parents? Why didn't they want me?'

Sioned moved to sit beside him on the sofa; put one arm around his thin shoulders and took his hand again.

'We don't know Bach. We were never told. I don't think the Social Services knew themselves.' She paused, trying to recollect. 'No, hold on, I remember now. You weren't given up; you and your brother were found when you were tiny babies.'

'*Found?* What do you mean, found?'

'That's all we were told. And that an ambulance was called when you were discovered, and you were taken to hospital, and you were named after the ambulance men because no one had any idea what else to call you. So you were called the English Tom – no, it was Tommy – but we changed it to Welsh Tomos.'

It was all coming back to Sioned now. She and Glyn had been told the circumstances of the babies' discovery. But she couldn't tell her boy that. Not that he'd been left in a public lavatory of all places. Telling him all this was quite enough. Tomos had become quiet, digesting the shocking information. Then he said, 'Hold on a minute, you say there were two of us? What; both babies?'

'Yes Bach. You were both newborns, apparently. You were twins.'

There was another silence. 'So what happened to him, my brother?'

Sioned smiled, remembering. 'He was adopted by other people, I imagine. You two were taken to be cared for in a children's home in Liverpool. We'd been applied to adopt with the Social Services and had said we'd prefer a baby, and they let us know you were there.'

Tomos interrupted. 'Why Liverpool? Why did you go all that way to get a baby?'

'Because we were living there then. We spent a few years there. Your dad was trying to further his career in England. You were in a home run by the Salvation Army. What was it called now?' Sioned stopped to rack her brains. 'What's that Beatles song? Ah, yes, Strawberry Field. Not *Fields,* as in the song.'

'So, you went there and we were both there, and you adopted one of us – me?'

'Yes, that's right.'

'Why not both of us then? Shouldn't we have been kept together?'

'Well yes, ideally I suppose. They did try to persuade us to take you both. But we already had Lowri, and we didn't want to make it too hard for her, suddenly having two brothers out of the blue. And besides, we felt it would be a big enough commitment taking on one child, let alone two. It was a big responsibility.'

'So you broke us up. Just like that,' Tomos said, not a little bitterly. Sioned could feel his body tense beneath her touch.

'Yes, I'm sorry Bach. But we did what we felt was right at the time. Adopting was all a new thing for us. We didn't want to find we couldn't cope with two children or cause problems for Lowri. That would have been awful.'

'Well it still seems wrong to me. We got no say in it!'

'No, I know Bach. Perhaps you're right. But you were just babies, too young to know you were brothers. You were living in a temporary family of other children. You couldn't have known that you and – what was the other one's name now? . . . Wayne, that's it – you couldn't have known that you two had a particular relationship. It would have been different if you'd been older and knew you were brothers. That *would* have been cruel to separate you.'

'Yes,' Tomos conceded grudgingly, 'I suppose so.'

He became silent again, lost in thought. Sioned felt him relax a little; left him to his reverie. After a while he said, 'So what made you choose me rather than Wayne?'

Sioned gave him a squeeze. 'Because you were the most beautiful of course!' He smiled a little at that. Sioned breathed a secret sigh of relief.

She went on. 'But seriously, it wasn't easy to choose.' She smiled again too, nostalgically. 'I remember you two being so alike. Same features, same hair, everything. The only slight difference was that you were slightly smaller than Wayne, if I remember right.'

Tomos was agog now. 'What are you saying Mam? That we were

identical twins?'

'Oh yes, completely.' Sioned suddenly realised that she hadn't made that clear.

'Duw duw!' Tomos was dumbfounded.

Sioned sighed, remembering. 'Yes, there were the two of you at the children's home. Two beautiful little baby boys. Don't think we weren't tempted to take both of you, but as I say, there was Lowri to think of and adopting was a step into the unknown for us. We didn't want to bite off more than we could chew and end up being poor parents. So we felt we had to choose just one of you. I remember Wayne being introduced to us first. The superintendant of the home put him into my lap and he didn't like it at all. He howled. Both of us tried to placate him, but he would have none of it.

Then the superintendant fetched some little desert things – yogurt or something, I think it was – and you were put onto my lap and your dad fed you the stuff, and you were as right as rain with us. And I think that's what made us choose you. The fact that you came to us easily, so naturally, it seemed. Of course, it was probably cupboard love really; you were put at ease by the yogurt! Then Wayne joined us again and we had one each of you to play with, and Wayne was fine at the second try I have to say – he couldn't resist the yogurt either. But somehow, although it's a bit irrational really, we plumped for you; your accepting us straightaway gave you the slight edge.'

Sioned looked at her son, her eyes misted now. 'And we've never regretted it for a day Bach, not a single day. And Lowri thought you were absolutely wonderful too. Well she still does.'

A thought suddenly struck Tomos. 'Mam; so Lowri must have known I was adopted?'

'Yes, of course she did. I remember us consulting her before we decided to adopt, because we felt we should, and her deciding she wanted a brother!'

'And she's known all this time and not told me either!'

'Yes I know Bach. But we made her promise not to tell you until we thought it was the right time. Otherwise she might have just blurted it out without thinking and . . . well. Don't think badly of her, please.'

'No,' said Tomos, a little glumly, 'I don't.' But he still felt a tinge of resentment of the conspiracy of silence.

Sioned rubbed his hand. 'So how do you feel about all of this Cariad? I know it must be an enormous shock. I'm sorry if you think we should have told you sooner. Perhaps we should have. But we just wanted to make it as easy for you as possible.'

Tomos's voice was distant, as if he was indeed in shock. 'I can't help wondering who my real mother and father were, and why they felt they had to give me – us – away. Just leave us to be found like that. What if we hadn't been?'

'Well the main thing is you were, and I think they would have made sure you were. I suppose they felt they just couldn't cope, for some reason, and they didn't know what else to do.'

'Then why didn't they put us up for adoption properly; not just dump us!'

Sioned had to confess that she didn't know. Then another thought struck Tomos. 'What if it was a single mother, some kid who just got herself pregnant, and she had us both secretly and then just left us for someone else to find and look after? Perhaps we're actually illegitimate! Oh, Duw! We probably shouldn't have really existed! Oh for fuck's sake!' And the thought, the possibility of that finally tipped him over the edge of control, as he took his hand roughly from Sioned's and put it and his other one to his face, over his eyes, so that she wouldn't see his bitter tears.

Sioned twisted around awkwardly and pulled his head down onto her chest and held it there, and held him, let him weep, and mingled her tears with his. She rocked him like a baby. She spoke. 'Oh my poor Cariad. Don't torture yourself like that! It doesn't matter where you came from or how you were made. You're here now, in our lives; that's all that really matters. You're every bit as important as everyone else. You might have had a terrible life if you'd stayed with your natural mother or parents. But you were everything we could have wished for. Still are. And I know you've just been disappointed over a girl, so perhaps this was a bad time to tell you on top of that. I'm sorry Bach. But we do so love you; just as much as we do Lowri. Really! You're our son. We're your family and you're our precious boy.'

Sioned grabbed Glyn as soon as he came through the door. 'Glyn, I've told Tomos about . . . you know!'

'What, you mean . . . ?'

'Yes.'

'But I thought we were going to tell him together!' Glyn threw his car keys onto the hall side table angrily.

'Yes I know, but we were having a heart-to-heart – he's got girl trouble – and it just came out. You know we've been meaning to do it for ages though, haven't we?'

'Yes, well. How has he taken it?'

'I'm not sure really. He's up in his room now. He seemed reasonably fine at first, but then he got upset at the idea of perhaps being illegitimate.'

'Oh for Heaven's sake Sioned, you didn't tell him that?'

'No of course I didn't! What do you take me for? He thought of that possibility by himself.'

Glyn strode into the sitting room peeling off his jacket and tie. 'Well thank goodness this is Friday. He won't have to take your revelation to school with him tomorrow! I'll go up and talk to him.'

He took the stairs quickly and rapped gently on Tomos's door. 'Can I come in Tomos?'

There was a barely audible 'Yes.'

He entered. Tomos was slumped in his armchair, gazing listlessly at a quiz show on television. He sat on Tomos's bed.

'So your mam's told you then.'

'Yeah.'

'And how do you feel about it?'

Tomos reached for the remote control and muted the sound. 'Well, surprised, shall we say?'

Glyn ignored the sarcasm.

'Yes, I'm sure you are. That'll be putting it mildly.' His anger with Sioned was fading. At least she'd had the courage to take the plunge, do the evil deed. He searched for sympathetic words, but the best ones seemed to be hiding.

'It must be a hell of a thing to suddenly find out, son. I'm so sorry we didn't tell you before now. It was so difficult; trying to find the right opportunity.'

'Yeah, that's what Mam said.'

'And I'm sorry if your mam chose a bad time to tell you. You've been having a bit of girl trouble then?'

Tomos smiled thinly and turned the television right off. 'Well, I think it was a case of just misunderstanding something. I thought she was interested in me, but it turned out she wasn't. I made a stupid fool of myself.'

Glyn smiled too, in sympathy, in male solidarity. 'We all do that Tomos; believe me. It can be really hard to read signs sometimes, and really easy to get them wrong. It happens to us all. I had just the same trouble when I was your age. So don't do yourself down about it.'

Tomos looked at him for the first time. 'Really, Dad?'

'Yes, really. I was terrible! Women can be mysterious creatures sometimes! But then I suppose we are to them, too.'

Tomos fell into silence. Then he said, 'So I had a brother then. A twin.'

'Your mam told you that then? Yes, we had a choice. And we picked you. (Glyn formed a mental comment about choosing puppies but thought better of saying it aloud.) Did she tell you why we felt we couldn't take both of you?'

'Yes, she did. I can see why you didn't, I suppose. But I wonder what happened to him?'

'Yes, I've wondered that too.'

An idea began to form in Glyn's mind. 'I suppose you could find out, if you really wanted to.'

'How would I do that?'

'Well I think I read somewhere that the Salvation Army has a missing relative tracing service. Yes, that's it! It was they who ran that home you both were in. I remember now. They would be bound to have records of who adopted your brother, so it should be quite easy for them to track him down, I would have thought.'

Tomos looked at his father with animation back in his eyes. 'Do you think so Dad?'

Well I certainly think it's worth a try,' Glyn said, finding himself quite excited at the thought.

Chapter 10
Wayne

Wayne was bored with his job. By November the scant satisfaction of shelf stacking had worn thin; well, once you'd stacked the first hundred cans of baked beans or chicken soup or peaches in syrup, it did get just a tad repetitive. And okay, doing the limited-shelf-life stuff was slightly more interesting (pull the old stock to the front, fill in with as much as you can of new stock behind, pat the files tidy as you work across, stand back, admire) but it was still not exactly mentally taxing. It allowed your mind to wander, to daydream of more exciting occupations.

Over the past few days he'd often wondered how David was getting on. His friend had left for Catterick Camp the previous weekend. He'd gone straight down to York to the recruiting office when he got the literature about the army, after reading through it avidly and giving it serious thought for a good minute and a half, and signed on the dotted line. And there he was now, in the Yorkshires (not training for a trade or anything but that didn't matter) beginning his life of adventure and comradeship and serving his country. While Wayne was stacking his umpteenth tin of 400 gram minced beef with onions in gravy and envying him like hell.

So he stood there now, hands moving automatically and brain on autopilot, wondering how he was going to broach the subject again to Helen. When he'd mentioned the possibility of joining up before, she'd sounded distinctly uninterested. Not actually hostile, but certainly not encouraging either. He could sort of see her point, perhaps. They'd have less time together, because of course you had to live on camp and Catterick was eleven miles away. But surely, she'd want him to do what he most wanted to do, wouldn't she? She'd be a bit selfish otherwise. After all, if the situation was reversed and she wanted to join up, he wouldn't stand in her way. Definitely not. No way. Besides, he'd compromised with her over the scouting, many times. He'd given up weekend activities to be with her instead, when sometimes he would rather have been out with his mates really. He reckoned he was due a little pay-back. Well anyway, he was going to have it out with her tonight.

It was too cold in the evenings now to spend them outdoors, and too dark of course to go walking, so they usually spent them at Helen's. Mark and Susan, her parents, were surprisingly relaxed about them spending some of the time alone together in her bedroom if there was nothing on television that interested the youngsters. Susan knew the ways of teenagers though. She and Mark had had to marry in somewhat indecent haste when she had fallen pregnant with their first daughter, Gilly, when she was still just nineteen, and she'd been a stern teacher of the ways of responsible sexual conduct, first to Gilly in her turn and now, three years later, Helen.

She knew only too well that teenagers would be hormone-fizzing teenagers, but as long as they took sensible precautions it wasn't her place – and it would probably be futile anyway – to lecture her daughters about their morality. Parental finger-wagging certainly hadn't worked on her. Not that Wayne and Helen took advantage of this tacit sexual freedom. Wayne still felt constrained by his sense of decent behaviour; of parameters to stay within. They were both still virgins.

Tonight was a red letter one for Susan and Mark, as it was the occasion of their twentieth wedding anniversary; twenty years since their rather compulsory (although not later regretted) joining together one rather wet and windswept November Saturday morning at Northallerton Register Office in nineteen eighty-one. So they were going out for a meal to celebrate. Strictly speaking the proper day had been the previous Thursday, but they'd made it the Friday night to allow of late rising with possibly sore heads.

Gilly would be out with her boyfriend Craig too, doing the rounds of the pubs no doubt, and so Helen and Wayne had the house to themselves. So they were sitting close together on the sofa now, her head against his chest in his encircling arm, watching *Coronation Street* on the box. Wayne was psyching himself up to raise the subject of a life of adventure. He waited for the closing credits of the soap to roll. *Now for it.* He searched for a way in.

'It were busy in t' shop today.'

'Oh yeah?' Helen muttered distractedly, reaching for the remote control and programme guide to check out the televisual delights on offer.

'Yeah. Busy but boring.'

'Well, it's a job though.'

Wayne bristled inwardly. *Well it's okay for you to say that. You'll leave school in a couple of years with good qualifications and get a decent job.*

'I know, but I want to do summat with my life.'

'Well you should have worked towards something when you were at school,' Helen chided. She could be a bit inclined to be a bossyboots, Wayne sometimes thought.

'Yeah, I know. But I didn't know what I wanted to do then!'

'And do you know now, do you?'

'Yeah, I reckon so.'

'So tell me!' Helen was all undivided attention now.

'Well, I'm thinking of joining t' Yorkshires.'

He felt her stiffen under his arm. 'Oh.'

'Well my mate Dave just has. His brother and sister are in them too. They say it's great.'

'Well I can't see the attraction, personally. Anyway, have you spoken to them? How do you know what they think?'

'No, but it's what Dave reckons they say, any road.'

'If he says it, it must be true then.' Helen couldn't keep the sarcasm from her voice. Remembering him from school, she didn't like the bumptious, self-assured David quite honestly.

'So what have you got against it then?' Wayne was getting irritated. 'It's a good life. And t' money's quite good. Better than Tesco's at least. And there's all this terrorism now. Look at what happened in America. Something needs to be done about it, to keep t' country safe.'

'Well my dad reckons bombing other countries isn't the way to stop it.'

'So what is then? Does he know?'

'I don't know! I just don't like fighting, that's all. It's horrible.' Helen was getting tetchy too. And she didn't like having her father's opinions challenged.

'Well sometimes it just has to be done. If everyone thought like you we'd be living under the Nazis!'

'That's just silly, to say that,' Helen retorted. 'It's different altogether. And that was over fifty years ago anyway.'

'No it isn't! You don't want us to be bombed, do you? It's a matter of striking first before they hit us, that's all I'm saying! And besides, I thought you'd want me to be happy in what I'm doing, and make something of myself.'

Helen tried to calm things down; this was escalating into a row. 'Yes, of course I do. But if you joined the army you'd have to go and live in camp, wouldn't you? Then we wouldn't see so much of each other.'

'I'd still see you quite a bit,' Wayne insisted, 'it's not as if I'd be posted. I'd only be up in Catterick.'

Helen felt a prick of alarm as a thought suddenly came. 'You're not going off me, are you?'

Wayne tightened his arm around her; made it a cuddle. 'No! Of course not!'

She looked up at him, eyes wide with anxiety. 'Really?'

'Yes, honestly!'

'Well come upstairs and prove it then!' she said as she jabbed the remote control to turn the television off, got to her feet and pulled him to his.

They lay close together on her bed, naked (well, in his case apart from his socks), legs entwined, plump thigh over thin, as Wayne regained his breath.

He was overwhelmed. He was exhilarated. He'd seen and touched most parts of Helen individually during the past months, and with increasing familiarity as intimacy blossomed, but he hadn't quite been prepared for the glorious inviting softness of her beneath him as he frantically, fumblingly (and she fumblingly helped him to) entered her for the first exciting time.

Helen spoke first. 'How was that then?'

Wayne grinned, red-faced. 'Wonderful! Was it okay for you?'

'Yes, lovely,' Helen enthused, not altogether sincerely. (In fact it had hurt just a little, and where was the fabled climax all her mates went endlessly on about?)

'It seemed as if I hurt you a bit,' Wayne worried.

'No, it's okay, really. It does sometimes the first time. It's the hymen breaking.'

'How do you know that?'

'I just do. Girls know these things. It'll be great next time, honestly. And even better for you!'

'Oh, will it?'

'Yeah! Honest!'

Wayne felt suspicion nagging. 'How do you know?' he repeated.

Helen laughed. 'Well don't you boys talk about it all the time, like us girls?'

'Well, yeah, but . . .'

She stroked the side of his face. 'See what you'd be missing if you were away in Catterick most of the time, my lovely Wayne?'

Wayne felt his resolve crumbling, just a little. A small part of him whispered that she had a point. But no; he had to be firm. 'But it is what I want, Helen, to go in t' army. And any road, I don't see how us can do this very often. It was okay tonight with your mum and dad out of t' way, but we can hardly do it with them downstairs now, can we?'

But Helen would not be easily swayed. 'Oh, I'm sure we could find a way you know, if we really tried. But next time we really must take precautions.'

She moved her hand up to stroke his thick red hair. 'I do love your mop! I wonder where you get it from. No one else in your family's a ginger are they?'

'No.' The reply was curt.

'And there's no one further back that are? Or were?'

'No.' He paused. 'Well actually, there wouldn't be.'

'What does that mean?'

Wayne was silent.

'Come on, spit it out!'

She sensed him taking a deep breath. 'There wouldn't be because I'm adopted. And so is Poppy.'

Helen stared at him, shocked and surprised. 'Bloody hell! Really?'

'Yeah. My parents couldn't have kids themselves so they adopted me, and then Poppy too.'

'Oh, Wayne! And have you always known this?'

He smiled wryly. 'No, not always. They told us a year ago. When they thought Poppy would be old enough to understand, they said. They said they wanted to tell us both at t' same time; be honest with us.'

'Good grief! And how did you feel when they told you? Sorry, do you mind me asking?'

'Well it was a hell of a surprise.'

'Yes, I can imagine. Were you upset?'

'Poppy wasn't very much, really, but I was a bit, I must admit. I never thought for a minute that I wasn't theirs. It just never occurred to me.'

Helen ruffled his hair gently. 'Poor you! Well it wouldn't. And how are you now? And how do you feel about your parents – the people who you thought were your proper mum and dad?'

Wayne produced his wry smile again. 'Oh, I'm okay now. It took a while to get used to t' idea of not being theirs though. And I'm fine with my parents. I think the world of them really, even though my dad can be a miserable old git sometimes.'

Helen laughed at that and hugged him. Hearing this revelation completely out of the blue had made her feel oddly maternal, as if he were some Dickensian orphan in need of love.

Wayne went on, relieved to be baring his feelings. 'Shall I tell you what the hardest thing to take was though? When they told me I'd been found, and in a ladies' loo of all places. Just dumped, for someone to find, as if my real mum didn't care about me; didn't want me. As if I were worthless. That bloody hurt. I weren't even given up for adoption properly, like, or whatever they do!'

Helen hugged him tighter still. 'No, don't think that! Of course you aren't worthless. I'm sure your parents love you just as much as if you were their natural son. And I certainly do – love you I mean.'

Wayne lifted his head to stare at her. 'Do you Helen? Do you really?'

'Yes, of course I do. That's why . . .' She caught herself and steered the assurance along a safer track. 'Why I made you take me to bed!'

He grinned, complacent and preening a little. 'Yeah, you're a wicked woman Helen Micklethwaite. So you couldn't resist me, was that it?'

'Absolutely.'

Well I can't resist you either. He uncoupled his embrace and rolled away a little to look down at her white slightly podgy body. 'Bloody hell, you're gorgeous!' he breathed, as he felt another erection stirring. 'Can we do it again?' he asked, anxious, like a 'little boy asking for more; more newly-discovered ambrosia.

'Yeah, go on then,' Helen said, no less eager, as she settled into the middle of the bed and opened her thighs, and reached for him.

For all Mark and Susan's liberality, it wasn't easy to follow up on the discovery of each other's bodies' wonderful mysteries though. Not for a few weeks anyway, not until Helen reached her seventeenth birthday and, trying to sound casual, mentioned to Susan that she and Wayne were now In a Relationship, but still half-expected a shock-horror reaction. But there wasn't one. Susan knew perfectly well what was going on. She hadn't failed to spot the pink stains on Helen's bed sheet when she put it in the wash a few days after their anniversary night out. But she reiterated her warning to Helen to be careful and insist that the boy took precautions. This Wayne was a presentable-enough lad, and unfailingly polite, give him that. Her daughter could do a lot worse for herself really. At least he'd got a job, of sorts, which was more than could be said of many of the youths she might have brought home. But all the same, Helen was still at school and working for her A-levels. She really didn't need a pregnancy to scupper things.

And so Wayne and Helen fell into an easy routine through that autumn and winter of 2001. As there was so little to do in the evenings in Northallerton that they could – or wanted – to participate in together, they spent them at either Wayne's house or Helen's. Jim and Maureen were pleased to see Wayne with a steady girlfriend too, for all that he was still only sixteen (and thirteen-year-old Poppy was increasingly envious, as her own hormones began to kick in, of his comparatively adult status). They thought it broadened his outlook, got him out of the entirely male-oriented environment of scouting some of the time. At least that was Maureen's opinion. And mirroring Susan's approval of Wayne, she thought her son's girlfriend sweet and charming too.

As for Wayne, he could hardly believe that Helen's parents were so easy-going that they really didn't mind what often happened when, if uninterested in the television programme they were watching, she and he disappeared upstairs to her room. He tried to throw it off, but he nevertheless felt a tinge of inhibition during their impatient breathless coupling and when they lay naked together afterwards, acutely conscious of Mark and Susan sitting chastely below, separated only by floorboards, joists and plasterboard. He tried to keep quiet, and keep Helen quiet too, worriedly gagging her giggles and squeals, even though they always had music on her CD player loud, convinced that their sounds would carry downstairs; sure that her parents would just *know*.

But, he had to admit, it was a pretty good situation really. He could never have done this at home. He wouldn't have dared tell his mother – or his father for that matter – what Helen and he got up to. They must surely, confidently and trustingly, assume that he and Helen were virgins.

They were scrupulously careful about the Precautions though. It would be just terrible, Wayne thought if Helen fell pregnant. He'd imagined that scenario a couple of times, and it had frightened him to death. If it happened, perish the thought, they would simply have to get married, no two ways about it, quite apart from her parents (and if not them, his anyway) insisting on it. No; he was far too young for the responsibility of marriage and fatherhood. Although he could imagine the marriage bit in four or five years' time. Maybe then he could even contemplate having a child. It would certainly cement things between them; he'd have her bound to him for life then.

As for dreams of the army; well, maybe it had been a silly dream really. He'd got most of what he wanted after all. He'd got a job of sorts that wasn't too demanding but most importantly he'd got a girl who said she loved him, who accepted him, met a hidden crying need. Unlike that bitch who'd probably had casual sex without a thought for the possible consequences, with some bloke who probably didn't give a toss either, and he'd been the unwanted result. And he'd been just cast aside, like an unfortunate side effect. And left in a bloody women's loo, for Christ's sake! It still made him seethe with fury when he thought about it.

Anyway, in another eighteen months, when Helen left school with a few good A-levels (she was so much brainier than him, he knew that full well) she'd get a good well-paid job and then they'd be okay moneywise, and perhaps get engaged. And he might even (well, it could happen) find something a bit more exciting and a bit better paid to do job-wise himself. Something like a policeman, maybe. On the squad cars, perhaps, chasing villains at high speed and nabbing the buggers. Yeah, that'd be good! It was a thought. He'd have to look into it.

On the second of December when she got in from work, Maureen picked up from the door mat, along with holiday brochures and the gas bill, an envelope overprinted with the logo of SEEK Services. *What on earth is this?* she worried. *We aren't being chased for debt are we?*

She took the mail into the lounge and pulled the first brochure out of its clear plastic wrapper; stood, still wearing her coat, flicking through its enticing pages of sun-soaked Mediterranean villages, hotels with impossibly cobalt swimming pools and sad-eyed donkeys wearing straw hats. *Yeah, well, be nice if we won the lottery.* Looked at the other one; dismissed its offered delights too. Put the bill to one side. Tore open the other envelope, began to read and then sat down heavily in her chair. It was from something calling itself SEEK People Tracing Services. Very mysterious! She read:

Dear Mr and Mrs Harrison,
Firstly, please allow me to apologise in advance if this letter comes as a shock to you. Are you a Mr and Mrs James Harrison who formerly lived in Liverpool around 1995? I ask this because we have been approached by a Mr and Mrs Glyn Rees of Talsarn, Ceredigion, Wales, who have retained us to seek a brother of their adoptive son Tomos. We gather from them that their son spent some time as a baby in the Strawberry Field Children's Home in Liverpool in 1995, before being adopted by them.

We have also been informed by the Salvation Army, who run that Home, that your son Wayne was in the Home at the same time and is in fact the (twin) brother of Tomos, who was called Tom or Tommy then. Mr and Mrs Rees and their son Tomos would very much like to meet Wayne, and of course yourselves, provided, naturally, that you and Wayne would like to meet too.

Of course, I do not know whether (assuming that you are indeed the correct Mr and Mrs Harrison) you have made Wayne aware that he is your adoptive son, or indeed, if so, that he has a biological brother. Please do not feel pressured in any way by this letter. Whether you have made Wayne aware of his provenance or of the existence of a sibling is of course entirely your concern and no one else's.

If you are in fact the Mr and Mrs Harrison we are seeking, and together with your son Wayne would like to establish contact with the Rees family, please let me know, possibly enclosing your telephone number. I must stress though that Wayne's consent to this is paramount. Without it we are unable to take this matter further. Subject to his consent, I enclose a stamped, addressed envelope for your reply. I will then inform Mr and Mrs Reees, and I am sure they will be in touch. If however you do not wish to establish contact, I will tell Mr and Mrs Rees this and that will be the end of the matter.

Please be assured of my upmost discretion in this matter, and my apologies again if this has come as a shock to you.

My warmest wishes.

Yours faithfully,

Hilary Beale

Maureen read the letter through again, incredulous. She sat and gazed, unseeing, at the dead screen of the television, her mind racing. *Of course! We'd forgotten all about that other baby at Strawberry Fields, Wayne's brother. Not that we ever saw him. He'd already been chosen and gone to a good loving home, hopefully, by the time we got there. Just think; if we'd got there a few months earlier, before this Mr and Mrs Rees, we'd have got to choose instead of them. Or we might have taken both. Now there's a thought! They do say it's better not to split children up really, don't they? Not that the little mites would have been aware that they were brothers, of course. But anyway, things might have been very different if we'd been on the scene earlier.*

Not that we've anything to complain about, having just our Wayne. It's difficult to imagine another one of him though. I wonder what his brother's like? Is he like Wayne? Well I don't know about Jim and Wayne, but I'd certainly like to see this Tomos anyway. But that Mrs – or is it Miss? – Beale is right of course. It's got to be up to Wayne. I can't wait to tell him! I wonder how he'll react when he knows? He was pretty upset when we told him he was adopted though. More than Poppy. She just took it in her stride. But he'll surely be excited about this? Must tell Jim first though.

And when Jim came off shift and got home at ten fifteen, and she'd thrust the letter into his hands almost before he'd got through the door (Wayne was out of the way, he was over at his Helen's house), and when he'd taken off his coat and settled in his chair to read it, he was every bit as flabbergasted.

'Good grief! I'd forgotten all about them telling us there were another baby, Luv!' he said.

'Yes, and me. Funny that, isn't it?'

'Yeah, but I suppose it were easy done. Whereas these Rees's, they would have remembered t' other one because they must have seen both babies, I reckon.'

'Well obviously Jim, if they chose between them!'

Jim ignored the mild sarcasm. 'I wonder what Wayne will make of it though. It's going to be a hell of a surprise to him again. Just as much as being told he were adopted. And that didn't go down all that well, did it?'

'No it didn't,' Maureen agreed ruefully. 'Anyway, we'll have to tell him. We don't want him thinking we've been keeping it from him deliberately.'

'Yeah, right,' said Jim, as Maureen walked into the kitchen to put the kettle on, 'We'll do it when he gets back, shall us?'

Wayne walked in through the kitchen door at five to eleven, his usual sort of time when he was with Helen during the evening. It was a twenty minute walk across town from the Micklethwaites' to the Harrison's, and Maureen had garnered the information that Helen went to bed at ten thirty, so that was about right. They heard him walk through into the hall and make to go straight upstairs. Maureen called him into the lounge where she and Jim sat in slightly nervous anticipation.

His face registered surprise to find them still up; he was normally the last to bed now that he was a working young man. He looked at them suspiciously. What was this going to be about? But Maureen was all artificial bonhomie. 'Hello Luv. Had a nice evening?'

'Yeah, great thanks,' Wayne replied, guardedly.

'Good! Er, sit down with us a minute, will you?'

'Why?'

'We've got something to tell you. Sit a minute.'

Wayne sank down onto the sofa; looked from one to the other. *Come on then! Get on with it!*

Jim took over. 'Right. Um –'

'Spit it out Dad! Say what you want to say!'

'Right then. Well you know we told you and Poppy that you were adopted?'

'Yeah, yeah.' Wayne could hardly forget it.

Jim ploughed on, ignoring the rudeness. 'Well, there's something else. Your mum and me didn't tell you then, because we'd both completely forgot about it, but the fact is, you've got a brother.' Jim exhaled. *There. It's out now.*

Wayne's eyes snapped to his, round with shock and surprise. 'What?'

Jim shifted uncomfortably; muttered, 'Yes it's true.'

'But how come you know that? Or know but have conveniently forgotten?'

Maureen tried to placate, pleading, 'Yes, it's true Luv! We really did forget. It's a long time ago now. Sorry!'

'So how do you know that I have a brother?' Wayne demanded, repeating the question.

Jim answered. 'The people who ran t' children's home where you were as a baby, before we adopted you, told us that. It all comes back now. They said that there'd been another baby, your brother, there too. But he was adopted before we were told by Liverpool council that you were there. So we never saw him; he'd already been adopted by a couple from Wales.'

Wayne was agog now, but still suspicious. 'You seem to know a hell of a lot about all this, considering you'd forgotten,' he accused.

'Well that's why we want to talk to you about it, Son,' said Jim. 'We've had a letter from a firm that searches for people. They're working for the couple who adopted your brother. The letter says who they are. Mr and Mrs Rees from somewhere in Wales I've never heard of. They and their son want to meet you. But only if you want to meet your brother. It's up to you; you decide.'

Jim picked up the letter from the coffee table. 'Here's t' letter. Read it for yourself.'

Wayne took it and read, his expression flitting from brow-furrowed frown to wide-eyed surprise and back again. He looked up, at each parent in turn.

'Christ, it says it isn't just a brother I've got but a twin!'

'That's right,' said Maureen, 'I remember the superintendant saying that now – '

Jim interrupted her, excited. 'Hang on Mo. Bloody hell, there's another thing. I think I remember her saying the twins were identical too!'

Maureen stared at her husband, as more onion-layers of memory were peeled back. 'Oh Jim! Yes! You're right. She did say that!'

Wayne sat transfixed, his face ashen. 'So I not only have a twin brother called – what is it? – Tomos, somewhere in Wales, but he's *identical* too?'

'Yes, we think so,' said Jim.

'Yes, I'm sure that's what they said,' Maureen agreed.

There was silence, as the three of them digested the revelations that triggered memory had presented; snippets of information long forgotten. Then Jim spoke again. 'Anyway, so what do us do about this?'

The silence continued with each of them lost in thought. Finally Maureen said, 'But actually, it's for you to decide, Wayne. This Tomos is your brother. Your twin. What do you want to do? Do you want to meet him?'

A week later, in the evening, Maureen answered the ringing telephone.

'Hello?'

'Ah, hello. Is that Mrs Harrison?'

'Yes; speaking.'

The lilting Welsh voice repeated itself. 'Hello, this is Glyn Rees speaking. You've been contacted by a firm called Seek, I believe, on my behalf. About our adoptive sons, Tomos and Wayne?'

Maureen mouthed *It's them!* To Jim. He muted the sound on the television and hurried across to her chair, kneeling beside it with his ear close to the receiver, listening in.

'Oh yes; hello! Lovely to hear from you. I'm afraid Wayne's not here at the moment. He's out with his girlfriend. You know what they're like. We never see him nowadays!'

Glyn laughed. 'Yes, I do indeed. Our Tomos isn't courting yet but our daughter's been through all that! Tomos isn't here just now either, but perhaps it would be a good idea to talk things over between ourselves first anyway, do you think?'

Maureen agreed, and she and Jim and Glyn and Sioned, whose paths had so nearly crossed at Strawberry Field Children's Home all those years ago, who were bound by such a special commonality, spoke to each other, exchanged information, compared notes, laughed at similarities between their sons; boys who might easily have been just a single one had not, for some inexplicable reason, a microscopic cluster of eight cells divide but become two separate bundles of eight, which would grow into two beings, both red haired, both freckled, both shy with girls, both with lopsided grins. Boys who both might have become sons of one couple or the other, had circumstances been slightly different.

They talked on and on, particularly when Sioned came onto the phone to speak to Maureen. Finally it occurred to Glyn to call Tomos down from his room to say hello to the parents of his brother. He took the telephone nervously and spoke first to Jim, shy and awkward, and then to an impatiently waiting Maureen whose voice was by turns shrill with excitement and soft with wonder.

They agreed (although it would have to be cleared with Wayne of course; Maureen couldn't wait to tell him about the phone call when he came home) to meet in Northallerton over the Christmas period, on one of Jim's days off duty that coincided with Wayne's day off work. Maureen apologised that she wouldn't be able to accommodate them overnight, the three of them, in her modest house. Glyn assured her that it was no problem; they could stay in a guest house.

After what seemed to Jim several hours (but was actually an hour and twenty-five minutes), Glyn rang off (Sioned would never have done so if she'd still been on the line), with Maureen's promise to confirm the meeting date: the day after Boxing Day.

When Wayne arrived home at ten past eleven (he was getting later nowadays) Maureen, who'd stayed up, couldn't wait to tell the news, sitting him down and pinning him to the sofa with a fusillade of excited chatter: how she'd spoken to Tomos (what a nice boy he sounded, ever so polite; sounded just like him, same tone of voice and everything except for the Welsh accent of course) and how nice his parents sounded too. Eventually, to Wayne's relief, she ran out of steam.

'Well, what do you think then Luv? Do you want to go for it? Can I phone and say we'll meet at Christmas?' She looked at Wayne, willing him to say yes.

'Yeah, great,' he said. 'Let's do it.'

Chapter 11
Tomos

It's three-thirty on a chilly afternoon, the twenty-seventh of December, in North Yorkshire. Tomos and his parents have arrived in Christmas lights-bedecked Northallerton. It's been a long journey – some of it familiar from years gone by; the route up through mid and then north-east Wales via Wrexham and Chester, then onto the motorway to the Runcorn turn – but sailing straight past this time and onward into new territory, to skirt Manchester (stopping at Services to eat because they weren't sure whether a late lunch would be offered and they didn't want to presume) and then on again to Leeds and the die-straight Scotland-bound A1.

But at last they've arrived. They park in the street outside Jim and Maureen's modest but immaculately-kept Edwardian terraced house, getting out of the Ford Focus, gasping at the unaccustomed cold wind blowing straight from Siberia, to stretch limbs and gather mentally for the encounter to come. Glyn, as senior male, leads the way to the dark blue front door and rings the bell, as Tomos and Sioned hover nervously behind.

The door is opened by Maureen, presumably; surprisingly tall, pretty and blonde for all her thickening hips and matronly late-forties years. Her face lights up immediately, creasing into a broad grin. 'Hello! You got here then!' she welcomes, stating the obvious. 'Come in out of the cold!'

She stands aside, eyes going immediately to Tomos, to let them enter, pressing herself against the wall of the narrow hall as they crowd in and stand uncertainly, waiting for her to close the door. Then she leads the way through an open door on the right, into a cosy, warm-as-toast lounge. The small room seems to be full of people already, and apart from a Christmas tree sparkling with lights in the corner, the furniture consists mainly of chairs. A tall thin man with a curly grey hair-rimmed pate and bright gimlet eyes heaves up out of an armchair and moves forward, hand extended in welcome. Two girls occupy a three-seater sofa that has been pushed back against a side wall to create more space. One, a child of about thirteen years, is mousey-haired and bespectacled and staring, unabashedly curious. Beside her in the centre of the sofa sits an older girl, a bit plump, stub nosed, rosy-cheeked and with a haystack of jet black untidy hair. She is blatantly curious too. She emits an audible gasp, quickly trying to suppress it, at the sight of Tomos.

But the visitor's eyes are drawn magnetically to the young man in clean blue jeans and what looks suspiciously like a Christmas present rugby shirt, rising politely from beside the black-haired girl. Tomos senses Sioned's quick intake of breath beside him. He stares; can't help himself. It really is extraordinary. It's like looking in the mirror. He's seeing a doppelganger. A slightly taller and sturdier carbon copy, true, and this facsimile has shorter hair (although exactly the same rufous red). But the face; look at the face! It's Tomos's face: a perfect duplicate. The same freckles, the same wide-ish nose between the same green eyes. And, yes, now he's shyly smiling, and it's just the same slightly lop-sided grin.

Jim shakes their hands warmly, lingering over Tomos and looking deep into his eyes as if he just can't believe what he's seeing. Then he remembers his manners and introduces the young people: Poppy, Helen and, quite unnecessarily, Wayne. The girls murmur 'hi's' but Wayne seems to be completely dumbstruck. He's staring fixedly at Tomos, as for that matter is the rest of his family too. Tomos is beginning to find all the attention uncomfortable, as if he's some kind of freak.

There are three dining chairs supplementing the normal furniture, forming with it u-shape around the periphery of the room, and at a not-very-subtle-sign from Jim the youngsters vacate the sofa making it available to the visitors; Wayne and Helen relocating side by side next to Jim's armchair opposite the sofa and Poppy next to her mother's chair facing the blazing, roasting coal fire. The visitors shuffle off their coats and hand them to the hovering Maureen, who takes them from the room and then returns to sink with a sigh into her chair. She beams at the visitors sitting adjacent to her, but her eyes are still all for Tomos.

'Well, this is lovely!' She enthuses. 'I just can't get over this! Fancy us meeting after all this time. And especially meeting you, young man! I really can't get over you; you're the spitting image of our Wayne!'

Jim interjects, a little tiredly, 'Yes, well he would be really, Luv, being as how t' boys are identical twins.'

Sioned says, 'Yes, but I've seen identical twins round our way but you can just about tell them apart if you look really closely. But these two; they're just extraordinary.' She hasn't taken her gaze off Wayne either. 'The only thing is, Wayne,' she says, you're just a little bit bigger. I wonder why that is?'

Wayne takes that to be a question directed at him, and replies, with his shy smile, 'Dunno really.'

Jim says, hinting heavily at Maureen, 'Well anyway, what would you good people like to drink, tea or mebbe summat stronger?'

Sioned, already on first name terms says, 'Oh I'd love a cup of tea please Maureen,' assuming she'll be the provider of hot drinks.

Glyn, finally able to get a word in, says, 'I'd love a beer if you've got one Jim.'

Jim has of course, in various varieties, and proceeds to apprise Glyn of the selection on offer. All the youngsters opt for tea and Maureen rises again to go and put the kettle on.

With everyone furnished with drinks and mince pies, conversation resumes. It quickly returns to the twins. They are, after all, the reason for this visit. Sioned says, slightly guiltily keen to compare Jim and Maureen's twin with her own, 'And you've left school now then, Wayne?'

Wayne mumbles a yes, but he'd rather not enlarge on the topic. He knows what the next question is likely to be: what he's doing job-wise? But Sioned doesn't go there. She knows what he does, from speaking with Maureen on the phone that first time. She suspects (well, there's no disguising the fact really), with an odd mixture of smugness and sympathy, that Wayne is less academically gifted than her Tomos. But she doesn't want to embarrass the lad. Instead she brings Helen into the conversation.

'Have you left school as well then Helen?'

Helen, who has been a wallflower up to now, sends silent thanks for the inclusion. She pulls her gaze away from Tomos. 'No, I've stayed on to do A-levels.' But she leaves it at that; doesn't want to expand either, it seems.

Maureen says, 'And what about you Tomos,' (she has to make a conscious effort not to say Thomas) 'Your mum says you're hoping to be a doctor?'

'Well yes, if I do alright with A-levels and get accepted at university,' Tomos says modestly, trying to play his aspiration down.

He doesn't want to flaunt his ambitiousness over his twin. He's surprised indeed that in this respect Wayne and he seem quite unalike. His brother doesn't appear to have a similar intellect. Presumably Wayne sets less store by learning of the academic variety. And is he also less idealistic? Tomos has read about the nature versus nurture debate – genetic predestination as opposed to influences of upbringing and environment – especially since discovering that he's got an identical twin brother. He's read of cases like his own, where twins have been separated in babyhood and brought up in different adoptive families. In some cases twins have diverged dramatically in their personalities and outlooks suggesting that nurture is the dominant factor as far as character development goes. But in others he's read, separated twins remain uncannily similar. On first *impressions, Wayne and he seem to fall into the first category.*

He's jolted out of his reverie by Jim talking. 'Well, good for you, Tom (he cringes; hates being called that), we certainly need all the doctors we can get. Don't get me wrong, I've nothing against all the foreign doctors we've got over here – after all, where would the NHS be without them? – but it'd be good to have more home-grown ones.'

Tomos smiles non-committally and darts a glance at Wayne, checking for his reaction. But he doesn't seem offended that his twin is being lauded. Or is he? He's staring fixedly at the coffee table in the centre of the room and its empty mugs (Jim and Glyn are nursing refilled beer glasses) and solitary plate containing four remaining mince pies. Does he feel a little diminished by his more intellectual brother? It's impossible to tell.

Then Glyn speaks. 'Anyway, we came here so you boys could get to know each other a bit. It's been sixteen years since you last saw each other. I don't suppose either of you can remember each other at all, can you?' He looks first at Wayne and then at Tomos, only half-expectedly.

Sioned sighs; says, 'Well of course they wouldn't remember each other Glyn! They were only babies!'

Wayne ponders and seems to be struck by something. But then appears to dismiss whatever it was. Tomos, intrigued by the thought, racks his brain, but he can't dredge up memory from so far back.

Jim takes up Glyn's original observation. 'Yes, that was the point of you coming. Wayne, perhaps you and Tom would like some time alone together? What say you two go for a walk or something? Show Tom the wonders of Northallerton.'

Wayne laughs. 'Well that wouldn't take long! Penny's caff might be open though. We could walk down the town and see if she is. It's a bit parky to be walking around.'

'"Caff?"' says Tomos, puzzled.

'Yeah, caff – cafe,' Wayne elucidates, surprised that his Welsh brother doesn't know the English slang.

'Oh, right,' Tomos says politely.

To Tomos's great relief, because Wayne was quite right about it being 'a bit parky' (in fact, being used to more southerly and milder Wales he's found the walk into the town centre numbingly cold), the 'caff' is indeed open. He wonders why it is though; only two other tables are occupied. A mournful-looking elderly man sits at one with an empty mug at his elbow (perhaps he's there just for the warmth and a modicum of human contact) and a young couple with a small boy are arranged triangularly around another, determinedly working their way through a plate of scones and cakes. They aren't day trippers, surely? Perhaps escapees from hospitality-wearing-thin family festivities, more likely.

They find themselves a table next to a radiator and shed their coats. Wayne, knowing his manners, orders teas and Yorkshire parkin for his guest. Tomos remarks that it's quite like a similar Welsh delicacy: bara brith. Now it's Wayne's turn to look puzzled, so Tomos translates: speckled (because of the dried fruit) bread.

They sit on opposite sides of the small round red gingham table clothed table, hands wrapped around mugs, taking each other in. Helen had wanted to come too, but Maureen had gently suggested that, this first time, the boys might prefer to be alone together. Tomos had felt a twinge of disappointment when Helen had conceded the good sense of that; he wouldn't have minded if she'd come along at all. Wayne breaks the silence that has fallen since the food small talk.

'Well I just can't get over this: us being identical twins an' all, can you?'

Tomos agrees. 'Yes, it was a pretty amazing discovery. I don't know why my parents didn't tell me sooner. About being adopted and having a twin as well. Then we could have tracked you down before now.'

'Yeah, true. Poppy and me have known about the adopted thing for over a year now, but not about me having a twin.'

Tomos says, 'It's funny how it's worked out, isn't it? Just think, my parents went to that children's home before yours, when we were there together, and if they'd decided they wanted both of us, we'd have stayed brothers and been brought up together. That's quite a thought isn't it?'

Wayne grins. 'Certainly is! I always wanted a brother really. Poppy's alright, she's a good kid, but she's just at that awkward age now, you know? She's a pain in t' neck sometimes, quite honestly.'

Tomos smiles too, enjoying the male camaraderie. 'Yes, my sister went through a phase like that too. In fact it was a long phase with her; lasted until she was eighteen and went to uni!'

The smile on Wayne's face slips just a fraction. 'Your sister though; she's a lot older that you, isn't she?'

'Yes, nine years. And she's my parent's biological daughter. Although my parents treat us equally; always have done.'

'That's good,' Wayne says approvingly. 'It would be horrible if they favoured her. Do you get on well with her, her being so much older and everything?'

'Yes, I do really. Although she's left home now, anyway. She teaches at the uni she went to, in Cardiff.'

'Yeah, right.'

Tomos expands. 'Yes. Actually I went on a demo a couple of months ago, with her and her partner. To London. Protesting about the bombing of Afghanistan.'

The smile deserts Wayne's face altogether now. He repeats the monosyllable, but unenthusiastically. 'Right.'

The implication is clear: this isn't a subject upon which minds will meet. There's an awkward silence. Tomos searches for another topic of conversation. 'Er, what do you do with yourself in your spare time?'

Wayne brightens. 'Well, I go to Scouts quite a bit. Not quite as much as I used to though, now I'm going out with Helen.'

'She looks a nice girl,' Tomos says politely, feeling not a little envious.

'Yeah, she's great,' Wayne enthuses, his eyes alight again. 'I'm lucky, I reckon.'

He pauses, debating whether to confide in his brother. 'Only thing is, she's not keen on me joining t' army, so I might try for t' police instead.'

Now it is Tomos's turn to find empathy dulled a little. With a lovely girl like Helen to call his girlfriend, how could he even think about the army? That would mean a lot of separation, surely? Especially if posted overseas? Duw; it might even be to a war zone. How could he do that?

'Yes, well I can imagine the police being quite an interesting career. You'd have good opportunities for promotion, I should think.'

He stops. Hell; am I sounding superior; patronising? He looks at Wayne anxiously, but his brother doesn't seem in any way offended.

'Yeah, that's what I thought,' Wayne says equably. 'It'd certainly beat Tesco's, any day of t' week.'

Tomos nods agreement. He thinks almost anything would beat that. The conversation drifts onto other things as they explore each other for commonalities of interest or outlook, but don't, as far as Tomos is concerned (and he's a little disappointed) find very many. Wayne asks Tomos whether he's got a girlfriend and he has to confess that he hasn't, the admission of which he finds a little humiliating. They talk about their childhoods, exchanging early memories of growing up in such different environments. Wayne seems very impressed by Tomas's bilingualism and he basks modestly in the flattery, although he's always taken it completely for granted, as no big deal.

Wayne gets onto the subject of their mysterious biological mother and rather shocks Tomos with the vehemence of his resentment of her. As far as Tomos is concerned, having a good family, adoptive or otherwise, is all that matters; where he came from is neither here nor there. They speculate as to whom they inherited their red hair from: their real mother or father. They compare notes about being teased about it, and it seems that Wayne's experience is worse.

At five-thirty when they are left, the residue of the day's clientele, and the presumably titular owner of the cafe is making unsubtle signs that she's given up expecting any more customers and wants to close, they make their way back to Wayne's home. Things have become very convivial in their absence, with Sioned and Maureen having joined the men on stronger drink. Poppy and Helen, bored, have crept away to Poppy's bedroom and her new-for-Christmas record player. There are too many people to sit formally down to table, so Maureen conjures up a buffet-style meal of curried turkey, hot sausage rolls, Christmas pudding with ice cream and Christmas cake (the remains of which will be recycled yet again the next day).

Finally, at ten in the evening, a taxi is summoned (Glyn being well past the point of legally-permissible driving) to convey the Rees's to their Bed and Breakfast. It has been, all the adults agree, a wonderful getting-to-know-you.

Tomos lies in bed in the chintzy bedroom of the B and B and takes stock. He's been eagerly anticipating this meeting for the last eighteen days, but now he doesn't quite know how to feel or what to think. He tries to think it through; analyse his reaction. What had he been expecting? A perfect carbon copy; a clone, of himself? Reason says that that would have been unlikely. Impossible, probably. Wayne and he might be genetically identical, and they certainly are astonishingly similar physically, even down to the mannerisms, except for his brother being a touch taller and more stocky of build, but they are separate beings after all (or they are now, anyway – he's read how monozygotic twins come into being). They're now distinct individuals with brains, with personalities that have been moulded by different influences; they've trodden different paths of learning and development.

He wonders what would have happened if his parents had adopted both of them. Would they be so disparate now? Surely not, if they'd been brought up in the same environment? Wayne had said that he wished it had been so. But how does he, Tomos, feel about that? He isn't sure. After all, you can't rerun time and sample an alternative life-line, can you? And the moral outlook thing. He hadn't failed to notice his brother's mute disapproval when he'd mentioned the demo with Lowry. Well, if you'd grown up immersed in outdoor activity and the camaraderie and nascent *patriotism of scouting, which quite often (or so he believed) led on to joining the armed services, you'd be bound to take a different view about going to war.*

But then, that could simply be a different form of idealism really. So perhaps Wayne and he were both idealists, deep down; they had that predisposition in common. It just manifested itself in different ways. And as for Wayne's different intellectual level: well, it was just down to parental influence he supposed. His own parents always encouraged him to do well at school, although they would never, with their political outlook, have sent him to a private one even if they could have afforded to. Perhaps Wayne's parents, although nice people, simply weren't pushy in that way.

On the other hand, he does find Wayne likeable. And the sort who'd be very loyal, he imagines. Perhaps he would have been a nice brother to have had, had things turned out differently sixteen years ago. But that was just conjecture now. Obviously.

And that Helen! Since Wayne and he had returned from the cafe he'd hardly been able to keep his eyes off her, although he'd tried not to be too blatant about it. There was just something about her; the animation in her chestnut eyes, the ready smile never far from her lips, the slightly husky Yorkshire burr to her voice when she spoke, although that hadn't been a great deal. Perhaps she'd felt slightly the odd person out, being the only one present not a member of either family. She isn't ravishingly beautiful, Tomos muses, but she does have a very appealing, earthy and pleasantly plump sort of prettiness, with her funny snub nose and red cheeks (what would you call them; apple cheeks?). And that crazy hair! What's the English expression now; 'looks like it's been pulled through a hedge backwards'?

There's one thing he and his brother have in common anyway, he thinks ruefully: their taste in girls, although this one is very different from that Mair, the girlfriend-who-never-was. Yes Wayne, he thinks, you really are lucky to have a girl like that. Why on earth would you want to go in the army and leave her behind?

But then, he thinks, with a tinge of sadness and disappointment, my brother and I are chalk and cheese really.

Chapter 12
Wayne

At three-thirty on the twenty-seventh of December, Wayne is sitting nervous beside Helen on the sofa in the cosy, warm-as-toast lounge of his parent's house, awaiting the arrival of the guests. He's been waiting for this in a mounting fever-pitch of anticipation for eighteen days now. Suddenly the front door bell chimes. Wayne nearly jumps out of his skin, although they've all been expecting it for the last hour at least (they'd had only a general idea of an ETA). Maureen leaps up from her chair and moves to peep out of the window. There's a red Ford Focus parked outside; she thought she'd heard a vehicle pull up.

'It's them!' she exclaims, exited. She hurries to open the front door. A short dark stocky man is standing on the doorstep. Behind him hover an equally short and tubby woman, middle-aged, brown haired and complementing her husband perfectly, and, several inches taller than either of them, Wayne's double. Her face lights up immediately, creasing into a broad grin. 'Hello! You got here then!' she welcomes, stating the obvious. 'Come in out of the cold!'

She stands aside, eyes going immediately to Tomos, to let them enter, pressing herself against the wall of the narrow hall as they crowd in and stand uncertainly, waiting for her to close the door. She leads the way through into the lounge, as Jim heaves himself to his feet in welcome. Poppy stares, open-mouthed. Helen is blatantly curious too. She emits an audible gasp, quickly trying to suppress it, at the sight of Tomos.

Indeed everyone's eyes are drawn magnetically to the young man in black cord trousers and blue denim jacket, standing awkwardly before them. Wayne stares too; can't help himself. It really is extraordinary. It's like looking in the mirror. He's seeing a doppelganger. A slightly shorter and skinnier carbon copy, true, and this facsimile has longer hair (although exactly the same rufous red). But the face; look at the face! It's Wayne's face: a perfect duplicate. The same freckles, the same wide-ish nose between the same hazel eyes. And, yes, now he's shyly smiling, and it's just the same slightly lop-sided grin.

Jim shakes their hands warmly, lingering over Tomos and looking deep into his eyes as if he just can't believe what he's seeing. Then he remembers his manners and introduces Poppy, Helen and, quite unnecessarily, Wayne. The girls murmur 'hi's' but Wayne is completely dumbstruck. He can't take his eyes off his twin.

At a not-very-subtle-sign from Jim the youngsters vacate the sofa making it available to the visitors; Wayne and Helen relocating side by side next to Jim's armchair opposite the sofa and Poppy next to her mother's chair facing the blazing, roasting coal fire. The visitors shuffle off their coats and hand them to the hovering Maureen, who takes them from the room and then returns to sink with a sigh into her chair. She beams at the visitors sitting adjacent to her, but her eyes are still all for Tomos.

'Well, this is lovely!' She enthuses. 'I just can't get over this! Fancy us meeting after all this time. And especially meeting you, young man! I really can't get over you; you're the spitting image of our Wayne!'

Jim interjects, a little tiredly, 'Yes, well he would be really, Luv, being as how t' boys are identical twins.'

Sioned says, 'Yes, but I've seen identical twins round our way but you can just about tell them apart if you look really closely. But these two; they're just extraordinary.' She hasn't taken her gaze off Wayne either. 'The only thing is, Wayne,' she says, you're just a little bit bigger. I wonder why that is?'

Wayne takes that to be a question directed at him, and replies, with his shy smile, 'Dunno really.'

Jim says, hinting heavily at Maureen, 'Well anyway, what would you good people like to drink, tea or mebbe something stronger?'

Sioned, already on first name terms says, 'Oh I'd love a cup of tea please Maureen,' assuming she'll be the provider of hot drinks.

Glyn, finally able to get a word in, says, 'I'd love a beer if you've got one Jim.'

Jim has of course, in various varieties, and proceeds to apprise Glyn of the selection on offer. With Glyn's preference ascertained he gets up to fetch glasses and cans from the kitchen. All the youngsters opt for tea and Jim returns with glasses and an armful of cans as Maureen rises again to go and put the kettle on. Poppy goes with her, ostensibly to help but actually to talk about Wayne's incredible and exotic identical twin brother. She's never seen the like. She pulls the kitchen door closed and murmurs conspiratorially, 'Isn't he amazing! He's the spit of our Wayne!'

'Yes, unbelievable,' Maureen agrees.

'How can two people be *so* alike?' Poppy wonders.

'I don't know, Luv,' Maureen confesses, as she opens two more packets of mince pies and arranges them on a plate. 'Some twins just are, but others aren't at all.' She thinks she's read somewhere, probably in a women's magazine, why that is, but she's forgotten.

With everyone furnished with drinks and pies, conversation resumes. It quickly returns to the twins. They are, after all, the reason for this visit. Sioned says, 'And you've left school now then, Wayne?'

Wayne mumbles a yes, but he'd rather not enlarge on the topic. He knows what the next question is likely to be: what he's doing job-wise? But Sioned doesn't go there. She knows what he does, from speaking with Maureen on the phone that first time. She probably suspects (well, there's no disguising the fact really) that Wayne is less academically gifted than her Tomos. But she doesn't pursue the question. Instead she brings Helen into the conversation.

'Have you left school as well then Helen?'

Helen, who has been a wallflower up to now, sends silent thanks for the inclusion. She pulls her gaze away from Tomos. 'No, I've stayed on to do A-levels.' But she leaves it at that; doesn't want to expand either, it seems.

Maureen says, 'And what about you Tomos,' (she has to make a conscious effort not to say Thomas) 'Your mum says you're hoping to be a doctor?'

'Well yes, if I do alright with A-levels and get accepted at university,' Tomos says modestly, as if trying to play his aspiration down.

Jim joins in. 'Well, good for you, Tom, we certainly need all the doctors we can get. Don't get me wrong, I've nothing against all the foreign doctors we've got over here – after all, where would t' NHS be without them? – but it'd be good to have more home-grown ones.'

Tomos smiles non-committally and darts a glance at Wayne, who's staring at the coffee table, unwilling to engage. This talk about Helen and his brothers' academic aspirations rankles somewhat. He feels excluded from the conversation, afraid that he has nothing to contribute. He feels a catch of jealousy, although he'd angrily deny it if challenged.

Then Glyn speaks. 'Anyway, we came here so you boys could get to know each other a bit. It's been sixteen years since you last saw each other. I don't suppose either of you can remember each other at all, can you?' He looks first at Wayne and then at Tomos, only half-expectedly.

Sioned sighs; says, 'Well of course they wouldn't remember each other Glyn! They were only babies!'

Wayne ponders that. Tomos's mum is right of course. He doesn't remember his brother, obviously. Or that place, that children's home with a name like a Beatles song. But there is something, not really a memory but just a faint impression, like a tiny far-away voice barely heard, of being in some sort of frightening situation from which he'd been hurriedly withdrawn.

He comes out of his reverie as Jim takes up Glyn's original observation. 'Yes, that were the point of you coming. Wayne, perhaps you and Tom would like some time alone together? What say you two go for a walk or something? Show Tom the wonders of Northallerton.'

Wayne laughs. 'Well that wouldn't take long! Penny's caff might be open though. We could walk down the town and see if she is. It's a bit parky to be walking around.'

'"Caff?" says Tomos, puzzled.

'Yeah, caff – cafe,' Wayne elucidates, surprised that his Welsh brother doesn't know the English slang.

'Oh, right,' Tomos says politely.

To Wayne's great relief, because it would be a bit brass-monkey just traipsing around the streets, Penny's is indeed open. He wonders why she's bothered to though; only two other tables are occupied. A mournful-looking elderly man sits at one with an empty mug at his elbow (perhaps he's there just for the warmth and a modicum of human contact) and a young couple with a small boy are arranged triangularly around another, determinedly working their way through a plate of scones and cakes.

They find themselves a table next to a radiator and shed their coats. Wayne, knowing his manners, orders teas and Yorkshire parkin for his guest. Tomos remarks that it's quite like a similar Welsh delicacy: bara brith. Now it's Wayne's turn to look puzzled, so Tomos translates: speckled (because of the dried fruit) bread.

They sit on opposite sides of the small round red gingham table clothed table, hands wrapped around mugs, taking each other in. Helen had wanted to come too, but Maureen had gently suggested that, this first time, the boys might prefer to be alone together. Wayne breaks the rather awkward silence that has fallen since the food small talk.

'Well I just can't get over this: us being identical twins an' all, can you?'

Tomos agrees. 'Yes, it was a pretty amazing discovery. I don't know why my parents didn't tell me sooner. About being adopted and having a twin as well. Then we could have tracked you down before now.'

'Yeah, true. Poppy and me have known about the adopted thing for over a year now, but not about me having a twin.'

Tomos says, 'It's funny how it's worked out, isn't it? Just think, my parents went to that children's home before yours, when we were there *together, and if they'd decided they wanted both of us, we'd have stayed brothers and been brought up together. That's quite a thought isn't it?'*

Wayne grins. 'Certainly is! I always wanted a brother really. Poppy's alright, she's a good kid, but she's just at that awkward age now, you know? She's a pain in t' neck sometimes, quite honestly.'

Tomos also smiles, relaxing a little. 'Yes, my sister went through a phase like that too. In fact it was a long phase with her; lasted until she was eighteen and went to uni!'

The smile on Wayne's face slips just a fraction. Bloody hell; here we go again! He forces himself to be civil. 'Your sister though; she's a lot older than you, isn't she?'

'Yes, nine years. And she's my parent's biological daughter. Although my parents treat us equally; always have done.'

'That's good,' Wayne says approvingly. 'It would be horrible if they favoured her. Do you get on well with her, her being so much older and everything?'

'Yes, I do really. Although she's left home now, anyway. She teaches at the uni she went to, in Cardiff.'

'Yeah, right.' Wayne wishes he'd stop talking about sodding university.

But Tomos expands. 'Yes. Actually I went on a demo a couple of months ago, with her and her partner. To London. Protesting about the bombing of Afghanistan.'

The smile deserts Wayne's face altogether now. He repeats the monosyllable, but unenthusiastically. 'Right.'

He feels any newly-discovered sibling affection evaporating. Oh, really, he thinks darkly. One of those, are you? What do they call them now; conscientious objectors or something? You think we should just stand by and let these murdering terrorists do what the hell they like, do you?

There's another awkward silence. Wayne feels disinclined to talk. But they can't just sit and say nothing. Tomos searches for another topic of conversation. 'Er, what do you do with yourself in your spare time?'

Wayne brightens a little. 'Well, I go to Scouts quite a bit. Not quite as much as I used to though, now I'm going out with Helen.'

'She looks a nice girl,' Tomos says politely.

'Yeah, she's great,' Wayne enthuses; his eyes alight again, back on uncontentious ground. 'I'm lucky, I reckon.'

He pauses, debating whether to confide in his brother. 'Only thing is, she's not keen on me joining t' army, so I might try for t' police instead.'

'Yes, well I can imagine the police being quite an interesting career,' Tomos says rather icily.' You'd have good opportunities for promotion, I

should think.'

'Yeah, that's what I thought,' Wayne says levelly. He hasn't failed to spot the tone of Tomos's voice. 'It'd certainly beat Tesco's, any day of t' week.'

Tomos nods agreement; makes no comment. The conversation drifts onto other things as they explore each other for commonalities of interest or outlook, but don't, as far as Wayne is concerned (and he's a little irritated by it) find very many. Wayne asks Tomos whether he's got a girlfriend and gets a curt, lets-not-go-there, 'No'. They talk about their childhoods, exchanging early memories of growing up in such different environments. Wayne has to admit to himself that he's impressed by Tomas's bilingualism, and tells him so. He can't really get his head around the idea of a part of Britain speaking another language, and is astonished when Tomos says that his perfectly-spoken (and better than Wayne's, actually) English is his second language, and waves the flattery aside as if it's no big deal.

Wayne gets onto the subject of their mysterious biological parents.

'Do you know owt about our real mum and dad?' He stares at his brother, hoping he knows more than he does, which is bugger-all, really.

Tomos smiles wryly; shrugs. 'No, very little. They seem to be a complete enigma.' He notices Wayne's blank, faintly hostile gaze. 'Er, a total mystery. I think my parents know nothing about them. All they know is: we two were abandoned. In a ladies toilet in Liverpool. You weren't told that then?'

Wayne's eyes are wide; irises perfect white-bordered orbs.

'What?'

'Yes, apparently so. That's what my parents were told.'

'Bloody HELL!'

Wayne's voice has risen, angry. The couple with the child cast disapproving glances in their direction.

Tomos semaphores him to keep his voice down. 'Well they just don't know really I suppose, if we were foundlings. There may not even have been a couple. Perhaps just a woman. Or a teenage girl who just couldn't cope. Who knows?'

Wayne's face is drained, stricken. 'Jesus Christ! The bitch! So we were just dumped, like? Like a litter of unwanted pups or summat?'

Tomos is rather shocked by the vehemence of his resentment. 'Well, as I say, no-one seems to know the facts. But it sounds as if it was probably a pretty desperate situation. Perhaps we shouldn't judge them or her too harshly.'

'Judge?' Wayne cuts in, furious. 'Why the hell not? It's diabolical! Don't you think so?' He glares at his brother, daring him to disagree.

Tomos raises palms in supplication. 'Yes, of course it was. But we did okay, as it turned out, didn't we? We ended up with good adoptive parents who love us. Well I certainly did. Didn't you?' He looks at Wayne, anxious that it might not be so.

Wayne is slightly mollified. 'Yeah, right. Us did. Can't complain, really.'

He grins, but with teeth gritted. 'But even so, the thought of it. Being just chucked away like that. Not wanted.'

'Yes, I know,' Tomos sympathises. They lapse into private silences.

Tomos picks up the conversation. They speculate as to whom they inherited their red hair from: their real mother or father. They compare notes about being teased about it, and it seems to Wayne that his experience has been worse.

At five-thirty, when Penny ejects them from the cafe, they make their way back to Wayne's home to find the adults getting along famously. Helen casts slightly accusatory looks at Wayne when she reappears from Poppy's bedroom. Maureen, with Helen's help, conjures up her buffet-style meal.

Finally, at ten in the evening, a taxi is summoned to convey the very mellow Rees's and their son to their Bed and Breakfast. It has been, Jim and Maureen agree too, a wonderful getting-to-know-you.

Wayne walks Helen back home. They walk briskly, hand in hand, as the temperature has dropped even further and it's too cold to hang around. There'll be a hard frost in the morning. They seem to have hardly spoken to each other since the Rees's arrived.

'So what do you think of your brother then?' Helen asks.

'He's alright,' says Wayne, trying to feel enthusiastic.

Helen looks at him sharply. 'Is that it? Just "alright?" This is your long-lost brother for goodness sake!'

'Yeah, well, he's more different than I thought he'd be.'

'Different? He's the spit of you!'

'Yes I know. He is, ent he? Even got t' same grin. But I meant in character. Well, what do you call it? Outlook, or something.'

'How do you mean?' Helen sounds slightly peeved. 'I expect you two have had a good chat, but I didn't get a look-in. I don't know why I couldn't have come to the caff with you too. I've been bored out of my brain.'

Wayne ignores that barb. 'Well we're not very alike as people. He was telling me he'd been on a demo about us bombing Afghanistan. He's obviously one of the anti-war brigade.'

Helen goes quiet. Then she says, cautiously, 'He's got a right to his opinion though. A lot of people are against it. My mum and dad are. They think it won't do any good; might even make things worse.'

'Well okay, I suppose he has,' Wayne concedes, but grudgingly. 'But I've got a right to mine too. At least I care about what happens to my country! And I think Al Qaeda has to be stopped; murdering bastards. Look what they did in America.'

Helen tries conciliation. 'Alright, so you don't agree about that. But apart from that, you're pretty similar aren't you?'

Wayne is still in curmudgeonly-mode though. 'Dunno about that, really. He's a lot brainier than me. Wanting to be a doctor an' all.'

'So what's wrong with that? At least he's got some ambition!'

'Yeah, and I have too!' Wayne retorts. 'It's just different to Tomos's!'

'Okay, calm down Wayne!' Helen soothes, although there's a sharp tang to the placating words.

The rest of the walk is completed in ill-tempered silence sparsely punctuated by desultory small talk. Why can't Wayne have a bit more of the drive and intelligence of Tomos? Helen wonders. What has he got that I haven't, Wayne frets, resentment gnawing like a toothache. They reach her house and hover uncertainly outside. It's too late for Wayne to be invited in really and he doesn't feel particularly inclined to be amorous tonight anyway. They kiss goodnight with a level of intensity just above perfunctory, Helen goes inside and Wayne trudges back home.

The Rees's return the following morning, for their leave taking. Glyn and Sioned thank their hosts profusely for their hospitality and promise to stay in touch. A reciprocal invitation to visit is given, perhaps for Easter. Wayne and Tomos eye each other, slightly warily. Wayne has no idea what his brother might be thinking, but he isn't too sure how he feels about things. He doesn't want to be disappointed, but it's there, lurking, like an unwelcome gatecrasher at a party. How different it might have been if they'd grown up together, like proper brothers, but with the added bond of being identical twins. Gone to scouts together, been real mates, looked out for each other. Instead they've grown up separately and become very different people. This Tomos (and it's a bloody silly name; why couldn't he just be called Tom?) is no more like him, apart from in looks, than Poppy is, really.

He really isn't sure whether he wants to stay in touch, particularly. But he and Tomos mumble the expected pleasantries, not quite making eye contact, and Wayne's brother and his parents climb into their flashy one-year-old Ford Focus, and the Harrisons wave them off, back to Wales and their very different lives.

Part two

Chapter 13
Wayne

Wayne had made his mind up. He couldn't stand much more of Tesco's. It was all such a bore, and his supervisor had begun to notice his lack of application. Twice now he'd gone into the storeroom and come out with a load of stock, only to find the shelves already nearly full. It had happened again yesterday. Puzzled, he'd checked his list again and finally it had dawned on him that he'd completely misread it. How could you mistake chicken for vegetarian chickpea soup? For crying out bloody loud! Mind not on the job, that was the problem. Cross with himself, he'd returned the stock, slamming it down and reloading the trolley with the chicken.

'Get out of t' bed the wrong side today, did we?' Christine Wallace had asked, sarcastically.

'No,' he'd mumbled, 'just picked up t' wrong stock that's all.'

'Well sharpen up a bit, sunshine, will you?' Christine could be a right cow sometimes. 'There's plenty of others who'd gladly do your job if you don't want it.'

Wayne had bitten his tongue, before words like *well they can bloody have it if they want* came out, and quietly seethed. She'd had it in for him (he'd no idea why) ever since he'd joined the payroll back in August, and it was now March, nearly his birthday, and he'd had to put up with her bullying for six months. So he'd made his mind up. On his next day off he was going to the police station to enquire about recruiting.

The sergeant on the reception desk looked at Wayne slightly askance, as if he were taking the Mickey. 'You can't walk in here off the street and join just like that, lad.'

Wayne was deflated. 'Oh; what do I do then?'

The sergeant rootled around beneath the desk. 'Well I can give you all the guff about it if you want. It tells you how to apply and everything.'

'Right,' Wayne said, 'thank you.'

The sergeant looked at him again. 'How old are you, lad?'

'Seventeen. Well, seventeen in a week's time.'

'Ah. Well you're too young anyway. You've got to be eighteen.'

Wayne's face fell. 'Oh,' he said aloud. Inwardly he said, *Oh, bugger!*

'Never mind,' the sergeant said kindly. 'It's only a year to wait. If you want it badly enough you can wait that long. And you look a bright lad. It's a good career. What do you do at the moment?'

'Work in Tesco's' Wayne said, embarrassed to admit it.

'Right; okay then. I'll give you the stuff to look through anyway. Stick at your job because it'll look good on your application, and come back to us in a year's time.'

Wayne thanked the policeman and left. *Another year to wait!* He thought disconsolately as he trudged home. *I really don't think I can wait that long. And I don't think I can stick it at Tesco's much longer either. So what to do? Maybe try and find another job; something a little more exciting. Then maybe try and make myself wait to join the police.* Changing his mind, he walked back to the town centre and the Jobcentre. There was no harm in looking for something. He sat and waited for a computer to become free and looked through the vacancies. There was very little going really. Well, for the totally unskilled in anything, anyway. There were bricklayer's jobs, and someone wanted an apprentice plumber. But he didn't fancy that.

And then he spotted it. A job as a lifeguard at the leisure centre. Yes! He could do that alright. He was a strong swimmer. That was more like it! He quite fancied himself diving gallantly into the pool to rescue someone in distress (especially a girl). Think of the kudos that would bring. He'd be a hero. It was a perfect job, tailor-made for him! Excitedly, he sat and waited again for an advisor to become available. When his turn came he told the young woman which job he was interested in. She looked at him through her wire-framed spectacles, barely managing to suppress a weary sigh.

'Yes, okay, we've had a lot of interest in that one.' Her tone didn't sound terribly encouraging. 'Have you got any lifesaving qualifications?'

Wayne was taken aback. He hadn't expected that. 'Well, no, not really.'

She frowned. 'Okay. Any in swimming then?'

He began to form the word 'no' but caught himself in time. 'I've got some medals from scouts?' he offered.

She was clearly unimpressed. 'No, I meant more . . . competitive than that? Most of us can swim,' she added; a touch patronisingly.

Wayne had to admit that he hadn't, irritated that scouting awards seemingly counted for nothing.

'Okay then,' the advisor said. 'Well you can apply if you want to, but to be perfectly honest, the Sports and Leisure Department is looking for qualifications really. They have to consider public safety, you understand? And there are a couple of applications in from people older than you who do have diplomas in lifesaving.'

Her voice softened in sympathy. She'd dealt with many young hopefuls over the last few days; fit young men and women who had been drawn to this job like wasps to a jam jar. 'I do think you'd be wasting your time really. Are you sure there's nothing else we've got that might interest you?'

'No, there ent,' Wayne said, not even trying to keep the hurt and indignation out of his voice. He thought that he was perfectly well qualified for the job, with his scouting background and everything. He got up, gave the advisor a sullen 'Thanks' and left.

That evening, as they lay together on her bed, he was ill-tempered and out of sorts. 'Well when you think about it,' she said reasonably, 'You don't see policemen that young, do you?'

'No, of course you bloody don't. But there's training first. You don't go out on t' beat straightaway!'

'Even so, the training doesn't last that long, does it? You'd still be under eighteen by the time you trained, probably. How many eighteen-year-old policemen do you see around?'

'No, well; not many, I grant you. But I don't see why not. What does age matter anyway, as long as you're fit and keen to do the job? And as long as you're a good driver?'

Helen snorted. 'Yeah, well, how many teenagers actually *are* good drivers? They might think they are, especially the lads, but being fast isn't the same as being safe. And besides, there's the dealing with people and situations thing. You've got to be pretty mature to do that, I would have thought. Be able to use your initiative.'

'Well I'm mature, I reckon! Scouting teaches you that!'

'Maybe. But they obviously think seventeen's not old enough.

Couldn't you just wait another year and a bit?'

'No I bloody couldn't! Staying at Tesco's much longer will really do my head in!'

'Well then,' Helen said, trying to maintain calm, 'all you can do is keep on the lookout for something better, isn't it? A year will soon pass!'

Wayne wasn't convinced. 'No it won't,' he grumbled. I'd have to wait 'til at least next March. That's ages away.'

They fell silent. After a while Wayne said, 'It's a shame about that lifeguard's job, an' all. I could have done that alright.'

Helen squeezed his arm. 'Yes, it is. Maybe you could train for something like that; get the qualifications. What do you reckon?'

Wayne sighed. 'Yeah, but how could I? I'd have to stop work. Ask Mum and Dad to start supporting us again. And I'd have no money. I don't see how I could do that.'

'No, I suppose not.' Helen wished she could suggest something else helpful. But she could think of nothing.

'Well there's only one other thing,' said Wayne. There was an edge of defiance in his voice.

Helen felt her heart sink. She knew what was coming. 'You don't mean . . .'

'Yeah. The Yorkshires.'

There it was, the bald statement; spoken with no offer of negotiation, no accommodation, no compromise.

Helen felt as if she'd been slapped. 'So . . . you're going in the army?'

'Yeah. Well there's nowt else. And any road; you were just saying about training. The army trains you on t' job.'

Helen laughed mirthlessly. 'Oh yes; it does that alright. Trains you how to kill! That's a hell of a skill to have, isn't it!'

Wayne was affronted. 'No, don't say it like that! There's lots of things besides that; lots of things you can learn. Lots of trades.'

'Really? The Yorkshires are infantry, aren't they? They just shoot guns. What trades?' Her sarcasm was palpable.

'Well, I dunno,' Wayne admitted. 'I'd have to check it out.'

'But you don't really want that do you! You just want the playing soldiers bit, running round shooting people, don't you! Admit it!'

'No, it bloody ent just that!' Wayne could feel the familiar rage welling up. Why did talk about soldiering always end in a row like this? 'It's about defending the country. Somebody's got to! There's that bloke in Iraq; Sadam Hussein. He's got those weapons of mass destruction, so t' Government reckons. He's got to be stopped. And there's Afghanistan. So have the buggers there. Surely you can see that!'

'No I can't see that at all. My dad doesn't think it's true about the weapons. Well, the paper he reads doesn't anyway. He reckons they just want to invade Iraq because of the oil.'

'Well that's just bollocks,' Wayne retorted. 'Which paper does he read, the bloody *Guardian*?'

'Yes he does, actually. So which does yours read? One of the right wing crappy tabloids, I'll bet. Yes I know he does. I've seen it by his chair!'

She tried another tack. 'But don't you worry about the danger? I would! Worry for you, I mean!'

But Wayne brushed that aside, confident in his airy bravado. 'That's just the risk you have to take sometimes. Soldiers know that when they join up. Goes with the territory. Everybody can't just sit at home leaving to the others.'

'So you've absolutely made your mind up this time, have you? You'd rather have your sodding army than me?'

He looked at her, shocked. 'It's not a choice is it?'

Helen's tears were flowing, bitter, now. 'Why, Wayne? Don't you like what we've got? Don't you think it's special?'

'Yes, of course I do! But why can't I have what I want to do and you an' all? Why not? Why won't you support me in this?'

Helen got up, angrily shucking off his arm from across her stomach. 'You just don't get it do you! You want to have your cake and eat it! Go off and have your stupid dangerous adventures and crawl back home to the faithful little girlfriend now and then for rest and recuperation and oats; never mind that she's worrying herself fucking sick over you! You're just selfish, Wayne Harrison. Selfish! Selfish!'

Wayne sat up too. His arm went around her shoulder. 'Aw, come on Baby! Don't be like that! You know you mean a lot more to me than that!'

She wriggled out of his arm again, furious. 'Do I now! I mean so much that you'd rather be off risking your life in your bloody army than with me, it seems! Well you can just piss off then!'

'You don't mean that!'

Helen sat forward, forehead against her raised knees, hands in her wild black hair. When her voice came again it was calmer; resigned. 'Oh yes I do. Why can't you be more like your brother; have aspirations like him? Why can't you want to do something important with your life?'

'Oh, right; so defending my country from the bad guys isn't important then? And don't bring bloody Tomos into it!'

'Alright, I won't. Well, you obviously think what you want is the most important thing, whatever I think about it. And I can't do anything to change your mind. So really you'd better just go.'

'What; now?'

Her voice was a whisper. 'Yes; now.'

Helen put on her pyjamas and got into bed. She pulled the duvet over her head, shutting out the world. She didn't want to think. Didn't want to replay Wayne's angry leaving, her parent's raised, surprised voices and the sound of the front door slamming shut. Didn't want to think about what she'd just done; the ramifications of it. But the dismal thoughts came anyway; they wouldn't be denied.

So that's it. Goodbye Wayne. Oh bloody hell! Should I have sent him away like that? I don't know. But I couldn't bear the thought of him being a soldier. The danger of it. I don't think he realises how much there is. When you're sent to war anyway. He probably thinks it's all some exciting adventure, like young lads always do. He's right I suppose, in his way; as he sees it there's an enemy out there that has to be defeated and he wants to be heroic. Well let someone else do that, if they want to, not him! It's not like the country's going to be invaded, is it? That'd be different. Of course he'd want to go then. I'd be proud of him then. I think. But this Iraq thing. And Afghanistan. They're not the same. Dad's paper doesn't think so anyway.

And apart from that, there's the separation. I'd never see him. Well, I won't see him at all now. Oh well; there's other fish in the sea. Somebody else will come along. They're bound to. Oh Wayne! Why couldn't you have been like your brother? Why did you turn out so different? Tomos isn't rushing to join the army because he can't think of anything else to do. He knows what he wants and he's going for it. And he has principles. I wish I could have gone on that demo to London. They looked great, seeing them on telly. I bet most of the people there were students. Well, it's what students do. Try to change the world and everything. I wonder if I'll be a student one day?

The thoughts chased each other around in her head as she tossed and turned, longing for sleep and oblivion. She tried to empty her brain but it was impossible. She tried to think of happy things, but nothing sprang to mind. Well what was there to be happy about, anyway? The thought suddenly hit home. *I've just finished with my boyfriend. Now I've got no one. I'm alone again. What'll I do?*

And finally her self control crumbled. She surrendered to bitter self-pitying tears; sobbing as though her world had fallen in.

Wayne wandered home in a daze. He couldn't believe what had just happened. Helen, lovely sweet Helen, had kicked him out. Told him to go. Given him his marching orders. He smiled grimly at the irony of the phrase. She didn't want him anymore. Just because he'd finally decided to follow his dream. She'd made him chose between the army and her. How could she do that, if she really cared for him? How could she be so selfish and cruel? Well okay then, he *would* bloody choose if that was how she felt. And it wouldn't be her. Selfish cow! He'd be down to York on his next day off and straight into the recruiting place; to hell with her. He'd walked by the window of it many a time and gazed longingly at the displays there. This time he'd damn-well take the bull by the horns. He wasn't going to let anyone come between him and doing what he wanted to do.

But then the enormity of what had happened sank in. *I'm alone. I've just been thrown over. I haven't got a girlfriend any more. Christ, what will I do?* Self-pity overwhelmed him quite as completely as it was doing Helen, as he walked away from her, leaving her in his past. He felt his throat catch painfully, almost choking him. And then the bitter tears came.

He lay in bed thinking about the future. Well he might be girlfriendless now, but he was free to do what he wanted. And he couldn't wait. To hell with the police. He wasn't going to waste another year buggering about waiting to join them. His mate David reckoned the army was a good life, anyway. Hard, yes; the basic training was tough, but then it had to be. He could handle that alright, no problem. And the discipline. Scouts trained you for it, after all. He smiled, remembering a story David had told about his first night in training camp. The sergeant was a right bastard apparently and had threatened to have their guts for garters if their beds weren't absolutely perfectly made when he inspected in the morning, so they'd all slept on the floor leaving the immaculately made beds that had awaited them unsullied, as they didn't trust themselves to be able to meet the sergeant's exacting standards (well, they were used to having mums for stuff like that: bed making). But then when the sergeant had discovered them sleeping on the floor they'd got a bollocking anyway!

He knew he'd have to get his parents' consent though, as he was under eighteen. Bugger it. What a stupid, neither-here-nor-there age seventeen was! You felt like a man (well you were shaving regularly now and doing all the other stuff, including – until a few hours ago at least – getting your end away), but you weren't considered 'mature' enough to join up! Ridiculous! So you had to be a kid still and ask your parents! He thought his dad might be okay about it (after all, he'd encouraged him to join the Scouts, and this was only like that but more so, really) but he wasn't quite so sure about his mum. Women were so stupid and lacking in understanding of men sometimes. But maybe she'd come round.

So he planned his big ask for the following evening. It would have to be at tea time, when they were all sitting quietly together at table, before the telly came on and starting a conversation became a losing battle. He toyed with his Irish stew nervously, waiting for an opportunity, waiting for his dad to stop blathering on about some difficult patient they'd had to deal with that day (some old dear who was a bit senile and had kept trying to get off the trolley as they wheeled her to X-ray, apparently). Finally there was a pause, the subject closed, and he leapt in.

He looked at his father. 'I'm going to leave Tesco's.'

Jim looked up sharply, mid-mouthful; chewed to clear the way for speech. 'Oh; why's that?'

Wayne faltered; his nerve threatening to evaporate. 'Cos I'm bored with it.' The reason sounded pathetic.

'Well a lot of jobs are boring, lad. Mine is sometimes.' Jim looked at Wayne quizzically. 'So what are you going to do instead?'

'Well I want to go in t' army.'

He sensed Maureen's sharp intake of breath on his left, but kept his gaze fixed on his father, his ally. Or so he hoped.

Jim said levelly, 'So what's suddenly brought this idea on?'

'It's not a sudden thing. Been thinking about it for ages.'

Maureen spoke. 'But why do you want to do that, luv? What's wrong with Tesco's? It's a nice steady job you know.'

He couldn't bring himself to look at her. 'I just said. It's boring. And the pay's crap.'

Jim said sharply, 'Don't speak to your mother like that! And watch your language!'

'Sorry. But it is. It's boring, doing the same thing every day, and the pay *is* rubbish.'

'Yeah, well, if you leave school with no qualifications what do you expect? You're not in much of a position to command high wages are you lad?'

Maureen began to say, 'Unlike your . . .' but thought better of voicing the sentence; left it unsaid.

Wayne pretended not to notice. 'But that's the thing about t' army. You can learn a trade. Learn on the job, like. And earn good money while you're doing it.'

Jim said, 'So what do you reckon you'd do? Learn, I mean?'

'Dunno. Maybe become a mechanic. The First Yorkshires is armoured.'

'But you can learn to be a mechanic in Civvy Street,' Maureen protested. 'You don't need to go the army to do that!'

'Yeah, but the training's better in t' army. So they reckon, anyway. And besides, I might learn it in Civvy Street and then not get a job at the end of it!'

Maureen tried a different angle. 'But what about Helen? What does she think about all this? You'd be apart a lot, I imagine. It wouldn't be very nice for her, would it?'

'Well it doesn't matter what Helen thinks. Not now. We've split.'

Maureen looked shocked. 'Oh Wayne; I'm sorry!' She was silent for a moment. Then: 'Because you want to go in the army?'

'Yeah. She didn't like the idea at all. She wouldn't support me. So we've finished,' Wayne answered bitterly.

'So you chose the army over her, did you luv?'

'Wayne shifted uncomfortably. 'Well, yeah. She just didn't understand.'

'Understand what?' Jim put in.

'Well, that I need to do this. Want to. Someone's got to stop the terrorists. I want to do something with my life, something for my country, not waste my times at Tesco's!'

'So your mind's made up, is it lad?'

'Yeah. And if you won't let me go in now I'll just wait until I'm eighteen, then you can't stop me!'

Wayne looked at his father, defiantly, hopefully, anxiously.

Jim returned his stare. His expression was unfathomable.

He spoke. 'Well I can't fault you for being patriotic, lad. If it's what you really want to do, I won't stand in your way.' He glanced at Maureen. 'I don't know what your mother thinks.'

Maureen sighed. 'Well, you're going to do it anyway, aren't you, regardless of what us silly worrying women think about it. Men always do. I won't hold you back. Do the basic training anyway; then see how you feel about it all. I should have known when you joined the scouts it would lead to this. It often does. But just please be careful, won't you? Please!'

Wayne exhaled a long sigh of relief. 'Yes, of course I will Mum. 'Course I will.'

The smiling, balding, middle-aged recruiting officer at the centre in York was a lot more positive than the police had been. He sat Wayne down and put him at his ease; didn't ask awkward or difficult questions. It didn't feel like an interview at all really, just like a friendly chat. He wanted to know a little of Wayne's background. Had he been in the cadets at all, or anything similar? No, Wayne had to admit, but he'd been in the Scouts since the age of nine. The officer nodded approval at that. 'Good, good. So you know about taking orders, working as a team and respecting authority then.'

'Oh, yes Sir!' Wayne confirmed eagerly.

The officer smiled condescendingly. 'Fine. But you needn't call me Sir. You haven't joined us yet, er,' he glanced at his notes, 'Wayne.'

'Oh, sorry, er,' Wayne floundered.

The officer was still beaming. 'I'm Captain Bainbridge to my friends.'

He went on, 'Now I have to ask you this Wayne; it's nothing personal. Have you ever been in trouble with the police? Anything involving violence?'

'Oh, no Sir, er, Captain! Never!' Wayne replied, not a little offended by the very thought.

Captain Bainbridge repeated 'Good, good.' He seemed quite satisfied with Wayne's credentials already. 'Splendid,' he added, as if for good measure.

As if the application process were now considered over, he went on to describe life in the modern army: the camaraderie, the sense that it was like a big extended family, that you looked out for your mates, as they did you. That there was training available, free, if you wanted it that would stand you in good stead in later civilian life. That it was dangerous, yes, sometimes, if you were in a combat zone, but every precaution was taken to maximise safety, and if you did become a casualty the medical treatment available was the best in the world. 'Only the best, *for* the best in the world!' he said with an evangelical gleam in his piercing blue eyes. Wayne had noticed the colour. Well, he could hardly fail to, as he was watching this role model with such rapt attention.

Wayne listened avidly, basking in the notion of joining such an elite body of people. But then his mind began to wander, fantasising, imagining the adrenaline high of combat; perhaps the selfless heroism of recuing fallen comrades; the relaxation and chaffing over a beer later back at base; the proud head-held-high marching through streets lined with cheering flag-waving townspeople on return from tour. Yes, he wanted some of this. . .

He suddenly became aware that the captain was speaking again.

'. . . you do understand that your parents have to give consent to your joining us, as you're under eighteen?'

'Oh, yes, Captain. They're all for it!' Well, his father was guardedly pleased at any rate, but that would surely count as approval.

The officer was still smiling. 'Good. Splendid. Well take all the bumph home with you to read, and perhaps your father could come back with you to do the signing on the dotted line when you're ready. Is that alright?

'Yes Captain!' Wayne beamed. It certainly *was* alright.

He bumped into Helen eight days later, in the High Street, as he was coming off the early shift in mid-afternoon. He was sauntering along, gaze fixed unseeing on the ground, mind miles away engaged in something heroic in some Middle-Eastern combat zone, when he almost actually did. He looked up and there she was two metres away, emerging from a group of people in front of him, her head down too, coming towards him on a collision course unless he took evasive action. He moved to the right, nearly falling off the kerb into the road. As she was about to draw level she raised her head too. It was too late for either to take cover in a shop doorway to avoid embarrassment. But neither could they simply walk on by.

They stopped, uncertainly, neither really wanting to meet the other's eye.

Wayne spoke first. 'Hi, Helen.'

She shifted uncomfortably. 'Hello Wayne.'

'How's it going?'

'Okay. You?'

'Yeah. Good.'

'Right. What've you been doing with yourself?'

'Oh, you know. The usual.' He knew very well what she was asking without actually saying the words. He'd just have to come right out and say it. 'I've signed up. Dad came with me last Saturday to do it.'

He'd been looking at her furtively, trying to gauge her reaction. She looked up too. Her eyes were glistening. When she spoke her voice was flat, expressionless. 'I see. So what happens now?'

'I wait for a bit, until t' next cohort is ready to go for basic training, at Catterick.'

'Yes. And what do you do until then?'

'Keep on working at Tesco's. As soon as I know when t' army wants me, I can give in my notice.'

She didn't reply. Her head went down again to study the pavement. She was making it difficult for him.

He wanted to tell her all about it, share his bubbling excitement with her. But knew he couldn't. It would fall on deaf ears. The silence dragged on. He knew he'd have to break it.

'Right. Okay then. I'll have to go. Things to do. See you around then?'

'Yeah. Right. Bye then.' Her voice was little more than a whisper.

She gave him another quick glance, and now her eyes were shedding fat blobby tears onto her redder-than-usual cheeks. She didn't bother to wipe them away. Simply walked away from him, head down again, defeated. He looked after her, at her hunched unhappy figure. He wanted to run after her, stop her leaving him like that; plead with her to be happy for him, thrilled for him. Give him love and support. But it was too late; much too late.

His happiness shattered, *his* eyes pricking too, he trudged home.

Chapter 14
Tomos

Sioned looked at her son anxiously. He was slumped on the sofa gazing vacantly at the television, clearly not taking its delights in.
'All right, Bach?'
He gave her a thin smile. 'Yeah, thanks Mam.'
Well he certainly didn't look it. If this was what volunteering in India during your gap year did for you, they could keep it. It wasn't worth making yourself ill over. But that was her Tomos all over; mainly at his sister's instigation (again!) he'd agitated to spend a few weeks as a medical volunteer in Madurai, in Tamil Nadu. She and Glyn had been a little surprised that not only had they had to pay his airfare but also a fairly hefty sum to cover his board and lodging and other expenses too. But they'd found the money, willingly. It was a once-in-a-lifetime experience for him, after all.
And how could they have said no, anyway? After all, it was a good and appropriate way to spend some of the hiatus between leaving school and going up to university, as he was going to do medicine. It would be a valuable experience in more ways than one. It had been a shame though that right at the end of his placement he'd caught a heavy cold, of all things to get in India! It could have been worse though; at least he'd been able to complete his stay there. And he'd really enjoyed his time at the hospital and staying with his guests.
'How's your throat now? Still as sore?'
His voice was a little husky, although perhaps not quite as much as when he'd first arrived back home, looking more than a little sorry for himself.
'A little better. Doesn't hurt quite so much.'
Sioned wasn't altogether convinced. 'Yes, well, I still think you should go to the doctor with it. It looks like more than just a cold to me. Besides, you wouldn't expect to get a cold in a place like India, would you?'
Tomos sounded a touch patronising. 'Colds aren't caused by *being* cold Mam! They're virus infections. They just happen more

often in winter because the bugs spread more easily.'

Sioned wouldn't be fobbed off though. 'Well, whatever it is: cold, throat infection; you get yourself to the doctor if it doesn't clear up soon, alright?'

'Yes, okay, I will,' Tomos replied, tiredly.

But there was no need to; it did get better. The soreness lessened during the next few days. Tomos was all for volunteering again, but Sioned put her foot down. He was over eighteen now and legally could do as he pleased, but she worried about him returning to a disease-ridden place like India. (You heard of such dreadful illnesses being caught over there, like leprosy and such-like.) Besides, there was the cost. They weren't made of money. She sought the support of Glyn, who agreed that another thousand pounds or so for more funding was out of the question. Tomos had had a taste of volunteering; had sampled altruism for a short while, anyway. Now he must begin thinking of his training and his path in life.

On the other hand he had to do something with the rest of his gap year. They didn't want to be miserly and clip their son's wings altogether. Sioned had an idea. Tomos could complete his year in Houston, Texas. Her brother Huw was a pharmacist there in a large hospital, private of course, and would probably offer his nephew a little work experience for a few months. He'd offered it before, actually, but Tomos had preferred the Indian opportunity. There'd only be the cost of another return air ticket; he'd be able to stay with Huw free. It would be a far cry from India, but all the same another window on the world and a chance to sample life in America. Talk about two extremes! So what did he think about it now? Yes, fine, Tomos said. He'd like it.

Sioned put in an international call to Huw. Huw said yes, the offer still stood. It was November now; get Christmas out of the way and he could start in the New Year. And so it was all arranged.

Lowri phoned at the beginning of December to invite Tomos to Cardiff for a weekend after the university closed for the Christmas break.

'Come on Bach,' she said (she still tended to mother him a bit sometimes; still used the endearments his mother did, as if he were still a child), 'It'll give you a break; get you out from under Mam's feet for a while. We'll paint the town red. What do you say?'

She was becoming more and more anglicised in her speech of late, he noticed, her conversations laced more and more and more liberally with English idioms, spoken in English, making her speech sometimes jumpy and disjointed. It was the sophistication of living and working in the capital, he supposed. She was forgetting her roots. He didn't altogether approve of that and wondered what his grandfather would have made of it. Not a lot, probably. But he fancied the idea of a weekend in Cardiff, all the same. He still thought the world of his big sister (and he'd always regard her as 'big', because she was so much older, even though he towered lankily over her now); she would always be a role model. And besides, she and Will were going to his parents for Christmas, so he wouldn't get to see her for ages, probably. He wanted to tell her all about India.

'Yes, great,' he said. 'Like to.'

'Wonderful! The Manics are gracing us with their presence in a couple of weeks before starting their UK tour. We could take in their gig if you want.'

'Love it! Diolch Lowri!'

He'd always liked the Manic Street Preachers; aped his sister in admiring their leftist attitudes. He wasn't interested in vacuous music; it had to be radical, have meaning, have an idealistic edge. And they were Welsh boys. Not from Ceredigion, true, but the next best thing to local heroes all the same.

'Okay then Cariad. We'll do that.' Lowri sounded pleased, almost suspiciously so. 'I'll see about some tickets. Bring yourself here the weekend after next then.'

So twelve days later he found himself sitting on the sofa (having first cleared a space in order to be able to) in Lowri's cluttered, chaotic flat. He smiled to himself. *Nothing changes!* He wondered how Will put up with it. But then, presumably, he wasn't the tidiest person in the known universe either, otherwise he and Lowri would never have got on.

Lowri proffered a scalding-hot mug of coffee, keeping the handle herself, obliging him to wrap his fingers, wincing, around the body of it. He put it down quickly on the coffee table, its glass top decorated with the dry brown souvenir rings of spilled drinks, like a disordered and repeated Olympic Games logo.

She sat down opposite and beamed fondly. 'So, how's the throat now? Still sore?'

'No, fully recovered now, thanks. It was a bit of an infection I think. Mam got very worried about it; said I should have gone to the doctor, but you know what she's like!'

Lowri laughed. 'Tell me about it! She never quite forgave me for taking you on that demo, you know!'

Tomos grinned too, remembering the fuss there'd been over his little incident. Lowri's name had been mud for weeks afterwards.

Lowri sipped her coffee. 'Anyway, how was India?'

'Oh, brilliant. I loved it! You should see their hospitals compared with ours though Lowri, and the sheer numbers of people they have to treat.'

Lowri smiled, sympathetically. 'Yeah, I can imagine. And people grumble about our health service. Don't know how lucky we are, do we?'

Tomos nodded. 'We certainly don't. The poorest people get treated here but they certainly don't over there, necessarily. Not in the remote villages. They can't afford to pay for it, apart from anything else.'

'I know,' Lowri said, 'that's the injustice of it. Still, that experience will be good for your CV though. Well, so to speak. I know you haven't actually got one yet. But you know what I mean.'

'Yes and the people were really nice. I stayed with a lovely family. They had six kids: two boys and four girls. I slept in with the boys. It was a bit crowded with us all together in a tiny house but we managed. All the girls wanted to become doctors and the boys wanted to do IT! I would have liked to have stayed longer, but Mam and Dad could only afford to pay for me to be there for ten weeks. And anyway, then I got this damn throat infection, so I couldn't really have stayed after that anyway.'

Lowri nodded. 'No, I suppose you couldn't really be doing healthcare stuff if you were breathing germs all over the place, could you, even if our parents could have paid for you to be there longer.'

Tomos had to admit the logic of that. 'No, I couldn't really, that's true. I thought it was just a cold though, and I'd soon get over it when I got back home, but it did seem to hang on. It took quite a while to shake off.'

'Mam was right; you should have gone to the doctor about it you know. Got some antibiotics or something.'

'Well yes, I know,' he said sheepishly, not meeting his sister's eye. 'She did keep on about going but then it did go away of its own accord. I feel fine now. Well, apart from a little bit tired.'

Lowri reached for his empty mug (he'd been gasping for a drink and had quickly drained it) and rose. 'Okay. You're typical though, you males. Seem to have a pathological horror of going to the doctor. Will's just the same. Now, speaking of the Devil, he'll be back soon and we'll have a main dinner meal, then it won't be long before we have to leave for the gig. Is that alright?'

Tomos put on a hard-done-by expression. 'Yes, I suppose so,' he said doubtfully. 'Think I can last until then.'

Lowri looked down at him in mock-pity. 'Oh, my poor little deprived brother who never gets fed! Shall I make you a sandwich or something, to keep the hunger pangs at bay? You look as though you need feeding up a bit, anyway!'

'Oh yes please!' Tomos said, relieved that the suggestion had finally occurred to her. Have you got cheese and pickle; something like that?'

She smiled tolerantly and reached to ruffle his red hair. 'Well as it's you, I'll see what I can find.'

She moved towards the kitchen.

'Oh, by the way, we've got someone else joining us for the gig. Just to make up a tidy foursome, so you don't feel like a bit of a spare.'

'Oh, who's that?'

Lowri tapped the side of her nose, theatrically. 'Just wait and see.'

In fact, the mystery guest arrived an hour later, having been invited to join them for early supper too. When the doorbell rang Will leapt to his feet to answer it, a smile suddenly creasing his face. Tomos heard him greeting the visitor then closing the outer door. A young woman looking slightly embarrassed came into the living room. She scanned the room, finding him quickly, as Lowri emerged from the kitchen to give greetings.

Tomos was taken aback. Mair! She looked different. Well, it had been two years since he'd seen her last. Then she'd been, what, eighteen, nineteen to his sixteen? Now she must be twenty, perhaps twenty-one. Her hair was different: gone was the plaited, Tyrolean look. Now it was short, styled, a bit boyish, although it suited her. And she seemed to have filled out a little – was still slender but less wraithlike now – and as she unpeeled her coat a tight sweater displayed, he couldn't fail to notice, a small neat bosom.

'Hi Mair!' Lowri greeted. 'Nice to see you again! How's it going?'

'Hey Lowri,' Mair answered a little distractedly, 'Good, thanks.'

Her eyes were still on Tomos. She spoke again, her voice small, shy. 'Hello Tomos. How are you?'

Tomos rediscovered the power of speech. 'Hello, er, Mair. I'm fine thank you. And you?'

Lowri interrupted fussily, 'Okay, we've done all the solicitous enquiries as to wellbeing. Glass of something preprandial Mair? Wine? Or lager?'

Mair grinned. 'I could kill a Stella if you've got one Lowri!'

'Your wish is my command,' Lowri came back. She looked at Tomos, grinning. 'One for you too, little brother?'

'Um, yes, thanks,' Tomos mumbled, having temporarily forgotten what 'Stella' actually was.

Ignoring Mair's coat draped across the back of the sofa (she'd be putting it back on again soon after all), Lowri disappeared briefly into the kitchen, returning with a four-pack of silver cans, one for each of them. She distributed them, snapped off her ring-pull and raised her can in a toast. 'Cheers one and all!'

Everyone echoed 'cheers!' and drank. Tomos and Mair still stood awkwardly, looking at each other.

'There's no charge for sitting down, you know!' Lowri told them. 'Now I must return to my culinary labours, if you'll excuse me.'

'Oh, can I help?' Mair offered.

'No you bloody can't! Lowri said, shocked. 'Sit and talk to Tomos. That's what you came here – er . . .' She trailed off, flustered, and then beat a hasty retreat to the kitchen.

Tomos resumed his seat on the sofa. Mair took Lowri's usual armchair, facing him. He searched frantically for a topic of conversation. Nothing suggested itself. Mair seemed to be having difficulty too. After a lengthy silence, Will from the other armchair came to the rescue (It hadn't occurred to him to make himself useful helping Lowri). 'So how's the job going Mair?'

Mair seemed to sigh with visible relief that the silence had been broken. 'Good, thanks, Will. It's a bit of an eye-opener though, I must admit, actually doing social work properly now. Different from just sampling it on work experience from uni. They don't really prepare you for the messes some people get into with their lives. It's all very well learning about it in theory, but when you get involved with real people it's something else. Still, it's good; very satisfying – most of the time anyway. You feel you're really helping people, apart from those who don't want to be helped!'

Will smiled. 'Yes, it was ever thus, I'm afraid.' He glanced at Tomos, inviting him to join the conversation. 'But then your India experience must have been even more revealing Tomos, I suppose? Talk about How the Other Half Lives!'

'Yes, absolutely it was,' Tomos agreed, grateful for being included. He looked at Mair. 'As you say Mair, you don't really realise until you see the reality.'

'No,' she said, 'you don't.'

She held his gaze, seeming to will him to say more.

'So where are you working? Here in Cardiff?'

'Yes, for Social Services at the city council? (she still, Tomos noticed, tended to make statements questions). I'm working with abused and at-risk children. Well, teenagers really. Been there nearly four months now! Already!'

Tomos was impressed. He looked at her admiringly. He'd forgotten how actually quite pretty she was, in a slightly porcelain sort of way. Her eyes were quite strikingly blue and she opened them very wide, showing white all around those beautiful irises when she spoke animatedly. She was very different from that Helen, his brother's girlfriend (assuming she still was). She was lovely too, in a more voluptuous sort of way, he seemed to remember. But also out of reach, dammit. Why was he always fated to want the unattainable?

I really am a bit sad, a bit pathetic, he thought, *ending up attracted to women I can't have. Perhaps I should be a bit more competitive about it. Just grab what I want. Duw; it's all very well to say that though. I couldn't be that ruthless. Could never tempt someone else's woman away from them. It would be like stealing; just plain wrong. But a different matter if their relationship were already over, I suppose . . .*

He suddenly realised that Mair was speaking to him.

'. . . your Indian thing sounds interesting. Lowri was telling me about it. I wouldn't have minded doing that, actually. Not medical stuff like you did – I'm too squeamish – but something.'

'Yes, well, I'd better get used to the sight of damaged bodies if I want to be a doctor, hadn't I? It's what doctors do every day, after all; look at bodies.'

Mair regarded him steadily, smiling. Enigmatically, was it? Tomos felt a blush rising. He'd been staring at her even when lost in his reverie, and sometimes his gaze had surrendered to gravity and dropped below her face. And an idle conjecture had refused to be suppressed: how would she look without that pale blue skinny-ribbed sweater on? Or that brighter blue (tweedy?) skirt finishing demurely just above those petite, pretty knees, decorously closed, enhanced by those shiny purple tights?

He caught himself, alarmed. *Hell; what am I thinking? She'll think I'm being lascivious! And she has a boyfriend. She told me so. Well, she did two years ago anyway. But then why isn't he here? He'd surely like music, wouldn't he? But perhaps there isn't anyone now. But how can I tell? Duw! Well there's only one way to find out, I suppose.*

She was still holding his gaze; still doing her Mona Lisa.

'Um.' It was so difficult, coming out with the bald question. 'Um; how's the boyfriend these days?'

Mair looked puzzled. 'Sorry?'

'Didn't you tell me you had a boyfriend?' It was coming out wrong. It sounded like an accusation.

'No . . .' her eyes widened beneath a pale furrowed brow. It creased delightfully, Tomos thought. 'Oh, you mean Derek. No, we finished ages ago. It didn't work out. I've been single since then. Concentrating on getting my degree, and then starting the job?'

'Oh, right.' Tomos didn't know whether to commiserate or not.

'And what about you?'

'What about me?'

'Got a girlfriend?'

Tomos studied the carpet. 'No. Not at the moment.'

'Okay,' she said, enigmatically again.

Lowri appeared in the doorway, casting glances at both of them before addressing Will meaningfully, 'Are you going to come and give me a hand then, Sunshine?' She frowned, jerked her head in the direction of the kitchen, from which wonderful smells were drifting, in emphasis.

Will grinned and rose to his feet. 'Okay lover. I'll be there now.'

She pushed him into the kitchen ahead of her before throwing back, 'Be ready in five minutes, okay?'

'Great!' Mair exclaimed, 'I've been waiting for this all day!'

'Well that's more than my little brother has!' Lowri rejoined, making Tomos blush again. 'Mind you, I don't know where he puts it. He's such a beanpole.'

She pulled the kitchen closed, leaving the pair of them to their conversation.

Mair spoke first. She seemed visibly more relaxed now. 'Well you do surprise me, not having a woman, Tomos,' she teased. 'Why is that then?'

Tomos tried to affect nonchalance. 'Oh, you know; same reason as you I suppose: there hasn't been the time, what with doing A-levels, and now I've got a busy gap year, which will soon be halfway through already. I'm off to America after Christmas, to work in a hospital again. Well, work experience, anyway.'

Mair seemed only half-interested. Indeed, oddly, a little deflated. 'Oh, that'll be some more good experience then. A bit different from India, I expect.'

Tomos smiled. 'Yes, it certainly will. It'll be good to see yet another different sort of health system though. And to compare it and India's with ours.'

'Yes, I suppose so.' Mair sounded subdued.

The conversation seemed to be floundering. Tomos tried a change of tack. 'So you live here in Cardiff now, do you?'

'No, a little bit out. On the other side of the motorway. Nantgarw, on the road to Pontypridd. I can't afford to live in town, not on my starting salary. I'm not as well off as Lowri and Will!'

The kitchen door opened and Lowri appeared again. 'Ears are burning! What are you saying about me?'

Mair laughed. 'I was just saying I can't afford to live in Cardiff like you and Will!'

Lowri smiled sympathetically. 'I know; the rents they charge in the city are a scandal. They should bring back rent controls, in my view. We've got Labour in charge at the Assembly so I don't know why they don't do it. Anyway, enough of that. Dinner is served; come and get it.'

They got to St David's Hall in Will's tiny Fiat (the same one; Will declared that he was running it till it dropped) in plenty of time for the gig. Lowri had got good tickets for the auditorium, just a few rows from the front. Taking charge of course, she strode ahead looking for their seat numbers. They were on the end of a row. The party milled around a little uncertainly, unsure how to arrange themselves. At least Tomos, Mair and Will did. Lowri had it all worked out though. She ushered Mair in first then propelled Tomos after her. She took the third seat and Will sank into number four on the aisle.

Mair divested herself of her parka again, balling it up in her lap, as Tomos shed his duffle coat too. She gave him a grin, and for the first time he noticed that she smelled very nice indeed. She must have put something on, some sort of perfume, when she was getting ready to come out. She settled herself deliberately (was it?) nudging his shoulder with hers. He had an almost irresistible desire to put his arm around her slender shoulders, but fought it down. They'd need their arms free for waving, anyway.

The band, of course, was brilliant, but Tomos found it difficult to give the music his undivided attention. He was lost in the aura of Mair; her perfume, her presence at his side, the way she seemed automatically to turn her body towards his so that their thighs touched too. He reciprocated, subconsciously resting his weight on the buttock nearest her, and soon found it uncomfortable, but he didn't want to move away. It was intoxicating: Mair, the music, the occasion. Everything. He looked at her frequently and often caught her already looking back. Her face was flushed, her eyes wide with excitement and she seemed to be positively beaming at him. He joined in singing along with the band on the familiar numbers when invited to, at full volume (although he had a terrible singing voice), completely abandoned. Mair seemed to be in the same state. Lowri looked at him now and then, grinning in a big-sisterly way, clearly pleased about his happiness. Yes, he was certainly having some of that, all right.

They drove back to the flat. Tomos's mind was in a complete whirl, still full of music; still full of Mair. Scrunched up in the back of the Fiat because of Tomos's long limbs (but satisfyingly close together), Mair took his hand. There was another slightly awkward hovering outside the front door. Mair seemed uncertain whether to bid them goodnight and climb into her own little red Citroen and depart. Although she certainly looked as though she didn't want to.

Lowri took the initiative again. 'Coming in for coffee are you, Mair?'

Mair's relief at being asked seemed almost palpable. 'Yes, love one, please, Lowri.'

Oddly, Lowri seemed relieved too. They settled down in the flat again; this time Tomos and Mair together on the sofa, sitting close, with Lowri in her customary armchair and Will busying himself in the kitchen making coffee.

Lowri kicked off her boots, slumping and stretching her legs. 'Well, that was a brilliant gig, wasn't it?'

Everyone murmured agreement. When the coffee had percolated Will brought it through, with a plate of cheese and grapes and biscuits, of both the sweet and savoury variety. They chatted contentedly; Lowri and Will about university politics, Mair about her job, Tomos about his hopes for the future.

They finished their drinks and nibbles. Lowri heaved herself up and disappeared into the bedroom, reappearing with bedding for Tomos's slumbers on the sofa and dumping it in the vacant space next to him. 'It's okay Mair,' she assured, this isn't a hint for you to go or anything. Head off whenever you feel like it.'

Mair smiled. 'Okay; right.'

'Right then,' Lowri said, shooting another meaningful look at Will, 'we'll bid you two goodnight. Nice to see you again, Mair.' She moved towards the door but then paused, as if remembering something. She looked at Mair with an expression that Tomos couldn't decipher. 'Oh, and should you need anything, look in the bathroom cabinet.'

Mair looked briefly puzzled. 'Sor . . .' But left the question unformed, as if a penny had dropped.

Lowri closed the bedroom door and they were alone. Tomos cast Mair a furtive, still shy glance. *Now what? What happens now?*

But, thankfully, she was already doing the same. And she was smiling.

'Erm . . .'

She was suddenly practical. 'Get up a minute; I'll help you make your bed.' He did, and watched as she threw the scatter cushions onto the floor, spread the bottom sheet and duvet and placed the pillow. She sat down again and reached for his hand, pulling him down too.

'There we are. That's tidy!'

'Erm, yes.' He said uncertainly.

She leaned back resting her head against the high sofa back, head turned towards him. 'Well this is a funny turn up for the books, isn't it?'

'How do you mean?'

'Well, you know; meeting up again like this?'

Tomos smiled ruefully. 'Yes, I suppose it is.'

Mair took his hand again. Her touch was so delicate; hardly there. But it still felt wonderful. 'Tomos . . . I'm really sorry about hurting you before. I wouldn't have done that for the world.'

'That's okay. I was just a kid, getting the wrong end of the stick.' He tried to sound more magnanimous than he felt.

'Yes, well, I suppose I was being a little bit ambiguous really, ringing you up like that. But I was worried about you. You seemed to bang your head so hard. It really spoiled my day, to be honest with you?'

Tomos risked a little hand squeeze. 'It was a kind thought, anyway.'

She squeezed back.

A thought suddenly struck him. 'How come you got invited to the gig tonight?'

Mair giggled. 'Well, I happened to run into Lowri a couple of weekends ago. We went for a cappuccino and got talking? She told me about your Indian thing and how you were back home now, and then she suggested we all have a get-together, as the Manics were going to be doing a gig.'

'Yes, but did she know you hadn't got a boyfriend now?'

'Oh yes, that ended quite a while ago, before I finished my course. And I always got on really well with Lowri. I thought of her more like a big sister than a tutor sometimes. Told her all my troubles. So she knew Derek and I had split.'

Tomos pondered that. 'So . . . she set this thing up then? But why?'

Mair laughed aloud now. 'What you mean; *why?*' She's very perceptive, your sister! She doesn't miss a trick. I suppose she could tell by my interest in you that I . . .' she petered out; looked embarrassed.

'That you what?'

She hesitated; bit her lip. 'That I . . . I . . . had feelings for you. There; now I've said it.' She paused, suddenly seeming shy. 'Do you know, sometimes when I was with Derek I'd find myself comparing him with you? He was a nice guy and everything, and quite considerate in some ways, but his main preoccupations seemed to be beer and rugby with his mates. I felt a bit of a widow sometimes. He was never going to want to change the world. Unlike you.'

Tomos said, wryly, 'Perhaps he had the right idea. It's easier if you don't want to. You don't get attacked in the street, for a start.'

Mair smiled; put her other hand over his, holding it captive. 'No; don't say that. The world needs a few rebels to prick apathy. Challenge the powerful. Don't you think?'

Tomos lifted his free hand to stroke her cheek, astonished both at the softness of it and his own boldness. 'Yes, I suppose you're right really. Anyway, you want to make a difference too, don't you, doing what you do?'

'Yes, I do. I'm lucky; I have a good loving family. But some aren't so lucky are they? I want to help them.'

She fell silent, regarding him solemnly. Then she freed her hand and took it to the back of his head, and closed the short distance between their faces and kissed him, lightly, feather-soft, then kept her lips against his, as if reluctant to break contact, smelling of whatever that perfume was she was wearing and chocolate digestive biscuit.

'Tomos,' she murmured, 'Do you think – would you think me awful – if we got under your bed covers?'

He was taken aback. 'Er, no. No. No, not at all.'

She disentangled herself and sat forward to remove her boots. Tomos followed suit. She drew him to his feet and pulled his sweater over his head, dropping it on the floor amongst the cushions.

'Oh! Do you mean, er . . .?'

She laughed. 'Yes, of course I do!'

Her slender fingers unbuttoned his shirt, baring his thin hairless chest; pulled it from his shoulders, as she reached behind him to slide it down his arms and off. He began to tremble, coldness and excitement mingling in equal part.

'Your turn,' she said.

She raised her arms to let him remove, butterfingered, her sweater too. It joined the growing pile on the floor. Her small breasts were held high and tight in a red lace-edged bra. He looked at them, captivated, then into her eyes, mutely seeking permission. 'Yes,' she said, 'go on.' He found the clasp and fumbled it open, inexpertly drew the straps from her shoulders and, gasping, pulled the garment away. He stood transfixed, panting a little, taking her in.

'Do you like?' she said.

'Oh yes, yes!'

'Good,' she said. 'You can touch, you know.'

He bent to cup one soft, exquisitely soft orb and kiss its pink quickly hardening tip as she pulled him to her, giving him the breast like some gangling oversized suckling. She moved urgent hands to undo his belt, the waistband of his jeans, his fly and pulled them down, as his erection tented his boxers, straining to be free.

'Hold on a minute,' she said, sounding a little breathless too, and went quickly to the bathroom, leaving him standing there contemplating his tumescence, feeling a little ridiculous.

She returned, throwing a small package onto the sofa after taking one item from it. He stared. 'Really? Are you sure?'

'Of course I am,' she said. 'Aren't you?'

'Um, yes. Yes,' he managed through chattering teeth.

She came close again, arms going around his neck. 'Right, now my skirt. Zip, at the back,' she added helpfully as his trembling fingers searched, ineffectual and inexpert and uncertain.

He managed to unzip; lowered the skirt for her to step out of. She kicked it to one side. Now there were just her shiny purple tights and knickers. He fumbled them down as one (it seemed the obvious thing to do) as her small tuft of lower belly hair came into view. Astonishingly, it was ginger. She laughed. 'Yes, we have something in common!'

She took his hand and placed it in her soft, so soft and slippery secret place as its mouth yielded to his fingers. At last, having made him wait so long, she unhooked his shorts from his erection and quickly dropped them. He felt ridiculous again, standing naked with that normally flaccid organ now so absurdly, disproportionately engorged and rampant. It felt as though it would burst.

But she didn't laugh; didn't make fun. 'My, what a big boy you are!' she breathed. 'What a lovely big boy.' She held him and planted a kiss, then quickly took the condom and rolled it on, as he gasped in pleasure, in desperate need, almost in pain. His heart was thumping wildly. She moved back to pull the duvet to the end of the sofa, lay down, opened her thighs, brazen, lascivious, pulled him down too, took him in hand, guided him to where he had to go now, enveloped him in virginity-stealing bliss.

Tomos wanted to stay between her thighs. It was a wonderful place. He could have lain there forever, cradled in soft flesh, regaining his breath, waiting for his heart to stop hammering. But for all his thinness he must still be heavy on her ribcage. He would have to move. He raised himself, not quite sure where to move to as the sofa was so narrow.

'Are you going to put the light out?' Mair said languidly.

'Oh, are you staying?'

'Well, yes, that's the general idea.' She suddenly sounded anxious 'Do you want me to go then?'

'Oh no! Not at all! I was just thinking of Lowri . . .'

Mair seemed to find that highly amusing. 'What do you mean, "thinking about Lowri?" She's not your Victorian mother you know. Not that I'm suggesting your mam's puritanical of course. Lowri'll be quite relaxed about this. In fact she'll be really pleased for you. She did offer the condoms, remember?'

'Oh, right.' Tomos got up from her, feeling quite bold and grown-up and unembarrassed now about his dangling penis, and toured the room switching off the table lamps. He groped his way in the nearly complete blackness to the bed, tingling again with anticipation. Mair had shifted onto her side, back against the back of the sofa, holding the end of the duvet. He settled in, on his side too, tightly against her, intertwining arms and thighs with hers as there was no other way to lie on the narrow seat cushions. She pulled the duvet over them; sighed contentedly. His left arm settled around her slender shoulders, holding her in tight possession, his right hand intimate on the hill of her flank.

She raised a hand to cup and stroke his hot face. 'Oh, Tomos, I've been aching for you all evening, I really have. What a beautiful boy you are.'

He squeezed her to him. 'And you're lovely too, Mair Jenkins; simply gorgeous.'

Her other hand, trapped down between their thighs, found its way naughtily to his groin to caress his quiescent genitalia, dormant now, but there might have to be a repeat performance before too long, when he'd recovered and recharged.

'This your first time then, was it?'

'Yes, afraid so,' Tomos admitted, a little sheepishly.

'Well I'm glad you lost it with me; that's all I can say.'

'Yes, me too,' he replied, fervently.

Chapter 15
Wayne

Although she hadn't really thought she would, when it came to it Maureen had to secretly admit that she'd quite enjoyed the passing out parade. It was a surprise to her really. She certainly hadn't been greatly enamoured of the idea when first, five months ago, Wayne had announced that he was definitely going for it now; he was joining up. In fact she'd tried feeble dissuasion, whilst knowing deep down that she was wasting her time really. But, she'd argued, what about Helen; she wasn't really all that keen, was she? But of course then he'd said that she'd left the scene anyway.

So Helen's departure had removed all her ammunition, really. And she'd known better than to try the Oh-but-*I'll*-worry ploy. That wouldn't have cut any ice. Jim hadn't been much moral support for her either. He'd seemed positively pleased about it. That was probably only to be expected though. After all, he'd been keen to encourage Wayne into scouting as a way of funnelling some of his energy. And this was like a next stage along the same path, really.

Wayne had looked so proud today though; so happy, striding with his compatriots, his back ramrod-straight, eyes bright and fixed resolutely forward. He'd seemed distinctly taller, somehow. She'd really been able to see the fierce patriotic determination firing him. She'd picked him out on the parade ground immediately. His hair was much shorter now, as militarily decreed, but there was still enough of it to be seen below his cap for it to be unmistakeably his. No other young man had hair quite that colour.

When it was over and all the marching was done, and all the speechifying too, and the newly trained young men and women had been given permission to dismiss to join their families, he'd stridden towards them, looking so smart in his uniform (a far cry from the sartorial disaster he'd always been in his school togs) grinning from ear to ear, fairly radiating pride. Jim had looked pretty pleased too, as if basking in his son's reflected elation.

'Here comes the soldier boy!' he'd exclaimed. 'Here's the

warrior!' Because it had somehow seemed the right thing to do, he'd taken Wayne's hand and shaken it, and then enfolded him in a manly hug too. He'd never done either of those things before. Wayne had looked momentarily perplexed, but his grin had widened even more. And of course Maureen had hugged him too, and kissed his cheek, and then had had to find her hankie and spit on it and clean away the red ring of her lipstick, so as not to embarrass him. Even Poppy had hugged and pecked him in a rare show of tactility.

He'd stood amongst them, a peacock, relishing being the centre of attention, enjoying his big day.

'You made a grand show, all of you,' Jim had enthused. His admiration had bordered on the embarrassing.

Then there'd been photos to take, using Poppy's state-of-the-art mobile phone, which even, extraordinarily (the things technology could do these days!) took pictures. Poppy had taken one of Wayne with Maureen, then one of him with his dad, then one of him with both of them, which she kept framing wrongly and getting Wayne's and Jim's heads chopped off, so had to do several times. Then they asked nearby proud parents – well actually another proud sister, presumably, who knew how to operate the device – to take one of them all together, with short Poppy standing scowling a bit in front of her tall parents and beaming brother, but not so as to obscure Wayne in his finery at all.

Yes, it had been quite a day, Maureen thought now as she lay in bed next to the already snoring Jim, who had hit the whisky bottle a little too enthusiastically on their return. Wayne had been granted leave after his gruelling fourteen weeks' training, prior to joining his regiment, and arrived home later, and Jim had already laid in celebratory supplies of beer and spirits and Babycham for Maureen and Poppy (well, it wasn't every day that your son got inducted into the Army, was it?). It was a rite of passage into manhood for the lad, if ever there was one.

Yes, she reflected, *Now he's actually done it and there's no going back, I feel better about it now, strangely. I'll probably always worry of course. What mother wouldn't? But he's doing his thing, as they say. Jim and I could never have talked him out of it. And now he <u>has</u> done it, I'll give him all the support he wants. Jim will too. His face was a picture at the parade today. He got quite emotional at times, when they were* doing the speeches. His fingers went to his eyes a few times, He might have thought I didn't notice, but I did. I could tell he was feeling really proud. Well, I think I do too. Yes, I definitely do.

Puzzled, Wayne turned the envelope over in his hands, looking at the back as if that might give any clue as to the sender. It didn't. He turned it back again. The handwriting of the original address (to his home; his mum must have forwarded it) was large, clear, loopy, written in blue ballpoint. Vaguely familiar. He took it back to the room he shared with Lee, Pete and Craig, sat on his bed (he would straighten the cover when he got up again so as not to incur SM Morris's wrath), tore the Basildon Bond envelope open. On matching notepaper read:

14, Bedale Road,
Northallerton,
North Yorkshire.
27th January, 2004.

Dear Wayne,

I'm sorry if this comes as a shock to you. I sent this to your home, as I didn't know where you would be now. I presume you joined the Yorkshires, did you? Someone told me that the 1st Battalion is in Warminster, so if you did that I suppose you are down there now. But I suppose this will have got forwarded on to you anyway, wherever you are. I hope so.
   So how are you enjoying army life? I hope it's turning out to be everything you hoped it would be. Well I won't beat about the bush, as my Dad would say. The thing is Wayne, I'm sorry I gave you your marching orders back last summer. (Sorry, that's a very bad pun). I know now that it was a very stupid and selfish thing to do. I was just thinking of myself, not of you. You had every right to want to do what you wanted with your life. It wasn't for me to dictate to you, or blackmail you like I did. You must have been very hurt and I'm really really sorry for what I did. I'm such a stupid cow sometimes
   . So I'll come straight to the point. It really is miserable without you Wayne. I miss you so much. I tried to forget you. I even tried to get myself another bloke, but it wasn't easy. I'm not exactly a glamour-puss. No one wants me. The only one who ever really did was you. I did

go out for a little while with Mark Symonds (remember him from school?), but it just wasn't the same. It was like just going through the motions, not that we ever did – you know. I just didn't want that. He isn't kind and considerate like you, in fact he's a complete pillock. So that didn't last long. Since then I've been alone. Have been for three months now.

So what I'm saying is, can we start again? Please? I wouldn't be so possessive again. I promise. I really wouldn't. I've left school now of course. I didn't do brilliantly well with A-levels after all (well I was always getting distracted!) but I got a job with the council, in the tourist office in Thirsk. It's alright, it's a job, anyway. But wherever you may have moved to, I'd pack it in and move to be near you like a shot. I'd do it tomorrow. I could probably get another job alright, now that I've got one under my belt. And after all, I'm turned 19 now so I ought to be independent. Leaving home wouldn't bother me at all.

But I don't know whether you've got another girlfriend by now. I suppose I wouldn't blame you if you had. So if you have, just forget all this. It probably all sounds a bit pathetic anyway. If there is someone else in your life now, she's a very lucky girl.

Will you write to me though, please, either way, and put me out of my misery? Please? Oh Wayne, what a silly fool I was to let you go! Perhaps it's too late now and I've messed up big time, but I hope not. I'll always love you. I was such a stupid bitch, not realising what I'd got.

Love from

Helen

Wayne stared at the three sheets of paper for a long minute that grew into many, re-reading and then re-reading again. With brain on autopilot he refolded them; replaced them in the envelope. Unlocked his bedside cupboard and stowed it safely inside, away from prying eyes. Locked it again. He rolled onto his bed (he'd just have to completely remake it now before inspection) and lay on his back, gazing without seeing at the ceiling.

Thoughts began to churn. *Oh, bugger! This is a bolt out of the blue, or whatever the saying is. Helen! I thought you'd gone forever, after dropping me like that. I really did. I waited to see if you would change your mind. Waited ages. But you never got in touch. And I was buggered if I* was going to change my mind again. You got your own way the first time. And now this! Just when I was getting my head sorted. Just settled into the routine here. And besides, there's Rachel now. Okay, she's very different to you (well obviously, as she's a soldier), but she's nice; a really nice kid, in her way. And she's quite sweet on me, I think, judging by the way she seemed more than ready to go beyond kissing the other night. Well beyond. But we have to be very careful about stuff like that. It's definitely frowned on. If she got in the club and Morris knew I'd caused it, he'd go ballistic.

Not that I'd want to cause that anyway. Of course I wouldn't. After all, me and my brother happened like that. It still narks me, that, when I think about it. Okay, we were lucky to find good families to adopt us, but even so, it's not the best way to get made. But then again, if it hadn't happened, however it was, we wouldn't exist. All the same, when I have a child it's got to be done proper, with a wife. Like maybe with you, Helen. Do you really want me back? Do you want to be there for me? And you'd move down here, and everything? You'd really do that? Oh, Helen!

Well you do knock spots off Rachel, really, if I compare the two of you. She's nice but a bit of a tough nut in some ways, but then I suppose the lassies have to be really, to want to join up. I don't think I could see myself living with her, if I'm honest. We'd probably always be arguing and fighting. No; if it's between you and her, it certainly isn't her. I'll just have to tell her, that's all.

Wayne saw her later in the recreation room, although he didn't particularly want to. She sidled over as he finished a game of pool with Lee, having lost badly. He'd been unable to concentrate; mind elsewhere. He declined the offer of a return match and Lee wandered away, a little disgruntled, knowing he was on a winning streak.

'Hi Wayne, how's it going?' She looked at him expectantly, eyes questioning, asking more than the simple phrase. Her large bony frame wasn't enhanced by her t-shirt and fatigue trousers. She hadn't bothered to change into civvies, except to put on trainers.

'Oh, hi Rache.' This was going to be difficult.

'Get you a drink?' she offered.

'Um, no thanks. You're alright.'

She sounded disappointed. 'Okay. Want to watch some telly then?'

'No, not really.' He paused, gathering courage. 'Er, look, can us go somewhere quiet and talk, like?'

She frowned; said uncertainly, 'Well alright. Go for a walk?'

They found their combat jackets and walked out into the chill February evening, crunching along the immaculate gravel path around the camp perimeter.

'Go on then,' Rachel said; her gaze fixed determinedly ahead, throwing the ball back.

'Well, er . . .'

'Come on, spit it out!'

'Um . . .'

Rachel was no fool; took no prisoners. 'You're dropping me, is that it?'

'Well, we never really got started.'

'Oh, really? What was last night all about then? Or did I just imagine it?'

'Well, it weren't owt really, was it? Just a snog.'

She laughed bitterly. 'Well for you maybe, but not for me.'

'I'm sorry, but you know how it is. They don't really encourage it, do they?'

'Oh, bugger them! They rule our lives quite enough as it is. They aren't going to tell me whether I should have a love life or not!'

'No.' God, this was hard! 'Look Rache. I think you're a really nice girl an' all but . . .'

She rounded on him, her plain face reddening. 'Yeah, I know, spare me. There's always the "but." I've heard it all before. Story of my fucking life, it is. It's why I joined up really. Thought I might get some respect. Thought people might accept me for who I am, not for how sexy I am. Or sodding aren't.'

Her face had reddened; her bottom lip was quivering, for all her masculinity.

'I'm sorry,' Wayne offered. 'I really am.'

'Oh, it's alright. She sighed dramatically. 'I'm used to it.'

Then, in a sad, quiet voice she asked, 'Is there someone else? I've just been assuming that you were on your own.'

Wayne hesitated. It was bad enough, uncomfortable enough, telling this girl he didn't want her, except as a colleague and friend. But to have to confess that she came second in a contest with someone else for love; that was really turning the knife. It was probably better to be honest about it though.

'Well, yes. I had a regular girlfriend before I joined up. But she didn't like t' idea; didn't want us to. But I joined up anyway, and she dropped me. Now she's changed her mind though; says she'll accept it an' everything.'

Rachel stopped dead; stared at him. She was nearly his height (and weight, for that matter) so was virtually at eye-level. 'Oh, right. Let's get this straight. She hasn't got the decency to support you in what you want to do and gives you the boot 'cos she can't get her own way, but now all of a sudden she says she will, and you're going to crawl back to her?'

Wayne squirmed. 'No, it's not like that!'

'Well it bloody sounds like it to me!' Rachel retorted, voice rising, shrill. She glared. 'Well okay then; piss off back to her. Honestly, you are *so* weak! And don't think I'll be waiting if she dumps you again!'

She darted him a last venomous look and stormed away, furious, back in the direction of the female living quarters. Wayne closed his eyes; exhaled long and hard. Set off back to his room. He had a letter to write.

Warminster Barracks,
Wiltshire.
1st February, 2004.

Dear Helen,

Thanks for your letter, which came as a great surprise, I can tell you! I thought I'd blown it completely with you, you seemed so dead set against me joining the army. It was a really difficult decision to make, but it is what I always wanted to do. I'm sorry if that seems selfish, but it's just the way I feel. I know it's not easy, being the wife or girlfriend of someone in the services, but someone has to defend our country and I want to be one of them doing it.

Anyway, thank you for changing your mind. I miss you too, lots. We had some great times together didn't we, and I'd like to have lots more. It would be wonderful if you could move down here. I'm at Warminster Barracks with the 1st Bat. Yorkshires. Maybe you'd be able to get a job down here, and a flat in the town or something. I would be able to see you in the evenings when off duty and at weekends. I think it would be alright to spend whole weekends with you (except when away

on Exercise of course). Some blokes do. Wouldn't that be great!
Shall I keep an eye open for jobs going in the town? I could send you all the job ads from the local paper. And I could also look in the Jobcentre and keep a lookout for flats and stuff. Oh Helen, this is just great! I love you too, lots.

Lots of love from

Wayne

There was nothing going job-wise in Helen's specific line just then, but Wayne tipped her off about general office work being advertised, ironically in the Warminster branch of the supermarket that he had so hated. It would be an employment toehold in the town at least. Helen applied by post, then, feigning sickness, took a day off work (thankfully it was a Friday) borrowed her father Mark's car and motored down for interview. Wayne had found a cheap bed and breakfast for her to stay overnight. There was no alternative but to spend that evening together visiting a pub with as quiet a snug as could be found on a Friday night, for a meal, a lot of hand-holding and a lot of talk, and for her to later drive him back to barracks. It wasn't the sort of reunion they would have really wanted, but it would have to do.

Four days later she heard from Tesco's that the job was hers. Thrilled, she rang Wayne with the news. She could tender and work out her notice at the tourist office. Now there was just the matter of a roof over her head. Wayne found a reasonably decent flat (one bedroom, living room/kitchen, bathroom, no pets allowed) on the first floor of a small Edwardian villa out on the Salisbury Road. The rent was reasonable; they'd be able to manage it (although it would be in Helen's name of course). He borrowed the key from the estate agent and went to do a recce. It wasn't luxuriantly appointed, and was furnished, in clean but uninspiring fashion, so not what Helen would have really wanted (she would have preferred her own stuff, although of course that had to be acquired) but again it would be a start. It looked alright to Wayne, anyway, to be going on with. When Helen found a better-paying job, and with him chipping in too, even if he was officially living in barracks, she – they – would be able to move a rung or two up-market. He met the downstairs tenants: Sue and Jack, and their baby son Bradley. Sue explained about taking it in turns to keep the communal lobby inside the front door clean. They showed polite interest that he was a soldier and that the flat would actually be for his girlfriend. Sue offered him a getting-to-know-you cup of tea, and he accepted. They seemed very nice.

Near the end of February Helen left her tourist office job and the girls she'd come to know (and collected a glowing reference for future use), and on the following wet-but-who-cared Saturday, with the help of Mark with his car chock-a-block full of her possessions, she moved to Wiltshire and back into Wayne's life.

After collecting the keys, which had been left in the charge of Sue because the letting agent would be closed in the afternoon, it didn't take too long to bring her things (mainly clothes, a small portable telly, a CD player, a laptop) into her new domain. When all was safely in Mark drove back into town in search of a fish and chip shop, and convenience store for essentials for the next day, as they didn't want to be bothered with cooking just then. After eating (after unpacking Helen's mum's donated crockery and cutlery), Mark made sure that the television got a reasonable signal. It wasn't brilliant, but it would do. He stayed over for the night (it would have been a long, long, dark drive back home otherwise) sleeping a little uncomfortably on the two-seat sofa. Helen offered him the bed, but he refused. He didn't want her sleeping her first night as an independent grown-up on a bloody sofa.

He was still there, feeling a bit stiff, sitting at the red Formica-topped kitchen table eating marmalade on plain bread (Helen would have to get a toaster) when Wayne arrived at twenty past nine the following morning. Wayne had rather been hoping that he would have set off home by then; he wanted Helen all to himself. But thankfully, with a long hug and kiss for Helen and an instruction to take care delivered from a tight throat, because he'd suddenly realised that his daughter was a woman now and had just left home; and with a manly slap to Wayne's bicep, Mark was soon on his way.

After they'd stood at the downstairs outer door to wave him off and out of sight heading back into town, and Helen had felt her throat clench too, because now she, too, saw the no-going-backness of her father's leaving, they went back inside, into the tiny lobby, through the cheap white-painted door to the left at the foot of the boxed-in staircase, up the slightly dingy carpeted stairs to the rooms that had suddenly become home.

They went into the living room with its sputtering gas fire and uninspiring pictures not quite straight on the magnolia walls, its uncomfortable stripy-brown sofa and single non-matching chair, a pinewood, floral-cushioned rocker that had seen better days. Helen sank down onto the sofa, pulling Wayne down with her. She kept hold of his hand, tightly.

'Well, here we are then,' she said, 'Home Sweet Home,'

'Yeah,' Wayne said, suddenly emotional, unable to conjure a fitting response.

They sat and looked around, taking everything in. It all looked fine to Wayne. Helen imagined how it might look, with some personalisation, after a few DIY store trips. She looked at Wayne, solemn; raised a palm to cup a familiar cheek. 'I won't do it again. Not ever.'

'Do what again?'

She smiled, eyes glistening. 'Let you go. You're stuck with me now, Wayne Harrison.'

He smiled too, bottom lip trembling just a little. 'Well that's okay then.'

They sat for a long time more, not speaking. Nothing needed saying. Neither needed to suggest getting up, going next door to the bedroom, closing the curtains against the still rainy winter afternoon; it was the natural thing to do.

Chapter 16
Tomos

In the spare bedroom of his Uncle Huw's house in the smart, leafy, Memorial area of Houston, Texas, Tomos sat down with his host's borrowed laptop and composed an email to Mair.

Mair, my Sweet,

Well I've arrived here, after a very lengthy fight. Cousin Bryn was waiting at the airport to meet me, thank goodness; otherwise I wouldn't have had a clue how to find my way to his very nice house in Memorial. It's been years since I last saw Uncle Huw and Aunt Bethan, and when I saw Bryn and Anwen last they were small kids, so I hardly recognised them.

We've just had a really nice typical Texan meal (apparently) of barbeque ribs, baked beans, coleslaw, and apple pie (with cream, not custard!) and iced tea, and lots of catching-up-with-news-type talk, until finally I tore myself away, feigning tiredness, and asked if I could borrow a computer to mail you. I could have handwritten a letter, but ordinary mail takes forever to cross the Atlantic they tell me. And I can't wait that long!

Well wasn't that an absolutely brilliant weekend again! Of course my mam and dad wanted to know why I was so keen to visit Cardiff again so soon, so I had to tell them the reason: you! I couldn't have come over here for several weeks without seeing you again. My mam was really pleased and says she can't wait to meet you. I think she was a little put out (for purely nosy reasons!) that you didn't come to visit me in Talsarn But, although my parents are fairly liberal-minded, I don't think they would have been altogether comfortable with us sleeping together at this early stage. But Lowri has no such qualms about it! She's great, my big sister. Wasn't it good, having _two_ nights together on her uncomfortable, narrow sofa? I don't know about you, but I don't mind having to lie really close together at all – even if I do wake up with a stiff back! And I didn't mind that you pretty well wore me out. It was the most (and very pleasurable it was too) exercise I've had in years!

The plan is for me to have a few days just chilling out, getting over the jet-lag and all that and generally getting acclimatized to things (it's really warm over here, like our summer) and then start going to work with Uncle Huw at the Methodist Hospital. I can't wait to do that. It'll be great experience, although very, very different from India of course.

I miss you loads already. I came here with very mixed feelings really!

Love from

Tomos X X X

Tomos certainly enjoyed his first day in the pharmacy of the Hospital. As he expected it would be, it certainly *was* a world away from the Subcontinent. It was huge, with a mind-boggling array of pills and potions, shelf after shelf of them, carefully catalogued according to some baffling system that his uncle began to explain, arranged by general type, such as antibiotic or analgesic, then further classified by sub-groups that were themselves arranged alphabetically. It all seemed an awful lot to take in to Tomos. He was introduced to his uncle's assistant, Krystal, a small pretty red-bespectacled black girl with large tight-curled hair, who beamed at him maternally, although the top of her frizzy head was no higher than his shoulder. She would be taking him under her wing, Huw said. Krystal guffawed in delight at that.
 He quickly discovered the general routine. Frequently, orderlies would appear from the various departments bearing requests for supplies of some mysterious drug or ointment or medicament and Krystal would glance at the scrawled request, know immediately what was being asked for and move unerringly and quickly to

find it, a mother hen trailing Tomos in her wake. She explained what malady each tablet or bottle or unguent would be used to treat. Her knowledge seemed encyclopaedic. Tomos could do little more than follow her around, up and down, up and down the shelves, listening intently to her rapid-fire drawled explanations, trying to understand what she was saying and absorb and remember it all. He quickly realised that he was floundering. It was all too much; a barrage of information, delivered too quickly, to take in and retain.

When they broke for lunch in the staff cafeteria, which seemed as opulent as a five-star restaurant (it wasn't called a canteen, apparently), Tomos slightly disconsolately admitted that he was struggling. Huw looked up from his sandwich (ham and cheese on wheat) and grinned. 'Ah, don't worry about it. It took me several years of training for my degree to learn pharmacology in general, then quite a few weeks here before I could find things quickly. Although now I'm in charge, Krystal does most of the legwork these days. I'm mostly doing admin. – ordering in supplies and so on. And also, there are new drugs coming on stream all the time, given the okay by the AFDA, that you have to become familiarised with. It's a constant learning curve. You certainly won't learn it in a day.'

Tomos heaved a sigh of relief. 'Oh, right. Thank goodness for that!'

He smiled ruefully; added quietly, 'But pharmacology's only part of what I'll be learning in September. It's such a lot to take in. I don't know whether I have the brain for it.'

Huw, short, dark and well-fed swarthy, stopped chewing and regarded him, still smiling. 'Of course you have, boy, judging from what I've heard your mam say about you! You sound brighter than my two, to be perfectly honest – although they're good kids, don't get me wrong. Besides, pharmacology is a specialism, like any other aspect of medicine. I don't know, not having done a general medical degree, but I should imagine you get taught a good working knowledge of it and that's it. Get to know all the basic drugs. It's only if or when you decide to specialise in something that you need to know that specialism's particular pharmacology. It's only us druggies who have to know it all!'

'Oh, I see. That doesn't sound too bad then.'

Huw beamed. 'No, you'll sail through it, a bright boy like you.

Just you see!'

'Well, I don't know about that,' Tomos said, modestly.

'Of course you will! Where are you going to uni, Cardiff or Swansea?'

'I'm down for Cardiff; where Lowri works. Different department, obviously.'

'Yes, obviously,' Huw agreed, a tiny bit patronisingly. 'What is it she teaches now; sociology isn't it?'

'Yes, that's it.'

'Well I'm sure Sioned and Glyn are very proud of you both. Well, *will* be proud of you Tomos. You've got the potential.'

They lapsed into silence, finishing their food. Then Huw suggested a stroll in the hospital grounds. Tomos didn't feel keen. He felt a little lethargic, really. Perhaps it was the chasing around following the supercharged Krystal all morning.

'No, that's alright thanks, Uncle. I'd rather just chill somewhere.'

Huw looked faintly surprised. 'Oh. Right. Well let's go and sit in the staff lounge for half an hour then.'

He got up, brushing away imaginary crumbs.

Tomos's emails to Mair were becoming regular. How quickly he'd fallen into the comfortable routine of it. It was so good to be able to ask for the use of Huw's laptop every evening, provided that he wasn't already using it of course. But, anxious not to abuse his uncle's offer of it, he tried to keep his correspondence within sensible limits. After all though, better a shortish letter every day than wait forever, like three, even four days, for a long one.

Hello, Sweet Mair,

Well that's a week of work – well, work *experience* anyway – under my belt. It's surprisingly hard work, or perhaps I'm just not used to doing anything very active! This Krystal, Uncle Huw's assistant, is a ball of energy. She doesn't do walking at all. At least, not walking at a steady pace. When we're fulfilling requisitions (getting asked-for drugs off the shelves in British English) she always has to do it virtually at a run. Talk about a human dynamo! When we come home in the evenings I'm exhausted!

She's the most exuberant person I've ever met, I think (even more so than Lowri, and that's saying something!). Perhaps she's so ebullient and pleased with life because she's got a new boyfriend. Well I know the feeling there of course, substituting 'girlfriend' for 'boyfriend'! Apparently he's a trainee football player for the Houston Texans. She says he's going to be famous one day and make megabucks, and keep her in luxury. She's forever going on about him; it gets a bit tedious sometimes. I escape as often as I can to talk to Uncle Huw about the drugs and things we've been dispensing that day (he monitors everything that goes out) – after all, that's what I'm supposed to be there for, not talking about football players. And I can't understand what Krystal says half the time, anyway, as she talks so quickly. I'd rather be sitting quietly with Uncle, speaking Welsh. It seems a bit strange doing that in an all-American place like Houston!

Apart from Krystal wearing me out though (although I'd rather it was you, doing it in your special way!) it is all very interesting. I'm astonished at how much Uncle knows when you get him started about something. When he starts going on about how many different forms of cancer there are, for example, and all the many drugs that are used to treat it, it's just mind-boggling. Hopefully, after this I'll have a little bit of a head start in pharmacology at least. It's really good of Uncle and Auntie to give me this opportunity, anyway.

But I'm going on about myself too much. How are things with you? Are they still working you into the ground? I shouldn't grumble about being tired, you do proper work, not just experience, and with stress thrown in as well. I know you can't talk about cases too much, but how is it with those two brothers you were telling me about? Did you get an order to take them into care? I hope so, if they were being abused like that. It sounded dreadful. I suppose Wayne and me might have finished up like that, in a terrible dysfunctional family, if we hadn't been abandoned. We were lucky to have been, as it turned out. Speaking of Wayne, I think I really ought to make a bit of an effort to keep in touch with him. After all he is my brother and there ought to be a bit of a bond, in spite of us being such different characters with little in common, apart from having once shared a womb. I think he and I do rather prove the nature/nurture theory: that even if you're genetically identical you can grow into very different sorts of people if you grow up in very different circumstances.

Well, it's back to the grindstone on Monday – and the frenetic Krystal! I'm going to try and slow things down a bit; go at my own pace. Otherwise I'll never last the eight weeks! Actually I think I might be coming down with something; my legs feel a bit achey and I get breathless very quickly. Maybe it's 'flu, which seems very unfair coming so soon after that infection or whatever it was in India. If it is 'flu, I don't suppose they'd allow me to work in a hospital if I was breathing germs all over the place, so perhaps I'll have to take some time off.

To tell the truth, I wouldn't mind too much if I had to be sent home early again. Then I'd get to see you sooner. Oh Mair, I do really miss you! I feel like one of those Romantic poets we did in school, pining for love.

Well I'd better close now or I'll be accused of hogging the laptop!

Love from

Tomos X X X

Huw looked at Tomos with some concern. 'Any better today then?'
   'Not really,' Tomos mumbled. If the truth were known, it actually felt worse. He felt hot, and achey, particularly in his knees, and increasingly tired. And for some strange reason, he was becoming clumsy using the computer.
   'Okay,' Huw said, 'you're going to see my friend Cyrus at the hospital. He's an emergency room physician and not a specialist, but even if he doesn't know what's wrong with you himself he can point you at someone who does. This looks more than something like flu to me. It doesn't matter about the cost; we won't involve the insurance company.'

Tomos didn't argue; he felt too wretched for that.

Cyrus Hamilton listened carefully to Tomos's tale of woe. He produced a thermometer and took his temperature, frowning at the reading. 'It's elevated a couple of degrees,' he drawled. He pushed his spectacles back up his suntanned, aquiline nose. 'Mm.' He drew the syllable out, making a sentence of it. 'And and how long have you been feeling like this?'

'About a week I think. I keep thinking it's going to go away, but it seems to be getting worse. My uncle thought I ought to have it checked out.'

'Mm. And you haven't felt unwell before now?'

'Well, no, not really, although I had a bit of a cold or something when I was in India recently.'

Hamilton looked at him sharply. 'Did you have a sore throat at the time?'

'That's right, although I didn't feel as bad as this. And I didn't feel hot then. Well, I don't think so. It was difficult to tell as it was so hot anyway.'

'And how long ago was this?'

'Er, I came back from there two months ago.'

'Mm. Were you fully inoculated before you went?'

Tomos looked puzzled 'Yes, I think so. Presume so anyway. I had several jabs.'

'Okay. Do you know what they were preventative of?'

'No, sorry. I can't remember.'

'Right.' Hamilton reached for a stethoscope and stood up. 'Take off your shirt for a moment, please.'

Slightly surprised, Tomos stood and did so, and the tee-shirt underneath it at the doctor's nod to his mute question. He flinched at the cold metal of the instrument on his chest. Hamilton listened carefully, moving around to the back to sound there too.

'Mm.' Hamilton did another lengthening. 'How's your general health normally. Do you feel pretty good?'

Tomos pondered. 'Yes, I think so. Apart from the tiredness. It's quite hectic work in Pharmacy, usually. And I get out of breath quite easily.'

The doctor smiled thinly. 'Huw's a bit of a slave driver, is he?'

'Well, not my uncle so much as his assistant. She's a bit of a whirlwind. Does everything on the run and I have to try and keep up with her!'

Hamilton's smile faded. He ignored the levity. 'Mm. Right; here's the plan. I want you to see my colleague, Dr Ashford. He's a cardiologist. He'll have a look at you and possibly run one or two tests.'

'Cardiologist? Why do I need to see a heart specialist?' Tomos would have settled for his knees to stop hurting.

'It's just precautionary, nothing to be too concerned about. Your heart seems a tad arhythmical so it might need checking out.'

'But you can't give me treatment here, can you?'

Hamilton put his insipid smile on again. 'Well not a great deal of it, obviously. I wouldn't have thought you'd have insurance cover, would you?'

Tomos shook his head uncertainly. He had no idea what had been arranged between his uncle and parents as far as that was concerned.

'But that doesn't mean we can't give a bit of unofficial diagnosis for relatives of staff members. Apart from anything else, the hospital wouldn't want you here if you were dangerously infectious.'

'Oh, right,' Tomos said, rather anxiously.

'Anyway,' Hamilton said, I'll talk to Dr Ashford and get something set up, and liaise with Huw about it. Okay?'

'Yes, right. Thank you.'

Hamilton steered him towards the door. He was probably a very busy man. 'Well, nice to meet you. And how is Wales these days? My wife and I had a vacation there a couple of years ago. It was a nice part of England but it rained a lot of the time we were there, I seem to remember.'

Tomos bristled. 'It's not part of England; it's a separate country.'

'Oh, sorry. I tend to confuse England and Great Britain. Wales and Scotland and Ireland aren't, like, states of the UK then?'

'No . . .' Tomos let the sentence peter out. He couldn't be bothered to explain.

The doctor ploughed on. 'Yeah; we had ten days in England. Did London of course, then Yorkshire, then Shakespeare Country and then drove over into Wales, to Snowdonia.'

'Really?' Tomos wanted the conversation to end. He needed a sit down again.

'Yeah, we did the Snowdon railway, and that cute little place with the crazy long name, and the village where that dog, what's his name, is buried?'

'Gelert.'

'Yeah, that's the one. Then we went to Aber-something-or-other. What's it called? Quaint seaside place. Gotta cliff railway.'

'Aberystwyth?'

'That's it! The sun finally came out when we were there.'

'Right...'

'Right. Well I won't keep you. So you're going to do medicine, Huw tells me?'

'Yes, I hope so.'

'Cool! Good for you. Well I wish you all the best, fella.'

'Thank you,' Tomos said, and made his escape.

Dr Ashford, sleek and dapper in his thousand-dollar Brooks Brothers suit, looked up from the notes written by Cyrus Hamilton. 'So, er, Thomas...'

'It's Tom*o*s, actually,' Tomos said, a little irritated again. 'The Welsh form.'

'Oh, my apologies,' Ashford said, slightly peeved too. He was accustomed to a certain degree of deference from patients. After all, he didn't have to grant this for-free consultation.

'So Tom*o*s,' Ashford repeated with a touch of sarcasm, 'you've been to India recently and seem to have picked up some sort of infection, which looks as though it's flared up again. Possibly because it wasn't diagnosed and treated adequately in the first place.'

'Yes, but I don't understand why...'

Ashford ignored the question, asking one of his own. Do you have any other symptoms? Lack of co-ordination; anything like that?'

'Er, well, I'm a bit clumsy on the computer at the moment. Tending to hit the wrong keys. But it's my knees that bother me the most.'

'Really? Drop your pants a moment, will you?' Tomos sat nonplussed for a second, before realising that the doctor meant trousers. He stood up and undid and lowered his jeans. The doctor told him to sit again and articulated and gently prodded his inflamed-looking knees with soft pudgy fingers. Tomos winced.

Ashford straightened up. 'Mm; a touch of arthritis there.'

He sounded Tomos's chest too, and murmured non-committally. 'Right; I'm going to run a few tests and we'll get the results in a couple of days.' Ashford instructed the attendant nurse to take him for an electrocardiogram and to give a blood sample and submit to other procedures he'd never heard of. And with that he bade him good day.

On instructions from on high, Huw grounded his nephew, forbidding him to return to the hospital until his malady, whatever it was, was diagnosed. Two days later he came home with the test results. He came straight to the point.

'Well, young man. It seems you have rheumatic fever. That's what's making you feverish now and giving you arthritis, and why your heart's a bit all over the place. They could treat you for it here but it would cost a fortune as you don't have insurance. There are only so many free favours you can get because you're my relative. So we'll have to get you repatriated back to Britain straight away.'

Tomos looked at his uncle in alarm. 'Oh, Duw.'

'Yes, but don't worry about it. I'll ring your mam now, and book a flight. And tell her to fix a visit to your GP so he can organise for you to be seen straightaway if possible at Aberystwyth hospital. They'll soon get you sorted out. Okay?'

'Yes, alright,' Tomos said, feeling far from confident about it.

Steffan Jenkins, senior cardiac consultant at Bronglais Hospital, Aberystwyth, pored in his turn over the notes sent with Tomos from America and at the ECG and other tests he'd done too. They confirmed Dr Ashford's view. It definitely seemed to be rheumatic fever.

A North Wales boy, Jenkins was a Welsh speaker and they fell naturally into their mother tongue. 'You very probably picked up a streptococcal throat infection in India,' he informed the anxious Tomos. 'Rheumatic fever often follows it, with a delayed-action effect. If you got your infection eight weeks ago that makes it about right. And you're displaying the classic symptoms: short-term arthritis; breathlessness because your heart's a bit compromised;

growing clumsiness, which is a neurological thing; and now signs of Erythema Marginatum, that rash that's starting on your arms.'

Tomos stared at the consultant in disbelief. He'd always thought rheumatic fever didn't happen in the Developed West. 'Oh. And can all these things be cured?'

Jenkins smiled, oozing professional reassurance. 'RF is an immune system malfunction, which is why it shows such a variety of effects. We can manage it reasonably well with anti-inflammatories to reduce symptoms and antibiotics to minimise re-infection, and often with simple drugs like aspirin in high dosage. It usually involves a lengthy course of medication, anything up to five years, to guard against it coming back. And you really don't want that to happen.'

Tomos sat stunned. 'So all of this is happening just because I got a throat infection?'

'Yes, I'm afraid so.'

'Duw, Duw!'

'It's easy to be wise after the event, but it's a great pity it wasn't picked up earlier, but that's the problem with it. It doesn't manifest itself, if it's going to, until some weeks after the original infection. If your infection had been tested and identified as streptococcal after it had happened, any early signs of RF appearing could have been got on top of sooner. But as it is, it's been allowed free rein to develop. And unfortunately it's affected the mitral valve of your heart.'

'Oh. Is that serious?'

Jenkins chose his words carefully. 'Well, it can be. It's produced carditis – inflammation of the heart – manifesting itself as congestive heart failure. That's not good of course.'

'Oh bloody hell! You mean my heart might stop?'

The consultant smiled, without warmth. 'No, no; the term always sounds worse than it is. It simply means it's working less than optimally, hence your breathlessness. I'm surprised you aren't having a little chest pain too.'

'Well actually,' Tomos confessed, 'I am getting twinges every so often now.'

'Ah, yes.' There was a faint note of triumph in Jenkins' voice, an unspoken thought-so. 'I thought you might be.'

He continued, 'Have you always been fit and healthy before this happened? There've never been suspicions of any problems? You're a pretty slender lad.'

'What, do you mean regarding my heart?'

'Yes,' Jenkins said, bluntly.

'Er, no, I don't think so. I've never been very athletic though. Soon get out of breath, so I was never into sport or anything.'

'Mm. Interesting.'

Tomos suddenly remembered. 'Actually, perhaps there is something; it happened a couple of years ago. I went on a demo to London.'

'Oh, what was that in aid of?' Jenkins interrupted.

'Against the bombing of Afghanistan.'

'Really? Well good for you. I'm sorry; carry on. You were saying?'

'I was attacked in the street and fainted from the shock, and fell and knocked myself unconscious. They took me to hospital and told me afterwards that my heart had become a bit unstable.'

Jenkins leaned forward, suddenly interested. 'I see. But you had no diagnosis of anything? No treatment?'

'No, they said my heart had stabilised itself and I was discharged the following day. I forgot all about it after my head stopped hurting!'

'Mm.' The consultant studied Tomos intently. 'Well that tends to fit with you being underweight. You've never had a very strong constitution, by the sound of things.'

'No,' Tomos said, wryly, 'I'm certainly not as beefy as my brother.'

'Why do you say that?'

'Well, we're twins. Monozygotic. You'd think we'd be just the same in build, wouldn't you?' Tomos felt a little smug, knowing the technical term.

Jenkins was still staring fixedly. 'Mm. Very interesting. Obstetrics isn't my field of course, but I believe sometimes monozygotic twins share a common placenta. If that were so in your case, you might have developed less well than your brother. You might always have had a rather compromised heart but sometimes it takes a trauma to point it up. Very interesting.'

Tomos could feel irritation rising again. It happened a lot lately. Perhaps that was another strange symptom. He didn't feel like an interesting case study. He just wanted to be made well.

'So can my heart be cured of this, what's it called, Carditis?'

Jenkins looked grave. 'Well, we should be able to bring all your sorts of inflammation under control, but unfortunately, once heart tissue has been damaged that's it. It doesn't regenerate.'

Tomos could feel his heart pounding alarmingly. *Duw, it's not going to stop, is it?* 'So what happens now then?'

'Well, you've got normal function of about forty-five percent. I don't know how much you had before, unfortunately. It would have been interesting to know. But anyway, people have lived with less than that, under a comprehensive drug regime.'

'So, will I have to take drugs for the inflammation and others to guard against re-infection, and more again for my heart?'

'Yes, I'm afraid so,' Jenkins confirmed, gently. We can give you diuretics and beta blockers and so on for your heart, and they'll have to be taken long-term.'

'Do you mean . . . for the rest of my life?'

'Yes, I'm afraid so. Well, with our present state of knowledge anyway. Of course there are new treatments being developed all the time. In the future there may be stem cell therapy, for one thing. The work that's being done there looks quite promising.'

Tomos stared at his hands, utterly drained of emotion. It felt somehow safer being cocooned in lethargy. Best not to think or feel. Easier to simply curl up, submit to fate, give up, now. He forced a reply, trying to sound interested. 'You mean growing tissue, that sort of thing?'

'Oh, you seem to know something about it.'

'Well, not very much. I'm interested in medical stuff, that's all. I'm doing medicine at uni later this year.'

Jenkins' expression shaded to sadness. 'Yes, well, let's concentrate on getting you as well as we can first, and keeping RF away from you again. Then you can think about that. Alright?'

'Yes, okay,' Tomos muttered, disconsolately.

Chapter 17
Wayne

Helen turned her left hand this way and that, admiring the ring. Letting the significance of the three tiny (well, one was a reasonable size but the adjacent ones were miniscule) diamonds sink in. It was about time too, she reflected. For goodness sake, it was March 2006; four years and nine months since she and Wayne had taken their first shy fumbling steps into a relationship together. She was twenty-one and Wayne was too, now, as of last Thursday.

It had been a big day for him of course, notwithstanding that the age of majority was eighteen for pretty much all purposes nowadays. But somehow, twenty-one still *felt* like fully attaining adulthood. It certainly had done when she turned that age last November, anyway. You felt you really were, absolutely, now fully grown with a mental maturity to mark your years.

Last weekend had been brilliant. Wayne's parents, with their conservative ways, had certainly regarded twenty-one as more significant than eighteen anyway, and insisted on throwing a party back home in Northallerton on the nearest point to his birthday that he could take leave. Which was pretty close, actually, on the second weekend in April. In fact, they'd suggested to Tomos's parents that they make it a double, collaborative effort, to celebrate his majority too, but they'd demurred, apparently. They'd said Tomos wasn't really feeling up to any sort of big do; they were just going to have something really quiet for him. She'd felt a slight pang of guilty disappointment at that; she would have liked to see Wayne's brother again. It was a shame that they'd seen each other just the once, never followed up on their meeting four years ago.

But it had been a great do, all the same. A few of Wayne's old mates had been invited, and a couple of hers too (some had partners and one or two actual spouses, like her friend Becky, who'd married Steve and was now huge with her second pregnancy). It had been really good seeing their old friends again and catching up.

Naturally, Wayne had regaled his mates with tales of life in the army and they'd got into earnest, although increasingly alcohol-fuzzy, opinionated discussions of the Iraq war. And of course Poppy had her new bloke, Darren, in tow. He'd seemed a nice enough lad, in a slightly gormless sort of way. Her parents had been invited too. There'd been rather too many of them to all squeeze into the Harrisons' little terraced house, so the function room of the *Duck and Drake* had been hired, which neatly met the twin requirements of accommodation and booze.

And then, when it had got to eleven in the evening, when Wayne's dad, looking very red in the face and rather the worse for wear, had called for a brief cessation of music and (relative) silence in which to formally congratulate his son and propose a toast wishing him long life and happiness, and an unsubtle wish that he might in the fullness of time make an honest woman of herself, Wayne, the bugger, the sweet man, had sprung his little surprise.

He'd excused himself from the company saying that he had to 'just fetch something from his coat,' then returned with his right hand tightly balled, concealing something. He'd taken her right hand with his left, and turned to address his puzzled parents.

'Well, funny you should say that about Helen and me. I know you're always going on about it, Mum. I know what it is; you just want grandkids!'

Maureen had blushed, lost for a repost. Jim had said, 'Well, it is about bloody time you know!'

Her dad, showing male solidarity, had chimed in, 'Aye; I'll second that!'

Wayne had ploughed on. 'But 'happen as like I've been thinking a lot about it lately. And mebbe it is about time we, like, did summat about it.'

And then he'd done it. Actually done it. Got down on bended knee and looked up at her and said, apprehensiveness making his voice tremble, 'Right, um . . . Right. Okay. So will you, Helen Micklethwaite, marry me? Please?'

Helen smiled, remembering. It had been a total shock. They'd touched on the subject occasionally – well, she'd tentatively suggested it now and then – but something, some caution on his part, had always chased it away. So she'd pretty well resigned herself to not looking beyond partner status. And after all, the present situation, the status quo, hadn't been so bad. She'd got the job at the library; They'd pooled incomes and bought a one-year-old, low-mileage, as-good-as-new car, a little Ford Fiesta, together; she had upgraded to a better flat (a ground-floor one with a pocket-handkerchief garden, which she tended assiduously); and she and Wayne were to all intents and purposes cohabiting already. They usually had weekends together, unless he was on exercise, and most evenings too. So it was tantamount to being married anyway. And besides, she'd learned that you couldn't always have things quite as you might have wished in life.

So to see his earnest face looking up at her, pleading, doing the traditional proposal thing, had, well, melted her heart, as they always said in the romances she occasionally, guiltily, dipped into at work. Her reaction had been mixed, really. She'd felt tremendously touched, both by the fact that he was actually saying the words and the absurdly theatrical way in which he was delivering them. At the same time she'd also nearly lost control and burst out laughing, but managed to keep a tight rein and had resorted instead to flippancy.

'Yeah, go on then,' she'd said, putting her free hand on his hot cheek, 'let's do it.'

Of course the room had erupted then, with exclamations and gasps and ooh's and ah's from most females present and cheers from the men, and his mum had looked as though she were about to burst into tears. Indeed her own mum too had quickly put a hand up to mask her mouth, whose lower lip had probably become suddenly unstable too. But Wayne hadn't finished. He'd unclasped his hand to reveal a tiny blue box. He'd let go of her hand and opened the lid to reveal the small sparkly object nesting in white satin within. He'd lifted it out and held it up to her.

'Er, right. Shall us get engaged then?' I hope this is the right size. I told t' girl in t' shop you had a sort of average-sized finger, like. Well, I said it might be a little bit on t'chubby side. She said I could always change it if it's wrong,' he added, anxiously.

She'd taken it from him, gingerly, as if it were some priceless artefact. 'Oh Wayne; it's beautiful!'

She'd tried it on the third finger of her left hand. It had slid on easily, feeling just right. And of course then she'd had to show it to all the females in the room, in descending pecking order: her mum, Wayne's mum, Poppy, her friends, Wayne's mates' women, and so on. Everyone had gushingly opined that it was beautiful too.

So here she was now, on the Tuesday following that eventful (to put it mildly!) weekend, waiting for Wayne to arrive. He wouldn't be too long, because it was his turn to have the car. He generally arrived at around seven-thirty. It was funny, she sometimes thought. His job was really quite pedestrian in some ways, the way he could simply walk out of camp, in civvies, once off duty, to join the outside world.

He hadn't been able to join her the previous evening as he'd been on guard duty; the late shift. She didn't mind that though. She'd come to accept that it went with the territory, was simply an aspect of his job, As would being posted away on tour, if necessary, although that wouldn't be a very appealing prospect. She hadn't liked it very much when he'd been sent away on exercise in Britain, like to the Brecon Beacons, never mind abroad. And not to mention the possibility of active service. But she tried not to be selfish about it and give him a hard time. It was all part of his job, after all.

But being alone last night had given her time to think. She'd been so bowled over by his proposal that she hadn't had time to consider the nitty-gritty: the timescale and everything. She was going to tackle him about it tonight; like when it could happen, and how big a do they'd have, and so on. But, she supposed, that would be largely down to what her parents could afford. They weren't made of money. Her dad was only a schoolteacher (although a head of department, admittedly) after all. And her mum's wage wasn't all that great. It wouldn't be fair to lay a hugely extravagant affair on their shoulders, it being up to them to shoulder most of the expense as parents of the bride. And it wouldn't be fair to expect Wayne's folks to contribute a lot either. They had much less coming in than her parents, she imagined.

She really wasn't bothered about a big splash though, and she doubted whether Wayne would be. After all, they'd been together – living together – for two years anyway. The wedding would be really just a technicality, a sort of legal endorsement of the commitment to each other they already had. It wasn't as if they were getting married as virgins, to begin shacking up for the first time. Well, did anyone do that anymore, anyway?

And yet, in a funny sort of way, it did sort of put a different

Slant on things. Like the question of starting a family. Well, why not, now? Big sister Gilly had little Suzie (dear little soul, she was) and now had a second, a little boy apparently, due in a couple of months. Her future with Craig was all mapped out: a soft-focus, romantic vision of cosy secure domesticity. She, Helen, wanted a bit of that too. Yes, what she and Wayne had was nice, in a low-key, familiarity-of-years sort of way. There was the emotional security of it, and all that. But how much better it could be with the patter of tiny feet around the place! She'd lain in bed last night; hand on the empty pillow next to her, imagining it. Two kids would be nice. Or maybe three, if the first two turned out to be either both boys or both girls. Perhaps a third would balance up the genders. And of course one, at least one of them, would have to have red hair, like their dad. As long as the other didn't have an unruly haystack of black hair like their mum, God forbid.

Yes, she was definitely going to put it to Wayne when he came home.

She'd made Wayne's favourite, sausage and mash. It was sitting in the oven keeping warm, the potato topping becoming crusty and brown, as he let himself into the flat. He walked through into the living room and did a surprised double-take. The table in the corner, a recent acquisition from IKEA in Bristol, was laid with a red paper tablecloth and their souvenir place mats from last year's holiday in Ibiza. The place settings included upturned wine glasses and there was a single tall, white, lit candle guttering softly in another souvenir from abroad, their wrought-iron candlestick. The only other lighting was from the table lamp furthest from the table. Snow Patrol was playing softly on the CD player.

Helen got up from the sofa, which was also Scandinavian. She came to give him a kiss and hug. He pulled back and looked at her appreciatively. For once she wasn't wearing jeans, but her slinky dark blue dress, the one with the breathtakingly low cut top that normally had to be worn with a modesty panel to hide what would be a good two inches of cleavage otherwise. Tonight though, Helen clearly wasn't feeling inclined to be coy. And she was made up. And she smelled gorgeous. It must be the scent from last Christmas.

'Hey,' he said, 'what's t' special occasion then?'

She grinned. 'Well, another little celebration after last weekend's bombshell. Just for you and me, this time. Okay?'

'Er, well, yes.' In his many-times-washed jeans and sweater, Wayne suddenly felt decidedly under-dressed.

He sniffed. Smells wafting from the kitchen were joining the ones coming from Helen. 'Is that what I think it is?'

'It certainly is! And there's a really wicked pudding too; Black Forest Gateau. With cream, to be really decadent. And a bottle of cheap supermarket red to wash it all down. How's that?'

'Wonderful!' Wayne enthused. 'Why don't we celebrate all the time?'

Helen giggled. 'Steady on! If we did that, then we'd never have special treats would we?'

'No, suppose not,' Wayne had to concede.

She pushed him further away. 'Right then; you do the wine and I'll dish up. Are you hungry?'

'Starving!' he said, enthusiastically.

Later, in bed (although not very much later, as Wayne was easily enticed), Helen steeled herself to bring up the twin subjects that needed discussion.

'So when are we going to do it then?'

'Do what?'

'You know what. You know perfectly well! Get spliced, of course!'

Wayne was feeling drowsy, having drunk the greater part of the wine, and having had quite an energetic day, not to mention the recent ten minutes.

'Oh; yeah. Dunno really. When do you think?'

'Wayne! Come on! It was your idea after all. You can't leave all the decisions to me now!'

Helen could sense him grinning in the dark. He was teasing but she wanted him to be serious.

'Weddings are for t' womenfolk though, aren't they? You love all this stuff.'

'Yes, well, let's leave out the sexism, shall we? We've got to discuss this!'

Wayne removed his hand from her breast and squeezed her shoulder. 'Okay luv; sorry. But really, when do you think would be best? I suppose it should be ASAP really, shouldn't it?'

'Well, it all depends how big a do we have, doesn't it? The bigger it is the more planning there needs to be. So the longer a lead-time there'd have to be.'

'Okay, I can see that. So how much of a splash do you want to have?'

'You keep putting the onus on me!'

'Alright; so what do you want me to say?'

'Well tell me what *you* want.'

'Well, I don't know. Nothing really grand, I suppose. Think of t' cost, apart from anything else.'

Helen sighed, secretly relieved. 'That's what I was thinking. Although a lot of the cost – the reception and everything – falls on the bride's parents, traditionally. I suppose it's like a hangover from the days of dowries.'

'What's that?'

'It's like a sort of payment the bride's parents give to the other parents, or something. I think it still happens in some societies.'

'You mean like a sort of bribe to get their daughter safely married off?'

Helen giggled. 'Yeah, something like that!'

Wayne sniggered too. 'Well I wouldn't need bribing at all, petal!'

'Oh, I'm pleased to hear it! But seriously though; I think our Gilly's do cost my parents a fair packet, and she didn't mind asking them to stump up. She wouldn't though. But then she had a big wedding, as you know; the full church thing with white dress and bridesmaids and a flash car and everything.'

Wayne remembered. He'd been dragged along, just a few months after they'd got back together and Helen had moved down to Warminster.

Helen continued. 'No, I wouldn't want all that stuff anyway, so don't worry. And I wouldn't ask my mum and dad to find all that money again.'

'That's fine by me,' Wayne said, relieved too. He paused, mulling things over. 'So what sort of a do would you want then?' he repeated.

'Well, nothing really special, to be honest. Just a quiet little register-office thing, and a families-only reception, maybe at my parents' house, after. That would do me. What do you think?'

'Sounds good to me,' Wayne said, hastily, before she could

change her mind.
'Okay then. So when shall we do it?'
'Dunno Luv. It's up to you.'
'Wayne! Well, what if we say in the autumn – September; something like that? That'll give us time to save a bit; get some more furniture, for a house, and save for a nice honeymoon too, somewhere warm.'
'Yes, great. Let's go for it. That's settled then, is it?'
'Right then.'
They lay in silence for a while. Wayne wanted to settle to sleep. He'd have to be up early tomorrow to get back to camp in time for parade. He'd cut it too fine once before and missed it and received a high-decibel earful from the RSM. If it happened again there'd been hell to pay; the mother of all bollockings from higher up and very probably punishment, like confinement to barracks. He couldn't risk it.

Helen wondered whether she dare bring up the subject of babies. It was tempting to give it a try, as Wayne was in a mellow post-coital mood. Which had been her cunning plan, of course. But she hesitated. Hadn't she just been terribly sensible and suggested a reasonable engagement period during which to get some money together and set themselves up in a nice little house, probably married quarters? After all, this flat, although nicer than the first one, was still only one-bedroomed. Not big enough if there were a baby on the scene too. But best to put any little scheme involving family creation on hold for a bit. One thing at a time. She kissed him on the cheek, said 'Night, night' and turned away.

It was easier said than done though, now she had the thought in her brain. By September the marriage plans had been finalised (they'd tie the knot in early October) and married quarters been enquired about. There would be a house available, although Helen didn't really see why they couldn't have it now, as they were formally engaged. But the rules were strict, apparently. They would just have to wait. Meanwhile they'd bought (well, some of it was on credit) more furniture, a new washing machine and a better fridge that incorporated a full size freezer, one of those tall ones. They'd be able to run to a decent ten-day honeymoon (Wayne had applied for and been granted the leave) somewhere a little up-market from Spain; and the costs they didn't feel they could load onto Helen's parents could be comfortably met.

But as far as her secret wish went, it didn't help that, alone again tonight as Wayne was on duty, there was a thing on the box about someone giving birth. The classic tableau: exhausted, rapturous mum seeing her tiny, red-wrinkle-faced offspring for the first time; equally ecstatic, doting dad. It promptly set her off thinking. Well, wedding arrangements-wise, everything was pretty much done and dusted. There was nothing else to think about. But there was plenty of time to daydream about their life together; properly together, with all the fulfilment that would bring. Time now to fantasise about all the golden days to come. And so now, like a tempting little devil sitting on her shoulder whispering slyly in her ear, *Yes, but you know what you really want, don't you?* the tempting thoughts came back. Well, why not leave off the contraception now? Even if she fell straight away, which would probably be unlikely anyway, the marriage date was only three weeks away. Even if she'd conceived, it certainly wouldn't be showing, so there'd be no embarrassment about the wedding looking as though it were a shotgun. Not that her parents would have been bothered in the slightest even if she were, or it did. Quite the opposite; they'd both be delighted. It wasn't as if she and Wayne were still sixteen-year-olds.

So now was the time to have another serious chat with Wayne, this time *definitely* about baby making.

The following night, having enticed Wayne to bed early (again, he hadn't required a lot of persuading) she took the bull by the horns. They'd switched off the bedside light and made love as they always did, in the dark. He'd turned to settle to sleep. She snuggled close, fitting herself foetally to him, right hand snaking around to caress the sparse pale hairs on his chest.

'Wayne . . .'
'Mm?'
'I've been thinking . . .'
'Yeah?'
'Well . . .'

Wayne rolled over to face her, lifting his arm for her to nestle into the angle of his shoulder.

'Come on, spit it out. What is it?'
'Well, now we're so nearly married and everything, what about .

. . er . . . starting a family?'

Silence.

Then, 'You mean, like, have a baby?'

'Well yes Wayne; it does usually involve that!'

'Oh. Right.'

Another silence.

'So what do you think?'

'Well, yes . . .'

'You don't sound very sure about it!'

'No. Yes. I mean, I am. But is this a good time, do you think?'

Helen felt tiny icy fingers squeezing her chest. 'Why shouldn't it be? We've been together years and we can afford it, I reckon, now the wedding's mostly paid for and we've got most of the stuff we need for a house. Why wait any longer? There's no need to, is there?'

'No, I suppose not.' Wayne did not sound entirely convinced. 'But there's always the possibility of getting posted; like to Iraq or Afghanistan or somewhere. There still needs to be a lot of sorting done out there.'

Helen felt the fingers squeezing harder. 'Yes, but why should that make any difference? Lots of servicemen have children. It doesn't have to be a choice between the two, does it?'

'No,' Wayne repeated. 'But it would be quite tough being out there knowing I'd got a kid at home. I'd, like, feel I should be here, really.'

Helen felt anger rising. She fought to keep her tone level, her voice calm. She really didn't want a blazing row about it.

'Yes, well, that's always the way it is when you're in the services, if you've got a family. Which do you put first: family or duty? You have to have divided loyalties'

'Well obviously,' Wayne said levelly, 'but if we were posted that would be it. I wouldn't have any choice in t' matter, would I? That's what I mean though. It'd be bad enough just leaving you, never mind a bairn as well.'

They fell silent once more; an uncomfortable, accusing silence a wedge between them. *Here we go again,* Helen brooded, *me competing against the bloody army. It's just so unfair. He wants everything his own way.*

She wasn't going to take it, not again. 'Well anyway,' she flared, blatantly ill-tempered now, 'what about what I want? How many years do I have to wait until you feel ready for fatherhood? I want a child now, not when your sodding army career allows it!'

'Well so do I,' Wayne assured, appeasing. He hated rows. 'It's just that . . .'

'No! Just nothing! Why don't you consider *my* feelings for a change! Our Gilly's got her Suzie and another one coming, and I want some of that too. It's all right for you, with your soldiering, your mates, your 'family' as you call it, but I want a family, a sense of belonging to!'

'But you've got a family; what are you on about?'

'Wayne you know what I mean! Like an *immediate* family to be around every day – kids, for Christ's sake! People to live with and care for, *especially* if you're off somewhere sorting out the world. Can't you see that? It would be something to take me out of myself for one thing; stop me worrying.'

She stopped, biting her lip. Tears were bubbling to the surface. But she was damned if she was going to lose control; succumb like a typical weepy, clingy female. Wayne brought his free hand up to cup her cheek.

'Yeah, okay Hel. You're right. I expect I'm being a selfish bugger really. I can see what you mean. Let's go for it then.'

Helen lifted her hand to clasp his. Tightly.

'Really, Wayne? Can we?'

'Yeah, it would be good, wouldn't it? And if I did get posted, it'd be something even better to look forward to when I got leave.'

Helen felt relief surge through her. 'Yes, and you'd be a brilliant dad too.'

'Do you reckon?'

'Absolutely sure you would. Look how good you are with little Suzie.'

Wayne grinned in the dark, preening a little. Well, she was certainly a sweet little two-and-a-half-year-old. He hadn't seen her that many times, but she knew him and came to him readily, climbed onto his lap, when they did.

'She's a cute little thing. What's not to like?'

'Yes, she's gorgeous. So wouldn't you like one like that of your own?'

Wayne had to concede the point. 'Yeah, I suppose I would

really.'

'Well there you are then.' Helen pressed her advantage home. 'Which would you rather have; boy or girl?'

'Oh, girl. Yeah, little girl. Definitely. Followed by a boy, probably.'

Helen laughed; relaxed now. 'Yes, well, we can't order them just like that. It's the luck of the draw really.'

Wayne chortled too. He'd been won over, she could tell. 'No, I know, luv. It wouldn't matter really, as long as it had all its fingers and toes.'

'That is a joke, I take it?'

'Yeah, 'course it is. Seriously though; that's all that matters, ent it? As long as he or she is healthy?'

Helen disengaged her hand and returned it to his ribcage, hugging.

'Yes, true. Of course we'd want that. And ideally,' she added, teasing, 'one would have to be a carrot top, like their dad.'

'Aw, Hel, don't say that. Poor little bugger! He – she'd get teased rotten!'

'Oh, come on. People aren't so stupid about it nowadays, surely.'

'Well they were ten years ago, believe me. Some stupid kids were, anyway.'

Helen smiled in sympathy, remembering their schooldays. 'Well if I heard a kid teasing ours like that they'd soon get a good clip around the ear, no problem,' Helen declared, mock-crossly.

Wayne laughed again. 'Yeah, I can believe it. You should have been a soldier, Hel. You've got t' right instinct for it.'

Helen ignored that; it was a blatant wind-up. They lay for a while in silence. Wayne broke it. 'Okay then; the deal is: the other one has black hair that always looks like a bloody haystack. How's that?'

She lifted her hand, balled her fist and thumped him on his muscular bicep. 'Bugger off Wayne!'

They lapsed into silence again; Wayne chuckling quietly. Helen broke it this time. 'What about names then?'

'Hells bells luv, you aren't even in t' club yet!' he expostulated.

'I know, but we can have a few thoughts on the subject, can't we?'

'Okay, go on then. What do you fancy?'

'Um: Chloe perhaps, if it's a girl. Or maybe Emily. One of my nans is an Emily. Or if it's a boy: perhaps Daniel. Or Jack. They'd all go well with Harrison.'

'Okay. Yeah. Great.'

'But don't you have any thoughts?'

'Well, the subject's only just come up. Give us a chance. But it sounds like you've been thinking about it!'

'Yes, well, just idly mulling a few ideas over.'

'So it seems!'

'Well, you have some thoughts too.'

'Right.'

'Good.'

Helen moved her hand down over his hard stomach, through the hair of his groin, found his penis. Recognising the familiar touch, it responded quickly. She moved to straddle him, leaning forward as his hands reached for her heavy pendulous breasts.

'Okay' she said, beginning to pant, tingling with anticipation, 'let's give baby making a go, shall we?'

Chapter 18
Tomos

It could hardly have been a worse Christmas, really, Tomos reflected miserably, as he lay listlessly watching but not seeing the television on its bracket on the wall. He would have switched it off, but the remote control was out of reach on the far side of the bedside cabinet and he couldn't work up the energy to reach across for it. But then who *would* enjoy spending it in University Hospital, Aberystwyth? Alright; the staff members were doing their best to whip up a modicum of seasonal spirit; trying with somewhat pasted-on grins to look as though they'd really rather be in here, on duty, than at home with their families tucking into turkey with all the trimmings. (Not that he really envied normal, healthy people that, at the moment, anyway. The very thought of a huge plate of food made him feel like puking, to be honest.) There were a few decorations strung in desultory fashion around the walls of the three-bed side ward he was in, fortunately alone because he really didn't feel like talking to people, but their half-heartedness served only to lower his mood if anything, not raise it.

He'd thought he was going on alright too; adjusting to life with a heart condition that would never go away now. Mr Jenkins the consultant had pretty much got his daily cocktail of medication right, weighing efficacy against side-effects to strike a satisfactory balance; achieve an acceptable long-term status-quo. He had a reasonable quality of life, although thoughts of studying medicine had had to go by the board. But he'd not given up on medical ambition altogether. When it had become disappointingly plain that the rigours of six years' medical training followed by the pressure of being the lowest of the low, a junior hospital doctor, would be beyond his modest reserves of stamina, he'd applied instead for a pharmacology course in Cardiff. Well, he'd quite enjoyed his truncated work experience with Uncle Huw in Houston, and after all, pharmacology was an important aspect of medicine. As he was now finding, in a very real and practical sense.

Of course there had had to be other slight compromises too, mostly regarding Mair. Specifically, their sex life. Mr Jenkins had urged sensible restraint in matters of exercise. It was a matter of avoiding great exertion, which generally speaking wasn't a great problem or a case of having to radically change his lifestyle. After all, he'd never done sport. He was that rare animal: a young Welshman with no interest in Rugby. He didn't even like walking, particularly.

But Mair was a different matter. The discovery of sexual love with her had been a glorious revelation. But since diagnosis he had had to be careful. She did try to dampen his ardour as much as possible by not over-exciting him; tried to keep it low-key. And when, sometimes, he – they – just couldn't resist each other, took the active role. But she must surely have sometimes wished that they could really surrender to complete abandonment. He'd worried about that sometimes; feared that she might lose interest and be tempted away by more virile lovers, even when she insisted that his lack of virility really didn't matter. And so he clung to her desperately, as much in gratitude for her acceptance of his inadequacy and her support, as in wanting to give his own love.

He'd been a year and a term into the university course, looking forward to a second properly-together Christmas with Mair, and then this: developing a persistent cough in early December, greater than usual breathlessness, fatigue, a nagging chest pain that couldn't be ignored, much as he tried to deny it, and then, one morning, coughing up blood; Mair's frantic ringing for an ambulance and ten days spent in intensive care at Cardiff's University Hospital. Somehow, in spite of the regular antibiotics taken to ward off another episode of rheumatic fever, he'd become exposed to a pneumonia-triggering bacterium which had wormed its way around their protective shield.

For a period whose length he couldn't define, but was days he'd later learned, he'd retreated from the world, lost in a limbo of pain alternating with dulled senses and oxygen flooding his struggling lungs, unable to find the will to fight, oblivious of everything, submitting to whatever might be coming, a cat's cradle of tubes entering his arms and orifices and sensors taped to his bare chest. Until a corner had somehow miraculously been turned, and now he became aware of anxious faces peering down at him: Mam and

Dad, and Lowri looking unusually red-eyed, and Mair, pale as a ghost and biting her lip in an effort to maintain control, trying to smile.

Gradually he'd returned to the land of the living. After a few more days he could breathe without assistance, although the lethargy he felt was leaden. He'd been transferred by a lengthy and tiring road journey to Aberystwyth and the care of his own consultant. Then another milestone was passed one afternoon (how was she able to spend so much time with him, away from her job in Cardiff, he idly wondered) when Mair walked into the ward wearing her pasted-on smile and bent to cup his face and plant a kiss on his forehead and he'd weakly said no, lips, and so she did, so gently, and for some reason that had made her cry, wetting him with her saltiness.

Since then he'd made slow, almost imperceptible progress until now it was Christmas Day itself. The family were due in soon, and of course Mair (who was staying with his parents). He'd tried weakly protesting that Mam and Dad and Lowri shouldn't sacrifice their Christmas for him, to which Lowri had retorted, 'Don't be so bloody silly, of course we're coming.' You didn't argue with Lowri. But of course he did want Mair here. Well, all of them of course. But especially Mair.

And because Mair was staying with his parents they all arrived together, at eleven-thirty: Mair, Mam, Dad, Lowri and even Lowri's Will. It was fortunate that the other beds *were* unoccupied, because the visitors' chairs for them could be borrowed. Even so, they were still a chair short, so after all the kissing from the females, a manly grasp of his shoulder from Dad and a tentative, uncertain shake of his hand by Will, Mair plonked herself proprietorially on the bed beside him. Sioned and Glyn sat in a row on one side with Lowri and Will mirroring them on the other, a small and intimate audience. All the women had brought in carrier bags, and it soon became clear why. There was present-exchanging to do.

Tomos felt a stab of panic. He'd done all his present buying in good time, fortunately before the onset of the pneumonia, but they were all in Cardiff. But Mair had thought of that. She reached into her bag and brought out four variously-shaped and sized gift-wrapped parcels, and, looking like an afterthought, a tiny fifth one.

'I wrapped all your gifts for everyone for you,' she said. 'I think I remembered which was for whom. Hope I have anyway. People can always swap if I've got it wrong!'

She handed them around, leaving the very small one lying on the bed. She picked it up and gave it to him. 'And this is from you to me' she said quietly. 'You can give it to me and I'll pretend it's a surprise.'

'But how did you . . .'

'. . . discover where you'd hidden it? You're not very good at hiding things, Tomos Rees! Fortunately.'

'Oh, right.'

'Well go on then,' she said, give it to me!'

Tomos's felt his spirits lift a little, although the plan had been to give it to her in secret. He picked it up and handed it to her. 'Right; Mair, this is for you.'

'Diolch Tomos, thank you,' she said, taking it.

Suspecting that it might be something highly significant, Glyn said, 'Er, do you two want to be left alone for a minute?'

Mair laughed. 'No, you're alright Glyn, thanks anyway.' But then she looked a little anxiously at Tomos. 'Unless you do, do you Caraid?'

'No, I'm fine,' he mumbled, just a little peeved. 'Seeing as it isn't a surprise now.'

Sioned and Lowri, also suspicious, had no such inhibitions and were all inquisitive eyes. Mair tore open her careful wrapping and withdrew the small white jeweller's box. 'I really did only have a small peek,' she assured Tomos. 'As soon as I twigged it was my prezzie, I didn't look any further. Honestly!'

Tomos smiled weakly. 'Alright; I'll believe you.'

She opened the box and gently took out the little exquisitely engraved silver locket; studied it at length; undid the clasp to open it. It held a miniscule picture of Tomos, smiling in monochrome back at her. 'Oh,' she said, 'this is so sweet! Diolch yn fawr iawn!'

'I know it's a bit corny really,' Tomos mumbled, 'but it is a genuine antique. Victorian, they said in the shop. It was quite expensive, anyway.'

'Really?' Mair looked a little tearful. 'I mean about it being Victorian. The cost doesn't matter.' She looked at it some more, held it up by its silver chain, then handed it to Sioned, who took it almost with reverence, cheekily opening it again to look at the picture of her son.

'This is lovely!' she cooed. 'Where on earth did you find such a tiny picture of yourself though Bach, and why is it in black and white? Couldn't you find a nice coloured one?'

Lowri had taken it now, a not-quite-disguised supercilious smirk on her face. Sentimental lockets were not her thing at all. 'Mam, you are clueless! Black and white is much more *de rigueur* nowadays. It would look like a holiday snap if it were coloured. How did you do this Tomos; on your computer?'

Tomos smiled tiredly. 'Yea. Scanned in a picture, minimised it as needed with the zoom in Word and then printed in black and white.'

'So it started as coloured to begin with but you wanted it like that?' Sioned was thoroughly perplexed.

'Yes Mam.'

'Oh, I see.' Clearly, though, she didn't.

Lowri handed it to Will, who said, 'Yes, very good, Tomos' and handed it on to Glyn, who seemed as puzzled as Sioned but also opined that it was 'very nice.'

'I wonder who it belonged to first?' Mair ruminated. 'I wonder whose picture was in there originally. Whose sweetheart? And how did it finish up in a jeweller's and not get passed down through a family?'

'Perhaps it did for a while, but a female line ran out. There was just no female to leave it to,' Lowri suggested.

'Well I think that's very sad if that's the case,' Mair said.

She took it back from Glyn. 'Anyway, I think it's quite beautiful. Diolch, Cariad.' She leaned across to kiss Tomos's rather bristly ginger cheek. Then she pulled another package from her carrier bag and placed it in his hand. 'One of these isn't quite as antique as my locket, but it is pretty old. Nineteen-oh-nine perhaps. So what does that make it? Not Victorian?'

'Edwardian,' Will informed.

Tomos pulled the quartering purple satin ribbon loose on the curiously shaped package, quite glad that it wasn't Sellotaped. Undoing that would have required some effort. He opened out the silver-snowflakes-on-red paper. There was a stack of two books, smaller sitting upon larger. The smaller one was clearly old, bound in slightly frayed-at-the-edges dark green Rexene. Silver-blocked lettering proclaimed it *An Anthology of the Works of the Romantic Poets, with foreword by J. S. Lewis.* He lifted it to look at the other one. It was a modern book, a hardback, pristine and new, a montage of faces on the dust jacket, most of whom he knew, like Robert Owen, Karl Marx, Kier Hardy and Aneurin Bevan, below a title that read in large red sanserif letters: *Socialist Thinkers Who Changed The World.*

'Oh, great; diolch Mair.' He tried to sound enthusiastic; appear pleased. He turned back to the old book and opened it. In the top left-hand corner of the marbled endpaper was written, in just-decipherable brown ink in loopy copperplate, a dedication:

To my Dearest Mildred
with great affection
from Arthur
Christmas, 1909

Mair could see that he was reading it. 'Isn't that just so sweet?'

Tomos found himself smiling, in of spite of being determined not to enjoy the proceedings. 'Yes, it is.'

'What is it?' Sioned wanted to know.

'A dedication,' Mair told her. 'Tomos will show you in a minute.'

'I wonder who they were,' Mair mused. And who was Arthur? Was he husband? Fiancé? Brother? It's so formal, you can't really tell.'

'Umm, boyfriend or fiancé, I should think,' Tomos said, 'judging by the content.'

'Yes, I suppose so,' Mair agreed. 'Nineteen-oh-nine. That's just five years before the first war. I wonder if he fought in it. If he survived.'

'Well if he did, I hope so,' Tomos said.

'I'll second that,' interjected Lowri. 'Poor bugger.'

Tomos flicked through the pages, languidly. He passed it to an eager-to-look Lowri, who opened it carefully and found the contents page, scanning it with interest. 'Oh yes, wonderful,' she enthused, glancing across at Sioned. 'They're all here. It's got Sonnet forty-three; Elizabeth Barrett Browning.'

Sioned looked blank. Lowri grinned at her. 'You know, Mam!

"How do I love thee? Let me count the ways." That one.'

'Oh, yes,' Sioned said, slightly uncertainly, although she knew the familiar first line.

Lowri turned to the page. 'I love the last bit, even if I am a heathen. *"Smiles, tears, all of my life; and if God chose, I shall but love thee better after death."* Ah!'

Will grinned at her. 'Crikey Lowri, I didn't realise you were so sentimental!'

Lowri glared at him. 'I'm not! But this isn't your modern saccharine crap. This is beautiful elegant timeless prose. Don't you bloody call me sentimental!'

Sioned cut in, placating. 'Yes, well I think it's lovely. Don't fight about it, you two! It's a lovely book for Mair to give our Tomos!' She turned her gaze to Tomos. 'Don't you think so, Bach?'

Tomos concurred, tiredly. 'Yes, it is, Mam. Lovely.'

'Right then,' Sioned said firmly, drawing a line under the discussion. She didn't want Tomos to feel agitated, not with his delicate health. Especially not on Christmas Day. She looked at the wrapped present lying on her lap. 'Can we look at ours now then Bach?'

'Yes of course,' Tomos said. He was finding the chatter of so many people a little wearisome.

Sioned opened hers. It was books too; two new paperbacks by two of her favourite romance authors (he'd checked that she hadn't read them yet). Glyn had got a sweater and so had Will. They looked at each other and then at Tomos, rather uncertainly, slightly anxiously, a silent question hanging in the air. Glyn gave it voice. 'Er, have we got the right ones?'

Tomos smiled weakly. 'Yes you have.'

'Thank goodness for that,' Mair breathed.

'Duw, yes,' Glyn said, palpably relieved. His was plain and dark blue.

'Yes,' Will agreed. 'Thanks, Tomos.' He was holding a boldly patterned sweater emblazoned with *HUG ME NOW* in unmissable lettering across the chest.

Lowri had got two CDs. 'Ah; wonderful, little brother! Diolch!' she hooted with delight and reached to grasp his hand, surprised to find it so cool and limp.

A catering person wearing a Santa Claus hat and beaming

A wide smile appeared, towing a drinks trolley. She asked Tomos what he would like to drink. He began to decline all offers but a stern look from Sioned, her mouth open ready to form a non-ignorable coax changed his mind. He accepted a cup of tea.

'Is this for us as well?' Glyn asked.

'Yeah, go on then,' the plump, jolly assistant said, 'as it's Christmas.'

'Is there anything stronger to go with it?' Will wondered, grinning.

The woman snorted good-naturedly. 'You'll be lucky! The NHS isn't made of money! Even at Christmas. It's what you see here or nothing, I'm afraid.'

'No, this is fine, said Lowri, 'don't take any notice of him. Thanks.'

The woman distributed drinks and, making a half-hearted attempt at refusal, accepted a five pound note as a Christmas tip from both Glyn and Will (they knew how shockingly low pay was in catering firms), wished them all Season's Greetings and trundled on her way.

The company sat and sipped their tea and coffee, and in Mair's case bottled water she'd brought in with her, and made small talk across Tomos's bed, glancing at him, inviting him to participate, but he didn't want to. He drank half of his cup of tea and put it aside. It was too much of an effort to finish it. Mair glared at Sioned, daring her to chivvy him to finish it. He could feel weariness inveigling in; his eyelids growing heavy. But then he always spent most of the morning asleep. He blinked, trying to keep his eyes open. It was rude to simply go to sleep on his guests, after all. But it was no good. He'd just close them for a moment. Mam was saying something to him, but she was fading away. And then the darkness came.

He opened his eyes. Mair's body had gone from his side. He looked around, irrationally panicking a little. But it was all right. She was sitting in a chair to his right, blonde head bent over, reading his poetry book. There was no one beside her. He looked to his left. There was no one else there either. The chairs had disappeared. She looked up. Smiled. 'Ah, Cariad. You're back with us, are you?'

'Where is everyone?'

'They've gone. You dropped off to sleep and your mam decided they should leave you to it. I stayed, so I'd be here when you woke up.'

Tomos felt his throat tighten. 'That's sweet of you. Diolch.'

She closed the book and put it on the bedside cabinet, within his reach. Took his right hand in both of hers. They were warmer than his. 'Well I couldn't leave you all alone, could I?'

'No,' he said, close to tears, ridiculously grateful.

'Well I'm glad they went, in a way,' she said. 'Your family are lovely and everything, but I wanted you all to myself.'

'I'm not much good to you, in this state,' Tomos grumbled, self-pity threatening to steal his voice completely.

Mair squeezed his hand, almost painfully. 'Don't say that!' Her voice was husky too. 'Of course you are. You're still my beautiful Tomos. Still my lovely boy. You being a bit poorly doesn't make any difference.'

'Yes, but I can't . . .'

'Can't what?'

'Well, you know. And I don't know when – if, I'll ever be able to again. Not the way I feel at the moment. We were having to take it really gently before, and now it'll be even worse. We might just as well just stop altogether.'

His lower lip was trembling, his jaw gaping into a rictus grin. He put his free hand to his face, ashamed of his sorrow. She rose and sat on the bed, bending to him; took his face in her hands, almost crying too, struggling to find enough strength for them both.

'Listen to me you silly boy,' she said, tears welling now, 'It really doesn't matter! We'll just do what we can; what your condition allows. I won't love you any the less just because you can't be all virile and rampant. That's not everything, believe me.'

'Really?' Tomos whispered. 'Really?'

'Yes,' she said, voice cracking, 'really.'

They were interrupted by the arrival again of the catering lady. She beamed at Tomos, a toothy grin splitting her dark round face from ear to ear. 'Hello sweetheart! You back in the land of the living now? I came before but you were dead to the world. Fancy some Christmas dinner now?'

'Yes. Thank you,' he said, not altogether certainly. 'Just a little then, please.'

The woman looked at her trolley doubtfully. 'Well we only do the one size. Standard portions and all that. Well never mind. You just eat what you can, leave the rest.'

'Right. Thank you.'

'And do you fancy some Christmas pudding? Or would you rather have fruit salad and cream? That would slip down nice and easy.'

'Yes, rather have that. Thank you.' Tomos said.

Mair rose from the bed and pulled the wheeled table across. The caterer placed the meal on it with a clatter of cutlery.

'Sorry there's not a nice bottle of wine to go with it,' she grinned. 'You'll be able to have one when you're better though, I expect.'

'Have you got another fork we can have?' Mair asked the woman. 'Er, what's your name?'

'Angel, for my sins!'

'Rubbish! I bet you live up to your name every day.'

Angel laughed. 'Working the NHS, it has to be mainly from the kindness of my heart, true. It's certainly not for the money, Darlin'!' She paused and added conspiratorially, 'Actually it's Angela, but I got called Angel as a kid and it kinda stuck.'

'Well you're doing an angelic job today, anyway.'

Angel thought that highly amusing too. 'Thanks! Mind you, I'm getting a bit sick of the sights of Christmas dinner, to be honest with you. And I've got my own to face when I get home.'

'When do you finish work then?'

Angel glanced at her watch. Mair noticed it was a Mickey Mouse one. 'Hour and fifty minutes time. 'Four o' clock.'

'And don't tell me you're going home to start cooking?' Mair was horrified.

'Good grief no! I've got a well-trained hubby. He just happens to be a chef. He'll have the turkey in the oven by now and it'll all be ready when I get back home, hopefully, provided the kids haven't eaten it all.'

'Yes, well you enjoy it! It's rotten, you having to work on Christmas Day.'

'Thanks, I will.' Angel sighed. 'Someone has to do it though. I don't mind too much really.'

Remembering the requested fork, she placed another one on the table and then poured Tomos another cup of tea.

'Right,' she said, grinning again, 'I'll leave you to it. Let you eat that before it goes cold.' She stepped towards the bed and touched Tomos's hand kindly. 'And you get well soon, Sweetheart.'

'Yes, thank you,' Tomos replied, weakly.

Angel wished them Happy Christmas again and trundled on her way. Mair set about cutting the turkey and roast potatoes and vegetables on the plate into small pieces.

'What are you doing?' Tomos asked, puzzled.

Mair smiled. 'Something I read once about preparing food for invalids. It looks easier to manage, more palatable, cut into small pieces.'

'I still don't think I can eat it all . . .'

'Never mind Cariad. Just eat what you can. I'll help you clean the plate. It's a shame to waste the food.'

'Aren't you hungry anyway? You've not had dinner, have you?'

'No; it's okay though,' Mair said. 'I was waiting for you to wake up. Anyway, I didn't suppose the NHS would run to giving visitors Christmas dinner so I brought my own supplies!'

She delved into her bag again and brought forth a selection of items: a plastic-packaged chicken-and-something sandwich, a Mars bar and three tangerines. Tomos smiled. 'You think of everything.'

'Yes, well; you've got to. I thought you might like the tangerines. And they're a bit Christmassy, aren't they? Anyway, come on, eat your dinner.'

Tomos set too, finding he'd got a modest appetite after all, with Mair occasionally, supportively, spearing pieces of turkey or vegetable for herself, to help out. The plate was soon emptied, even the mandatory Brussels sprouts. He sipped the now-almost-cold tea. Mair said, 'I think you could have something a little stronger than that,' and dipped into her bag yet again and produced a can of lager.

'Oh.' He was uncertain. 'I don't know whether I'm allowed that . . .'

'Come on,' she said, looking theatrically towards the door and dropping her voice, 'just have a drop; just a taste. They'll never know.'

She poured the water in his tumbler back into the water jug; snapped the ring pull of the lager can and filled the tumbler, fizzing, half full. 'Go on,' she urged, grinning, handing it to him, 'drink it quick before anyone comes!'

Tomos giggled and took a sip, gasping slightly at the sharpness and bubbles. It tasted wonderful. He couldn't drink it all down at one go though; it made him gasp all the more, and a little alarmingly. He handed the tumbler back to Mair.

She was contrite. 'Sorry Bach; shouldn't have rushed you. I'll hide it until it's gone flat. Tell me when you want some more.' She opened the door of his bedside cabinet and put it inside, away from disapproving eyes. 'Right', she said, 'What shall we do now?'

'Dunno,' said Tomos, feeling almost cheerful. 'Race you down the ward, if you like.'

'Mm; don't know about that.' Mair laughed. 'Now that *would* get me into trouble, I think, for getting you into bad ways.'

'Oh, okay then, we'd better not.'

'Do you want to watch some television?' Mair suggested.

Tomos wasn't keen though. 'No, not particularly. It's always the same old stuff on at Christmas.'

Mair agreed. 'Yeah, you're right. Shall I read you some poetry then? How about that?

'Okay, yes, that'd be nice.'

She picked up the book from the cabinet; opened it and gently turned the pages. 'It feels sort of, I don't know, almost intrusive, reading a book that was once a gift between two other people; doesn't it?'

'Yes, I suppose so. But then it's also a bit like a privilege, in a way. I wonder how long that woman – what's her name? – kept it.'

Mair turned back to the flyleaf. 'Er, Mildred. I wonder if she was called "Millie." Well all her life, hopefully. And hopefully, she spent it all with her Arthur.'

'Yeah.'

She turned again to the Elizabeth Barrett Browning poem; began to recite it, softly.

How do I love thee? Let me count the ways.
I love thee to the depth and breadth and height
My soul can reach, when feeling out of sight
For the ends of Being, and ideal Grace.

Tomos closed his eyes, letting the words lull him, as Mair

continued:

> *I love thee to the level of everyday's*
> *Most quiet need, by sun and candle-light*
> *I love thee freely, as men strive for Right;*
> *I love thee purely, as they turn from Praise.*
> *I love thee with the passion put to use*
> *In my old griefs, and with my childhood's faith.*
> *I love with a love I seemed to lose*
> *With my lost saints – I love thee with the breath . . .*

Her voice faltered, faded to silence. She wasn't finishing it. Tomos opened his eyes; looked at her. She had the book in her lap, closed, her thumb keeping the place. She was looking down at it; face stricken, teeth biting her trembling lower lip. She was blinking away tears.

'I'm sorry,' she said, 'I can't read the last lines.'

Friday the ninth of January. Mr Jenkins the consultant was wearing his sombre-but-trying-to-appear positive face. It wasn't terribly convincing. He was sitting in the visitor's chair at Tomos's bedside.

'Well there's no reason why you shouldn't go home to finish recuperating in a couple of days' time.'

'Really?' Tomos was dubious. I really don't feel all that well, still.'

'No,' said Mr Jenkins. He paused, weighing his words carefully. 'I'm afraid though that we've done pretty much all we can and there's no real point in you staying in hospital. We've got this bout of pneumonia under control, but your heart has taken a bit of a beating again.'

'But won't it recover?'

'Well, no, not in any real sense. There's too much damage now, I'm afraid. It's taken a triple whammy, really. First the congenital problems, then the rheumatic fever, and now this.' He smiled sympathetically. 'Heart failure can't really be reversed; you know that.'

Tomos felt irritation rising. 'I wish you wouldn't call it that! You make it sound as if it's going to stop any minute!'

Jenkins lifted his hands in apology. 'Sorry. It's just the term we use. Of course it doesn't necessarily mean that.' There was a pause as he searched for a gentler way of putting it, wishing he hadn't used the qualifying phrase. 'You know that your heart's efficacy has dropped further since this latest turn of events. And in spite of our best efforts it hasn't really recovered significantly. I'm afraid it will only have thirty-five, forty percent capacity for the rest of your life. But as long as you take it easy; do moderate exercise but don't go thinking you can run the London Marathon, you should be alright.'

'Well there's no chance of that; I was never into sport anyway,' Tomos said sourly.

'All the same, you should do some exercise,' Jenkins insisted. Say twenty minutes of gentle walking per day. Work your way up to that.'

'What about surgery?' Tomos wanted to know. 'You've mentioned it as a possibility before. Replace my mitral valve and be done with it?'

Jenkins sighed. 'Yes; with your degree of cardiomyopathy, you're getting close to the point where we'll have to start thinking about it. But not just yet. Like all operations, especially open-heart, the procedure isn't entirely without risk, so it's a matter of weighing probable benefit against possible complication.'

He paused again, letting Tomos digest his words. When Tomos didn't speak he resumed, 'But at the moment your symptoms are significant but not chronic. You get a bit breathless fairly easily, and I know you have some fatigue. But then you have just had pneumonia, remember. And you have some oedema in your ankles, but I've seen far worse. No, we'll keep a close eye on you, and give you a streptococcal inoculation to guard against the possibility of further pneumonia. I don't really know how that got missed before, to be honest. If any symptom gets markedly worse, then we *will* have to think about surgery.'

Jenkins looked at his unhappy young patient. 'Okay?'

Chapter 19
Wayne

Helen was on the phone to her mum, trying, as usual, to get a word in edgeways. 'Yeah, I booked it today. For the fourteenth of next month.'

On the other end of the land line, Susan smiled and sighed. She'd always rather prided herself about not being overly sentimental, but it *was* a wedding after all, even if it was a bit low-key. Still, that was the way the youngsters wanted it; it wasn't for her to impose her opinions on the matter on them. Although she suspected that Wayne's mum Maureen might be a tiny bit disappointed that it wasn't more of a do. But at least now, finally, after all these years (although she wouldn't have been terribly happy about them marrying much before now anyway) it really was going to happen. There was no going back for them now, short of cancelling and probably forfeiting the license fee, not to mention the booking for the reception in the same pub that had done Wayne's twenty-first.

Unless, of course, pigs were suddenly able to fly and Wayne chickened out at the last moment; did a runner. But of course he wouldn't do that. Not solid, reliable, slightly-dull-but-nice Wayne. It was unthinkable. No, it was pretty much all done and dusted now. Just the formality of the ceremony. Did you call register-office sanctioned marriages ceremonies? Well what else could you call them? They were understated, rather slight affairs, true, but ceremonies all the same.

She'd rather been hoping, secretly and a bit naughtily, that Helen might have been with child, in the Biblical phrase, by now. That would have really raised a few eyebrows, pricked a few respectabilities, certainly. Not that she herself would have been bothered in the least by a suspicious belly bulge. Neither would Mark. That was one thing about her and Helen's relationship; they could confide in each other completely, as equals, more like close sisters than mother and daughter, really. So when last April Helen had revealed, just in passing, like, that she and Wayne were now trying for a baby, she'd been quite thrilled at the notion, if she were to be honest. What a silly expression 'trying for a baby' was! She'd always thought that. She knew, obviously, that it simply meant laying off the contraception, but it always evoked images of them suddenly doing it more vigorously, more determinedly, eyes closed and jaws clenched in concentration; of them doing it at every opportunity, any time of the day or night.

   A baby would have been further cement for their coming marriage; extra underpinning, because she knew (Helen had spoken wistfully about it many times) that things weren't always perfectly okay between them. Helen had often confided that she sometimes felt she had to share Wayne with his army life and his mates a little too much. His other family. His comrades, as he might have put it if he were more articulate. And there was the increasing possibility, with the continuing trouble going on in Iraq, that Blair might suddenly decree that Wayne's regiment be sent overseas, to do actual real-life soldiering. Then there would be not just separation but worry overlaying it too. A baby to care for would be a distraction. To some extent, anyway.

   But, so far, it hadn't happened. Helen would certainly have told her, even if it were only a suspicion. If she were only a couple of days late she'd have been on the phone like a shot. She'd begun to wonder, vaguely, if there was something wrong physically with one of them. Possibly Wayne (she knew from their girl talk that Helen's periods were as regular as clockwork); perhaps he had a low sperm count, or something? After all, for goodness sake, they were young, at the height of their sexual prowess; at maximum fertility. Helen should be falling easily.

   Susan was snapped out of her reverie. Helen was continuing, taking advantage of the unusual silence. 'Yeah, just think, in less than three weeks from now I'll be Mrs Harrison!'

   'Well it'll be about time too,' Susan replied. 'And you've got your married quarters sorted, you say?'

   'Right. We've been allocated a house. Beats me why we can't move into it now, as getting hitched is definitely going to happen, but you know what the army's like. They have to do everything by the book. Can't have things like flexibility or common sense intruding, now can they?'

   Susan laughed. 'No luv; that'd never do. Got to enforce regulations. Can't have the common soldiery living in sin in army accommodation, you know.'

'Well I think it's bloody stupid, all the same. What possible harm can it do to their reputation, if that's what's worrying them?'

'Yes, I know,' Susan sympathised, 'but that's the military for you. Never mind though. It's not long to wait. After all, you've been waiting, what is it, five years? A few more days is nothing.'

'I suppose you're right,' Helen conceded grudgingly. 'But we seem so near and yet still so far now. After all, we live together nearly all of the time anyway. Have done for ages. It's not as if we aren't committed to each other.'

Susan laughed. 'It certainly does seem a long time. As if you've been doing it forever.'

She paused. 'There's no sign of, er . . .?'

'No, sod it.' Helen didn't bother to hide her exasperation. 'My present condition proves it. That's another egg that's going nowhere, except down the toilet.'

'Well, never mind luv. I'm sure it'll happen soon enough. Two healthy young people like you.'

Helen laughed bitterly. 'It's certainly not for want of trying, Mum, believe me.'

'No, I don't suppose so.' Susan smiled, then tried reassurance. 'But just give it time. Sometimes you can't rush these things. You just have to let nature take its course.'

'Well I wish nature would hurry up; I can't wait forever,' Helen grumbled.

Susan broached the delicate subject, carefully. 'Yes I know; you're impatient. But give it longer. Anyway, if you're worried that nothing's happening, you could always get yourselves checked out, you know.'

'How do you mean?'

'Well, make sure there's nothing wrong with either of you. Just in case.'

Helen's voice rose a couple of tones in anxiety. 'Well I must be alright, surely? I couldn't be more regular. And I bleed normally, as far as I know.'

'Yes, I'm sure, but it could be Wayne; you never know.'

Helen snorted the next reply. 'Uh, I'm pretty sure there's nothing wrong with him either. He can perform okay; believe you and me!'

Susan said gently, 'He might have no problems producing the

goods as far as you can tell, but his sperm count could be low.'

There was silence, threatening awkwardness. Susan hurried on. 'But I expect he's okay really, a man of his age.'

When Helen spoke again there was an edge to her voice. 'Yes, I suppose you're right. Bloody hope so, anyway. I can see it being hard to get him to the doctor if we were concerned about things. He'd never want to admit he might be defective in that department. Male pride, and all that.'

'No, well, as I say luv; he's probably fine. It's just a possibility to keep in mind, that's all I'm saying. Sorry I brought the subject up.'

Helen's reply was a grunt.

'Anyway,' Susan said, looking around for an escape route, 'I must get on. Get the dinner ready. Okay then. And don't worry. It'll be fine; you'll see. Right. Bye then.'

'Bye,' Helen mumbled distractedly.

Wayne was on guard duty, the evening shift, so he wouldn't be home until late. There was nothing that Helen particularly wanted to watch on the box and ages to go until she had to get dinner ready, so she rang friend Sally. It had been a while since they'd chatted. Helen missed seeing her around the library. They'd been good mates, and she'd been really sorry when laugh-a-minute Sally left to work as manager in the wine bar, which was an environment better suited to her ebullient personality. Sally was one of those people who found it difficult to remain quiet for longer than ten minutes at a time, so she and libraries had never really got on.

The phone was picked up quickly and Helen was relieved that it was Sally herself who said, 'Hello?' If she were perfectly honest she didn't really like boyfriend Chris all that much, with his overblown, over-muscled torso (not finely honed like Wayne's), perpetual tan, blond pigtail and tattoos. Talk about your personal trainer stereotype. And the way he always, *always* wore sweat pants with the obligatory stripe, only because, she suspected, they displayed his not inconsiderable crotch region attributes to best advantage. Although it completely turned her off, actually. Sal was welcome to him. Size wasn't everything. She found his constant inane grin and flirtatious full-of-himselfness irritating too, but Sal seemed to think the world of him. Well, each to their own.

'Hi Sal,' she said, it's Helen.'

Sally almost squealed with pleasure. 'Hel! Hi! How you doing?'

'Great thanks, Sal. You?'

'Yeah; good.'

Helen felt her spirits rising immediately. 'How's life in wine-bar-land then?'

Sally tittered. 'Oh, you know. About the same. A bit livelier than the library, anyway!'

A thought suddenly struck Helen. *Bugger!* Sal would probably be going to work any minute now. She'd forgotten that.

'Oh; you aren't just rushing out to work or anything, are you?'

Another giggle. 'No; you're alright. Night off. His Nibs is working though. Some old bird with a home appointment. I've seen her; got to be sixty if she's a day, so I reckon I can trust him.'

'No! Really?'

'Yeah; straight up! Makes you laugh, don't it? Still; it's easy money for Chris, working for the hopelessly deluded. He says she's knackered after five minutes.'

'Sal! Don't be a cow!'

'Well, it just strikes me as a bit pathetic, that's all. Anyway, how's your gorgeous soldier boy?'

'He's fine. He's on late duty too, guarding the barracks against attack from all sides.'

'Right. Hey, tell you what Hel; how about I nip round and see you in that case, bearing a free sample from work, as the cats are away? We haven't had a good chinwag for ages.'

'Yeah, great. Helen found herself grinning inanely. 'That'll be good. There's lots to tell you, like about the wedding and everything.'

'Wonderful! See you in a bit!'

Helen went to reply, but the line was already dead.

Helen opened the door to stifle a continuous ringing of the bell. Sal always did that; stood there with her finger on it. It was a running practical joke of hers. There she stood, hand dropping from the bell as it swung away, the same old Sal. As short as herself and blond-haired like her fella; chest well-developed too but in altogether a different sort of way. They were two of a kind, really, her and Chris. She was grinning from ear to ear, but then she almost always was.

They embraced, Helen reeling slightly from her friend's perfume.

What had she done; taken a bath in it? She led the way through into the lounge. Sally and her bottle followed. Helen had already set glasses and corkscrew waiting on the coffee table, as Sally put the bottle of Burgundy down and divested herself of her denim jacket, throwing it carelessly onto the sofa. She sat down beside it as Helen uncorked and filled their glasses, handing one to her.

'Cheers,' said Sally, raising it in salute.

'Cheers,' Helen replied, plonking herself down in the armchair. They drank.

'So,' said Sally, 'tell me all about it. The splicing's all arranged then, is it?'

'Yeah. Not that there's a great deal involved anyway. The register office, then a bit of a do at the *Duck and Drake*, our old local up in Northallerton, then we fly off to Lanzarote for ten sun-soaked days. Wayne managed to get the leave.'

'Mm; right.' Sally's interest sounded polite rather than enthusiastic. 'You didn't fancy the full church thing then?'

Helen grinned. 'Not really, to be honest. After all, it's only really a matter of making it legal, isn't it? I suppose if I'd really wanted all that, Wayne would have gone along with it, but I didn't.'

Sally seemed unimpressed. 'Yeah, well, if Chris and me ever take the plunge, I will. The bigger the better. It's only one day of your life after all. Might as well make it a blinder.'

Helen laughed, imagining her extrovert friend standing demure and pious; virginally white before a vicar. 'Don't you think it'd be a touch hypocritical though, you of all people coming over all religious just for one day?'

Sally looked puzzled. 'No? Why would it be? Everyone gets married in church, like they get their final send off in church. It's just what you do. Doesn't mean you have to be a regular worshipper or anything. But then you've got these strange leftie ideas, you silly cow. Like you're anti-war and everything!'

Helen delivered a swift kick to Sally's calf. 'No! That's different altogether. It's a matter of principle. Just 'cos you haven't got any! Bloody hedonist! Anyway, at least I'm honest about my atheism. Not two-faced about it.'

'Yeah, well; I think it's a bit weird, all the same. Why can't you just be like normal people?' Sally was grinning; it was only good-natured banter. She loved a good winding-up of Helen. She always took the bait.

'Anyway,' said Helen, 'You're still going to lower yourself to come to our heathen do, aren't you?'

''Course we are! Just you try and stop us. I've gotta see my old mate hitched now, haven't I?'

'And you don't mind making the trip all that way?'

'Nah, 'course not. I'll enjoy it. I've never been up north before. Well, not proper north, anyway.' Sally paused, considering. 'Although I went to Nottingham once, to my gran's funeral. Does that count as north?'

Helen was horrified. 'Bloody hell, Sal! No it doesn't! Honestly; you southerners! You think anywhere north of Watford is north!'

And so the banter continued. Helen unwound, basking in her friend's easy company. It was a therapeutic ambience; soothing and comfortable. At ten o' clock she announced that she'd have to begin getting dinner ready. Wayne would be home at twenty past, exhausted from guarding against the marauding hordes at the gate. Sally, pouting disappointment, got up to leave, reaching for her jacket.

'It's okay,' Helen said, 'don't go just yet. Come into the kitchen and talk to me.'

So Sally did, sitting at the kitchen table, nursing her jacket, chatting as Helen prepared vegetables and set pork chops under the grill, ready.

With complete predictability, they heard a key turn in the entrance door at twenty-one minutes past the hour and Wayne entering the living room, calling hello. Helen left the potatoes simmering and walked through to welcome him, Sally in her wake.

Seeing the unexpected visitor, Wayne's forehead furrowed. He looked openly displeased. 'Oh, hi, Sally.'

The words came out grudgingly. He cast a what-the-hell's-she-doing-here? sort of glance at Helen as she pecked him on the cheek, surprised at his brusqueness.

Sally sensed the atmosphere. 'Hi Wayne; how you doing?'

He didn't reply.

'Right. Okay, I was just leaving.' Sally risked a joke. 'Just been keeping my old mate company while you've been defending us!'

Wayne scowled.

'Yes, right; I'll be off then.' Sally put arms into jacket sleeves and headed towards the door, Helen following.

Helen opened it for her, as Sally said, giving her friend a sideways look, 'I'll see you again before the wedding then, I expect.' She looked back at Wayne, who had slumped down onto the sofa. 'See you, Wayne!'

He grunted. Sally gifted a parting, quizzical look, a final 'night' and departed. Helen closed the door and returned to the kitchen to set the vegetables boiling and the chops grilling. She called to Wayne, who was still lolling, hands clasped, examining his feet. 'Everything okay, love? Had a bad day?'

'No, it's alright,' Wayne answered, but morosely.

Helen knew him of old though. 'Well, tell me about it after dinner then.'

They ate in silence. He didn't eat with his usual gusto. He declined the fruit bowl afterwards (Helen always tried to persuade him to eat healthily). Something was bothering him, alright. She cleared the dishes away and washed up. Wayne rarely offered to help at the best of times, and seemed completely disinclined to tonight. And usually the box would be on by now. Helen tidied up and made coffee for them, bringing it through to set on the coffee table, sinking down beside him. Wayne was already wearing civvies, so there was no need for him to change.

'Ah; that's better.' Helen patted her belly. 'I was ready for that. Wish you didn't have to work late sometimes!'

Silence.

Clearly, she would have to wring it out of him.

'So what is it then? And don't say "Nothing"!'

He shifted uncomfortably. 'Er. . .'

She took his hand. 'Come on! Tell Mummy!'

He looked at her for the first time, gathering himself as if building courage. 'Well, the thing is, we're being posted.'

Her heart dropped like a stone. 'Where?' she managed.

'Iraq.'

His eyes had slid away again. She let go of his hand, irrationally blaming him personally. 'Oh, bloody hell; no!' She stared at him, stricken.

'Yeah. Well, us always knew it were on t' cards.' He was trying to make it sound like an apology.

She could feel her heart being squeezed, suddenly racing. 'Oh, for fuck's sake! She forced the question out, dreading the answer. 'When?'

'Next week. Tuesday. Fly out oh-six-forty-five.'

'Next *Tuesday?* But that's only, what, five sodding days away!'

'Yes, I know it is,' Wayne said patiently, trying to reclaim her hand. Helen was having none of it though. She crossed her arms, angry, folding it unattainably across her right bicep.

'Well it's not much notice is it?'

Wayne sighed, a little too audibly. 'I know, but t' top brass isn't going to ask us lads if it's convenient for us, are they? When t' order comes, we just have to go, at t' drop of a hat, like. Constant readiness, an' all that.'

'Yes, well,' Helen said, bad-tempered, it's still not long.'

He was getting angry as well now. It was what he'd been expecting though. He'd known she wouldn't be reasonable about it. He'd been dreading having to tell her all day. 'Well that's just t' way it is in t' services. You always knew that.'

Helen laughed humourlessly. 'Uh! Knew it maybe, but never liked it!'

Wayne tried cajoling. It wasn't easy though with his control slipping away. 'Ah, come on Hel! We've been through this before, many times. It just goes with t' territory. You know it does. Give us a bit of support, please!'

She wouldn't be mollified though; retreated into sullen silence. He tried again. 'Come on, luv. Please?'

Helen turned to face him, keeping her distance. 'Well it's alright for you, isn't it? You're finally going to get some action; do it for real. It's what you want, isn't it? I bet you're just loving this!'

'No I'm not! But it *is* what I've been training to do all these years. It's what soldiers do after all!'

'Yes; true.' Helen could feel control deserting her too; the pent up anxiety of years, always present but carefully contained and denied, just about, always hoping that he'd never be tested; now threatening to erupt like a volcano. 'But why do *you* want to do it? Why not leave it to the other silly buggers, who can't think of anything else to do with their lives? What's so wonderful about fighting, for Christ's sake? Why would you enjoy killing, anyway?'

Her voice was getting shrill, becoming a screeching falsetto. But there was no stopping the torrent of words now. 'Why can't you be like your brother? He never wanted to do the bloody army thing! You're so fucking different, you two!' You wouldn't think you were twins!'

The words hit him like a slap in the face. He swivelled to face her, too, glaring. 'Oh yeah; that's it, ent it! Bloody Tomos, with his education and his posh way of talking and his ambition and his strange lefty ideas! I allus thought you took a bit too much interest when he came to visit us that time!'

'Oh come on now Wayne! Helen spat back. Don't be stupid! Of course I took an interest. He was your brother for crying out loud. And I couldn't help but look at him now, could I? He was so the spitting image of you!'

'Yeah, well. Maybe so,' Wayne grumbled. 'But you were hanging on his every word as I remember. I bet you wish I *were* more like him really, don't you?'

'No! Of course not!'

'But you just said you did!'

'Yes, well, I didn't really mean that. It just came out, because I was cross. Sorry.'

'Um.' He sounded completely unconvinced. 'Anyway; you're really putting a dampener on things. Can't you at least try and be a bit pleased for me? For my sake? I'm finally getting t' chance to do what I've been training for these last few years and all I get from you is all this bloody clingy female stuff. I'm gonna be careful, for God's sake. Not do anything stupid. They teach us not to take unnecessary risks, you know!'

'Oh, *please!* Just listen to yourself! You're going to be putting yourself in harm's way and you say you'll be *careful?'*

'Yes, of course I will! It's not a game of cowboys and Indians, for crying out loud. It's serious stuff and we *are* careful. As careful as we can be. Any road, the worst of it's over, over there, now. The coalition's got things pretty much under control.'

'Um; yes, that's what the bloody government and Bush would have us believe.'

'Well they've got a better idea of what's going on than us.'

Wayne's complacency was driving Helen mad. He just couldn't be reasoned with. She gave up arguing. A black silence fell as each brooded, sullen, unbending in the certainty of their position.

A thought suddenly struck Helen. 'Hang on a minute. You know what this means, as well, don't you?'

'No; what?'

'Oh, that's just bloody typical! You aren't even thinking about it, are you? There's the small matter of getting married, if you remember! That's off now, too. Oh, *shit!*'

Wayne squirmed visibly, contrite again. 'Yes I know, Luv. Course I were thinking about it. That makes it even worse for you, I know. But I can hardly tell t' C.O. that us can't go now 'cos of getting married now, can I?'

Helen was calming down, anger giving way to disconsolation, resignation. But it felt like the last straw. She exhaled a long theatrical sigh. 'No, of course not. Don't patronise. But that too! It's too much. We'll have to un-arrange everything now. The register office. The *Duck and Drake*. Cancel the application for married quarters. Or I will, as I did all the arranging in the first place.'

'I'm sorry. Really. It's just bloody awful timing ent it?'

'Too right it is,' Helen agreed, miserably. 'Last April seems like a thousand years ago now. It was all going to be so good, wasn't it?'

Wayne risked reaching for her hand. She surrendered it. They both sank back against the cushions. 'Well, it still will be,' he said. 'You'll see. I'll just get this tour over, then we can do it. It'll be okay; I promise. We'll just postpone it for six months.'

'Yes, I suppose you're right. What's another half a year?'

Wayne smiled, relieved, trying not to look triumphant. She'd come round. 'It'll fly by; you'll see,' he said.

But actually, they hadn't got five days – evenings anyway – together before he left. There were five hectic days now of getting everything ready, preparing the snatch Land Rovers, the other vehicles, the armaments, the other ordnance; doing a thousand and one things as the military machine swung into action; years of practice now coming to well-oiled fruition. For those soldiers who lived off-base, Sunday and Monday nights away from barracks were forbidden. In effect they were under curfew.

So, as this was Thursday, Helen had only this night, Friday and Saturday to have him to herself. And as it turned out, He was home late on Friday and Saturday evenings too. There was just so much to do, he told her. They were rushing around like blue-arsed flies. But he didn't look unhappy about the pressure. There was a glint of excitement in his eyes when he came home, although he was trying not to show it. Indeed he was going out of his way to be considerateness personified. He wasn't completely insensitive. He knew she was hating it all, even if for him the prospect of for-real combat was thrilling, heady, the culmination of so many years preparing for it; endlessly practicing in exercises and mock-battles, longing nervously for the day when going through the motions, mere rehearsal, became actual performance.

For her part, Helen was determined to put on a brave face. There was no point, and it wasn't fair, to make Wayne's final two evenings and nights with her a misery of sulking, silent accusation. She'd said her piece, reacted in the only way she could. (She wondered how many other service wives or girlfriends reacted similarly, if they were honest, away from the public gaze and brave affirmations of pride and support.)

For the Saturday night she made a special dinner: a couple of nice steaks with fries, American style, onion rings, peas and tomatoes, and (the usual) a wicked Black Forest Gateau (with proper cream) to follow. Had it been any other occasion, there would have been wine too. Like if it was the celebration of homecoming, not the sedative of saying goodbye and impending loneliness. But Wayne had to keep a clear head; she knew that. He could hardly turn up at barracks on Sunday morning with a thick head. If he did, his life wouldn't be worth living.

Still determinedly cheerful, she put her sexiest dress, outrageously low-cut, on herself and their favourite music on the stereo. They ate in silence. The music excused it. Conversation would have been stilted anyway. Wayne had two helpings of the dessert, messily spooning it into his mouth, edging it white with the cream, mechanically and without comment. He seemed preoccupied. Understandably, she supposed. His mind was obviously elsewhere, probably already in Iraq. How was he feeling? Excited? Apprehensive? She felt stabs of jealousy, and then resentment because she felt jealous. But no; she must keep it hidden. Must put on every appearance of calm, at any rate, even though she didn't feel it. Mustn't spoil things for him.

He'd been late home again because of the preparations, and by the time they'd eaten (she'd had to wait until he showed up before she could start cooking, not knowing when it would be) it was past eleven-thirty. She steered him straight towards the bedroom. The dishes could wait until the morning. It would be something to do to occupy herself. She undressed first, quickly, and got into bed, naked. She must make the most of him. She watched him undress in turn. She'd never tired of doing that; always felt a bit smug that she, dumpy plain Helen with ridiculous hair and too-large breasts should have been so lucky as to find herself with such a gorgeous bloke, with his beautiful body honed to perfection by his training. The years of being together had certainly not bred familiarity, mundaneness. She drew back the duvet to let him in and opened herself, reaching urgently. He was already nearly fully erect. He knew exactly how to prepare her and entered quickly as her arms went around his broad back.

She tried to delay his climax, although that had never been easy; wanted to make the love-making last. Wanted to make the possession of him go on and on. And when he shuddered and came, one hand went to his buttocks, pulling every available millimetre of him as deep inside as he could go, feeling the spasm, the gush. Perhaps this time they'd make a baby. She wasn't sure whether it was the right time in her cycle, but perhaps it was. Perhaps there was an egg in a fallopian tube, obligingly ready and waiting to be invaded by a tadpole sperm. Wouldn't that be marvellous, if this night of all nights she might conceive; they might finally catalyse a child!

And after he had finished, and she had too, and he'd stopped panting, and even after he'd become quite flaccid, still she held him there, gripping tightly with arms and legs. He was heavy on her ribcage, but she didn't care. She just wanted to keep him there, in memory at least; remember his heat, his solidity, his sweet odour, his stickiness between her thighs. The wonderful completeness of him.

Eventually though he rolled away and turned his back to settle to sleep, but still she wouldn't let him go, and pressed close up behind him, arm around his chest, cupping the muscular swell around his left nipple, fitting foetal shape to foetal shape. She wanted to keep him awake all night; prolong this precious time, but knew she couldn't. He had to go and defeat Iraq, and save the world.

Chapter 20
Helen

Helen had decided. She was pretty sure. It had been eleven days now. Overdue eleven days. She hadn't wanted to mention it before now in her every-third-day (that was what they'd agreed; it wasn't fair to expect him to write any more frequently than that) BFPO letters to Wayne. She hadn't wanted to get his hopes up until she was sure of her facts. Or better still, until it was officially confirmed. Doctor-confirmed. And apart from anything else, he had enough on his plate, as the situation out in Iraq seemed far from resolved, without the uncertainty of not knowing whether she was or wasn't pregnant and he was or wasn't going to be a dad.

But she was going to do it all the same, tell him; she couldn't keep the knowledge – well, the hope – to herself any longer. Then tomorrow she would book an appointment at the doctor's. She couldn't wait to tell Wayne when it really was confirmed though. He'd be so pleased; she knew he would. So, after dinner on that Friday night in early December 2006, the box was switched off and she got out her stationery and pen.

Three weeks. He'd been gone three weeks already. Twenty-one increasingly lonely days. Already it felt like forever. But there were another twenty three of the buggers to go. She'd written to him six times already, although she'd only had four letters back. He'd apologised for not doing so more often, saying that it was 'hectic' out there, whatever that meant. She'd rather not think or speculate about it though; keep imagination on a very tight rein. Although frankly he wasn't, she knew (and preferred this as a reason) the world's best letter writer.

Her thoughts returned to the subject in hand. Tonight was letter writing night as it happened, so it wasn't as if she were writing specially. So best to keep it fairly light perhaps. Assure him that she'd be able to cope alright, although he'd be home well in time for the birth anyway. And besides, she wasn't absolutely certain. There was no point in going too over the top, raising hopes only to see them crushed.

She sighed and began to write.

Wayne sat in the mess hut, exhausted after the day's patrol. It wasn't that it was physically demanding. Far from it. After all, after the years of training, yomping around the hillsides of the Brecon Beacons or North Yorkshire carrying full pack, riding around in a snatch Land Rover was a piece of piss, really. No, it wasn't the physical aspect of things. But the mental tension was something else altogether. You couldn't relax for a moment. You daren't. Most of the Iraqi faces you saw around Basra seemed friendly enough, as far as you could tell. But you could never really be sure. Although Saddam Husain, both man and statue, had been toppled, there were plenty of his followers still around, lurking in the shadows, indistinguishable in appearance from the good guys and always ready to wreak unexpected and violent mischief.

He couldn't understand it really. You'd think they'd all be glad to be shot of Saddam, evil bastard that he was. But no; it seemed that only one section of the populace was grateful to the Coalition for delivering them from their oppressor; the other wanted the West out of there. He didn't completely get it, in spite of the lectures they'd had to sit through, but it all came down to religion apparently. Different branches of Islam, or something. Sunnis and Shias. He'd always thought that Islam was Islam was Islam (insofar as he'd ever given the subject much thought), like there was basically only one sort of Christianity.

Not that it was for him to question why he was there now; now the terrorist threat had gone, trying to keep one lot of Arabs from another lot's throats. And from *his* throat. But orders were orders; you went where you were sent and just got on with your job.

He rubbed the back of his neck. It ached like hell, partly from the helmet he'd been wearing all day but also, he knew, from tension; from the constant nervous keeping your eyes peeled and your ears pricked, always alert to danger that could come at any moment, sneaking up like a ravening black wolf in the night.

But he was safe now, back in base. Back with the other lads, relaxing, eating, drinking, joining in the relieved banter, the piss-taking, the joshing; the black humour. Relegating his fear firmly to the back of his mind. He hadn't really expected this. It wasn't something they told you about in training: that you'd spend a lot of the time scared shitless, quite frankly. Or that, perversely, patrolling was scarier almost than combat. At least with that you hardly had time to be frightened. There was the adrenalin rush. You were focused, wound up, confronting the situation. Incoming fire had that effect.

But now, this evening, no harm could come, not in this safe haven. And there was a letter from Helen to look forward to reading! He'd been saving it, envelope unopened, delaying the gratification. Shower first (the bloody dust seemed to get everywhere) some grub and then go to his bed, where it would be quiet, with no distractions. He felt slightly guilty (not that it was his fault) that it was impossible to have a proper, reciprocal conversation-by-letter. The letters from her appeared as regular as clockwork every third day, but as they took anything from three to five days to reach Basra, the answering had got completely out of synch. If he replied straight away, tonight, to whatever she had to say in her letter, it wouldn't begin its tediously long journey back to Britain until tomorrow and so not reach her until nearly a week's time, possibly.

Meanwhile, before it reached her, another one would be winging its way out to him, crossing, so it was impossible to communicate properly, really. But it couldn't be helped. The army and the country had more important considerations than a prompt mail service for squaddies.

He tore open the envelope, withdrew the several sheets (Helen couldn't write small to save her life) of blue Basildon Bond, unfolded them, lay back on his bed and began to read:

214 Salisbury Road,
Warminster,
Wiltshire.
4th December, 2006

My sweet Wayne,

Now then. There's something I have to tell you, but I'm going to make you wait until the end of the letter. Rotten tease, aren't I!? I'll tell you all the boring stuff first, and then hit you with it at the end.

Not that there's a great deal to tell, really. Life is pretty dull and boring in Warminster, as usual. Nothing much has happened in the library. Well, libraries aren't exactly eventful places to work in, are they? No terrorist attacks or anything. No, I shouldn't joke about things like that, after what happened in London last year. It's not funny at all.

Apparently they are going to expand the computer section at the library and have some better ones that are much faster, so they tell us. It always seems a bit odd to me, having computers in a library at all. Surely if people want to have computers they should have them at home. Libraries are supposed to be for books and newspapers, I reckon. But perhaps I'm just old fashioned. You have to move with the times I suppose. And I suppose not everyone can afford one, anyway.

It will be quite good when the army brings in email contacting, like they say they're going to do, won't it? Perhaps you'll feel a bit more inclined to write me longer letters then, as it'll be easier!

I had quite a good night out with Sal the other evening. I told you I was going to, didn't I? I'm sure I did. Although I felt a tiny bit guilty really, going out enjoying myself, knowing where you are and what you're doing. Yes, I know you told me to do it, act as normally as possible and not brood about things or worry, but it's alright for you. You don't have hours by yourself with nothing really to distract and keep the thoughts at bay. You've got your mates around you, their companionship, the camaraderie (had to look that word up to see how to spell it!) and you say you're very busy anyway. You perhaps don't have time to think very much.

Anyway, I'm not going to start grumbling and make you feel guilty. I'm alright, really. Liz from the library came as well. She goes back to the days when Sal was there, and so knew her of course. They were always big mates, like Sal and I are, so there was a great deal of ribaldry (that's, like, rude fun) going off. I felt a tiny bit out of things, to be honest. Although that sort of night out was never my thing really, as you know. Honestly, it was like a hen party at times! It's not that I'm a prude or anything (you know that!) but I began to wish they'd talk about something other than sex. But I suppose I was just envious.

It didn't help that Liz has just got a new boyfriend, and this one's The One, she kept telling us. Well, she says that about all of them. She doesn't exactly win prizes for sensitivity, does Liz. I'm sure she didn't realise what she was saying, crowing about how bloody marvellous her Dean is in the sack, with me there. And of course Sal, lovely though she is, isn't much better. They were egging each other on and not exactly keeping their voices down either. It got quite embarrassing at times. Honestly, you should have heard them, comparing the lengths of their bloke's dicks (surely they haven't actually measured them?) like they were fifteen-year-olds. Pathetic, if you ask me, considering that Sal's thirty next year (as she keeps reminding us, as if it's middle age) and Liz is twenty-seven too.

Anyway, enough of my silly friends. I can't put off what I want to tell you any longer. So here goes. The thing is, Wayne my love, I'm late. Know what I'm saying? Late. Late as in: period hasn't come. It's been eleven days now, and no sign of it. I know I can be a little erratic sometimes, but not this much! And the other morning, the Morning After The Big Night Out, I felt a little bit queazy (think I've spelled that wrong but sod it, can't be bothered to look it up). Okay, it might have been too much pop, but then I didn't drink that much. And my breasts feel a tiny bit sore, both of them.

So maybe, just maybe, it's what I think it might be. Oh Wayne, wouldn't it be wonderful if it was? Well we certainly did try hard, those last three days before you left, if you remember! When I began writing I was going to keep it quite low-key. Not go too over the top about it. I don't want to raise our hopes too much only for them to be dashed. Tomorrow I'm going to ring the doctors' and book an appointment, so let's keep our fingers crossed, hey?

I know this perhaps isn't what you want just at the moment, but then again, it's something to take your mind off other things isn't it; something to look forward to, hopefully. Perhaps I should wait before writing again (it'll give you a chance to catch up!) until I've been to the doctor and got confirmation. It'll be terrible writing again in three days time still not knowing for certain.

So there we are. I've been hugging this knowledge – well, this hope – inside myself for days now. I wasn't going to say anything until I was absolutely certain, but I can't restrain myself any longer. We'll just keep everything crossed, shall we?

I do miss you so. Please keep safe.

All my love, sweet Wayne

Hel

Wayne finished reading. Then scanned back through the large

loopy writing to read the important words again. As if doing that would fix them, cement them in fact. Or re-reading simply to make sure he hadn't misunderstood. But no; he'd read them right. She really was saying she thought she was pregnant! Bloody hell! At last, a baby! His heart had begun racing, hammering away like the clappers in his chest as though he were in a firefight. He gazed up at the drab ceiling, looking but not seeing. Christallmighty! He'd begun to vaguely wonder if there might be something wrong with one of them; it was taking so long for Helen to fall. Assuming the blame, he'd begun to think it might be himself, that he just couldn't deliver a decent package of wrigglers or something. Well you heard about it. Some blokes just couldn't. There was no shame in it really.

But no; it seemed that everything was okay in that department. A baby! He was going to be a dad! And then he felt guilty, in spite of the elation. This was what Helen had been wanting for ages now, but in the last few weeks, with the preparations for the deployment and then the excitement of at last being in the thick of the action, it had been the last thing on his mind. Even worse, he'd pushed Helen away. Well, not given her sufficient attention anyway in the hectic build-up to the tour. There had been just too much to think about then and there was too much going on in his brain now.

Rosy images floated into his mind. He imagined himself holding a tiny wrapped bundle, a morsel of life, so carefully, imagined the swell of pride and protectiveness he'd feel. Yes, this was what his job was all about; enabling all this to continue, unthreatened by murderous fanatics with cowardly delivered bombs. Through a soft-focus haze he pictured himself with a cuddly dimple-kneed toddler on his lap, tickling him, making him squeal.

But hold on. Would it be a 'him?' It could equally well be a little girl. Just think of that! A pretty little thing with button-bright eyes and a shock of black unruly hair, just like her mum! He'd be just as thrilled with that. And then later, after a few years, playing footie with his boy. What fun that'd be! Or for that matter, doing so with his little girl. Well, why not? Girls played football too nowadays. He wouldn't want her to be *too* sugar-and-spice, like in that rhyme he'd heard his Grandma Thorpe recite to sister Poppy when she was little. Whichever it turned out to be, he wanted his child to be his *mate* though. And his child would have the knowledge that his or her parents were their proper ones, they were not some accidental by-product of casual sex. Not that he didn't think the world of his adoptive mum and dad, of course.

Well he must write a letter straight back, no slacking this time, telling Helen (the thought of her now, possibly carrying their child, made him feel weak with love) how thrilled, how over the moon he was. How tickled, in the words of that old Liverpool comedian Ken Dodd who his gran used to rave over, he was. He wouldn't mention that IED incident the other day when two of his mates had been badly injured, one of them Rachel, his brief girlfriend during that estrangement from Helen all those years ago. No, the letter would be entirely positive, only upbeat.

He found his writing pad and pen in his locker and, sitting up on the bed with knees bent, back against the wall and with his dog-eared paperback that was taking forever to plough through as a rest, began to write:

1 Battalion Yorkshires,
C Company,
Basra,
Iraq.
10th December 2006

Darling Helen,

I'm really thrilled with the news! I wonder why you left it this long before getting yourself checked out though. Why haven't you done one of those pregnancy test things that you can do yourself at home? Then you'd know for certain, wouldn't you?

But anyway, its great, isn't it? I'm really chuffed to bits. I wonder what it is, boy or girl? I don't mind what it is though, so long as its got all its fingers and toes and everything! And all the important bits of course! And if its a girl, as long as its got your hair, not my bloody thatch. Well, I'd want that if it were a boy too! When can they tell which it is, do you know? I expect you will be reading up all about it now, wont you?

I feel a bit bad now sweetheart about neglecting you so much before I came away. I was very selfish I think. But there was so much to think about after us heard about the posting. Just think Hel, when this tours over and I am back, you will be six months gone! You'll be a proper little barrel by then! I have been thinking, after this tour maybe I will see about leaving the army, if I can. I dont really think I would want to stay in and perhaps be posted again if there were a kiddy on the scene as well. Its bad enough having to leave you. The armys alright for single blokes but its tough for us family men!

Well anyway, I cant wait to get back and see you. Maybe I will be able to hear the heart beating, or feel it kicking or something? You can do that cant you? That would be great. Now you just take it easy, no running upstairs or anything like that, promise me? I'm being very careful, so don't worry about me. We went out on patrol again today but it was very quiet. There were no incidents.

I wont sleep a wink tonight, thinking about you. Or about you two! Take care Sweetheart.

All my Love,

Wayne

P.s. if you have got to wait several days to see the doctor, why don't you do a pregnancy test? Then we will know for certain. Anyway, as soon as you do know for definite, write to me, promise? You know how bloody slow BFPO is!

Helen could have kicked herself. She hadn't thought about a DIY pregnancy test until, after being told at the doctors' that she'd have to wait over a week for an appointment because she wasn't an urgent case, the receptionist had reminded her about it. So she'd been straight into Boots that lunchtime and bought a kit. And then with difficulty made herself wait until the best time to do it, the following morning (up *very* bright and early, at a quarter to six) and into the bathroom to breathholdingly test her wee. And of course the test strip had turned the correct colour. She'd gone back to bed and just laid there, staring at the ceiling, as Wayne, because of the time lag, would do three days later, reading her first letter. There was no possibility of going back to sleep. Her head was spinning, emotions swirling; laughing one minute and crying the next. It was true! She really was! Oh, but if only Wayne were here though, not stuck out there in sodding Iraq. They should be sharing this joy together, like most couples did!

She had trouble concentrating at work that day, she really did.

Her mind was elsewhere, off with the fairies. All day long she gifted bemused customers with broad if often absent-minded grins, doing a Cheshire Cat impersonation for anyone who spoke to her. And in the end she just had to tell Liz, who had kept looking at her quizzically and saying, 'What?'

When she heard the excitedly-delivered news she gave Helen a big hug and told her she was extremely jealous, saying she wanted a bit of that too. Well, she was twenty-seven; knocking on a bit. She didn't want to leave it too late. Words would have to be had with Dean.

Later, straight after dinner, and although it wasn't strictly speaking letter writing night, she got the writing pad out again, noting with dismay that she'd forgotten to buy a new one. Oh well; she'd just have to try and write small.

She had an early night because it seemed more, well, intimate. She could imagine Wayne being there beside her; seeing the look on his face. Sitting propped up in bed, she began.

214 Salisbury Road
Warminster,
Wiltshire.
8th December, 2006

Hello my Sweetheart,

Well it's definite! I really am a dozy cow sometimes. It never occurred to me to self-test, until they suggested it at the doctors because they couldn't see me for about a week. They said to test myself, and if it's positive to make an appointment then, and they'll absolutely confirm it and set the wheels in motion.

And it is! I got a test kit yesterday and did the test first thing this morning (very first thing!) and the test thingy went the right colour. So there we are! You're going to be a daddy! Isn't that great? I've been checking it out; they can usually tell the sex at the twenty week scan (but not always) so we'll know what it's going to be then – if we want to that is. Well I say "we." You won't be back by then, which is a shame isn't it? Never mind though, it can't be helped. I'll write to you on the day of the scan so you know as soon as possible.

Listen to me! Way ahead of myself! That's ages away. Still, it's fun to speculate, isn't it? Shall we think of some names, both sexes, or is that tempting fate? But you're not superstitious about stuff like that, are you? Tell you what; as we can't discuss it properly, face to face, you think of some names and I will too, and we'll see if we think of the same one. If we do, that'll be it. Deal? But then, we might come up with the same boy's name but not a girl's, and it might be a girl. Or the other case. Oh well; if that happens we'll just have to thrash it out a bit more! Which would you rather have? Or don't you mind? I really don't, just having your baby is enough.

Just think though, when we get married I'll either be heavily pregnant or we'll have a little one. That'll raise a few eyebrows, won't it! Still, who cares? I know my parents won't and I don't think yours will either, will they? This is 2006 for goodness sake. Well, it'll be 2007 when he/she is born.

Honestly Wayne, I've been in a complete dream all day! It's a wonder old Marjory at the library didn't send me home on account of being useless, being unable to concentrate. I told Liz, because she knew something was up because of the goofy grin I've had on all day. She was really pleased for me and said she was jealous again, bless her. She's definitely going to have a word with Dean, she says! I haven't told Sal yet. I'll ring her later. I wanted to get this letter written first. And I must tell my mum as well of course. She'll be thrilled to bits.

So there we are my sweet. How does it feel knowing you're going to be a dad? Are you excited?

Well I'll close now. I'm writing this in bed, wishing you were here with me (but then I wouldn't be letter writing of course if you were!) I can't wait for you to come back; it's still bloody months to go! Take care, please, please take care. There's someone else relying on you as well now.

All my love, sweet man

Hel

Helen reached for her new writing pad. She had to shake off the dreadful lethargy, the black depression, and write. It was only fair. She couldn't keep Wayne in the dark. She still couldn't believe it herself. That sudden intense stomach cramping pain at work yesterday then a pressing need to pee and the blood in the toilet bowl. The urgent appointment with the doctor this morning and the dreaded confirmation, even before there was time to do so for pregnancy, of an early-stage miscarriage. So tomorrow there would have to be a hospital appointment for a D and C; curettage to remove all traces of lining from her uterus; make sure it was cleansed of any unwanted matter that might cause infection. Unwanted matter? For fuck's sake, how could a should-have-been baby be considered unwanted? It *was* wanted; God, how it was wanted! Had been wanted.

She had never felt so wretched.

She wrote:

214 Salisbury Road,
Warminster,
Wiltshire.
15th December, 2006.

My Sweet Wayne,

I'm so, so sorry to have to write with bad news now. There's no point in beating about the bush and I'll come straight to it. I've lost the baby. For no reason at all I suddenly got excruciating pain yesterday afternoon at work, and went to the toilet, and there was a lot of blood, like a really heavy period. Margery knew what it probably was because I'd told her about being pregnant too, and phoned the doctors' to make an appointment for me. It didn't seem to warrant calling an ambulance so they didn't. I didn't feel really ill or anything, but Margery sent me home.

So I went to the doctor this morning and she said yes, it was a miscarriage. She arranged for me to go into hospital this morning to have a D and C. That's a dilation and curettage, a procedure where they scrape the womb clean of the lining and everything that formed for the baby. A lot of it bled out but they like to make sure. It's just routine, she said, nothing to worry about. Doesn't mean I can't have children now, or anything. She said losing the baby actually happens a lot, sometimes after only a couple of days of the embryo implanting, so you think you're just having a period. Well maybe so, but it's still a lousy rotten thing to happen, when you think you've conceived. Although I suppose it wouldn't matter if it happened really early because you'd be none the wiser anyway.

Oh Wayne, I do feel so miserable now! And only yesterday I got your letter that replied to my first one to you saying I thought I was pregnant! You sounded so chuffed and excited about it, but now this. I'm so sorry. I feel as though I've let you down. The doctor said we could try again and there's no reason at all why I shouldn't carry to term another time, but that's not the point, is it? I wanted this one! I so wanted it. I wonder what it would have been, a boy or girl? Well we'll never know now.

But I suppose if it's going to happen, it's best at a really early stage rather than later when there's a recognisable baby. I can't imagine what it must be like to have a baby stillborn. That's just too awful. But even so, it's still a life that won't now be, isn't it? And it's so, so disappointing.

I do so wish you were here. I really do. Not stuck out there, fighting Bush and Blair's bloody war for them. Yes, I know; I shouldn't say that. I'm sorry. You believe in what you're doing. But it would be nice to have a bit of support just now, after all the times I've supported you.

No; sorry again. Shouldn't have said that either. I don't want to make you feel bad. Mouth running away with me. I know you'd be here for me if you could. Take no notice, I'm just upset. Well when you come back we'll just have to try again, my sweet, won't we? Lots!

Please don't be too disappointed or upset yourself, will you? You don't want any distractions. I'm just a silly tearful woman, who misses you like hell. Just keep yourself safe. Promise?

All my love,

Hel

Chapter 21
Tomos

Tomos wasn't greatly looking forward to Christmas 2006. He hadn't got the energy to feel enthusiastic about anything, for that matter. He wondered why Mair bothered with him really, as he was so depressed most of the time. He couldn't remember when he'd last smiled at her; spoken a pleasant word. And as for having sex, well, it seemed a distant memory. He sometimes wondered whether it had ever actually happened. Perhaps the increasingly hazy recollections of it were some sort of malicious false memory.

He almost wished, perversely, that she would finish with him. At least then there'd be no guilt. She could find some nice strong strapping *healthy* chap and get on with her life. Not have the burden of supporting an invalid with no future.

So he sat there now, slippered feet up on a footstool (it eased the oedema in his legs a bit) on the sofa in his parents' sitting room, gazing vacantly at the flames in the woodstove. Mam always kept it well fuelled and blazing nowadays, because he felt the cold so and also, he supposed, because she thought the dancing yellow flames would lift his spirits a bit. They didn't though. He felt crushed by a pall of lethargy. What was the point of carrying on, when was all said and done? Living on a cocktail of so many drugs to keep him clinging to a precarious existence, what with the captopril, lasix and lanoxin, to name but three? He almost rattled when shaken. There wasn't much of a life in prospect, either quantitatively or qualitatively.

But perhaps he was being churlish about Mair. She was sticking by him. And for goodness sake, she'd applied for and got a job with Social Services in Aberystwyth so that they could move in with his parents, after he'd had to abandon the pharmacology training following the last surgery, so his mam could share some of the caring. After all, Mair had to hold down a job. As for a career himself, or training for one, there seemed no point in even thinking about it. Dad, trying to sound optimistic and positive, had suggested that perhaps he could study pharmacology with the Open University, until he'd pointed out that they didn't do such a course, because there was a lot of practical work involved. And anyway, even if there was one, the mental effort would still be too onerous.

All he could really do was sit here, waiting on the transplant list, hoping guiltily that some poor bugger would lose his or her life having previously, altruistically, agreed to donate his or her now-unwanted heart if the unthinkable should happen. It was a hell of a moral conundrum. That someone would have to die that he might live. It wasn't like kidney transplantation, the only sort where you could have a live donor who'd be able to function perfectly well for the rest of their life with their remaining organ. He could only gain a proper healthy heart if someone else died. There would have to be tragedy for the donor concerned and pain and loss for his or her family.

Tomos ruminated glumly, reprising the familiar depressing thoughts that had taken firm root in his consciousness nowadays.

Yes, it was complicated. He knew it was. It was all very well to say, from the comfortable position of not actually having to face the situation, that the person concerned had sadly lost their life anyway but another (or even others, plural) would as a result have theirs saved. Some good would come from the tragedy. And easy to say too that the grieving relatives shouldn't really mind about their loved-one's organ or organs being used for the benefit of others; that indeed it might give them a measure of comfort to know that for someone else there'd be a happy outcome.

Yes, it was easy to say that.

But people didn't always act selflessly or rationally, especially when burning in the pain of unexpected loss. Although they'd be-oh-so-grateful if the boot were on the other foot; if it was *their* loved one being saved through someone else's misfortune. If only medical science were more advanced, so you didn't have to rather ghoulishly take replacement parts from the newly, suddenly dead. If only it had developed stem cell technology to the point where useless, damaged organs could be replaced with new healthy ones grown, seeded with cells from an umbilical cord or, better still, a person's own tissue, thereby neatly solving the problem of rejection. He'd read about that. He'd always thought it was fascinating from an academic point of view. Now though it was much more personal. But all that seemed to be years in the future, from what the researchers said. By the time such things became available it would be too late for him. He wanted it now!

How long had it been now since he'd woken up from anaesthetic in hospital in Swansea, after his heart valve operation, to be gently told hours later that it had been only partially successful? That his heart, when they actually looked at it for real, beating feebly and enlarged in his chest cavity, was even worse than they'd expected, what with the malformed tricuspid valve, the narrowed pulmonary and the mitral and the heart generally deeply scarred from the rheumatic fever and then the pneumonia. That, with no great expectation of success, they'd simply attached new valves to an ailing organ. But that it wasn't a long-term solution. That his only other option now, realistically, was a heart transplant

Nine months, give or take. It had been done in early March. Afterwards he'd been prescribed yet more drugs to add to his already large daily cocktail and after he'd recovered a bit from the operation, but with no significant improvement in heart function to show for it all, had been referred to the nearest transplant centre. He'd been taken by Dad (but Mam and Mair had insisted on going too) to Birmingham for interview, more tests, examination and assessment by Mr Petersen, the transplant surgeon.

There'd also been an interview with someone called a transplant co-ordinator: a kindly woman called Jan who had all his medical notes, blood group and all the rest of it, and whose job it was to match people waiting on the list with organs as they unexpectedly became available, matching organ with potential recipient as closely as possible and dealing with all the practical arrangements. Not to mention the emotional counselling. Subject to his being recommended for transplant, it would now be a waiting game, she'd told him.

As soon as a very good match showed up he'd be informed, pronto, (he must keep his mobile phone with him at all times if he strayed from a landline) and he'd be rushed (probably airlifted as he lived at the back of beyond) to Birmingham. Time would be of the essence; the heart would only be able survive for a few short hours in disconnected limbo outside the human body. Ideally, for the best chance of success, they should operate within four hours.

The recommendation had been confirmed and so the anxious wait had begun. Mr Petersen had been very encouraging, assuring him that the success rate for transplantation was very good nowadays and the rejection problem could be managed well with careful balancing of immunosuppressants. Tomos had wanted to ask how long he'd be likely to survive waiting for a heart to come along, but couldn't bring himself to, and the consultant, probably anticipating the question but looking relieved that he hadn't had to answer it, had said nothing. But Tomos knew that patients did die waiting for organs; it was common knowledge. There simply weren't enough donors. Although nine out of ten people professed themselves in favour of transplantation, only thirty per cent actually joined the register. And he hadn't discussed it with Mair or Mam and Dad, but he knew that they knew too. It was a subject assiduously avoided. No, only bright encouragement (you'll probably hear something next week Cariad!) was allowed.

And then there'd been that false dawn six weeks ago, when they'd had a call from Jan at three in the afternoon to say that a suitable organ had been located, and he was not to eat or drink anything but to be ready to be collected by the ambulance in twenty minutes, to be transferred to the air ambulance from Cardiff because the west Wales one was currently busy, rendezvousing in Llandovery, to be whisked to Birmingham. The mixture of dread and excitement had almost been too much. It was Last Chance Saloon time.

Mam had made him sit and try and stay calm, although his heart was going like the clappers. He'd been terrified it would pack up on him before he even got to Birmingham. He'd already got a bag packed anyway, to be ready at all times, so there was nothing to do except wait. Mam had phoned Mair, who was out of the office on a visit but been able to get her on her mobile. She would hurriedly try to arrange some impromptu leave. She'd also phoned Dad at the agents, who without ceremony had dropped what he was doing and driven at high speed straight back home.

But then there'd been that terrible anti-climactic let-down, when half an hour later, after enduring a very tense wait, an extremely embarrassed-sounding Jan had phoned again to say sorry; there was a change of plan. She'd been over-ruled by Mr Petersen, who'd decided that the heart should be given to a more ill patient who was also a slightly better match. Dad, furious, had taken over the phone and remonstrated with Jan. How ill did Tomos have to be, for Christ's sake? This was so unfair, to raise their hopes like this and then dash them. Jan had sounded really contrite. Yes. She fully understood how they must feel and she was desperately sorry. But it was always a juggling act, trying to make the best, most effective use of a limited supply of organs. If only more of the population were more donation-aware . . . and no, she shouldn't have contacted them unless absolutely sure of herself, but she thought she was. She'd stepped a little out of line and acted too much on her own initiative, because it was Mr Petersen's day off. But she was confident that another organ would become available soon.

Dad had desperately tried another last tack, although knowing that it was futile: wasn't Tomos's transport arranged now, and everything? No, Jan had said, she'd been spending the last half-hour urgently re-organising things and was sorry it had taken so long to get back to them. Finally Dad had muttered something about bloody inefficiency, and slammed the phone furiously down. Mam was in tears and he had been too. Tears both of relief, perversely, and disappointment. This had been the scene that greeted an anxious, breathless Mair who burst in five minutes later. She had taken him in her arms and, determinedly, professionally keeping her own in check, assured that it would be alright Cariad, it really would.

Yes, that had been six weeks ago. Since then things had got worse. The dyspnoea, the breathlessness, was present all the time now, even when completely still, and with it the persistent cough. Walking anywhere at all, even to the toilet (fortunately his parents had had the former dairy, latterly a utility room, converted into a downstairs bathroom for him) was a major excursion, undertaken very slowly and well in advance of actually feeling the need to go. And it had got to the point where Mair hovered slightly anxiously in the bathroom when he took baths now (it was easier sitting in the bath on one of those silly bathing seats that old people had than standing in the shower) and hauled him solicitously out afterwards to towel him dry as if he were a baby. It had been a little irritating to begin with, but he was getting a bit past feeling emotion now, to be honest. All the same, there was a slight but pleasant remembered intimacy in his being naked before her.

He could no longer lie flat and had to sleep well propped up on a mountain of pillows, in pretty much the same position in which he spent his waking hours. He hadn't been able to get upstairs for six months now. Dad had wondered aloud about having a stairlift installed, but he'd insisted irritably that it wasn't worth messing about with the old winding staircase, which it might be difficult to persuade to accept one, probably. He couldn't be bothered to go to all the effort of getting up there anyway. He had no energy at all.

The oedema was worse too, in spite of the increased daily diuretics, and for the first time in his life, he was putting on weight. But he knew it wasn't healthy weight; wasn't fine musculature. It was simply fluid retention as his ailing heart found it ever more difficult to keep his circulation moving.

So his world had contracted, to the parental living room. It was where he spent all his days, and nights too, on the three-seat sofa (well, it felt marginally more normal than having a bed in there). Technically, he wasn't yet bed-ridden. Not quite, although it was self-kidology really. He had everything to hand: books, his CD player (although he could rarely be bothered to play it; the music only reminded him of earlier, happier, healthier times, like when he had a sex life for example). Sometimes he languidly half-watched television, not really absorbing the sights or sounds.

Mair, loyally, had acquired a camp bed which she erected every night beside the sofa, after Mam and Dad had tactfully retired to bed early to allow them to be alone together. She built it up higher with the seat and back cushions from the armchairs so that it was more or less at the same level as the sofa. She couldn't bear to sleep upstairs, alone, she said. She held his hand as he drifted off to sleep, and often when he awoke was still doing so, lying there regarding him, rather pointlessly naked out of habit, the duvet pulled back to below her belly, because he still liked to look at her like that. He could at least still touch her. Her presence was a comfort, at least.

Dr Jones, his GP, who monitored his condition, supervised by Mr Jenkins from Aberystwyth, had said that if (but he probably meant 'when') his breathing got any worse they'd see about rigging up oxygen for him. Yes, that would be nice. How pathetic it was though; what a state to be reduced to, to be grateful for something like that. And of course there was always the looming spectre of hospitalisation, with more interventions to keep him alive, but he didn't want his thoughts to go there. That would be the end game, pretty well.

Mam came into the sitting room, having set the potatoes to boil for dinner. She perched on the edge of the sofa for a few minutes, smiling down at him. Her hand moved to tidy his unkempt red hair a little. Her eyes looked tired though (as did Mair's, for that matter). It must be the anxiety.

'Alright, Cariad?' she said.

It was always the more affectionate 'Cariad' nowadays, not 'Bach'. As if she wanted, needed to constantly remind him of her love. Of course it was an inane question, if well-meant. He was far from all right. But he had to fight down irritation and go through the rituals of polite behaviour.

'Yes thanks, Mam.'

'Good boy,' she said, as if awarding brownie points for it.

Tomos smiled wanly back.

'Nothing you want to watch on telly then?' she encouraged.

'No, not really.'

They always went through this. He could see what Mam was fumblingly trying to do: keep him interested in life. Keep him positive. It was alright for her though. She was a strong as an ox; always had been. What was he supposed to do though? Fight it, like they always spoke, those who hadn't experienced it, of 'fighting' cancer? If only it were that bloody simple!

She looked at his abandoned paperback. 'Is it good?'

'S'all right.'

'What's it about?'

'Afghanistan. Two boys growing up there. But one betrays the other. And kites. Something like that.'

'Oh; nice.'

Tomos knew that her interest was only polite. And again, she was only trying to humour him; keep him motivated. It wasn't her sort of thing. She liked a good romance if she read at all. Her interest in literature didn't extend far beyond that.

'Well, not really. It's far from sentimental. About the Taliban. It's pretty bleak in places,' he replied ungraciously.

Mam changed the subject. 'Anyway, I'm doing chops for dinner. Will you eat a little of that?'

'Yes, okay, just a little. I'm not very hungry.'

Mam opened her mouth to speak, thought better of it and closed it again.

She looked at him for another long moment; bravely smiling again, eyes bright with moisture. 'Yes; just try your best. I won't put too much on your plate.'

She patted his hand, got up and returned to her cooking.

Tomos managed half of what was on his plate: two potatoes, a few pieces of pre-cut pork and a small spoonful of peas. But he did finish the dish of Viennetta ice cream. Peppermint was always palatable, though. There was something about the clean, sharp taste. The three of them had had to start without Mair; she was late. She'd rung to say that she would be; they'd got a rather challenging emergency sectioning on. That meant 'unpleasant', reading between the jargonistic lines, probably involving police support. It was a tough job she had, sometimes.

She finally arrived at a quarter to nine, looking drained. Sioned had kept a plate of foil-covered dinner warm for her, but it would still be rather dried up. She heaved herself out of the armchair to get it, waving Mair's offers to help herself aside. Sioned had a proper sense of correct behaviour; her sort-of daughter-in-law looked exhausted. Mair settled on the floor with her back against Tomos's sofa, plate on her lap, devouring the food greedily. For a slight girl, she could certainly pack a lot of food away to great effect.

Sioned looked at her fondly. With Lowri away from home living her own life for several years now, it was almost like having a daughter around the place again.

She knew that Mair couldn't discuss her clients in great detail but she was curious. 'A tough sectioning, was it?'

Mair grimaced between mouthfuls. 'Too right. A chap who'd been mixing too much alcohol with his medication. He was away in La-La Land, but violent with it unfortunately. We thought we could support him out in the community but some you just can't. He'd been abusing his wife quite badly and there was always the risk the children would be next.'

'Duw Duw,' Sioned exclaimed, 'some people! It's terrible!'

'Yes,' Mair agreed. 'But he'd got significant mental health issues. He wasn't really responsible for his actions. He's been in hospital for some time and they presumably thought he was safe to be discharged, but obviously not.'

'Well I think you're very brave, to deal with situations like that, Bach,' Sioned said.

'Mair laughed. 'No, not really. For a start, I was partnered by Gareth, who's an old softie in some ways but can look after himself if needs be. He's six foot five and an amateur rugby player with the build to go with it. Plus there was a squad car, a van and six hefty policemen in support. The client did get very agitated, shall we say, after we first invited him to come quietly, but he was quickly subdued.'

'But even so . . .' Sioned began.

The telephone rang.

The landline was still by Sioned's chair. Well, most incoming calls were for her.

She grabbed the receiver in an instant. 'Hello?'

There was a pause.

'Oh, hello Jan?'

Glyn had muted the television in an instant; swivelled his head to stare at her.

There was silence as Sioned listened, open-palmed hand going to her cheek.

'Yes.'

. . .

'Right.'

. . .
'Really?'
. . .
'You do mean it?'

The conversation went on and on, Sioned answering monosyllabically, as the others watched, tense. She reached for the pen and notepad that was always to hand by the phone; scribbled something down. Finally, with a 'Thank you Jan,' she replaced the receiver.

Glyn spoke first, urgent, impatient. 'Well?'

Sioned couldn't meet his eyes. Hers were still fixed on the notepad; looking but not seeing. Her voice when it came was small, incredulous.

'They've got a heart for Tomos.'

'Oh yes? They said that before,' Glyn retorted.

'But it's true! Jan insists it is. She says she wouldn't falsely raise our hopes again, after what happened last time! It's an excellent match, she says.'

She looked up and across to Tomos. Her eyes were brimming with tears. 'Oh Tomos, Cariad! It's true! It really is this time! You're going to have a new heart!'

Tomos was stunned. His chest felt a squeeze of dread. This was it: make or break. His heart, his poor pathetic inadequate heart, was thumping violently. Mair had put her half-finished plate down on the floor and reached frantically for his hand with both of hers, clenching painfully hard. She was crying too.

Sioned tried to stay calm. 'It's all arranged. Ambulance on its way. They'll give Tomos something to calm him when they arrive. Then to Lampeter. The air ambulance – ours – is on its way too and landing on the rugby field. We're to meet it there. Oh Glyn! It's happening!'

Mair let go of Tomos's hands and scrambled to her feet, running for her mobile phone in the pocket of her coat hanging on the rack in the hall. 'I must phone Freda to tell her. It's short notice but she'll have to let me go!'

She fumbled it out of the pocket and opened the front door, letting in a cold blast, stepping outside and closing it behind her. The signal was better there. Glyn was galvanised into action too. He came quickly over and picked up the phone. 'I'll let Tim at work know, then phone Lowri.'

Sioned heaved herself out of her chair too and came to Tomos, perching on the edge of the sofa, taking his hand in her turn, reassuring. 'It's going to be alright Cariad; it really is. You'll see!'

She stayed for a moment and then rose. 'I'll just run next door and tell Nerys what's happening, and then get the bags out.'

Glyn had finished his call to his work colleague and was now onto Lowri. 'Don't stay talking too long Glyn,' she warned, 'the ambulance won't be long.'

As she dived out of the back door to tell their neighbour Mair came back in through the front, glancing anxiously at Tomos, who could only lie and let the urgent preparations happen around him. She raced up the stairs and returned moments later carrying her overnight bag. She'd maintained a state of readiness against this moment too.

Glyn finished his call to Lowri, with the promise to keep her informed. 'Right,' he said to Mair, 'I shouldn't think they'll let us all go in the helicopter, so if Sioned travels with Tomos, you and I can follow by car. Are you ready?'

'Yes, fine,' said Mair, who was back with Tomos, stroking his chest, soothing, as if that would make any difference, willing him to stay calm, to cling to life for another hour or so, please; her dinner plate still on the floor, forgotten.

Sioned returned, breathless. 'Right, that's done.'

She looked at the focus of their attention again. 'Okay, Cariad? Nerys sends her love. Says she'll be thinking of you.'

With their bags assembled in the middle of the living room floor (they had all been pre-packed) looking for all the world as if they were waiting to go on holiday, all they could do now was wait. It wasn't long. Five minutes later a distant dayglo yellow heralded the ambulance and in three more (Glyn having gone outside to make sure they didn't fly straight past), a paramedic was easing calming sedative into Tomos's arm.

In his drugged, cotton-wool state Tomos was hardly aware of the next couple of hours: the dash to Lampeter in convoy with Glyn and Mair following the ambulance by car; the arrival at the rugby field, where the floodlights had been turned on to facilitate easy landing for the helicopter; the waiting of five minutes again for it to arrive, dropping out of the dark sky like a noisy rescuing angel.

Tomos knew nothing of Glyn and Mair's slower (but high-speed, nonetheless – if they got pulled over by police they'd just have to try and explain) journey to Birmingham that night, along the frustratingly narrow twisting roads through the mountains, then the speed limit breaking hurtle along the motorway through Shropshire and then the West Midlands metropolis.

He barely registered his own rapid transport in the helicopter.

To Sioned, it seemed to be touching down at the Queen Elizabeth Hospital in a matter of minutes (but of course it was more than that). She remembered it all: the waiting reception party, with a wheelchair for the main attraction; the brisk but calm bearing of him to the transplant unit with her carrying their bags, scurrying anxious along behind; the re-acquaintance with Mr Petersen who'd had his evening relaxation interrupted, and along with his team would be in for a long night; his careful explanation of what would be happening, which she didn't really take in; the signing of the consent form on Tomos's behalf because he was too zonked out to do it himself and it would be another hour or more before Glyn arrived; Tomos's preparation; the following, gowned and masked, of her son into the anaesthetic anti-room, a rather pointless gesture really as he barely seemed to recognise her, but she craved every last minute of being with him. There might not be any more. Then his sinking into full anaesthesia before she was gently ushered from the room.

And then beginning the interminable wait, in a comfortable and bright waiting room, although she barely noticed it; waiting for Glyn and Mair to join her. As the hands on the clock on the wall registered their so-slow progress on that December night, with most of the good citizens of Birmingham abed, unknowing, the fighting down of her fear, waiting, hoping for her son's second lease on life to begin.

Chapter 22
Tomos

Tomos came back to consciousness completely disorientated. Where the hell was he? He was in a place he didn't know: a fuzzy place of bright lights, unidentifiable noises like clicking of machinery; murmured voices; a tranquil sort of place. A place of calm. Was this death? Or a sort of limbo, an hallucinatory state preceding it? Well fine, if it was. It was quite pleasant, except that his chest hurt a bit. Quite a lot, in fact. Everything was blurred though. He looked down. He was propped at forty-five degrees in a high bed, naked from the waist up and possibly below it too. Tubes led into his arms and mouth and up his nose and felt as though they might be inserted in other orifices also. There were attachments taped to his chest, down the centre of which ran a huge surgical dressing. Monitors of strange purpose clicked and hummed beside his bed. Another mysterious device, apparently some sort of pump, was pulsating rhythmically and connected via a tube to his mouth. His throat felt sore.

    He shifted his gaze further away. There were gowned people sitting to either side. He couldn't tell which sex they were. One of them began to speak but he couldn't make out the words clearly, except that they seemed to be in his mother tongue. Was he at home in Wales then? Yes, that must be it. He tried to recall what had gone before, but it was difficult. There was a faint memory of being somewhere enclosed and very noisy, then of a much quieter place, then nothing after that.

    Another figure appeared at his side, displacing the small one sitting there who got up to move out of the way. He felt a gloved hand on his forearm, squeezing very gently. The figure also spoke, in a different sort of voice. English, it sounded like. He wanted to speak, ask where he was, what was happening, but couldn't, because of whatever was in his mouth and throat, making him almost want to gag. The figure spoke to the seated ones in what seemed reassuring tones, and looked at the small standing one too, including it in the conversation. After a while, as the newly-arrived figure busied itself about his person, the original three got up to leave, each saying things to him that he couldn't quite catch. He had a vague idea that he knew them, but couldn't think how. They moved away, seemingly leaving, raising hands to bestow small waves, the small one blowing a kiss. He felt a surge of panic; for some reason, he didn't want them to go.

Yet another person appeared and again said unintelligible things to him, and made a big thing of looking at the machinery and monitors, then spoke to its colleague. He felt the slight scratch of a needle in his hand, and oblivion came.

Two days later he was able to breathe without the ventilator. And, without that intrusion into his airway, speak to Mam, Dad and Mair, although his voice was still a little slurred. His vision was getting better though, and he knew who people were now. Kelly, one of his ICU nurses, had told him this often happened after being on the heart/lung machine during the operation. It was due to microscopic contamination of the blood playing slight havoc with his brain, she said. He should recover fully in that regard though, a bright boy like him; most people did.

Time settled back into recognisable shapes of days. Mr Petersen, on his frequent visits, declared himself well satisfied with progress. The new heart was functioning well, he assured. In fact he was a star patient. He had a good healthy heart inside him now that hopefully should last his lifetime. Because it was a really excellent match, immunosuppressant management should not be a problem. When Mr Petersen told him so, with his parents there (with Mam all beaming smiles) he'd almost begun to say something but then glanced at them, received an almost imperceptible shake of the head from Dad, and stopped.

As for Mair, she looked radiantly happy too. She spent every possible moment with him (Mam and Dad discretely leaving them to it as often as they could). The worry had gone from her eyes. And the almost permanent irritation had left Tomos too. He found himself laughing with her again; weakly joking even. He could almost begin to imagine them resuming a sex life, eventually. But give it time. He certainly didn't intend to rush things and undo all Mr Petersen's good – no, miraculous – work. He intended to really look after this precious gift; take his consultant's advice and adopt a healthy lifestyle, one that included regular exercise. Not sport necessarily (he'd never been interested in that), but plenty of walking certainly. Duw; they might even get a dog.

The day after Tomos came off the ventilator, the Sunday, Lowri and Will drove up from Cardiff. Lowri too had wanted to just drop everything and dash up to Birmingham when the donated heart appeared, but once it was clear that all was well, the operation had succeeded, Glyn had persuaded her to wait a few days, until her brother was breathing independently and could at least talk. He would keep her well updated about things. Lowri had reluctantly agreed.

   No longer needing the same degree of intensive care, Tomos had been moved to the next grade down: a high dependency cardiothoracic ward. His sister and Will peeped a little apprehensively into the ward just after lunchtime. It was a small room containing just four patients and she quickly spotted Tomos and the ever-present Mair (Glyn and Sioned having paid a morning visit and departed to have a look around Birmingham). She was bearing the traditional offering of grapes, bought in a Services where they'd stopped for fuel on the way up the M5, hoping he was at the grape-eating stage by now. Well, it had been three days since his operation. How long did recovery take? They'd keep for a few days until he was ready, anyway.

To Lowri's astonishment, Tomos was out of bed, sitting in a chair. He'd spotted their arrival and raised a hand to gain attention, Mair swivelling to see who was making him smile. Lowri approached, her face wreathed in smiles, determined not to lapse into soppy tears of relief. She'd already done that, three days ago, when Dad phoned to say that everything was okay. Lowri fought to resist the temptation to hug him. Obviously that couldn't be done; he was fragile. Besides, they'd been warned to avoid actual physical contact as Tomos had little in the way of normal immunity, what with the drugs he was on now to prevent rejection of the heart.

So she could only convey how she felt through speech. 'Hello little man. How are you?' she said, voice quavering just a little, fighting down the mothering instinct he always provoked in her anyway, eyes smarting slightly.

   He grinned up at her. He looked tired and drawn, but not as

much as she'd expected. But there was a light in his eyes now that hadn't been there for a long while.

'Hello Lowri. Hello Will. Good, thanks. Really good.'

Lowri wanted to ruffle his hair but restrained herself. 'Great; that's my boy. Have you got your name down for the London Marathon yet?'

Tomos laughed. 'I'm working on it. Apparently they have a special Transplant Games. Perhaps I should go in for that. Take a bit of interest in sport, for the first time in my life.'

'Well why not?' Lowri enthused. It was so good to see her little brother happy. Actually indulging in banter. For the first time she noticed Mair, who had got up, offering her chair, to perch on the bed. (Will took the remaining one, beaming his pleasure too but staying discretely out of things. This was a family thing, after all.) 'Hi Mair; you okay?'

Mair nodded. 'Yes, fine, thanks Lowri. Certainly relieved, that's for sure.'

Lowri grinned. 'Yeah, I'll bet. This young man's caused us all quite enough worry, to be honest.'

She remembered the grapes and thrust them at Tomos. 'Oh, these are for you Bach. And don't tell me you don't like grapes. You have to have grapes when you're in hospital. It's compulsory. Otherwise Will and me'll have to eat the things ourselves.'

Tomos laughed again. 'Diolch Lowri. Yes, I'll eat them, don't worry. I've got my appetite back. I'll eat anything now.'

'Good. That's alright then. Perhaps you'll put some weight on now; not be such a bag of bones. Have something for Mair to grab hold of when you're back in harness.'

'Lowri!' Mair expostulated, pretend-shocked.

'Well, why not? You've got to think of these things,' Lowri retorted. 'Haven't you, Will?' she added as an afterthought, including him for the first time.

Will sniggered too. 'Absolutely! You'll have some catching up to do, Tomos.'

'Yes, well, you take it easy. Don't overdo things when you do.' Lowri was suddenly, uncharacteristically serious. 'Leave most of it to Mair; know what I mean?'

'Lowri! Mair shrieked again. Can we just stop talking about Tomos's sex life please?'

But she was loving it. It was nice to be normal; be talking about normal things. But when that happy day or night arrived, she certainly would be very gentle with him. Wouldn't risk anything.

'So,' Lowri continued, 'how long will you be in hospital? Have they said?'

'It's about two weeks normally, apparently,' Tomos said. 'Assuming there are no complications. But Mr Petersen says it's all looking good. He seems pleased with me. And I'm pleased with me. So maybe in about ten days' time.'

'That's amazing,' said Lowri, 'considering what a major thing it's been. Well I didn't expect to see you out of bed today, for sure.'

'Yes, they like to get you up as soon as possible. Tomorrow I can start a little walking, they say. Maybe even make it to the bathroom. That would be nice.'

'Well you take it easy young man,' his sister repeated, still solicitous. 'We don't want any relapses.'

'Yes, I will,' Tomos assured her. 'Don't you worry about that!'

'Seriously though,' Lowri mused, 'it must feel quite weird, knowing that you're carrying an organ that used to be part of another's body around inside you. Especially that one.'

Tomos smiled wryly. 'It certainly is, when I think about it. In fact it might not be from a man, necessarily. I suppose it doesn't have to be. As long as it's strong, and the right blood group and about the right size, and generally as close a match as possible.'

'Yes, well, let's be eternally grateful to whoever it was, for being on the donor register,' Lowri said soberly. 'It's just not something you normally think about, is it? Like getting blood. But it always has to come from some kind, generous soul.'

'Indeed,' Will put in. 'I've always thought I should go on the register, but never got around to it. I will do now. When the situation happens to family it brings it home, doesn't it?'

'Really?' Lowri looked at him sharply. 'You will? Well good for you, Love. And I will too.'

'And I would too,' said Tomos, 'but now of course I can't. I'm not and probably never will be in completely rude good health. I'll be on drugs for the rest of my life, apart from anything else.'

'But let's hope that neither of us finds ourselves donating though,' Will murmured. That's the paradox of it, isn't it? We want to do it, it's a good and noble thing, but we hope it'll never happen.'

Lowri laughed. 'Well, in my case let me live until seventy or so, then I'll pop my clogs and anyone will be quite welcome to any bits of me they want. If there's anything worth salvaging by then, that is.'

Will grinned too. 'Oh, I'm sure there will be my love. I can recommend some of them, anyway!'

Lowri thumped him hard on the bicep for his pains. She changed the subject. 'But anyway, here you are again, Bruv; in hospital at Christmas in three days' time. It's a bugger, isn't it?'

'Well, yes, but this time won't be as bad as last year.' Tomos was sanguine. 'This time I'm on the mend. I'll enjoy Christmas dinner this year, for one thing. And I won't be so miserable and feeling sorry for myself as I was last.'

Mair piped up. 'No, come on Cariad! You weren't really feeling sorry for yourself. Not excessively. You know depression's one of the symptoms of heart failure. And besides, who wouldn't be fed up, being as ill as you were then?'

'Quite right, Mair,' Lowri agreed. 'You were allowed to be a misery guts. But you aren't now. It's great to see you looking so chipper!'

'Oh Duw!' Mair suddenly exclaimed. 'I've just thought. All your prezzies are back home in Talsarn. We didn't bring them with us!'

'Yes, well,' said Lowri, 'I expect you had other things on your mind though, didn't you. Don't worry about it.'

'We did that, all right. What a night it was! I'd had a nasty sectioning at work and then the call came through at gone ten o'clock about the heart. It was panic stations, I can tell you!'

'I'll bet it was,' said Lowri. She paused. 'Hey, I've just had a thought. When this young man's back home, we'll have a delayed Christmas party-cum-welcome home. Have a real piss-up!'

'I don't think I'd be able to do that, said Tomos solemnly. 'I'll be on so much stuff . . .'

'Oh, you!' Lowri retorted. I was speaking figuratively, for God's sake!'

She was momentarily silent. But then all Lowri's silences were momentary. 'Ah, that reminds me. Something else for you.' She rummaged in her shoulder bag and brought out a bright red envelope. 'I couldn't think what to give you for Chrissie, as you were such an invalid before, so I've been very unimaginative, I'm afraid.'

Tomos took the envelope. 'Diolch, Lowri! Can I open it now?'

'Sure; it's mostly a card.'

As he might have expected, it wasn't the usual sort of Christmas card but a very ribald get-well-soon card heavy with nudge-nudge innuendo and with a picture of Santa Claus crudely stuck on. It was clearly a DIY job. And folded inside it there was a cheque, for a hundred pounds. Tomos picked it out, astounded. 'Oh, Lowri; you shouldn't have given me all this!'

His sister waved the objection airily aside. 'Nonsense! It's not every day your little brother gets a new heart. It's cause for special celebration. While you're here in a decent shopping place, when you're properly walking, you can go and do some serious retail therapy! I know you're a male, but you'd probably enjoy it.'

Tomos was lost for words. He could only mumble, 'Diolch, Lowri.'

Nine days later Glyn and Mair had to reluctantly take their leave. They both had jobs that needed attending to: his houses and Mair's clients. Mair didn't want to go of course, but she'd only been able to get two weeks' leave and some of it would have to count as part of annual holiday even so. The department, always overstretched, could not do without her for a lengthy period. And the same went for Glyn. Selling houses was hardly a vitally important occupation, but he was a key member of his small firm and could not be spared for too long either.

Mr Petersen opined that Tomos would be able to leave in a day or two too, although not to return to Wales. He would need to stay in the vicinity for another month for continued monitoring: blood tests, heart checks and the like. And just in case there was an unexpected complication. Mr Petersen thought that highly unlikely though. Indeed it looked as though the immunosuppressants could be reduced significantly; there were no signs of rejection at all and there was no point in Tomos suffering side effects unnecessarily or having his immune system unduly compromised, falling prey to every little infection that did the rounds.

So they scanned the local accommodation registers and found a nice little guest house not far from the Cadbury factory in Bournville (you could smell the sickly-sweet fragrance of chocolate on the air). It would be nice to avoid the busy city centre; they just weren't city types. And it would be simple to catch a bus up the Bristol road, heading back into the city, to the Queen Elizabeth for his checks. There would be a little walking involved but, taken slowly, no more than Tomos could manage. And the exercise would be good for him.

Their landlady, Margaret Symonds, sixtyish, short, plump, prodigiously breasted and peroxide blonde except where it was grey at the roots was a salt-of-the-Brummy-earth type, with a sing-song accent to match. She was a kindly soul and full of sympathy for Tomos with his recent trauma (but it's amazing what they can do nowadays, ain't it?). Her Eric had been in the QE too but had passed away the previous year, rest his soul, from lung cancer, although he'd never lost a day's work at the Austin in his life before that. And she knew Wales, she said. Eric and her had spent many a happy holiday at Butlins, Pwlleli or Pontins, Prestatyn when the babbies (our Craig and our Mandy) were little. (She'd never heard of Ceredigion though, although she knew where Aberaeron was.)

Sioned and Margaret took an instant liking to each other. She was a first-class cook too, and that first evening produced a veritable feast of roast beef with all the traditional accompaniments, followed by sugar-saturated apple crumble. They were her only guests, and rather than leave them to eat alone in the dining room invited them to join her in her private flat on the top floor, but only if they wanted to. They accepted with alacrity, touched by her hospitality. Margaret didn't seem to understand the concept of small dinner portions and Tomos's plate was piled high when she brought it, already assembled (none of your help-yourself-from-serving-dishes nonsense) to the dining table. She even produced a bottle of good Burgundy to go with it, which she insisted was on the house to celebrate Tomos's good operation outcome.

For the first time in three years Tomos attacked the food with gusto and cleared his plate, as Margaret rattled off conversation at high speed without pausing for breath, stopping only, reminded by good manners, to occasionally take polite interest in her guests.

After lingering gossiping over the rest of the wine (which mostly went down Sioned and Margaret's throats; Tomos restricted himself to half a glass) for an hour, they took a gentle stroll along Bournville Lane, Sioned walking slightly unsteadily with her hand solicitously and a little ridiculously under Tomos's elbow, although he hardly needed it. It was the opposite case if anything. They returned at ten past nine to find the guest lounge warm, inviting but empty and sank, sighing into Margaret's deep comfortable chintzy armchairs. Sioned found the television remote control and flicked it on. She hadn't been keeping up with her soaps lately. Within a few minutes, as if summoned down from on high, Margaret appeared asking if they'd like coffee.

To Sioned's 'Oh, yes please, Margaret,' she disappeared, to return five minutes later with coffee jug and accoutrements. She placed the silver tray on a coffee table, lifted the two together towards Sioned's chair and hesitated, hovering, ready for more conversation. Clearly she was a gregarious person; loved company. Taking Sioned's smile as invitation to stay, she sank into the end of a nearby sofa and continued telling her life story from where she'd left off fifty minutes earlier. Sioned found the controller again and muted the sound.

Sioned was beginning to feel sleepy. It was probably the huge meal and too much wine. Margaret was lovely, a wonderfully friendly host, but she was ready for bed. And before that she wanted some time alone with Tomos. Completely alone. With her boy. They drank two rose-patterned cupfuls as Margaret prattled amiably on. Sioned cast a surreptitious glance at the fake-antique grandfather clock on the Regency-stripe wallpapered wall to her left. Five to ten. She really must extricate them from Mother Hen.

She looked at Tomos, whose eyelids were drooping. He was probably tired too, poor love. It would be sleep time back in the QE now.

'Ready for bed now, Tomos?'

He smiled back. 'Mm; quite tired.'

Margaret joined in. 'Yes, I bet you are, Chick. Been a big day for you; first one out of hospital an' all that.'

Sioned pressed home the advantage. 'Yes, he really ought to be getting to bed. Mustn't overdo things. We'll be getting into trouble!'

Margaret heaved herself, panting a little, up from the sofa and came across to collect the tray. 'Right; well you get a good night's rest then my love, and we'll see you in the morning,' she said, not a little possessively. It was like being adopted again.

'Well thanks for the lovely meal and everything, Margaret,'

Sioned said. 'This feels just like home. It's a lovely guest house.'

'Thank you my dear; very kind of you to say so,' their landlady preened. 'I do try to make my guests feel welcome. Well I'll wish you goodnight then. Is eight o'clock alright for breakfast?'

'Yes, that's fine thanks. Goodnight.'

Margaret left them, heading with the tray to the kitchen, as Sioned breathed a long sigh of relief.

They went up the floral-carpeted stairs onto the floral-carpeted (but a different pattern) landing and found their designated bedrooms. They hesitated outside Tomos's door. He opened his mouth to say goodnight but she beat him to it.

'Get yourself into bed and I'll come in and see you.'

He opened his mouth again to ask why, but she put her fingers to his lips.

'Just do it. I'll give you five minutes.'

Sioned rapped on his door and opened it to his murmured 'Okay' a few minutes later. She hadn't changed for bed yet herself. He was sitting up in bed wearing his red pyjamas, leaning back against the buttoned padded headboard. She closed the door and came over to the bed, plonking herself down as he moved his legs aside.

'Tired now are you, Cariad?' She said. It was nice to be able to speak in their mother tongue after the remorseless Brummy-accented patter of Margaret, nice as she was.

'Yes, a bit, Mam.' Tomos certainly looked it, although not haggard and lifeless, as he'd done so recently.

'It's nice to be back in a proper bed though, isn't it?'

Tomos grinned. 'Certainly is. That hospital one was a bit hard, to be honest. And before that there was the sofa at home, when I couldn't even lie down properly. It's been ages since I was in a normal bed. This is Heaven!'

'I'm sure it is, Cariad.'

'It'll be even better to get back home and sleep in the bed there though. With Mair. That'll be wonderful.'

'Yes, I bet it will. But when you do, just go steady with . . . you know what. We don't want to be rushing back here in a panic.'

'Mam!' Tomos scoffed gently. 'Don't worry! I won't be that fragile! It is allowed for transplantees you know. You can get back to having a sex life remarkably quickly, apparently. That's what Mr Petersen has said. It's just a matter of knowing when you feel up to it. I won't do it if it seems to be too much, or hurts, or anything. Mair wouldn't let me, anyway.'

'No, I'm sure you're right. But even so.' Sioned just couldn't imagine Tomos indulging in anything as energetic as that again. But Mair was a sensible girl. She'd keep Tomos on a tight rein if necessary.

'How's your wound today?' she asked. 'Any pain?'

'No, none at all. Just a little itchiness. I keep wanting to scratch but I'm managing not to.'

Sioned laughed. 'No, don't; you mustn't.' Then she became serious. 'It's amazing how soon the body heals though, isn't it? To think that only two weeks ago you'd been sliced right open. Ugh; it makes me cringe to think about it!'

Tomos laughed again. 'Makes *you* cringe? How do you think I feel about it?

'Yes, well, it's all over now, lovely boy. All in the past. Let's just think of the future.'

'Indeed.'

A silence fell.

Then, 'Mam; what's this about?'

'What?'

'Well, you seem to want to have a heart-to-heart, or something.'

'I just wanted to have some time alone with you. Our landlady's very nice and everything, but in fairly small doses. This is the first time either your dad or me have had you all to ourselves, in private, with no other people around and without some nurse or somebody threatening to walk in on us.'

Sioned paused.

'Alright, there is something. 'Tomos, there's something you have to know. Your dad and I have known for a few days now and have been wanting to tell you, but there's never been the right moment . . .' She ground to a halt, flustered.

Tomos felt his breath catch, his heartbeat quicken.

Mam? What is it?'

Sioned reached for his hand; grasped it tightly with both of hers.

'Well it's about your heart.'

Another pause.

Tomos was alarmed now. '*Mam?* What about it?'

Sioned took a deep breath. 'Well, you know how Mr Petersen is so pleased that it's such a good match?'

'Yes?'

'Well it would be. The best possible. Because, Cariad, the heart is your brother's. It's Wayne's!'

Chapter 23
The One of Us

Sioned raised her head, reluctant to return his look. He was staring at her, eyes wide, mouth slack. He had gone deathly pale.

'*What?*'

She repeated, forcing herself to meet his shocked expression. 'Yes, lovely boy. The donor was Wayne.'

'But . . . how?'

'He was blown up by a roadside bomb in Iraq – Basra I think it was – two days before we got the call from Jan. He wasn't killed outright but very badly hurt. They flew him back to England – Selly Oak hospital here in Birmingham, where they bring all the wounded soldiers, I gather. He had very bad brain injuries – apparently he'd taken his helmet off for some reason – and had lost both legs. They had him on life support I suppose, must have done, but he just didn't make it. He died on the evening Jan rang us.'

Some of the colour was creeping back into Tomos's face. 'But how do you know all this?'

'Jan told us a few days ago. She thought it best if we told you ourselves, at the right moment.'

'So they knew it was Wayne and didn't tell us, didn't tell me, at the time? Bloody hell!' Tomos was angry now.

'No, Cariad, it wasn't like that. They wouldn't have withheld information like that, I'm sure they wouldn't.'

'Then how . . . ?'

'Jan said that they didn't make a connection between you two at first. Well there was no reason to. No one involved in looking after Wayne or you had seen both of you, so it wouldn't have been obvious you were twins. Besides, Wayne was so badly injured, they wouldn't have been able to compare you anyway . . .' Sioned trailed off, shuddering.

Tomos sat, still stunned, still staring at his mother. 'Bloody hell,' he said again, 'Poor Wayne!'

A thought occurred to him. 'Then how *did* they know about us?'

Sioned had recovered composure. 'Well, they didn't realise at first because of your different surnames of course. Why would they connect someone called Wayne Harrison from Yorkshire with someone else called Tomos Rees from Wales? And besides, on the evening Wayne died, all the transplant team was bothered about was that a heart had become available, from a donor, that was a good match for someone on the waiting list, particularly you, and the next of kin were alright about it. Well, reasonably alright, I suppose.'

Sioned paused again. 'But it must have been a devil of a thing to face. Bad enough to be suddenly losing your son. You'd hardly be in a fit state to be thinking about something like transplant, would you? Poor Maureen. Poor Jim!'

'No,' Tomos agreed, wryly. 'But I still don't see how they *did* make the connection.'

'Well, it was Jan who eventually put two and two together. Of course Jim and Maureen had come down from Northallerton when Wayne was brought back, and after he died and you were transplanted, a couple of days after that, she had a long chat with them before they went back, discussing funeral arrangements and everything, and they just wanted to talk to someone about Wayne, and told her he was adopted as a baby, in Liverpool, in 1985. Then, three days after your op, your dad and I were talking to Jan as well, and we brought up the subject of the Strawberry Field home for some reason, and how you were adopted and one of twins.

'She connected your ages, and Liverpool, and asked as a long shot if the names Wayne or Harrison meant anything to us, and of course they did. We were gobsmacked, as you can imagine! We told her our two families knew each other, and you and Wayne had met. Well, you should have seen her face too! It was a picture. She rang and double-checked with Maureen and Jim, and mentioned you, and asked them for a photo of Wayne. They e-mailed one to her and of course that clinched it for her.'

'Yes, I'm sure you were amazed,' Tomos said, a little acidly. 'But why didn't you tell me as soon as you knew? Didn't I have a right to know?'

Sioned squeezed the hand she was still holding. There was no return pressure. He was obviously upset. 'Well I know, Cariad. Yes, of course you did! But it was a matter of finding the right moment.

We wanted to tell you in private, not in a hospital ward. We didn't know how you'd take it. I've told you as soon as I could now, haven't I? None of us knew before you had the transplant, and would it have made any difference if you had? You surely wouldn't have refused it, knowing that, would you?'

Tomos smiled sadly, and now he did squeeze back. 'No, Mam, I don't suppose I would have. Not that I was very clear-headed at the time, anyway. Sorry. You're right. This is the best time.'

He lapsed into silence, gazing at the foot of the bed. Then, as if another thought had suddenly occurred, 'Does Mair know then?'

'No, Cariad, of course not!' Sioned assured, gently. 'We wouldn't have told her before you!'

She put a hand to slowly ruffle his hair. 'Poor boy; this is just something else for you to cope with now, isn't it?'

'Well it's certainly a shock, I must admit,' he murmured. 'So Wayne must have been on the donor register then. He was more the altruist than I supposed, in his different way.'

'Yes,' Sioned agreed. 'He was a good boy, sure enough.'

'Perhaps it's something that soldiers tend to do,' Tomos said.

'What?'

'Well, go on the register. As the possibility of dying young goes with the territory.'

'Mm; maybe. It's not something the rest of us give a lot of thought to though, is it?' Sioned bit her lip, suddenly realising what she was saying. Of course, her son *had* had it on his mind a lot lately. Must have done. She hurried on. 'Well; you know what I mean. People who aren't seriously ill don't.'

'No, Mam. I don't suppose they do.'

'How does it make you feel, knowing this? Sioned asked. 'It must be complicated enough anyway, knowing you've got a new organ because someone else had died.'

Tomos pondered that. 'Yes it is. I do feel mixed up. Very grateful, of course. But a bit guilty too. Especially as it's Wayne. Poor bloke. I still can't believe it. It's easy to say that soldiers know the risks they run and live with the possibility of death, but he still died. It's still just as tragic. And because of that I've got a chance of life now. It's like we've been recombined, sort of.'

'Yeah.'

'It's a bit ironic, in a sad sort of way,' he continued.

'How do you mean?'

'Well, you know, he didn't really seem to like me all that much.'

'Yes, well you only had that one meeting really, didn't you? And a few reluctant words on the phone sometimes when Maureen rang. You never really got to know each other, did you?'

Tomos sighed. 'I know. I regret it now. I wish I'd made more of an effort to reach out to him. But we seemed to be so different. In our attitudes and outlook and everything. So much for nature-nurture theory.'

'How do you mean?' Sioned repeated. He'd lost her, as he often did.

'Well, you know, whether children's personalities and intelligence and everything are due more to genetic inheritance or to upbringing; the family environment they grow up in. They've done studies of identical twins – they have to be identical so they're genetically just the same – who were separated at birth like Wayne and me, to see whether they develop into different sorts of people or grow up basically very similar.'

'Yes, I've seen things about that on the telly.' It had come back to Sioned now; the nature-nurture thingumy Tomos was talking about had thrown her. 'But don't they find that twins *do* tend to grow up the same?'

Tomos was talking animatedly now. 'It seems that often they do, sometimes to quite an extraordinary extent, but not always. I suppose me and Wayne are in the second camp. I read quite a lot about it when you first told me I was an identical twin, but I've forgotten a lot of it since. I seem to remember that it's not quite as clear cut as some scientists think though. It's really quite complex.'

'Yes, I see,' Sioned said, although really it was beyond her. She left that sort of clever scientific stuff to her clever son.

'Anyway,' Tomos continued, warming to his theme, 'I would have thought that childhood environment does influence how you develop a lot, even if identical twins do start off with the same innate predisposition due to genes. Maybe, if Wayne and I had both been brought up by you and Dad, we would have stayed very similar. But we weren't. We've grown up in very different sorts of families – even speaking different first languages, for goodness' sake.'

'True,' his mother agreed. 'Chalk and cheese, really.'

'And after all,' said Tomos, 'there were some pretty strong influences on me growing up, not least Lowri.' He chuckled. 'And no one could have ignored her!'

Sioned laughed too. 'You're right there Cariad. Poor old Wayne didn't grow up with her like you did!'

Tomos became serious. 'Yeah, when you think about it, Wayne and I had very different family situations. I wasn't remotely interested in outdoor activities or sport or anything, and we know why now, and you always encouraged me to be academic, so I did quite well at that. Not to mention the Lowri influence, as I say. But Wayne didn't have any of that.'

Sioned scoffed. 'But hold on Tomos; I wouldn't say your dad and me did a better job of bringing you up than Maureen and Jim did Wayne. He was a very nice boy, a nice human being, and that's the important thing. After all, look what he finally did, without knowing he'd be doing it. He lost his life doing what he believed in, and because of that and being a donor, someone else could live. And that person turned out by an amazing co-incidence to be his own brother.'

'Yes, true,' Tomos said sadly. 'This is the devil of it, isn't it? Someone else has died and because of that now I can live. It gave me complicated feelings before, anyway, and now there's the knowledge it was Wayne who saved me. Duw Duw! I really wish I'd been nicer to him now. Wish we'd been proper brothers!'

His eyes were tearing, lower lip quivering; the emotional reaction catching up.

'Yes I know, Cariad.' Sioned soothed as she moved closer and drew him very gently to her, not embracing too hard, letting him weep, as his arms came around her too, seeking comfort. 'I suppose it's our fault really. We should have taken you both.'

She caressed his shoulder blades. 'Do you know why we went for you rather than Wayne? Did I ever tell you? The first day we saw the two of you at the children's home; the lady who ran the place picked up Wayne to give to us first, but he bawled, the poor little love. He wasn't a brave little soldier that day; not at all. So he went back to the young woman who'd been holding him – I suppose she was a nanny – and she cuddled him, and he buried his face in her chest, and kept peeping out at us nervously, when all we wanted to do was love him. Poor little mite.

'So then the supervisor lady went and fetched some little tubs of yoghurt, and gave one to your dad, then picked you up and brought you over and got your dad to give you a spoonful, and it worked wonders! You sat on my lap quite happily, and your dad fed you the rest, and then he gave you the empty pot to play with and you smeared yoghurt all down my blouse, but I couldn't have cared less. And then we tried again with Wayne, and it worked with him too, thank goodness. So that first time we held and played with both of you. You were both such little sweeties. But we really didn't think we could take you both, so we had to choose, and we chose you just because you came to us more easily, but it was probably only the yoghurt talking, really. But yes; you're right. Perhaps we should have taken you both. I think we just weren't brave enough to take on the double challenge though.'

Sioned paused, considering that. 'But then, if we had done, Maureen and Jim wouldn't have had the joy that I'm sure Wayne gave them. So who's to say what would have been best, really?'

Tomos had stopped crying but they stayed in the embrace. 'You have actually told me this before, Mam.'

'Oh, have I? When was that?'

'When you first told me about being adopted. You told me why you chose me rather than Wayne.'

'Really? Oh, my memory! It isn't what it used to be!'

'That's alright Mam. But what you were saying about Wayne's parents. They would never have missed what they never had, I suppose,' he sniffed. 'And they might well have adopted another child just as nice. After all, they also adopted that girl. What's her name, now?'

'Poppy.'

'Yes, that's right.' He pulled away to lean back against the headboard; picked up a corner of the duvet to wipe his face. 'It's Maureen and Jim I feel really sorry for now though. It's a horrible situation for them, isn't it? Must be terrible to lose a child. Alright, not a child, but you know what I mean. So you haven't spoken to them at all then since it happened?'

'No, only through Jan. They were over at Selly Oak hospital of course, where Wayne was, and as I say they went back home soon after. There would have been no point in them staying around. I think the army's organising the funeral. It'll be a full military honours thing, I expect.'

'Yes, I suppose so. Poor Wayne; he didn't have the ceremonial homecoming the dead soldiers usually get though, paraded through the streets of Wootton Bassett and all that.'

Sioned sighed. 'No. He didn't get that recognition on the telly. Although it was announced on the news that he'd died, apparently. We missed it, because there was all the worry about getting you to Birmingham when the call from Jan came. We had other things on our minds. If we'd known, we'd probably have joined the dots and realised he was your donor straight away.'

'Mm.

Sioned put her hand to her mouth. 'Oh dear, I've just thought. The funeral must be very soon. I hope we haven't missed it! I expect it'll be on television. We must send Maureen and Jim a really nice wreath. And perhaps a special one from you, in the circumstances, don't you think?'

'Yes, of course. But I haven't got any money with me . . .'

'Tomos! For goodness' sake; that's not a problem! I've got my credit cards with me. Never mind about the money!'

'Alright then. Sorry.'

'Right; I'll see if I can get hold of Jan tomorrow. She'll probably know when and where the funeral's going to be. Or if she doesn't, I'm sure she can find out from Maureen and Jim. Then after you've had your appointment with Mr Petersen we can go and find a florist's, if you feel up to it, okay?'

'Yes, of course, Mam. Let's do that.'

'Right.'

They fell into silence again.

Then Sioned spoke. 'I feel so sorry for that Helen too.'

'Who?'

'Helen; Wayne's girlfriend. You remember her, don't you? We met her that time when we visited them.'

'Oh yes. Were they still going out together?'

Sioned delivered a gentle smack to his hand. 'Oh, you men; honestly! Just shows how much you two used to talk together – '

She stopped at the sight of his crestfallen face. 'Oh, I'm sorry Cariad. Shouldn't have said that. Yes, when Maureen phoned last, back in the summer they were, anyway. And it was a bit more than 'going out'. They've been together years. I think they were engaged to be married, actually. I'm sure that's what Maureen said.'

'Oh, right,' said Tomos. 'Yes, poor Helen. It must be awful for her. Really awful. I suppose she always knew there was the possibility of this happening to Wayne, but that can't make it any easier if it happens.'

'No, I'm sure it can't. I'm glad your dad was never a soldier. Or you.'

Tomos ignored that. 'And presumably Helen now knows about me.'

'Yes, I expect so.'

'Duw! I wonder how she feels about that?'

'I really can't imagine, Cariad. Like you, I suppose. Confused.'

'Yes, she must be. Poor girl. It makes me feel guilty again. It's going so well for me, now, but there's all that grief on the other side.'

'Sioned reached for his hand once more. 'Yes, well try not to feel bad. I'm sure Wayne would be pleased that his heart had gone to you.'

Tomos smiled, a little sadly again. 'Well I hope so. I hope he liked me a little, at least.' He paused. 'It certainly makes me feel thankful for what I've got. My health back. You and Dad and Lowri. And Mair. I've not been very nice to her, the last few months. I'm surprised she stuck with me, really.'

Sioned laughed. 'You don't understand women very well, lovely boy. She knows a good man when she sees one. But yes, she's a treasure. I'm sure you'll start appreciating her more now, at any rate.'

She planted a kiss on his forehead and got up.

'Anyway, I must leave you to your beauty sleep. I'm sorry if this has all been a bit of a shock, and you weren't told before. Am I forgiven?'

'Yes Mam,' said Tomos, looking as though he were going to cry again, 'of course you are.'

Chapter 24
Wayne

It was over. The day she'd been dreading. Helen lay on her bed, her ridiculously narrow single bed (the other one, to double the sleeping capacity, had mysteriously disappeared) in her old room in Mum and Dad's house, still in her sombre clothes. Hired dress, a tad on the small side. Black tights. Black heels kicked off, lying keeled over on the floor. Of course she hadn't driven all the way back to Wiltshire after the funeral, to that dismally empty flat echoing with too many memories. What would have been the point? She couldn't have found the energy anyway. And it was slightly, but only slightly, comforting to be back with family, even though they did seem to be tiptoeing around on eggshells, looking at her with that odd mixture of concern and embarrassment, daring tentative smiles, trying so hard to find the right thing to say all the time.

It was only nine o'clock in the evening on this chilly fourth of January. When she'd said she was coming up to bed, Mum had nodded sadly, said, 'Yes, alright Luv;' hadn't tried to persuade her to stay downstairs with them. Well, they must be sick of her zombie-like state. She stared up at the ceiling. It was looking distinctly off-white. Didn't look as though Dad had painted it since she left home. Since they had left home; her and Wayne. What the hell was she on about, thinking about the bloody ceiling? She switched the bedside lamp on, got up, padded across to put off the main light, came back to bed and climbed in, still clothed. Sod it; it wouldn't matter about creasing the dress. It would be dry cleaned and ironed ready for the next funeral-goer, after all.

She clicked the lamp off, drew the duvet up over her face. Her throat ached. Yes, this was retreating from the world, like a kid or a hurt animal or something, but who cared? Well it was a pretty shitty place, wasn't it? She closed her eyes, shutting it out.

But at least the second-worst day of her life was now over. The end of all that horrible anticipation, once the day had been fixed, after the inquest (why the hell did they need one of those? It was pretty bloody obvious how he'd died) and the military rigmarole and the normal funeral procedures that had to be gone through. Although it had been anything but an ordinary civvy funeral of course. It had had to be the full military-with-honours thing with all of Northallerton involved, because he was one of our heroic boys, a local lad, dying to defend his country. Had she been able to choose, she would have opted for the simplest, least visible ceremony. But it wasn't only up to her. His parents had wanted the best possible send-off for him, and the town had expected – no – virtually demanded it.

And of course there had been the extra dimension of his heart donation (as well as a kidney that had survived the explosion going to another recipient). That had elevated him almost to the level of a saint. The media had had a field day about it. For the local press and TV it had swelled a big story into a huge heart-string tugging, human interest one. And it had gone national. The satellite vans of the networks had camped outside Wayne's parents' house; reporters and photographers had congregated, microphones and telephoto lenses at the ready. They had intruded into the small front garden. More than one tabloid reporter had knocked the door offering temptingly large amounts of money for their exclusive 'story', she'd heard, until Jim, angry and upset, had gone out and told them all to bugger off.

So all things considered, it had had to be nothing less than the full works: the cortege processing through the banned-to-traffic High Street with the funeral director in his morning suit with top hat and cane walking ahead; her, feeling oddly emotionless, beside Maureen, Jim, Poppy and Wayne's CO, following the hearse with the union flag-draped coffin and dress uniform cap atop one end and a poppy wreath the other; the elderly men of the British Legion proud and grave with their berets and blazers and medals, dipping their standards as they passed. The flowers thrown by some of the hundreds who lined the way. The guard of honour at the door of All Saints' Church drawn from Wayne's comrades from Warminster, those not posted abroad, reversing and sloping their arms, with more as pall bearers and many more again packing the church. The awed-by-the-proceedings boy scouts. The many people standing outside; the sympathetic looks; many women dabbing eyes and more than one man doing so too. The omnipresent media again, with reporters talking gravely to video cameras.

The entry to the church to the strains of *I Vow to Thee My Country*; the vicar's gentle eulogy and the one from the regimental colonel: stout patriotic words about bravery and duty and honour and enthusiasm and loving his job, although she wondered if the man even knew Wayne; the final hymn, *The Day Thou Gavest Lord Is Ended* as he was borne by his comrades out again, to the graveside. The firing party giving their salute, frightening funeral-black crows out of the trees. The bugler playing the Last Post.

And then, afterwards, with the ceremony over and left, thankfully, to themselves, the viewing of the many wreaths and their messages, from Wayne's friends from scouting and soldiering days; from family unable to attend; from town dignitaries and organisations; from, touchingly, so very many total strangers.

And, most poignantly of all, the wreath from Tomos; a simple ring of white chrysanthemums and roses, and his message: With love from your Brother Tomos. There are no words I can say, except Thank You. Rest in Peace.

And then finally, at last a measure of relief – the wake; a more private affair away from the public gaze, the conspicuousness, the trying to hold herself together. But relief only slight, really. It had been nothing like her nan's funeral, who hadn't of course died tragically young but enjoyed a long and mostly healthy and happy life. So in her case there had been just a little sadness. But this was different. The military had organised the willingly offered Methodist Church hall, which was preferable to a noisy pub or something, and family and close friends had been segregated from the many other mourners. So Wayne's parents, Poppy, his Uncle Malcolm and Aunt Sheila with cousins Katie and Brenda; herself, parents and sister Gilly; Wayne's friends Billy and David from Scouts and pallbearers Lee and Pete from the army; and her mate Sal; had sat quietly, in her case feeling quite numb and detached, in the top-floor Rievaulx room while the soldiers young and old and boy scouts were catered for in the main hall.

The mood had been strained, sombre. Taking their cue from the chief mourners, no one had felt like small talk or the haven't-seen-you-for-ages-type catching up you always got at funerals. The

Methodist minister, the Reverend Matthew Sykes, had joined their group and sat with them, and encouraged Jim and Maureen to talk about Wayne, but only if they wanted to. She hadn't, she was still finding it difficult to talk, but the others had. Jim had got into a long sad reminiscence about their first sight of Wayne as a baby at Strawberry Field, how they'd wanted him immediately; about the way he'd made so many promises that day and embarrassed himself, and Maureen, twisting her screwed-up hankie, liquid-eyed had nodded her confirmation. Matthew (he'd insisted on being called just that) had nodded too; anxious to show his empathy and understanding. Jim had wished, mournfully, that he'd never encouraged Wayne to join the Services. Maureen had blinked and blown her nose, hard. She herself had felt only coldness, all emotion weirdly absent.

And then, at last, it really was all over; after the many final condolences offered and hugs bestowed on her, Maureen and Jim, funeral cars had delivered the families to their homes to resume their forever-altered lives. Mum, for once totally English and conventional, had made a nice cup of tea, and she and dad had made desultory conversation about what a lovely service, and ceremony generally, it had been (in spite of it not being their sort of thing normally). They'd had a simple meal, which no-one felt particularly hungry for. Dad had taken photos of a selection of the wreaths with his new mobile phone, including the one from Tomos, and he'd uploaded them to the computer and they'd looked at them, Mum murmuring comments as Dad clicked through the slide show. And still she couldn't cry.

Then Dad had picked up the television controller and asked if anyone wanted to watch anything. They'd looked at her. Clearly it was for her to choose. She'd shaken her head. She felt worn out and ready for sleep, weighed down with the lethargy she'd felt for the last nineteen days. She'd hardly slept the previous night. She'd made her escape and come up to bed.

Well that really is it now, she thought, from within her hurt-proof cocoon. *All over. That horrible anticipation of the funeral over and done with. Just a matter of getting back on track now. That's all. Adjustment to life alone. Without Wayne.* Her throat hurt so much she thought she'd choke. *Why haven't I cried properly yet?* she wondered. *Fuck it, I can let go now. No more face of the brave, stoical fiancée needed, to show to the world. No more bloody dignity.*

But then an image came. Wayne's coffin in its grave. The four red poppies handed by the funeral director to her, Maureen, Jim and Poppy, blood-bright on its lid where they'd thrown them. Her tears finally came. She curled foetally and sobbed and sobbed.

Chapter 25
Tomos

The following weekend, Jim and Maureen drove down to Birmingham to visit Tomos. Sioned had phoned them a couple of days after the funeral, when she judged (hoped, anyway) that they might be feeling a little less raw. It had been a slightly awkward conversation, obviously. Sioned couldn't begin to imagine, try as she might, how they must be feeling. Or course they would be pleased at his good progress after his operation, but there was the stark reminder, refusing to stay quiet, of the flip side; the necessary, enabling tragedy that had brought Tomos's salvation. Poor them, Sioned had thought, as she dialled their number and nervously waited for someone to pick up.

It had been Maureen who had answered, to Sioned's relief. She got on well with her, and conversations like this were better woman-to-woman. Of course, she had tried to keep the subject on Wayne, really tried to empathise, without being *too* poor-you about it. It was always such a difficult balancing act in these situations though, wasn't it? (not that she could remember a similar one, where a friend had lost a child, least of all had one killed).

She'd let Maureen talk at great length about it all, prompting with what she hoped were sensitive questions: her feelings, how Jim was coping (which wasn't terribly well, really), how beautiful the service had been and their amazement at the huge turn-out to it; how touched she was by Tomos's wreath and message. That had naturally turned the subject to her own son. Maureen had sounded genuinely pleased that he was getting on so well, although, obviously, there was an unmistakeable undertone of sadness.

And it was Maureen, not herself inviting, who'd said that they'd really like to visit Tomos. Sioned, surprised and pleased, had suggested that a good time would be whilst they were still in Birmingham for Tomos to have his follow-ups. It would be a much shorter trip than going all the way from north Yorkshire to west Wales. Maureen had agreed, sounding almost enthusiastic about the suggestion. They could meet up somewhere in the city centre, have a bite to eat, something like that. But when, later, Sioned had told Margaret of the plan, she would have none of it. Indeed she'd sounded almost affronted.

'No, you can't do that!' she'd protested. 'They can come here and you can have a nice visit in comfort. They can stay as long as they like, and I'll rustle up a little something for lunch. No charge for it of course, in the circumstances.'

Sioned had thanked her profusely for her kindness (and she knew what Margaret's 'little something' would be). And so, after another call to Maureen, it had been arranged for the coming Saturday, with elaborate instructions for finding Linden Lea Guest House (All En-Suite; if you get to Bournville Lane you've gone past it). Sioned felt almost excited about it. Tomos felt rather nervous.

At eleven-thirty (they must have made an early start) Margaret hurried to answer the Tyrolean chimes in the hall. Sioned and Tomos were in the lounge, waiting, she immersed in a repeat on the television, he trying to concentrate on a paperback. Margaret escorted the visitors in. Sioned scrambled to find the television controller and clicked it off. She and Tomos rose. Maureen stood, slightly uncertainly, as Sioned murmured, 'Hello Maureen,' and came to embrace, and kiss her cheek. Sioned turned and looked at Jim, who was gazing at Tomos, a faraway expression on his pale face. *Duw*, she thought, *He looks ten years older than when we saw him last. Has all this happened in the last few days?*

His hair, what was left of it, was completely grey, almost white. His face looked haggard and drained. He certainly looked in need of a comforting hug. Sioned moved to embrace and kiss him too. 'Hello Jim. How are you?'

His hands on her shoulder blades were listless. 'Not too bad thanks, Sioned.'

Maureen had moved towards Tomos. 'Now then; am I allowed to give you a hug, young man? You won't break, will you?'

Tomos smiled shyly. 'No, that's alright. Just not a bear hug.'

Maureen's arms went around him in a careful embrace, their bodies barely touching. But her kiss on his cheek was generous. Jim came forward too, and to Tomos's surprise also hugged him, gently, lightly patting his shoulder blades. He pulled back. His eyes looked tired; infinitely sad. 'Well you're looking grand, Tomos,' he said.

'Thank you,' said Tomos. Then, uncertainly, 'Um, I'm really sorry . . .'

The sentence petered out.

Margaret was still hovering, like a waitress. 'Right,' she said brightly, 'anyone like coffee?'

'Oh, love one, please,' said Maureen.

'Yes, please,' said Jim, politely.

'Right, make yourselves at home.' Margaret beamed and bustled away. She'd forgotten to offer to take their coats. They divested themselves and laid them across a nearby chair back and sat down together facing Tomos and Sioned, who had resumed their seats.

'Poppy not come then?' Sioned asked, unnecessarily.

'No, I'm sorry,' Maureen apologised. 'She's still not herself. You know what youngsters are. Taken it very badly, I'm afraid. I thought she might have made the effort, but you can't force them, can you?'

'No, you can't,' Sioned agreed.

Maureen remembered the etiquette. She smiled at Tomos. 'But what about you, Tomos? How are you feeling now?'

'Really well, thanks,' he replied, still feeling bashful and awkward.

'Well you certainly look it, I must say.' Maureen's eyes kept flickering to his chest, as if wanting to look at the heart that beat soundly in there. As if feeling proprietorial of it.

'Yes, he's doing really well. The surgeon's very pleased with him. Calls Tomos his star patient!' Sioned put in, before stopping abruptly, embarrassed. *Duw, this is so difficult! Mustn't crow too much about how well he's doing with his new heart. Wayne's heart.*

She was spared more difficulty by the return of Margaret bearing a tray with coffee mugs, accompaniments and a plate of biscuits: chocolate digestives and custard creams (Margaret always assumed that everyone had a sweet tooth like herself). Sioned had placed a coffee table centrally and she set the tray down on it. Margaret sank, sighing with effort, into another armchair, still smiling, mother-hennish as usual. 'I'll just sit a minute, then leave you good people in peace. I know you'll have a lot to talk about and you don't want me fussing around.'

'No, that's alright, Mrs –' Maureen began.

'Margaret, please!'

'Sorry. Margaret. We don't want to push you out of your own sitting room.'

'Don't worry about it,' Margaret insisted. 'I'll have to go and get a bit of dinner ready in a minute anyway.'

Sioned breathed a sigh of relief, hoping it didn't show. She knew what Margaret was like once you got her talking; Maureen didn't. She was a dear old soul but, yes, her presence was a little inhibiting.

There was a strained silence.

Margaret broke it. She looked at Jim, who was still staring at Tomos, then at Maureen. 'I am so sorry about your boy, my dear. It's a terrible thing it is, to lose them like that. Terrible.'

Maureen said, 'Yes, it is. But that was the job he chose to do. He loved doing it. And we're proud of him.'

'Yes, and so you should be. Our lads do a great job out there, they do indeed. Yes.'

Maureen didn't reply. Margaret ploughed on. 'And that was a lovely service you had up there in Northallerton. I saw it on the telly. And so many people there! It must have been some comfort to you.'

'Yes, it was,' Maureen said, already wishing Margaret would shut up.

But she was into her stride now. 'And I can't get over how alike your Wayne and this young man here are.' She beamed, motherly, at Tomos. 'I saw his picture on the telly. Talk about peas in a pod!'

'Yes,' Maureen repeated, gritting mental teeth. 'They are. Were.'

'Strange that, isn't it,' Margaret mused. 'How some twins are and others aren't at all.'

'Yes,' Maureen reprised once again. She couldn't be bothered to explain the reason. Across from her, Tomos had opened his mouth to speak, perhaps with the same idea, and then apparently changed his mind. She glanced at Jim beside her, who was frowning, looking as if he was struggling to maintain control. If this carried on much longer he'd lose his temper. It was a bit short nowadays.

Margaret was still at it. 'And the way he donated his heart like that, to his brother. I think that's just wonderful. What a good boy he was.' A tear squeezed out of her left eye, provoked by her eulogy.

Sioned was cringeing too. She'd explained to Margaret that it wasn't quite like that; wasn't a case of Wayne specifying any particular recipient for it (how could it have been?); was simply a remarkable confluence of events, but the sentimental old woman had probably not understood that, preferring to believe the schmaltzy tabloid version of things. She had to act, before Jim got upset. Maureen had said that he was very unpredictable at the moment.

'Can I give you a hand with lunch at all, Margaret?' she said, hoping her landlady wouldn't see it as a hint to shut up.

But if she saw it as one she didn't show it. Margaret heaved herself out of the chair. 'No, no chick. You stay and talk to your guests. I can manage alright, thanks.'

She gathered up the tray, handed the remaining chocolate digestive and two custard creams to Tomos (who had been eying them anyway but was too polite to take them) and shuffled out of the room. The two women exchanged glances as Sioned rolled her eyes theatrically upward. A faint smile played at the corners of Maureen's mouth. The conversation resumed, easier now, although Jim contributed little and Tomos even less.

At ten past one Margaret reappeared to announce that lunch would be in five minutes if Sioned would like to take the guests through to the dining room. Sioned breathed another sigh of relief. It wasn't going to be a cosy meal up in the flat then. And so they sat down to roast lamb with rosemary and garlic followed by spotted dick with thick sweet custard for pudding. Margaret didn't join them. She was being sensitive after all. Afterwards Sioned suggested a gentle stroll through Bournville. As they walked the women chatted and Jim brightened up a little, talking to Tomos now. Then they returned to Linden Lea. It had been enough exercise for Tomos; he was ready for a sit down.

Margaret was ready with afternoon tea and doorstep slices of cherry cake, and again she left them to it in the dining room. As the talk flowed it turned to Tomos, as if his visitors had suddenly remembered that he was the reason for their coming. Maureen found herself regarding him surprisingly fondly. Now that was odd, wasn't it? But perhaps not. For the umpteenth time she thought how he was so the spitting image of Wayne, apart from being thinner and having longer hair. It pained her in one way to be so vividly reminded of her son, but it was strangely comforting too. Looking at him took a little of the pain of loss away.

Sometimes their eyes met and he smiled his shy, crooked smile. Wistful reflections came to her. *Just think. Not so long ago Sioned and I both had one of these lovely red-haired boys. A copy each. But now there's just the one. Perhaps we can share? Well why not? Perhaps I can think of Tomas as mine too. Well, a small part, a vital part of him used to be mine anyway and it always will be. I sort of have a share in him. Sioned and I could be like joint mums. Two of a special sisterhood, or something.*

She wondered how he was feeling about all of this. It must be really difficult for him. It would have been hard anyway, going through what he'd been through. Well there was only one way to find out.

'So how are you feeling about things now then, Luv?' she asked gently.

He frowned a little, thinking about that, making some of the freckles on his forehead coalesce. Wayne used to do that, just the same.

'I don't know, really. Confused, I think. And a bit guilty, in a way.'

'Guilty? Why?'

'Well, because I'm now okay, but only because Wayne died. It's not the way I would have wanted it. It really isn't.'

His voice had dropped to a whisper and his lower lip was quivering a little. Maureen couldn't help herself. She rose and went to sit on the arm of his chair and put an arm around his thin shoulders. She raised her hand to stroke his head (it felt so, so like Wayne's) and he laid it into her neck. Sioned watched, her eyes glistening.

Jim suddenly spoke, animatedly. 'No! Don't feel guilty about owt lad! You've nowt to be guilty about. You were on t' transplant list anyroad, so it were always going to be like this. Some poor bugger'd have to die, unfortunately, so you could live. You knew that.'

Tomos lifted his head, looked at Jim, spoke quietly. 'Yes, I knew that. But you forget. *I* did, anyway. I was only thinking about myself; how lousy I felt before. And how scared. How terrified of dying. I wasn't brave; not like Wayne. So all I thought about was, would an organ appear in time? I didn't give a thought to how it would come about, what it would have to mean. But then when

Mam told me it was Wayne's, well . . .'

His voice petered out.

Jim continued, more subdued now. 'No, you shouldn't feel guilty, Tomos. I should be the one to do that. If I hadn't encouraged him to join t' Scouts all them years ago' – he looked over at Maureen – 'and if we *had* encouraged him more at school, Mo, he might have got his sen a decent job, not gone in t' army because he could think of nowt else to do.'

'But what has being in the scouts got to do with the army, Jim?' Sioned wanted to know.

Jim sighed wearily. 'Well, t' one often leads to t' other, doesn't it? It certainly does around Northallerton, any road. Us being a garrison town, and everything. A lot of Wayne's mates did that; he was always telling us about them.'

'Oh, come on,' said Sioned, sounding faintly exasperated, 'You men, honestly. You blame yourselves too much! Wayne just did what he wanted to do, because he believed in it, and probably would have regardless of what you thought. You know what young men are like. And he also had the imagination and good-heartedness to go on the donor register. I think that's really admirable. Most youngsters would never think of doing it. Or older ones either, for that matter.'

She looked at Tomos. 'And you too, young man. Jim's right. Your heart had to come from someone. None of us would have wanted it to come from Wayne, of course we wouldn't, but it just did, by a sheer fluke, and you shouldn't beat yourself up about it.'

Maureen, still on the arm of the chair, tousled Tomos's hair. 'No, you really shouldn't, Luv. If it was going to have to go to someone, Wayne would have wanted it to be you.'

'And also,' Sioned put in, 'it's still in the family, at least. 'We'll always stay in contact now, won't we Maureen?'

Yes, Maureen assured her, feeling teary again. 'Of course we will.' She smiled sadly at Tomos, the flesh-and-blood embodiment of her lost son. 'I want to see what this young man does with his life.'

She reached for his hand and he gave it, willingly. 'You will come and see us sometimes, won't you, Tomos?'

'Yes, of course I will,' said Tomos, blinking and smiling.

And then two weeks after that, just before Tomos was discharged from the follow up monitoring to return home, Helen visited too. Her supportive dad came along to drive her down; give company and moral support. (She'd now officially left Warminster, left her job and left her life there behind, and moved back home with her parents until she was emotionally back on her feet.) Again there was the kindness and hospitality from Margaret, who was of course keen to see all the actors in Tomos's poignant story. Again Tomos had to fight down his embarrassment and guilt, but Helen was fine. Sad and a little subdued of course, and Sioned's heart went out to her, but accepting of things. She expressed herself very pleased that Tomos was doing so well, and many of the same words that had flowed between the Rees's and Harrisons were repeated between Rees's and Micklethwaites. As with Maureen and Jim, Tomos promised to stay in touch.

Perhaps, Tomos suggested, she would like to visit, have a weekend in Wales, maybe sometime in the spring? Yes, Helen said, she'd like that.

Epilogue

Helen is back in the comfy armchair, replete after Mair's wonderful risotto, and tiramisu for pudding. They'd refused to allow her to help with washing up and now she sits there, mug of tea on the chair arm, smiling at her guests on the sofa and looking around the small tidy sitting room.

'This really is a sweet little house,' she observes. 'Are you buying it?'

'Good grief no,' Tomos laughs. We certainly couldn't afford a mortgage at the moment, or even to save for a deposit. Not just on Mair's salary.'

Mair begs to differ. 'Well, we could at a push, but you don't want me to do all the paying, do you? Foolish male pride!'

Tomos bristles slightly. 'No, well, I want to pay my share when we start thinking about that, but it'll be a while before I'm qualified and earning.'

'But who's paying the rent for this then?' Helen wonders, and then mentally kicks herself for her nosiness.

Mair giggles. 'Well okay, I am. But it's not very much.'

Tomos explains. 'This place belongs to my Uncle Guto. My gran used to live here, before she went into the old folks' home. She died a few years ago. Then Uncle rented it out but the tenants left last November. He was going to rent it again, but then my operation happened and he knew we'd need somewhere to live after. Well, we couldn't keep on living with my parents, much as my mum would have liked it. So he kept it for us and now we pay – okay Mair pays' (he grins at her mischievously) '– just a little because we don't expect to get it for free.'

'Oh, right,' Helen says. 'That's a good little arrangement for you then.'

'Yes, very satisfactory really. And my parents are just a few miles up the road, so everyone's happy. Mam doesn't like the idea of us living too far away. She's a great believer in family.'

'Yes, well nothing wrong with that,' Helen says, hoping Tomos doesn't notice the faint edge of bitterness in her voice. She's been very grateful for family too, recently.

Tomos is looking a little embarrassed. By the upturn in his fortunes, Helen suspects, compared with hers. She changes the subject. 'You said "qualified" just now. What do you hope to do then, career-wise?'

Tomos smiles. 'Well, it was always going to be medicine. I had high ambitions. But then I got ill and it took a couple of years out of my life, and I had to forget that. Maybe I could think about it again now, if my health stays good, but it would mean a lot of years of study. A big commitment of time. So I've lowered my sights a bit.'

'To what?'

'I did a little work experience in America, at a pharmacy, a couple of years ago. That was when I first got diagnosed with heart trouble, actually. Then I switched from grand ideas of medicine to pharmacology, thinking it might be less onerous. I began a course in it for a while until I had to pack it in too, when my condition really deteriorated. But I'm thinking I'll continue along that route now I'm feeling so much better. It's still perhaps more realistic than thinking of medicine again.'

'That's what I think too,' Mair puts in, grinning sideways at Tomos.

'I'm very impressed,' Helen murmurs approvingly. *If only Wayne had been more this way inclined, then he might still be alive, not squandered out in bloody Iraq for nothing,* the thought creeps in, insidiously, but she chases it away. No point in keep going over this ground. It's happened and that's that.

Tomos is still talking. 'I've started doing some of it again, a few hours a day, at Boots in Aberystwyth. I really like the work. If I show enough interest and demonstrate some aptitude – well, I've got a bit of a head start – they might take me on as a trainee. Then I'd actually get paid! Then that could lead to the company funding a pharmacy degree course, like I started before, if they still think I have potential. Then one day I might get into medical research. Perhaps cardiothoracic medicine; who knows? I feel I'd like to give something back.'

Mair interjects again. 'Steady on; I thought you were less ambitious now. Just slow down a bit!'

But Helen says, although there's a sudden nagging pain in her chest and a tightening in her throat, 'Well good for you, Tomos. That's really admirable. You go for it.'

Tomos smiles. That oh-so-familiar, slightly crooked smile. He speaks, cautiously, anxious about upsetting Helen. The subject of Wayne is never very far away. 'It's strange, this, isn't it? It's like as if Wayne and I have been recombined, in a way. We began as one, and now there's the one of us again.'

Helen smiles too, sadly. She's been thinking similar things lately. Had it been any other situation, Wayne would have been lost completely, gone forever. In this case though, a part of him lives on; will always be there, like a sort of tangible physical legacy. But no; that's not quite right. The red-haired young man sitting across from her actually *is*, partially, her Wayne.

She's reminded of the wish, the small request she's been holding inside ever since she arrived. The wish she hardly dare voice.

'Er, Tomos, can I do something?'

He looks at her, questioning. 'Yes. What?'

Helen is embarrassed. It sounds silly.

She pauses then blurts out, 'Can I listen to your chest?'

Tomos looks puzzled. 'Well yes, if you want to . . .'

Then he realises what she's getting at. 'Yes, of course you can,' he says, gently.

He gets up and Helen does too. He moves to stand before her. She steps close and lays the side of her head against his chest. But what with his thick sweater and her thick mop of hair, she can't hear anything.

Mair gets to her feet too. 'Can you hear it, Helen?' she asks; her voice soft with concern.

'No!' says Helen. She feels like crying.

'Take your sweater off, Tomos,' Mair commands.

Tomos looks at her uncertainly. 'Really?'

'Yes. Do it.'

Helen stands back and he peels it off.

'Undo your shirt,' Mair says.

Tomos unbuttons. 'It's not terribly pretty, I'm afraid.'

'Doesn't matter,' Helen whispers.

His long scar is still a livid red as he bares his chest, which is filling out gradually though. He must have been as thin as a rake before.

'Now try,' he says.

Helen pulls her hair behind her ear and lays it on his chest, his lovely warm male chest; so like another, although still thinner. Instinctively her hands fall onto his sides. She can feel his ribs. She would love to be able to really embrace him. His arms come lightly around her too. At first she can still hear nothing. She shifts position slightly.

And then, suddenly, yes, there it is! Wayne's, her sweet Wayne's heart, beating strong and true and loyal inside his brother. Her tears come, unstoppably. Tomos is getting very wet.

'I'm sorry', she apologises, laughing and crying simultaneously.

'It's okay,' he reassures. 'It's okay.'

Mair moves close. She's crying too. She joins them, putting an arm around each, tightly, pulling them close.

And so they stand united; united by Tomos. United by Wayne. Tightly bound in the fading light in that cosy little Welsh sitting room on that now-raining April evening; a trinity of bodies, of souls.

Strawberry Field children's home, run by the Salvation Army, really did exist. John Lennon played in the wooded grounds behind it as a child. He nicknamed that area Strawberry Fields (with an 's') and it was immortalised in the 1967 Beatles' hit *Strawberry Fields Forever*. The home closed in 2005 to become a church and prayer centre.

About the author

John Needham was born in Rutland in 1943 and brought up in Stamford, Lincolnshire. After study at Leicester College of Art he spent the first twenty-five years of his working life in graphic design and copywriting. Later he pursued his lifelong passion of renovating old houses, to end his career in landscape gardening.

Since retiring he has written three non-fiction books: two on house renovating and an autobiography. In fiction he has written *Convergence*, *Forebears* and *Another Spring*, a short anthology of short stories. *The One of Us* is his third novel.

He now lives in west Wales with his spaniel, Sali.

Thanks

My thanks go to Gwendlyn Kallie for encouragement, support and proofreading; Michael Hawke for constructive comment and editing; Chantelle Atkins, Steph Gravell, Marilyn Tomlins and Shirley Hardy for friendship and interest; Susan Keefe for promotional help; and my publisher, Autharium, for showing me to the world.

Printed in Great Britain
by Amazon